THE HERE OF THIS NOW

Science Fiction Stories

S. PARNAM-HARRIS

sparnam-harris.com

*For Ben Dave and Roz
I couldn't be prouder!*

Time is but the stream I go a-fishing in

— THOREAU

CONTENTS

The Here of This Now   1

Fish Girl   85

A Conversation With 'Last Resort'   160
The film script

Lovalott Intersolar Removals   182

The Time Travel Tree   259

Acknowledgments   325

Also by S. Parnam-Harris   327

THE HERE OF THIS NOW

I HAVE BEEN THINKING *about this story for quite a while; the places I have ridden out on Exmoor lend themselves to constant dreaming, awake or asleep. I see old, derelict stone houses in misty valleys where quiet ghosts still walk the rooms. The horse stops sometimes and watches someone I can't see amble in front of her. She doesn't mind, so why should I?*

Time, according to Einstein, 'is only a stubborn persistent illusion.' And somewhen, we all need another now.

Also, I have always wanted to put a body in a muck heap!

The song I associate with this story is, Moon River, sung by Patricia Gilpin. Because each note is a memory in time and string theory is music played by the cosmic orchestra.

MY BOSS WAS LOOKING at something on the holo screen that I couldn't see, which was odd, as I'm covered for highly secret documents. Even more shocking was the expression on his face, it was almost fearful. The man is usually only every afraid of his mother and quite rightly so, I have seen her pick up and throw a Europa sea-crab at an adversary. Even in low gravity those things are heavy and *really* nasty. It made a terrible mess of the subject we were pursuing, but the bounty was good and they didn't seem to mind that he arrived a little squishy when we turned him in. I was working with her at the time, which was how I met my current boss.

Baaz Webber is tall and very slim; he'd been born on Mars before the settlement domes had got proper gravity and become cities. His name means eagle in Punjabi so he mostly goes by his nickname, Eagle-eye, unless you're in trouble and then it's 'Boss.'

His dark eyes flicked from the hidden privacy holo screen, to me and back again and he was now far too pale for his usual skin tone.

I waited. Looking around, his office reflected the slightly too tidy and organised of the in-charge personality he exuded. There were old and therefore very expensive actual paper books on the shelves, some holos of famous people he was shaking hands with and a few of his family. The huge windows looked out over a bustling scene. Commercial submersibles docked and discharged their cargos. Tiny, power assisted, suited figures worked the deep, doing one of the most dangerous jobs in the port.

Mid Pacific underwater city was one of my favourite places to be. I have two associates who won't set foot in it or Mid Atlantic, citing a fear of drowning if it ever had a breach. But I point out, in what I consider to be a helpful way, that they'd be a jellied mess from the massive pressure at this depth, long before they would drown. I thought it was funny, though it never seemed to get a laugh. And considering both of them work on deep space freighters, I think it's a bit hypocritical of them, after all vacuum can be just as problematic, when it's *sudden*.

Eagle-eye turned the holo off without showing it to me and then leaned back in his chair and sighed. Grabbing a crystal information file, he slid it across the desk.

"Do you want me to look at this?" I was puzzled, he could have input it into the holo computer in front of him.

"Single connection, your eyes only, Ariadne," he said abruptly.

I winced, things must be bad, because he usually called me Ari like the rest of the team. Pressing on the comm attached to the side of my face, I saw a head-up display flickering into life. I don't like using them, which is why mine is detachable. I need my privacy, though most of the people I know have a permanent implant, including Eagle-eye. I tapped the crystal information cube and they connected.

The personal file scrolled in front of my eyes of a man I thought I vaguely recognised, who'd had a job similar to the one I had done when I worked for Eagle-eye's mum. But much better paid and only just slightly inside the legal lines. I shrugged, there was nothing unusual about it, rich people paid to have their problems sorted out for them without using the proper authorities. We all knew it happened and there was a regular, well publicised sweep to deal with it. So, I couldn't see what the issue was, as long as you didn't invite the man to dinner and give him a really sharp knife to cut up his food.

I paused the file and removed it, then looked at Eagle-eye for an explanation. He passed me another crystal, this one was an evil version of the first one, with pictures and diagrams. It was all horrible.

The deviant personality had undergone several illegal, physical identity changes, all of them very professionally done. He also seemed to have an endless amount of unspecified financial backing and a get out of gaol free card.

I finished with a grimace of disgust and disconnected the second file. I waited again. Eagle-eye said nothing. The crystal sat on the desk between us, making me nervous.

"I don't get it, who is he, where is he and what's it got to do with me?"

Eagle-eye sighed. "He managed to get a trip back and it's caused a blip in the system."

I went with the formal title, because it felt as if this was appropriate. "Boss, I'm strictly animal trafficking, I don't do people any more!"

"He's not a bounty, he just needs to be, er, returned." He was being evasive, and his usual piercing gaze, the one that had earned him the nickname, wasn't in evidence as he looked carefully down at the desk in front of him.

"How is he *not* in reprogramming, or been incarcerated and what sort of blip?"

I sighed with exasperation and went through the first file again of the mercenary, the one I recognised, checking the details. A name attached to his client list pinged up and a bell rang somewhere in the sludge of my memory. "You have got to be kidding me, he's worked for—"

"*Don't* say it!" Eagle-eye looked round. Even though his door was closed, the office had clear walls, and most of us, as part of our training, could lip read really well. The unit was nothing if not efficient when it came to communication and psychology.

"I still don't understand why you want me to do this?" I really didn't. My current role was strictly extinct species related. You wouldn't believe the number of people who would pay for a living velociraptor. The fact that the last one I'd rescued was a juvenile and only the size of an average crow, didn't stop it from being a nasty theropod, elaborately feathered, with sharp teeth and a vicious claw. It wasn't a bit grateful to be going back to its own now, I had only just survived the trip. I rubbed the scar on my arm where it had left me with a parting gift.

"Call it a favour." Eagle-eye was watching my micro expressions.

I thought carefully. "Is this Misha's doing?"

Eagle-eye's mother was always messing around with my life. I was working in the unit because of her; she had also taken an inconvenient interest in my partnership status. I found myself constantly bumping into 'suitable' prospects. It was my turn to sigh as I saw his lips twitch in a barely discernible wince. Eagle-eye was obviously dodging the mum thing himself.

"To whom am I doing this favour?" I was leaning back in my chair with a more evident level of body language, because it felt like an important question.

"The core flow, the unit and my mum," he smiled winningly, adding, "and not necessarily in that order."

The charm wasn't working on me and I decided to see exactly how high the stakes were. "*If* I do this, I get to make it my last job with the unit."

"Done!" Eagle-eye agreed much too quickly.

We looked at each other, both of us uneasy with the bargain we had just made.

"What's the first man got to do with the second?" I asked.

"Proximity," Eagle-eye replied tartly.

I gaped. "You're joking, why aren't you asking *him* to sort it out?"

Eagle-eye paused before he spoke, which seemed overly dramatic. "He's off the books."

I think all that came out of my mouth was a rather unimpressive, "Huh!" And then I eventually managed, "Is that actually possible?"

There was a silence that stretched and no answer. I waited, but it was clear I wasn't going to get one.

"Can I look at both of the crystals again?" I asked.

He nodded. "But you can't take either of them out of this room."

I was puzzled, some files were never removed from the unit office as it existed outside of the core flow, but I couldn't see why either of these should fall into that category. This was something else to add to the unusual status of the job.

The review didn't contribute any more information, but I was careful to give myself key thoughts to remember the details and memorised the facial expressions and bio mechanics of the 'job.' It's easy to change your looks and disguise your voice but the intonation and cadence when you speak and the way you walk are usually something no one remembers to do anything about. I'd had success in catching several bounties that way.

Apart from the murder and mutilation, which seemed to be his first choice for income, he was also a prolific smuggler of extinct species, I assumed it was why I had been asked. I'd never come across him before which confused me more than the favour I was apparently considering.

"How has he been covering up the animal trafficking?" I paused the crystal connection.

Eagle-eye gave made a very expressive shrug and huffed. I tried not to grind my teeth with frustration.

"Is this the way we're going to proceed; I ask you a question and try and work out if I'm right from your non-committal grunts?" I started up the file again. "You *could* just tell me what you know," I muttered.

I'm pretty sure I heard him say, "Where's the fun in that?"

I SAT in a café on the top level of hydroponics. The gardens spiralled down through the levels in the centre of the dome, mature trees were in full leaf and open flowers covered the ground with narrow paths between that led to seating areas. Natural sunlight was channelled down from the surface using a series of massive reflectors. We all needed our green, even in the deep blue.

Birds and insects cheeped and buzzed, doing the job of pollination and maintaining the precious biome. There were gardeners and biologists, but the farming was done outside the dome; mostly algae and seaweed at a shallower depth.

The fuel that kept the systems running was the usual cyanobacteria that we used on the land in cities for industry and domestically in every house, but instead of geothermal heating, the domes got theirs from deep sea vents.

The coffee was good, loads of milk and sugar and a plate of interesting chocolates to go with it. The proprietor, Hao, no longer asked me for my preferences, just grinned whenever he saw me sitting down. I paid with my still in situ, comm link and he waved his thanks when he saw it on his more permanent version. He made everything himself and often tested new chocolate recipes on me. His partner, Sarah, worked in the gardens. I envied them the quiet confidence in their choices and each other.

Leaning back, I looked up through the transparent graphene ceiling and watched a lazy whale spinning above me in the dark blue water over the dome. I sighed with contentment, for about as long as it took to rethink the job I had been offered.

The personal file had seemed thin on background information for a such a successful mercenary, which was what I would class him as. No, it just didn't seem right. I tried again. Thinking about the conversation with Eagle-eye, I wondered how you were able to go back and be off the books at the same time, and whether it was something to do with his associations. Our paths had never crossed workwise. My bounty role was strictly government related and therefore not so well paid.

As for the job, I couldn't understand why Eagle-eye had asked me. It felt so completely wrong that I was leaning towards refusing when I saw Svana coming towards me. She was obviously looking for a quiet place to eat her lunch and she hesitated when she realised who I was. Slim with plaited brown hair and bright intelligent eyes, she worked at the main core flow console and was a quiet voice during tense departures and fraught arrivals.

The unit actively sought out people on the spectrum, in fact anyone who had the ability to analyse emergency situations and find creative solutions. My intuitive skills stemmed from dyslexia, synaesthesia and the ability to see patterns and connections. Apparently, I didn't speak much when I was a small child, my mum said it was because I was thinking.

Going with instinct I asked, "Svana, do you know when Eagle-eye was last out of the unit?"

She thought carefully about her answer before speaking, which was part of her emotional makeup, a trait I very much wished was more common.

"Not for several days," she said eventually.

I nodded and she walked on to find a more solitary area of the garden.

MY FOLKS LIVE on the Cornish coast and farm seaweed for commercial and domestic use. The house has been in the family for generations and my brother Jago is set to take over the business when they retire, which would be never. They all get on; his partner Cadan and their children live with them. I had left home in the middle of the night the minute I turned sixteen and there was no danger of the local sheriff coming after me. No one actually minded me not being there.

There's only so much seaweed a girl can cope with and I wanted to see the worlds... all of them.

I didn't get very far on savings and as my folks felt it was important for me to understand life lessons, it wasn't long before I had to find paid employment, reality having set in rather abruptly. Something my brother never seemed to have to worry about.

To my family's stunned surprise (and mine) I had managed to reach Mars main dome and was working in a club in the seediest area, when I met Misha Webber. Or rather, I was using the illegal stun stick that was kept behind the bar on two warring tool pushers, who had both taken an interest in the same dancer. It was *that* sort of place.

As they were completely oblivious, due to a considerable amount of stimulant, the stunning wasn't having the effect I had hoped and things were getting interesting, which was when Misha stepped in.

The woman has an intimidating gaze and she's taller than her son, which meant a head and shoulders higher than the two Earth born men. Plus, there was the very large, only *slightly* more legal, bounty hunter stunner and things were quieter in an instant.

We talked a lot that night and for several days afterwards and eventually I agreed to be her apprentice. And I got to see the worlds after all.

REFLECTING on my past wasn't getting me any closer to the answers. I stood up and wandered back to my accommodation three floors down, a small studio on the very expensive ninth level, with a large, and even more costly, graphene window to the outside. The corridor was quiet, most people were working and I didn't really know my neighbours. The couple next door were marine biologists who usually argued all the time about plankton and marine snow. We just nodded good morning and evening if our paths crossed.

Lights reflected the water movement through windows set into the walls between the apartment doorways, making soothing patterns on the flooring. There were plants in flowerbeds nearby, which was to give you the illusion you were walking down a path in a housing block land-side. Personally, I preferred the view through the windows.

I tapped in my door code and sighed with relief as I set my things down. I don't carry much for work, just the essentials in a small backpack.

I sat down in front of the view and watched the port activity winding down between shifts. Not everyone likes to see the outside. I loved it. Curious, deep-sea fish came towards the light in hopes of an easy meal and watched me watching them. The distant underwater freighters looked just the same design as their space cousins and did a similar job, food distribution, industrial and commercial goods; though the people carriers in space had fewer windows.

My personal comm pinged and I waited for the ID before answering.

"Ariadne!" Eagle-eye was looking harassed. There it was again, the first name thing.

"Hey boss," I went along with the more official address in the hopes that it would lead me somewhere.

"You left without formally committing to the job," he smiled as he spoke, which was, quite frankly, unnerving.

I waited, when nothing else was forthcoming I sighed, "Okay, I'll do it." The look of relief on Eagle-eye's face would have been comical if I hadn't worked out just exactly how much trouble he was in. Which, I thought, was hardly a blip as he'd described it, basically it meant him being stuck in the unit until I sorted things out.

"When is departure?" I got up to make a drink and settled back on the chair by the window while he fiddled with crystal information files.

"Tomorrow, nineteen-hundred West Coast Pacific time, we need you to arrive at three am GMT." His voice was back to being clipped and efficient.

I spluttered hot liquid over myself and the furniture, I think there was even some on the window. He waited patiently while I got the resultant choking under control.

"Are you out of your mind? I can't do a beat up in, "I looked at my comm clock, "twenty-four hours!"

He tried for a patient tone but his exasperation and apprehension got in the way. "You're going back home, the differential is not that much, people, language, geography, it's all the same, you'll be fine!" I wondered who he was trying to convince.

"I come from Cornwall, not Somerset and it's just after the first Covid pandemic, there are whole countries back in that now that no longer exist in this forward, of course there will be a noticeable degree of difference!" I was trying to clean up the mess I'd made.

His voice was oily. "You could use the box."

I stopped what I was doing and turned round. "I am *never* going to use the box and you know it, that thing is dangerous. Linking up to the mainframe computer and asking it to download straight into your brain, how is that ever a good idea?"

"You are fully aware that there is no empirical evidence that it's bad for you." Eagle-eye had the grace to look away while he said it.

"Tell *that* to Simon Wetheridge's partner," I replied waspishly, as I sat down.

He shuffled a bit and the rather odd look of discomfort on Eagle-eye's face made me pause for a moment of thought, though I didn't know why.

I added, "I'll cram tonight, I could use the history lesson and hopefully I'll get some help from Ash when I get there."

"*We* don't contact *him*; you'll have to do that yourself when you arrive." Eagle-eye disconnected abruptly.

I sighed and paused to think about how that would feel, to be completely detached from your own now. I shuddered; after a shower and some more of Hao's chocolates to keep me awake, I set up the non comm holographic computer in the living area and got to work.

NOT KNOWING how long I was going to be away for meant I had to do some personal maintenance, not much, as there were no dependants or animals. My family existed in a state of blissful disinterest in my whereabouts and my job description, therefore no misinformation was needed.

Neither did they know, like most of the general public, about the secret organisation set up to track the criminal activity in smuggling extinct species forward and tourists travelling back. We also monitored the legal de-extinction programme and the rarely permitted trip, which was usually for observation purposes only. In my tenure I had only ever seen one of those.

Pearl Chanter, who worked in the recovery of ancient artifacts that had been destroyed by catastrophic events, spent months, sometimes years, providing conclusive evidence of the loss, before a highly scrutinised, single visit back could be attempted. She was small, with very dark hair and skin, and a powerful body honed from years of living in a high gravity environment. I have seen her arrive forward with a stack of books that weighed more than I do without pausing for breath and usually nothing fazed her. Except of course, for the bureaucratic shenanigans of those lacking imagination.

It was after midnight before I gave up on the history files, but it's important to do it effectively.

I didn't think for a moment that Eagle-eye would let me leave afterwards. My training must have cost a fortune and those of us who travel back and forward well are not easy to find. I have a team-mate who is nearly incapacitated by the trip on each attempt, when I asked him why he carried on, he told me that all the pain and discomfort was worth it to see other nows.

Daniel Roper was a deep time expert and had been very helpful with the velociraptor, I usually consulted him if I needed any advice or information further back than the Palaeolithic and he had seen me off on the last trip and waited for me to return. The sort of unit member you really relied on. Particularly when you're bleeding copiously from a gash; he had tutted as he slapped a gel dressing over the gaping wound and issued a directive to the medic for a specific anti-microbial nanoparticle treatment. Velociraptors from the Cretaceous period not being much known for clean nails.

I rubbed the still-visible damage on my arm, the searing pain refreshed by the memory; I hadn't had a moment to visit the doctor for some scar removal therapy.

SLEEP CAN BE the avoidance of reality and my dreams were telling me something that I couldn't remember when I woke up.

After doing all the usual bathroom stuff and breakfast, I got back to the history and tried to use the patterns and connections that work in my brain as keys to keep the information fresh and natural.

I don't usually come into contact with the smugglers, and there is no one else around to notice the fact that I'm not 'local' on the few occasions when I've chased them through the undergrowth. The extinct species don't care, unless you look particularly tasty.

The hours passed and I wandered restlessly around, reorganising my already tidy life. It was a relief when the moment came to go into the unit offices. Svana called me on my comm as I was heading out of the door.

"On my way," I said. She nodded her agreement and closed the connection. I had always found her complete lack of extraneous conversation very restful.

The corridors were evening quiet, most people stuck to the obligatory circadian timings, essential and mandated for brain and body health. The unit, however, was busy with technicians and scientists, all doing the necessary roles for a successful trip back.

I could see Eagle-eye tapping away at a holo computer in his glass box of an office, watching everything without seeming to do so.

The medic on duty came over and ran a portable scanner over me. He nodded to Svana that I was good to go and she added it to the list on her display. My travel clothes were handed to me and I changed behind a small screen. I was used to the complete lack of real privacy. Another technician checked me for any items that I was wearing that might cause a problem. He also used a scanner. I stood patiently, with my mind fixed on the job and breathed in and out slowly.

People came and went, the list on the holo computer lengthened and the results were all reassuringly positive. My backpack, containing appropriate kit and my information brief, was handed to me and I put it on my shoulder.

A red light began to flash and the beeping informed everyone who didn't need to be there to leave.

I saw Eagle-eye standing next to the office door, his expression unusually tense, he saluted and I tapped my forehead in acknowledgement.

The small round shimmer of light formed between three zero-point energy fields and grew to become a large, upright, dark puddle, full of shapes and shadows. The green light flashed, Svana pointed at me and I stepped through the link, into the core flow. And back.

I HAD NEVER EXPERIENCED any of the things my unit co-workers talk about. There is no whooshing, or tunnel of light, no strange sounds or cold, no space or stars. Just once when I was extremely tired after a particularly difficult day, I thought I felt, I don't know, *something*, for a brief instant, as if I was with an old friend, which was odd, because I don't really have any.

The slight step down was onto crisp grass and it was countryside quiet, comfortingly empty of people, and after the noise of the unit control room it felt stunningly silent. The low moon through the trees made interesting shapes around me and I waited for a second to listen to the wind ruffling the leaves. There was a late autumn chill in the clear air and a frost on the ground. I could hear sheep and cows in the neighbouring fields and a distant mechanical car.

It takes a moment and a lifetime to get used to being somewhen else.

I TOOK the brief out of the backpack and studied it with a small button-controlled torch. Written on wood-based paper, it was further instructions and the details of the house where I would be staying. It was set out as if I was on an extended holiday, looking for a change of life somewhere with a slower pace after burnout; it actually used those exact words. I snorted, and apologised to the nearby oaks for the paper. I looked around, over by a clump of trees I could see a small stone dwelling surrounded by fencing with an open wooden gate.

We never, *ever*, arrive back inside a building. The possibility for ending up enclosed in a wall was too high. *Always* outside. This of course can lead to problems of its own.

The crepuscular light lent itself to atmospheric shadows and I realised a small black and white border collie was watching me from the fence line. It looked interested and as it came to investigate, I realised it was a puppy, no more than six months old. My parents had given one to my brother when I was growing up. He worked the farm with Jago, I remembered being told off for cuddling him and giving him treats.

The dog sat down in front of me looking up, though it was dark under the trees the field was moonlit and I could see that he had a blue eye and a brown one, his head tipped to the side and he grinned with joy at meeting me. An odd sensation thumped in my chest, I knelt and we eyed each other. He leaned in and a wet cold tongue swept across my face. I laughed.

"Badger, that'll do," a quiet voice said.

I freaked and grabbed the nearest stone, ready to either throw or use as a bludgeon. Badger was instantly embarrassed for both of us. His strategy was to roll onto his back and offer his rather tubby, puppy tummy for inspection. When I wasn't instantly delighted, he whined, then yipped.

The man was tall for this now, with a slim build and wearing the Exmoor country uniform of waterproofs and muddy wellingtons. He pointed towards the building. "How about we talk inside, it's freezing cold."

"Ash Grey," I said, "I was thinking *I* would have to come and find *you*." I got to my feet and tried not to let my shaky voice betray me. Badger did his best to make me feel more comfortable by trying to launch himself into my arms.

Ash picked up his wriggling, delighted dog and we walked in silence to the small cottage.

He made me nervous, I didn't know him that well, our paths hadn't crossed at all, but I felt the uneasiness, because I knew exactly how many people he had terminated. All of them were authorised, but still. I'd never done it, unless you included the creep who got eaten by a mosasaur, and I didn't.

We walked around the outside of the cottage to the front door which faced a low stone wall with a gateway, there was the shadow of a sloping track the other side and I could hear a slow river close by. It was dark inside and out and I hesitated in the doorway and waited until Ash had walked through and turned a light on. He used a switch by the kitchen counter, my brain registered that there was no voice activated system. I shook my head and did the breathing exercises and counting backwards that helped me connect to my adjustments. By the time I had reached three I was standing in the main room and had shut the door behind me.

I put my backpack down on the chair close to the fireplace and looked around. One big living area with skylight windows in the ceiling roof. The sitting room was a single chair and a small sofa set on either side of the fireplace. The kitchen was at the other end, with an oblong table acting as a room divider. Large windows looked out to the field I had arrived in and onto the track. There was a narrow set of open stairs up to a balcony bedroom which was above the kitchen.

"Bathroom?" I asked hopefully.

"Upstairs through the bedroom." Ash was lighting the fire and adding wood to bring up a blaze, which made me cringe a little for a moment. But the morning was late autumn cold and I stuck to the exercises for the mental fine tuning.

"Okay?" Ash had moved over to the kitchen and began filling a kettle with water from the sink tap. He indicated his question by pointing at his head and then me.

"I didn't have long to do much preparation, Eagle-eye was in some-thing of a hurry." I moved my backpack and sat down in the chair. Badger had curled up in front of the warming fire and sighed with contentment. It smelt of pine needles and comfort. I have no idea why; I had never sat by one before.

"I'll just bet he was," Ash snorted, as he found cups in a cupboard without actually having to look for them.

"What?" I was puzzled.

"Eagle-eye, in a hurry," Ash clarified.

I waited, it's part of my training, the trouble was it had been essential in Ash's too. He put cups on the table, a tea pot and some biscuits. Milk from the fridge and sugar in a chicken shaped container. He indicated the chair opposite him and sat down, helping himself to three biscuits.

Sighing, I got up from my cosy place by the fire and moved over to the table. He poured me a cup.

"I don't usually drink tea," I said petulantly.

"Well get used to it, it's Exmoor!" He grinned.

After some rummaging around in one of his coat pockets he pulled out a large envelope and emptied the contents onto the table. Mobile phone, credit cards, driving licence and passport all in my own name, Ariadne Bickerstaff. I wasn't sure how usual or wise this was, it didn't feel very much of either.

"Your bank details are on the phone under 'personal stuff,' the contract for rental is there too."

"Who am I renting from?" I drank the tea, it was strong with an underlying smoky flavour. Rather nice. I took a biscuit and bit into it, chocolate ginger, my favourite. Instantly I was apprehensive again.

"Me, I bought several hundred acres and the two derelict buildings from the local farmer on the promise that I would renovate the dwellings and give him the grazing rights to the land." Ash was sitting back, relaxed, the greying hair now matched his dark grey eyes. He looked at home, something that made me oddly envious for a moment.

I turned on the phone and scrolled through the information. It was set up with great attention to detail. Looking around the cottage, I could see interesting books on the shelves by the windows and framed photographs that were both appealing and thought provoking. The décor was simple and expensive, white walls, wood flooring, nice furniture, green kitchen cupboards, clever lighting. I glanced back to Ash who was watching me, his face expressionless, grey by name and nature.

"Exactly *how long* have you been here in this now?"

"You got there really fast!" He snorted.

"WHAT'S GOING ON?" I don't like being manipulated. The tea was bitter on my tongue, fear stimulates adrenaline production which tastes of metal. My ignorance was making me angry.

"I can't do this on my own, you're better at putting things together. And you have a certain attitude to dealing with problems that I can work with."

"What do you mean?" I squeaked, causing Badger to get up and worry his way over to me. A cold tongue rasped over my hand for moral support.

"Throwing that man to the mosasaur." He grunted his satisfaction.

I was incredulous, first it had been a unit action and highly secret, and secondly it was technically inaccurate. "I didn't *throw* him in, he fell!" He had; I just didn't pull him out. "The creep had provided an extinct aquatic reptile for some equally awful business people, who had paid astronomical amounts for the privilege of the sport; and he was baiting the water with—" I stopped abruptly and looked at Badger who was smiling up at me with puppy adoration. Hiding my finger from him with my other hand, I pointed down.

"I read the statement." Ash's tone made the dog look at him in alarm.

I didn't ask him how he had been able to read a secret unit report and took another biscuit ignoring the whine of interest. Ash offered Badger a chewy treat from a bottomless pocket as compensation and he took it over to the fire and began making a spectacular mess. My tiredness swept over me. It happens when you go back, as if all that core flow is full of the energy you spent along the way.

"It's early, have a bath, get some sleep and I'll talk to you later on this morning. I'm about fifteen minutes' walk along the riverbank. Follow it upstream." He pointed out of the dark window, where I could see precisely nothing. "People will be starting work soon," he added helpfully, as he went through the doorway. Badger followed him out, pausing to look back at me, he seemed to be wondering why I wasn't coming too.

"It's good to have you here Ari," Ash's voice was so quiet I wasn't sure I had actually heard him.

IT TOOK PRECISELY three seconds after I had secured the door with an actual key, to register the word 'bath,' excessive water use being really frowned upon forward. Despite the fact that most of the facilities are powered by the massive pressure of the ocean depth and desalination is a part of everyday life landside, underwater, dome and space living. And there's plenty of it.

I ran up the stairs, threw my backpack on the bed, opened the bathroom door and stopped. If there had been a crescendo of music to announce the spectacle, it couldn't have been more wonderful. Shower, basin, loo... and a freestanding bath. I whooped.

Hot water up to my neck, the window open to the cold air, I listened to the outside, the wind in the trees, an owl, a creaking of wood fencing or a gate, the water in the river over stones. Then oddly a noise that didn't belong. I sat up. Water and bubbles slopped over the side. It sounded like a big cat calling. It was so unlikely that when it stopped, I just lay back and dismissed it as part of the adaptation process. If you go back and forward, you pick up memories that don't quite belong to the now that you are in.

The bed was firm and warm and I could see the embers of the fire through the balcony. I'm not sentimental but it felt as if a part of me was home. Sleep came quickly, but the dreams were full of unanswered questions.

THE SCRATCHING WOKE me and I sat up, dizzy for a second or two. I had never spent more than a few hours somewhen else. This was different. A whine had me out of bed and down the stairs. The house was warm though the fire had gone out. I could feel the heat through the wood floor on my bare toes. Ash really had gone for all the best ecological fittings.

I unlocked the door and opened it slowly. Badger looked up at me, a huge grin on his face, I moved it far enough so he could get in and then checked behind him. Nope, he was alone.

"Are you allowed out by yourself?" I asked him. He wagged his tail and assured me he was. "Really?" His head went down and he looked sheepish which I thought was clever considering his profession.

He watched as I did my morning routine and followed me around the kitchen. We shared some breakfast, me coffee, fruit and cheese, him doggie treats which had been conveniently left on the table from the previous evening. I felt different, as if everything was the same, except me.

The cupboards in the bedroom were full of appropriate country wear. In my size. Not perfect but still, creepily close enough. I could feel the apprehension rising again as I dressed in suitable layers, under-wear, trousers and a long sleeve t-shirt, jumper and thick wool socks. A scarf and some gloves were in a drawer.

Everything was natural fibres and a good brand, and fell into the practical and not decorative area of design, which made it only slightly less weird. An interesting combination of walking, riding and farm related clothing. I examined the trousers, jodhpurs really, and wondered what part of the cover story would include horses. The mobile phone started ringing as I pulled my hair into loose plaits. It was windy out and I don't like it in my eyes when I need to see clearly.

I picked up the phone and accepted the call, fully expecting Ash to be asking where his dog was.

"Badger's here," I stated helpfully.

"Er, well, that's good, I'm Roberta Tippet. Ash gave me your number; I hope you don't mind that I'm calling so early?"

I checked the time on the kitchen clock, missing my comm version, eight-fifteen. The noise coming from the phone was incredi-ble. "Are you at a football match?" I asked, holding it away from my ear.

"No, I'm at breakfast!" She snorted. "Just a second." There was the sound of doors opening and closing and the racket faded slightly, but not much. "Sorry, they're off to school and it's always chaotic first thing. Better?" she asked me.

"Much," I said, wondering at the number of children she had. "How can I help?"

"Well Harley usually lives in your field in the winter, he gets really tired and needs a break from us and I thought I'd check before I got someone to bring him over?"

"One of your *children* lives in the field *all* winter?" I re-examined the briefing information in my mind and couldn't find anything that would be helpful, except possibly a reference to child social services.

There was a stunned silence, then a shout of laughter. "Ash said you had an odd sense of humour. Harley's a pony!"

"Oh, sorry, I er—"

She interrupted me, "That's okay, he said you were suffering from burnout and it was affecting you in lots of different ways—" she swore. "He also said not to tell you I knew!"

I was about to ask what else Ash had said when the football game passed her on their way to school and there followed a verbal waterfall. "Have you got your PE kit, well it was washed last night, go and get it, if you don't brush your teeth they will fall out and I will have to call you gummy for the rest of your life, *homework* over there!" This last instruction was yelled. I winced.

Badger waited patiently by the door and I mouthed an apology, he sank dramatically down and sighed. A dog with people problems.

"I'm back, is it okay?" she said.

"Um, is what?" It felt as if the conversation was going to get me into trouble and I was wary.

"If I bring Harley down later this morning, he won't be any bother, he likes a bit of alone time, do you see?"

"I don't think it's me you need to be asking, Ash is probably the person to deal with as it's his field."

"He told me to ask *you*!" she sounded exasperated, and really busy.

"In that case I would be delighted to share," I tried for light hearted as practical wasn't working and I had no idea what Ash was up to.

"Thank you!" She sounded relieved, as if she had expected to produce more evidence for her case and had won on a technicality.

I found myself listening to air and I looked at Badger. He sighed. "What was that about?" I asked him. He sat up, head on one side, his eyebrows raised. "And what are the chances of me getting some more information from Ash?" Badger didn't think they were very good, it was my turn to sigh. "Eagle-eye is going to owe me one."

There was a selection of boots by the door in a low-down cupboard that looked as if it had been designed for the purpose. From a choice of three, I picked the ones that seemed to be waterproof.

Outside was something of a surprise, as the cottage had looked rather overshadowed by trees when I had first seen it. Actually, there were none really close to the building, with plenty of space between it and several groups of mature foliage scattered around, providing shelter from the wind and rain.

The low wall to the front had been cleared and restored and a small garden planted to the right side, with three miniliths, common to Exmoor. I fished about in my memory; it was something to do with the scarcity of large stones available to the neolithic and bronze age communities.

Both the house and garden were fenced off from the field, the gate I had come through at the back was still open. Badger watched me with puppy impatience and yipped to get my attention. I followed him to the river, it flowed peacefully downstream, whispering gently, but there was evidence in the undulating banks to either side and the memory on stones of a violent torrent in the colder months. A small wooden bridge went over to a sloping dirt road and more fields. Badger led me across, which explained how he had arrived relatively dry, then on up the incline to a gated field on the right of the road.

The wooden five bar gate was not padlocked but instead of opening it, I clambered over the top. The dog slid easily through the gaps and we set off.

The field had sheep on the upper level enjoying the clear autumn morning, or they seemed to be anyway. All of them looked up to watch us pass by, then went back to eating, they were small and grey with shaggy coats. I wasn't sure of the breed but my information suggested

Herdwicks, which I knew was unusual for the area. It was boggy in places and Badger led the way along a safe route only he could see.

On the other side of the river it was dense with trees and foliage. I could see why the dog had chosen this path. The walk was warming me up and I removed the scarf and gloves and put them in my pocket. Further up the slope I could see a dirt and grass road curving off the moor and down between the fields. There was a moss and lichen-covered stone bank on one side and fencing on the other. I stopped for a second but Badger wasn't pleased and barked to get my attention.

Two wooden barriers were spaced out over the river, presumably to stop debris but allow the higher water levels to flow easily through. It was well organised and gave me a good sense of someone looking after the land and the animals with thought.

I was on the wrong side of the river. The farmhouse, if you could call it that, was a messy wade across and there was no handy bridge. Badger splashed through the shallow water. "Fine!" I said, hoping my assessment of the boots was correct. They were waterproofed, but the water sloshed over the top and into my socks, and I swore, using the same word I had heard Roberta Tippet say, as it seemed appropriate.

Badger waited for me and then shook himself thoroughly, my coat, I discovered, unlike my face and hair, was also waterproof.

He trotted off up the incline and through the open gate to the left of a stony moss-covered path, just wide enough for a horse or a quad bike. I stood on one leg and emptied my boot, then did the other one before following him.

Ash was leaning on the wood balcony that surrounded the house on three sides, drinking a cup of tea or coffee, the swirl of steam curled up and dissipated into the cold air. Looking comfortable and at home in wool shirt and cord trousers, with his feet covered in thick stripy socks and no boots. I was instantly envious and also wary.

He held up a hand in greeting and I paused, watching the thoughts that came suddenly into my mind coalesce into words, "Ash, I really need to know, how long have you been back in this now?"

"Nearly three years." He grinned. "Coffee?"

WE DANCED around watchful words for the duration of the coffee making. The kitchen/living area was one long room on the front balcony facing part of the house. Actual other rooms could be seen through half open doors. It looked like two bedrooms with bathrooms. There was plenty of light coming in through ceiling glass tubes as the whole back of the house was built into the hill behind. A layer of insulating earth and moss covered the roof. I was guessing it had the same ecological profile as the cottage.

"Nice," I waved an admiring hand around. "Who designed this?"

"I did," he said. "I brought in some expensive Scandinavian builders, who flat packed it and shipped it over."

"Of course," I muttered sarcastically into my very tasty coffee, full of heated frothy milk and sugar, which is just how I like it.

"Do you have a file on me?" I asked him, indicating my clothes.

"Yes," he said, adding, "your hair and eyes are a darker brown than your ID."

There was silence. I slurped hot liquid and looked around as he went over to a desk with a lid and opening it, set out a very small computer with a flat screen. Tapping actual keys, he turned to me.

"This is what I've got," he pointed to the scroll of information that appeared in a hologram.

I did a quick search in my information. "Is that allowed?"

"It's technically possible but not in wide use yet," he replied.

I pulled a wooden kitchen chair from the table and sat next to him. The man in question was turning around on the holo as if for inspection. "Is this what he looks like?"

"I have no idea and it cost the life of an associate to get it." Ash was grim. "I'm guessing, but I think it's unlikely."

"Is the computer secure?" I was worried. People had died in my previous occupation *and* the current one, but not often and it was always a blow as we were a limited group.

"It's what is called air gapped, so yes." Ash waved his hand in the timeless signal for 'sort of.'

"*Terrific*!" I read the scroll of words; it was pretty thin. "Eagle-eye said he's causing a 'blip in the system.'" I wasn't looking at Ash but I heard the slight sniff of derision.

I leaned back in the chair and drank the rest of my coffee. The house was warm and I stood, rolling up the sleeves of the jumper and the t-shirt, my wet boots had been removed when I came in and were gently steaming on the heated flooring, the jacket hung on a stand by the door. Growing up on a farm, I was well house trained. Walking about, I started thinking. Ash watched me as did Badger, who was curled up by the fireplace, one eye open, the blue one. Small flames flickered enticingly. I was tired, but sometimes that was when I did my best connecting.

"How are you speaking to the unit?" I turned to look at him.

"I put a message into the dark web and it stays in an encrypted file and can only be opened with a date sensitive key."

"It appears forward at an appropriate moment?" I'd had a rough idea.

"You've never been back for long anywhen have you?" Ash had obviously read a very extensive file on me, he knew the answer, but we were having a conversation for some reason.

"No, I've been returning extinct species to their rightful location and the odd pursuit of smugglers in inappropriate places." I wandered around the room picking up personal items and collecting more information.

In the end I went with, "*Three years?* I'm going to throttle Eagle-eye!"

He smiled. "You're good at this, which is just as well."

I huffed. Badger could feel the tension and was now up following me as I continued my meandering and contemplation.

"What's the plan?" I said eventually, pausing long enough to hug the anxious puppy.

"You're going to have to stop doing that, it looks creepy." He waved a finger around his temple.

"Thinking is creepy?" I snorted.

"It is when you do it," he said, crossing his eyes.

I laughed, despite my best efforts not to. I really didn't know if Ash was on my side, or how important the stuff he was keeping to himself was. It made me nervous, which meant I looked for more information. This time I concentrated on not losing focus.

"Better," he said.

The phone pinged. I had left it in my coat pocket but I went to check it. "Roberta Tippett, says she's ten minutes away."

"Is she bringing Harley?" He closed the computer down and was finding boots and a coat.

"You set it up!" I tried not to sound paranoid.

"It's a good way to make friends around here." He handed me a pair of socks that were huge, I looked down at his feet, they matched in size.

"I didn't know I needed to," I muttered, removing my wet socks and putting them in the pocket of my coat along with the phone. The dry version was wonderful, like a warm foot hug.

"That's one of farming life's special feelings." Ash grinned at me and when I looked puzzled, he pointed at my feet. When I didn't react, he added sarcastically, "Ease yourself into it then, but don't take too long."

I tapped keys on the phone to say I was on my way back from Ash's house and would be there as soon as I could.

"You'll need this." He handed me a watch. I remembered my grandfather wearing a similar item, but most people forward relied on their comm. "You can't count on a phone connection and no one in this now knows exactly what the time is all the time without it."

I did up the strap, it felt odd for a moment or two but something about seeing the numbers and the moving hands was comforting, as if I had finally made a connection, though to what I didn't know.

"I'll give you a lift back on the quad bike. It'll be quicker." He was dressed and out of the door while I was putting on my boots, one of them still slightly squishy inside.

Badger decided to join us and sat himself firmly in front of Ash with his paws on the middle of the handlebars. It looked as if he was driving. The trip back through the river was wet but fast and the bike raced along the field. I held on behind Ash, Badger yipped in delight, his nose down, ears flat against the wind.

We arrived at the field gate and I hopped off to open it. "I'll leave you here." Ash turned the quad bike around as he spoke, gunning the engine. He looked at me, then down, patting the dog's head. "You weren't supposed to be activated yet, but it wasn't my call." It seemed to be some sort of apology.

"What does that mean?" I couldn't find anything in my briefing information or anywhere else that used the word and it filled me with disquiet, though I was betting I knew whose decision it *had* been. There were clearly knowledge gaps, either by chance, or more likely, design.

"Do you think you could manage one of these?" he asked me, indicating the squat, muddy vehicle and avoiding the question. I nodded. "I'll bring my spare over later, it's the easiest way to get around." He left, Badger still in the driving seat.

I was just about to open the gate when I heard the clip-clop and whinny of horses on the slope. I climbed over, walked across the bridge and waited by the river.

Four horses and two riders came into view. My first impression on seeing both of the women was shock. I leaned down and splashed my hands in the cold water, it helped to distract me.

The reason I was here was staring me right in the face.

"YOU HAVE GOOD HERBAGE, plus Ash checks for the usual problems, like ragwort and foxglove, the oak leaves and acorns are out of their reach." She paused, looking at me, as did the young woman standing patiently holding one of the saddled horses. The ponies had head collars and lead ropes.

Harley examined my outstretched fingers with polite interest, even to the point of an investigative nibble. "Manners!" Roberta said sharply.

He wandered off up the lane and through the cottage gate, stopped at the standing stones and the garden to check for possible threats, then into the field. His companion trotted after him without a backward glance for any of us.

Both horses were an unusual mix of Exmoor and something else. Harley was the bigger of the two but not by much. They had glossy, honey-coloured coats and light manes which gave them an exotic air compared to the actual Exmoor breed; and were small in comparison to the two saddled horses.

The one Roberta had been riding was a huge dark bay with an enormous head and meltingly beautiful brown eyes. He came over, stared for several seconds, sniffed my hair and the air around, then blew snot in my face. I took it as a great compliment and stroked his nose.

The women laughed. "His name is Bertie," Roberta said, with an expression of undiluted love and affection.

"Does anyone call you Bertie too?" I grinned.

"Not if they expect me to answer!" She said with a sniff.

I liked her immediately, but then I was also very fond of her descendant Daniel Roper, whom she so closely resembled. Tall and slim with red-gold hair and blue eyes, she could have been his sister, they were so alike. Even her voice had the same intonation. DNA is always amazing, but this was something more.

"It's Tippi, when you get to know her, but the farmers round here call her 'Tippi-teethi, because she's the local equine dentist." The younger woman was smiling at me after much the same level of scrutiny as Bertie, though I was hoping there would be no snot this time. "Hannah," she said, pointing at herself. She spoke with a lyrical European accent. Stunningly attractive with several bits of hay stuck in her long, dark, shiny hair and also holding the reins of a large horse, though it was not as big as Bertie. She patted its neck and then hopped back on with impressive skill. "I'll go back and get the stables mucked out, while you settle them in."

We stood looking at the horses in the field. Bertie had joined Harley and the companion, who was called Ernest.

"Do you ride?" Roberta was watching me, not the horses.

"What did Ash tell you?" I was genuinely interested in the answer.

"That you grew up on a farm in Cornwall, you had horses but they were used for work not recreation and you could ride when you were a child but hadn't done any since then."

I nodded; it was accurate. I had not been encouraged to develop any affection for the horses, but I couldn't resist spending time with them in the stables, it was always warm with that comforting smell of equine sweat and sweet hay. They were my companions and my consolation in a difficult home environment.

"What do you know about the miniliths in the garden?" I leaned forward as Ernest came up to me and asked for a stroke, I obliged, scratching his neck and smoothing his mane.

"They're called the Alger sisters, after a long-ago Saxon land owner. There's a convoluted story about a war between settlements, the tribe being massacred and the sisters enslaved, so their mother had the stones erected. She would come every evening to look at the stars and see her 'children.'"

"Oh, that is really sad!" I hugged Ernest and he didn't seem to mind.

"Or... it *could* be the local farmers just having some fun at the expense of the walkers who are here in the summer!"

I laughed out loud and she joined in. Harley came over and so did Bertie, because horses are highly sensitive to emotion and light hearts is one of their favourites.

"Is there anything else you need me to do?" I asked her.

"Just check they haven't got themselves into trouble and talk to them, they like good easy company, which is just not us at the moment, they're worn out with people sadness."

"Is that why you have them?" I was curious.

"Didn't Ash tell you I run a therapy centre?" She looked at me with that piercing blue gaze.

"No, it seems the personal stuff was strictly one way!" I said drily.

"I look after damaged horses principally, but it seems it works for people too—" she interrupted herself, "what are they *doing*?"

Harley and Ernest were standing stock still and looking at the place where I had come through the link in wary curiosity. I know horses are acutely aware of places where alteration occurs, they often follow things with their eyes that we can't see. The smaller pony lifted his upper lip and tasted the air for information.

"Flehmen response," I said helpfully.

"Yes, but to what?" Roberta speculated. Turning to me she did her own version of sensory perception that all good teachers have and most parents when they know something is wrong, but not what, and they are *absolutely* going to get to the bottom of it eventually.

I tried to distract her. "How far along are you?"

"Five months," she patted her small bump.

We removed their head collars and the lead ropes and I hooked them over my shoulder.

"I'll keep these here, just in case," I said, as I walked away from the horses, who had lost interest in the link area for now and were peacefully cropping grass. Roberta had one more look around then followed me.

"Do you have other children?" I asked her. Reminding myself not to mention the challenges of a licence and testing in my forward now.

"Three and a half, Alphie is seventeen, Toby fourteen and Abbigail is nine, then the bump," she pointed at it, smiling.

"*Seventeen*, how old were you?" I stopped talking, incredulous.

She laughed, "thank you, but I'm forty so it was legal!"

Not forward it isn't, I thought, then dismissed it, be in the here of this now or lose yourself.

"Alphie and Abbigail are all mine, Toby is from Luke's first partner, and the bump is both of ours," she explained.

"How well does that work?" I was curious.

"It's not too bad, Alphie is a teenager, he lives in the attic room subsisting on cheese flavoured noodles and doesn't speak, just grunts. Toby loves the moor and anything wildlife, is always rescuing small furry things and Abbi is a genius and frightens Luke by asking him questions about quantum mechanics."

It sounded awful but I was no judge of happy families. "It's complicated then," I said pragmatically.

"Christmas can be something of a trial, but we manage," she snorted. "I've been given strict instructions by Abbi that this must be a girl!"

She was making a joke, but I nearly tripped myself up by making a comment about genetic decisions and I had *never* met anyone who had four children. I covered with a question. "Tea?"

We arrived at the cottage door, and Bertie, who had wandered out of the field and was standing waiting patiently in the lane, seemed to be watching something across from the building on our side of the river. The trees and impenetrable autumn gold foliage were thick and came right down to the bank. A cold wind rustled in the leaves and bushes and it made me shiver for a moment. I really felt as if we were being watched. The horse whinnied his nervousness and both of the ponies in the field looked up, alert for possible predators.

"I have to get home, another time though." Roberta climbed onto the wall and slid across to the saddle, Bertie stood completely still until she was comfortable. I didn't say anything about her riding while pregnant and with no helmet, the horse looked smart enough to keep her safe. And it was clear the trust went both ways. Plus, she was obviously not someone you told to take it easy.

"Come up to the stables tomorrow Ari and meet the family, coffee and cake provided!"

I indicated that I would without actually saying anything. Bertie turned once after he splashed through the river, as if to say goodbye. But I don't think he was speaking to me; both of the other horses in the field lifted their heads for a moment of silent communication.

THE NOISE of the quad bike interrupted a lunch of cheese and buttered oatcakes that I had found in the fridge and cupboard respectively. I waited until I heard the scratching at the door and a demanding bark for attention.

"Well," I said, looking down. Badger responded by launching himself at me as if we hadn't seen each other for some time instead of a few hours. Ash was parking the vehicle behind the cottage.

Badger asked politely for a treat and I took one from the bag on the table and offered it to him, he waited for a moment, then lifted a paw for me to shake.

"Did you teach him that?" I asked Ash, when he came in and interrupted the handing over ceremony.

"I think the training is the other way round," Ash said dryly.

He pointed at the kettle and I nodded. While he was at the sink filling it, I got the cups out and added milk and sugar to the picnic on the table, and another plate and some jam to go with the oatcakes.

I waited until he sat down and the tea was poured before I said it. "Why didn't you tell me?" It came out with a certain level of quiet fury that I hadn't been aware of. Badger disappeared under the sofa by the fire.

Ash scrubbed his face, leaned back in his chair and looked at the ceiling. "I wanted you to see for yourself."

"Give me a—" I stopped before I swore, then was silent, waiting.

"Are you okay?" he said eventually.

"Because this conversation is going so much better than you thought it would?" I enquired politely.

"Well, yes," he said with a grin.

"How genetically direct is the connection?" I said, trying not to fall for the Ash Grey charm and nearly succeeding. He didn't answer me but buttered an oatcake and added a thick layer of jam.

I thought about it, sifting information and came to a horrifying conclusion. "How many?" I whispered.

He snorted, "you're *really* good at this, I can see why Eagle-eye— there are two direct and another two, possibly three, indirect."

It takes a lot to render me speechless, but this was it. I drank the aromatic tea and ate a piece of cheese. Badger came out from his hiding place and checked our faces. Satisfied, he went back to his favourite spot by the unlit fireplace and began making a mess with the chew treat.

I sighed. "I am from the forward of this now. It doesn't make me smarter; it just means I have some knowledge."

We both watched Badger devouring the scattered crumbs with a pink tongue. Ash pointed to the visible scar on my arm. "You tried to cuddle a velociraptor?"

"It's a long story," I said dryly. Word had travelled, literally. And it confirmed again that he had the file on my individual, highly secret project details. He was grinning again. I explained. "You already know that it was stolen as a juvenile and it looked tiny and a little, I don't know, *lost* when I returned it to its appropriate now moment." If anything, his grin was wider.

"I don't trust you," I said, after another pause when tea was drunk and he had crunched another laden oatcake.

"I don't blame you; I wouldn't trust me either," he sounded exasperated, and oddly sad.

ASH CHECKED me out on the quad bike. I looked carefully before I got on, it was similar to the version my family used, but without a bio fuel cell. Turning the engine key switch to make sure it was in neutral and pressing the starter button, the noise was wincingly loud. I released the parking brake and held onto the rear one, kicking the gear into first and moving off slowly. Ash watched me in the field along with Harley, Ernest and Badger, who all gave me their approval, then I ran it up and down the steep lane in front of the cottage. This time Badger decided he wanted to come too and he scrambled up, sitting between me and the handlebars. I cuddled him, he licked my face and then we were off again.

I struggled with the clutch and gears a few times, making Ash cringe as they grated in protest, until I got the hang of changing up and down with my right hand and left foot. He was leaning on the stone wall by the gate to the lane as I put the parking brake on and turned the engine off.

"How long do we have to sort this out?" I asked him. The trees rustled overhead and a few leaves scattered around us, like the golden reminder of a sleeping winter on the way.

"Days," he said eventually, watching my face for a reaction.

"No wonder Eagle-eye was frightened, he must realise that he could disappear at any moment if he stepped out of the protection field, never mind the unit and the effect on the core flow." This was shockingly honest, something I had done deliberately. Ash's face didn't change, so he knew about that too.

"Let me park it behind the cottage, it's a bit narrow and it's best if you don't leave it too exposed, there are gangs around here who steal to order and this is one of their favourite items." He got back on the quad bike and started it up. "You don't look surprised?"

"I'm not, I come from a now where people steal baby dinosaurs if they get the opportunity."

"THERE'S a helmet and goggles in the boot cupboard, if you're going further than my farm and onto the roads, I suggest you use them. Most of the young farmers around here don't bother, but I think it's important to respect the fragility of your cranium!" Ash opened one of the cupboard doors and pointed out the safety items.

"Thank you," I said politely. "Tea?"

He removed his coat and boots, filling the kettle while I sat down at the table. I was suddenly exhausted again. I usually got a few days off after I'd been back and forward. This was something new.

"It takes a bit of getting used to Ari," he muttered sympathetically, patting my shoulder.

My phone pinged and I checked it. There was a message, 'coffee tomorrow, ten-ish, come and have a look at the stables.' Followed by a tiny yellow circle with eyes and a grin. Ash snorted with laughter at my expression. I tapped a few keys to confirm that I would be there.

"What did you *say* to her?"

"That you worked for a charity that deals with animal trafficking and you'd had several really bad experiences with awful people that she mustn't ask you about, you were emotionally shattered and in need of a break, and I was an old family friend with a cottage."

I nodded, it was as close to the truth as possible and therefore easier to remember, as long as I didn't mention the type of creatures I had helped back to their natural environment.

"Why am I so tired?" I yawned and so did Badger in sympathy.

"It's the time differential between back and forward," Ash explained.

"It's not that much surely?" I said, puzzled.

"It is if you spend more than a few hours back," Ash clearly thought I knew, which I didn't. I was stunned.

"What's the difference if you've been here three years?" I was suddenly full of fear again.

He sighed, "It's slower here so I've been away nearly six years forward."

I tried not to look too shocked, but didn't succeed.

"You understand the three zero-point energy fields?"

I tried to recall the information and I know my expression must have been squinty because he snorted and rolled his eyes. "Quantum systems constantly fluctuating, even at absolute zero, matter fields, as in leptons and quarks and force fields as in photons and gluons, these are two of the transmission mediums or aether and the third is dark energy."

"So, no?" he grinned.

I laughed, "Svana says the vacuum holds the key to the link."

"She's right, but the problem has always been the time dilation field that begins to develop when we go back and forward. As you know, the universe is speeding up, that's caused by dark energy and the longer you're back it really makes it impossible to—" he interrupted himself, "you know you do look worn-out why don't you have a bath and go to bed?"

The suggestion made me yawn even more, and I let my mind lose the thread of what he had been saying because the ripple of apprehension was crawling up my back again.

I LAY IN THE BATH. Badger had decided to stay and Ash had said he would find his own way home in the morning if he wanted to. The puppy had listened to the wind rattling the windows and the rain battering the roof and made a decision that he would be fine with me. I felt almost guilty when Ash had left to trudge back to his farmhouse alone. We had eaten a meal that had been made from the seemingly endless kitchen contents, a vegetable rice dish that had been precooked and just needed reheating; I was too weary to actually taste it.

Ash had produced a bag of dog food from his coat pocket, which made me realise it was a set-up, though I didn't mind.

After a quick visit outside, and a wipe down with a towel, Badger hopped onto the bottom of the bed and turned around before settling down to sleep.

It was midnight dark and the rain had stopped, a bright half-moon was peering through the skylights of the roof. I sat bolt upright and so did Badger. Whatever had woken me was silent, but the horses were whinnying nervously in the back field and Badger's closed mouth growl added to the obligatory breath holding.

I slid back the covers and went over to the window looking onto the field. Standing carefully to one side I peered out, hoping not to be seen. A silhouette flitted through the trees and bent down, lifting up something bulky in each hand. It was difficult to focus, there was so much shadow in between the patches of moonlight, like a sinister chiaroscuro photograph inside my head. I watched but the figure had disappeared into the trees by the river. The horses waited and then eventually went back to sleeping upright, though they had moved nearer the fence by the cottage.

I turned round, Badger was settling down and snuffling grumpily. I got back into bed and he sidled up and curled close to me while I stroked his ears. Who was comforting whom, I wasn't sure.

I WAS UP EARLY and out, much to the puppy's delight. Badger sniffed the horses and in return they blew gently into his face as a greeting. The treeline looked benign in the cold, frosty light, and the clear blue sky and light winds made the day look easy and uncomplicated.

With my coffee cup resting carefully on a fence post as I didn't want to spill any and it was too hot to gulp down, I scrambled over to examine the mulch surrounding the trunks for any sign of disturbance.

Badger's happy yelp alerted me and I stood up. Ash wandered over and so did Harley and Ernest, they trailed after him with Badger, looking like a group on a mission. It made me laugh out loud, I sounded a bit rusty and it startled all of them.

"What are you doing? his voice was worried, not curious.

"I had company last night," I explained, going back to checking the ground.

Ash hopped dextrously over the fence, his long legs making it look easy. I snorted in annoyance. My height was considered to be short compared to my family and indeed most of the people at the unit. At least in this now I looked comparatively normal.

"Anything?" Ash saw my cup and helped himself to a swallow, then grimaced.

"What's wrong with the coffee?" I was really irritated.

"I can assure you," he said with asperity, "this is not caffeine, it seems to be a milky sugary sludge that might have seen a coffee bean in a past life!"

He handed me what was left, which was not much and then started casting around. I drank absent-mindedly as I tried to recall exactly where I had seen the figure.

It was Badger of course who sniffed out the evidence. He yelped to get our attention and then plopped his back end down, looking pleased.

"Well," I said, when I could finally speak.

"Do you have any idea what that is?" Ash was squatting by the tracks and he held a hand out carefully to measure the paw print.

"I do." I was struggling with the feeling of being suffocated. At least they were very, very small. I had studied them for a return trip back a few assignments ago. I spoke my thoughts out loud, "Daniel Roper is always really helpful with research, his expertise doesn't just cover deep time, he's also interested in the early Pleistocene epoch, more commonly referred to as the 'Ice Age—'"

Ash cut in, "Ari, get it together!"

"Smilodon," I said.

"ARE YOU SURE?" Ash was white with worry and Badger began to whine. "I thought all cats had retractable claws?"

"Not this one, kittens, two of them." I felt as if the grown-ups had left the room and I was completely alone.

"I'm out of my depth," Ash said, disconcertingly tapping into my thoughts.

I was muttering to myself as I tried to catch up with the information that was flooding my brain, "How did they get through, and why?"

Ash walked up and down looking for more tracks. He stopped. "Someone must have picked them up here." He pointed at a footprint. Then lined his own up against it to measure the size.

I snorted, "Give me a break, your feet are the same size as a stegosaurus!" I laughed as he looked affronted.

"They're not *that* bad," he muttered, relinquishing his place.

I did the same thing using my own foot as a comparison. "So, maybe a woman?"

"Hmm," he said, "or possibly a teenage boy."

"Do you know who this might be?"

He sighed. "It would make sense."

"Not to me it doesn't." I was cross again, with that feeling of not being able to quite catch up.

"Why would the kittens be here, I don't mean here in this now, I think I understand that part, but in this actual field... unless—"

"What?" Ash was sharp.

"It's possible that the scent receptors in the breed give them an enhanced view of the world. And they might have been able to detect the core flow." I pointed to where I had come through the link from forward. "Daniel did some research on evolutionary change due to back forward activity, but I haven't read the results."

Ash rolled his eyes and then sat down abruptly on the ground, causing Badger to leap around in misplaced delight. "And the reason why they're here?"

"It adds another layer of disruption to forward." I shrugged. It was not really my area of expertise and I was just speculating, but it seemed likely. Whoever had brought them forward from their own now had clearly been aware of the possibilities.

"Well, there's one good thing at least," I said, sounding oddly positive.

"What?" Ash wasn't convinced.

"Their mum isn't around."

"How do you know?" He was stroking Badger who had discovered treats in his pocket and was helping himself with an investigative nose.

"Because you'd have found great big versions of that!" I pointed to the kitten paw print.

"LET ME GUESS, you prefer that I should see for myself and work it out rather than you tell me?" I was sitting on the quad bike ready to go.

Ash was standing by the gate, he nodded and sighed. "It's better if you do." He held out the safety helmet.

"For whom?" I said sarcastically, putting it on. I had checked the online map using my phone, the stables were helpfully marked with a blue horseshoe.

I left in a cloud of high dudgeon and engine oil smoke. Badger watched me depart with a wagging tail and lolling tongue, Ash not so much.

THE RIVER HAD RISEN from the night's rain, but I sped through it and up the hill, along the bumpy track leaving spurts of washed down stones in my wake. I was glad I'd decided on wearing the helmet, as it felt precarious. I found myself standing up and leaning over to one side or the other depending on the camber, in the hope that would be slightly safer.

It levelled out at the top and there were fields on either side with sheep and cows. The sky was clear with a thin layer of high cloud. I shivered in the creeping autumn cold. A farmhouse, complete with a cheerful lady farmer checking on her animals, appeared on the left and she waved. I returned the gesture. The house was a single story, plain and neat with large barns to one side.

The track ended at a gate which I hopped off to open and then closed behind me. A tarmac road felt much smoother and safer and it curved around and down towards the village. A smaller dirt lane mean-dered off to the right and I stopped, orientating myself. The signpost said Cheriton and Furzehill, checking my phone map and the view I realised it would lead out onto the moor and then over to the right of the trail would eventually get back down to Ash's farmhouse. The other way was the village and Scoresdown.

Houses and farms were scattered along the downward steep hill road, which had me dropping a gear. I turned into the small village centre, really only a dozen cottages, several people waved from windows and gardens. It felt odd, and comforting at the same time, as if I had arrived in a now that made sense. I shook my head to clear the thought and changed gear again to go uphill.

Crossing the main road, the narrow lane opposite had grass growing down the middle. Hedges to either side made it difficult to see, but I could hear horses calling to each other, and a curious face peeping over a gap in the hawthorn confirmed that I was in the right place. I turned onto another bumpy track, then through an open gate and up to a large farmhouse, tucked carefully below the curve of yet another hill.

To my left there were barns and farm buildings. I decided to try them first. The quad bike was so noisy that by the time I got to a second, this time, closed gate, Roberta was already there. She grinned and waited until I had turned off the engine before she spoke, "Great, I'm gasping for a cup of tea!"

"Good morning to you too!" I laughed.

The farmhouse was enormous with high ceilinged rooms and big windows. She led me in through the back door into a utility room, where clothes and dirty boots were divested, and onto the kitchen.

Two terrier dogs looked up from their place by the warm range and didn't bother to move. One of them huffed an almost bark but closed his eyes immediately and went back to sleep.

"We live in here come the winter; the rest of the place is a pain to heat." Roberta filled the kettle and put it on the top of the range.

I sat down at the huge wooden table. It was covered in files and the usual unidentifiable detritus of farming with animals and having children. It was somehow reassuring that she was comfortable with herself and didn't excuse the mess or try and clear it away.

Alongside the more prosaic variety required to run a successful enterprise, as in actual paperwork, there were signs of technology, a laptop computer and a mobile phone that pinged messages alerts constantly. On one wall was a very large year planner with an eye-watering number of reminders in various colours. I found myself studying it with fascination. If ever a person needed an integrated communication device with a head up display, it was this woman.

"You should be here when we do the family meetings," she said wryly, as she made tea for herself and coffee for me and put a pile of wonky homemade biscuits on the table. "We're lucky enough to have good broadband, but that's down to Ash, he paid to put a tower on his land that we can all access. There are people around here trying to run their own businesses who worship him like a god, and I'm one of them!" She snorted with laughter at my expression.

"I hope the coffee's okay, I don't usually drink it, even without the peanut," she pointed at her bump, then added, "The biscuits are a moving in present from Abbigail."

"Thank you." I took one.

"Don't thank me until you've tasted them!" Roberta laughed. "Abbigail has many fine skills and is brighter than all of us put together, but she can't cook!"

The pale green walls were decorated with the most amazing two-dimensional photographs of local wildlife, birds of prey and hares caught in their perfect moment, and several of the Exmoor ponies marking the seasons with colts and shaggy coats.

Roberta saw me admiring them. "They're done by Toby."

"He has a real talent," I said, beginning to work out the possibilities 'for myself,' as Ash intended.

A knock at the back door and someone came through the utility room. I was instantly on alert, but Roberta looked as if this was the usual form of entry.

The young man, really no more than a teenager, came into the kitchen. I tried not to gasp, but did a bad job of disguising it. He smiled.

"Gethin Roper!" Roberta said suspiciously. "What brings you here at this time of the morning?"

"Well Ms Tippett, I was wondering if Alfie had overslept?" He spoke quietly and with a reasonable and calming voice, as if to an unpredictable animal.

He was right to do so. Roberta's face went white and then very pink. Slowly, she got up from the table, and both Gethin and I held our breath. Every inch of her was 'mother on the warpath.' The two terriers sleeping by the range were abruptly on alert and out of their basket, slithering, ears down, into the utility room.

She disappeared into the main hallway out of sight. Suddenly, and in a voice several sizes too big for her, "Alfie, get down here, *right now*!"

Gethin grinned at me, looking so much like his descendant, Eagle-eye, I felt as if my expression would give me away. He must have misinterpreted my feelings of apprehension because he whispered, "Don't worry, her bark is worse than her bite."

"Good to know!" I said, as quietly as I could manage.

Alfie appeared after thundering down several sets of stairs. He was tangled up in his clothes, so he must have dressed on the way. Red-gold hair like his mum's, but spiked and face pillow marked.

Roberta followed him into the kitchen. Her reasonable countenance didn't fool anyone.

"If you mess up this apprenticeship, there will be consequences of epic proportions." Her voice had a thread of menace. We all nodded our understanding.

The two young men prepared to leave and as Roberta was filling a flask and handing over thick, healthy-looking packed sandwiches, enough to feed an entire unit team, or one teenager, Alfie managed to give me a small scrap of paper without his mum seeing. He looked at my puzzled face and put a warning finger to his lips. I pocketed it. Gethin, with what must have been long practice, did a good job of not noticing.

I heard Alfie say as they left, "That didn't go as badly as I thought it would."

Then just as they were nearly out of my hearing, Gethin asked, "Are you going to tell me what it was about?"

And the even fainter reply, "Little brother stuff."

His mum's hearing was clearly as good as mine. "Have *you* any idea what my eldest son was up to?" her expression was sharp, with an edge of worry.

I shrugged. "As a survivor of sibling conflict, I'm wishing he was my big brother!" I felt, for a moment, as if I had neatly dodged the possibilities for a problem.

"Hmm," she said, and left it at that, but her face was not in agreement.

Roberta sat down as the sound of the car faded into the distance. She shook her head in exasperation. "They both work at the boat yard in the harbour, Alfie is boat-building and Gethin is doing a marine mechanics apprenticeship. His mum is the local lifeboat coxswain." She sighed, "I'm really hoping all that positive influence is going to rub off on Alfie."

"I'm sure it will," I said, grinning at her scowling face, aware that the whole thing had been planned to deliver the screwed-up bit of paper I had in my pocket. I couldn't think why, there must have been easier ways to get me a message. But I remembered being fourteen. Everything is complicated.

Into the next pause, Hannah bounded through the utility room, leaned into the kitchen with her dirty boots right on the point of crossing the invisible line between the two. "I have a slight problem with Rudy, can you come and have a look?"

"Would you like to see the stables and horses?" Roberta was already on her feet.

Hannah looked at me and then at the coffee cup and there was an imperceptible shake of her head and raised eyebrows.

"Yes please!" Puzzled, I gulped my coffee down and tried not to choke, it was awful. Hannah grinned mischievously.

"What?" Roberta was checking the pinging phone.

I dissembled, "Nothing, the drink was a bit hot." Then grabbed a handful of biscuits, which I shared with the smiling Hannah on the way to the yard. We walked up a small incline and around some massive old trees growing between the house and the stables, almost in a full circle from where I had come up the lane and parked. There was an alternative entrance to the buildings down another short steep hill, that led off from the main road across the moor.

The sliding doors were open and a wonderful smell of warm horses and dry haylage greeted me. It was as if the best bits of my childhood had returned, without all the misplaced feelings of not belonging.

The barn was several individual stalls on either side of a wide central space, with a large floor to roof opening at each end. The horses leaned over the hinged doors with bright inquisitive looks. I could see the tack room full of labelled bridles and saddles to one side of the main entrance, and a feed storage area on the other. There was a big chart on the wall with the horses' names and the list of feed supplements and special treatment schedules. Some of them with a warning highlighted in red marker pen.

Rudy was not looking over at me, he stood quietly, head down, breathing slowly. Roberta stopped abruptly, the soft words she spoke made the horse prick up its ears and as she went through into the stall, he lifted his head and sighed.

My throat caught, I could see the ugly, oozing, sarcoid growth on his hind leg close to the hoof and where there was one, there would be more. "Do you have any calendula ointment?" I asked Hannah.

"There's some in the feed store in the medicine cabinet." Roberta said, without looking away from Rudy, who was now leaning his considerably large nose on her shoulder. She staggered a bit, but didn't seem to mind.

"What about milk thistle, mistletoe and if you have it, comfrey and horsetail supplements?" I said, thinking back to the herbal remedies my aunt Rosie, the single relative of whom I was inordinately fond, had used on our horses.

"Same place," Roberta said to Hannah, as the young woman left to find the items. "Is this something you know about?"

"Not really," I spoke carefully, trying not to give too much away, which considering what had happened after the third global pandemic, was a lot, "my aunt Rosie was an herbalist, this was a treatment for our horses to help them with autoimmune conditions." I didn't add that in my forward now, we had medical nanobots for the more difficult illnesses.

"How is it that you have all this available?" I said, as Hannah came back with the various containers. I was expecting her to have to order most of it from an online site.

"My grandfather had an interest in herbal medicine too," Roberta said. "I don't have any knowledge myself but a lot of the farmers around here use a variety of these remedies along with the more conventional medicine. Where do you stand on Liverpool cream?" she asked me curiously.

My alarmed expression made her laugh. "It's toxic, so just make sure you wear gloves before you slather it on, otherwise your baby is going to be born with two heads!"

We three stood watching Rudy. He sighed and blew gently down his long soft nose, ruffling Roberta's tousled hair. There was a silent, expressive moment, when the beautiful bay made a decision to try and live for the love of the person standing next to him. The lump in my throat for the memories of my forward past came back to me in quantities that were difficult to swallow.

I turned suddenly, breaking the emotional quiet and said, "How many horses do you have here?"

"Go and introduce yourself!" Roberta was smiling as I began wandering up one side towards the back entrance to the barn. Hannah handed me some treats and then went into the feed store.

Eight stalls to each side, and a variety of horses from small Exmoor ponies to a Clydesdale of *epic* proportions. I've seen smaller mammoths. A wipe clean chart on each stall marked the issues and treatment for each horse.

They all had problems and some of them were people related. On one was written in red marker, 'don't go near Ethel with anything that looks like a stick or whip!' I held out my hand with a treat and a soft nose reached out carefully and with delicate lips nibbled gently. I patted her neck and talked to her; the strawberry roan seemed delighted by the attention. I have always been amazed at how forgiving animals are. Sometimes we get the love we don't deserve.

Through the large double back barn doors, I could see an enormous muck heap near the lane gate and some huge covered bales of haylage stacked to one side. The still fields spread out towards the coastline and into the sea beyond in layers of green and misty blue. I took in a deep breath and found myself with the odd misplaced sensation in my chest again, of belonging in another now.

"It gets to me every time and I was born here," Roberta said, making me jump. "Sorry, I could see you were lost in thought."

"Impressive muck heap," I countered, pointing.

"It goes tomorrow, the local farmers put in requests, and we let them have it for their fields," she sounded proud.

"Premium horse shit!" I laughed.

"Exactly!"

"What does Hannah do here?" I was curious. We walked back towards the main entrance, and I handed out treats and shared warm breath with the horses on the other side of the barn.

"She's a physio, and works mainly with the people who come here, but she has amazing horse skills too, I will miss her when she goes home. There are two other therapists, but they're local and come on an individual basis, that is, horse therapy for one and person client for the other!"

"You really have it organised," I was impressed.

"I'm glad you think so, it's actually a logistical nightmare and bill paying panic, both I and my partner have to work other jobs to keep the lights on!" Roberta sounded stressed and a bit tearful.

"I'm sorry," I couldn't think of anything else to say.

"It's okay, I'm pregnant and full of *very* inconsistent hormones." She smiled, but the worry was still there. "I have horse teeth to clean and file on one of the neighbour's farms, do you want to come with me?"

"I'd better get back, I have some work to do of my own and I can't put it off any longer, but if you want company another day I'd love to come and watch. Or help if you need me to, er, hold anything?" I finished lamely. She grinned and I felt awful, my intentions weren't exactly altruistic, it was the best way to get a good look at as many people as possible, I really needed to find the deviant personality.

I heard a shout and several of the horses pricked up their ears. "That's Luke, my partner, I was hoping you'd be able to meet him before you left this morning."

Luke arrived with several carrier bags in each hand. I tried not to wince, first there was the paper, now the plastic.

"Hello," he introduced himself. Tall and slim with green eyes and lots of dark hair, the genetic resemblance to another one of my unit team members was gaspingly worrying. Though their skin colour was different and the build, due to her high gravity dome living, he and Pearl were clearly related.

"What's in the bags?" Roberta asked him suspiciously.

He sighed, "Paperwork." He looked at me. "I run an online office management business, several of the local farmers are my clients." He opened one of the bags and we peered inside.

"Is that marmalade?" Roberta spoke after careful scrutiny.

"Yes," Luke frowned, "*and* coffee and I think that *might be* calving fluids." He sounded pragmatic.

"Eeuw!" I said helpfully.

"Yep," Luke agreed, shrugging. "I'm off down to the house. Don't worry, I'll peel them apart in the study, not on the kitchen table."

He left after shaking my hand again and I inspected my fingers once he'd gone as surreptitiously as possible. I don't mind marmalade and coffee, but there are limits.

"If you want you can meet some of his clients, when he goes out again next week? Roberta was being incongruously helpful. She added abruptly, "I can't find anything about you on social media?" Then, as if the thought had just occurred to her, "Is that because you were under-cover and people are after you for the animal trafficking investigative work you do?"

"What did Ash say?" my mouth was a bit dry with nerves but I had already intuited the answer.

She squinted and then repeated what must have been verbatim, "That you needed a distraction from your experiences, if I could get you involved in the local area and introduce you to as many people as possible, you might not have another meltdown. Oh, and you weren't a danger to us."

I gasped, "Well, er, thank you for your honesty!"

"I'm *always* honest." Roberta looked shocked.

"Yes, you are!" Came Hannah's laughing voice from one of the stalls.

THE RIDE back to the cottage was peaceful and I waved again at the folk going about their busy farming and country working day. I stopped three times for different vehicles to pass on the narrow lane through the village, coughing and spluttering on a shocking level of petrol fumes.

Ash was standing by the river with an ecstatic Badger, who waited no more than a second after I turned the engine off before jumping onto me and trying to clean my face with his pink tongue. I squeezed him until he yelped with delight, wriggling and yipping as if we hadn't seen each other a few hours ago.

"Well?" Ash said, he was washing his muddy wellington boots by sloshing his feet back and forward in the fast flowing water.

"*That* is a *lot* of genetics in one place!" I shook my head, incredulous. "The biological reality is, I can see more than four direct connections."

Ash swore. "How could this get any worse?"

"He knows we know?" I said helpfully.

"There's that."

Badger stood still, watching us both and feeling the uneasiness, but not understanding why and then we all turned to look at the river, as if the answers were there.

"Why is this so," I hunted for the right word, "meandering?" I examined the banks again and the gated barriers to collect debris when the water level was high, this time with more careful eyes.

"I'm rewinding it." He explained, "The area is prone to flooding and the old ways work best here."

Ash grabbed the worried puppy and walked over the bridge; I got back on the bike and made my way carefully through and up to the cottage. I left the quad bike outside for Ash to park round the back and went to check on Harley and Ernest in the field. The ponies were pleased to see me, it wasn't quite in Badger's league but they came up to me and hunted for the treats that I had saved. Happy munching followed and I texted Roberta by sending her a photo of them. The reply pinged back almost immediately with a thumbs up picture, in the obligatory yellow. I snorted.

Lunch was the usual table picnic, but Ash didn't seem to mind and

I don't care as long as it has food value and tastes nice. He indicated the small freezer and when I opened the door, I could see it was full of precooked meals, all helpfully labelled.

"One of the local farmers makes them as another income stream, he bakes the best cakes and biscuits too. I put some in the cupboard."

"Does everyone around here have more than one job?" I was buttering fresh crusty bread and slicing a really nice smelly blue cheese. Ash boiled the kettle and made the tea; we sat down.

"Yes, it's difficult to live on what the farms make in this now." Ash sounded sad.

"How is he going back and forward?" I asked Ash, wondering if he would tell me.

"My guess is he isn't," Ash said ominously.

I stopped eating.

The connections lined up in front of my eyes, like a synaesthesia of thought and shape and I tried not to look too creepy while I studied it. "Then this isn't just about someone seeing an opportunity tied to those stables to get rid of the unit's collective past for money or power." He understood, because he nodded but he waited for me to speak. "It could be revenge," I said, still working on my process.

"What do you make of the massive number of antecedents in one place?" he asked me eventually.

"We have a genetic bottleneck occurring forward after the next global pandemic, *and* the one after that, it's possible that an anomalous number survived in this area."

He ate his food and let me think. I watched Badger sliding surreptitiously up onto one of the chairs, where, with one single sigh of contentment, he settled down to immediate sleep, in true puppy fashion.

"Why are *you* here in this now? I mean, you know what's coming and I wouldn't have thought it would require your usual skill set." Then, because he didn't, I answered my own question, "Maybe that's why you're here, because you don't fit the profile."

"It's a confluence of continued events and people." He sat back, teacup in one hand and sighed, "which won't happen if I can't fix this."

"We," I snapped.

"What?"

"If *we* can't fix it." I was suddenly angry. "That's why I'm here, isn't it?"

"Yes," he said, looking uncomfortable. He hunted for the right words. "I am aware that if you work things out for yourself, you're more likely to believe it."

I had read his profile, but clearly, the one he had on me was more extensive.

"What next?" He finished his tea; it was as if we were talking about crop rotations or the seasonal worming of stock. He really looked the part of a local farmer. Comfortable in this now. I pondered the thought, but decided to peruse it when I was alone.

I took the crumpled note out of my pocket and flattened it out on the table so I could read it.

"WHERE DID YOU GET THAT? Ash said warily.

"Toby; he persuaded his big brother Alfie to pull a ruse of over-sleeping, so he could hand it to me behind his mum's back." I grinned.

"*Why*, it's a bit complicated?" his face was incredulous.

"He's fourteen," I explained.

"Ah, okay," Ash said, with not a whit of understanding.

I read the note, in a neat hand were the words, 'Please help, midnight in your field, come alone.' Short and to the point.

"Why midnight?" Ash was really being dense.

"*Fourteen!*" I said again, exasperated.

"Right," he drawled the word, then added unhelpfully, "His mum would be really worried if she knew."

"I imagine the idea is she doesn't know." I thought about it. "How dangerous is it around here?"

"Well, normally I would say not very, a bit of sheep stealing and the odd rave, and we've had some nasty dog attacks recently, but with the deviant," he finished on a high note, rather like someone asking a question.

I pondered, then came to a conclusion. "Tracking er, subjects," I delicately avoided the word target, "is your skill set, so, you'd better follow him from as close to the stables as you can get, to here."

He snorted, "He'd probably spot me in the first five minutes!"

"Then be more careful!" I snapped unhelpfully.

He sighed, "Sure, why not. I'll go back to the farm and get some work done. See you later."

After Ash left with a reluctant and sleepy Badger in tow, I wandered around the cottage, looking at pictures and photographs, flicking through interesting books and opening drawers and cupboards. It was as if I had written a list of requirements. But there were also things I found that were, the word that came to mind was 'pleasing,' as if *I* had spent time browsing for art and collectables and had been making a home for myself. The thought was increasingly disturbing; it had a longevity about it.

I lit the fire and made another cup of tea, adding the farmer's homemade biscuits to a tray. Opening an old book, I sat and read until the evening made a lamp necessary to see the words on the page. My drink had a cold skin over it and the plate of biscuits were uneaten. I couldn't remember the last time I had done nothing but lose myself in a good story.

WORRYING about Toby started soon after the sun had set, so I went for a hot bath and contemplated the possibilities for child endangerment. I comforted myself with sandalwood, scented bubbles and the fact that he probably knew the area better than a poacher. Several of the photographs on the walls of the farmhouse kitchen were of crepuscular or nocturnal animals. His mum must have known he was wandering the moor in the dark when he took them.

I waited until a few minutes before midnight, then went out into the field. Ernest came over to me immediately and asked for treats. I found one in the pocket of the warm jacket I had been wearing on the bike. He munched with delight then asked for a neck scratch and a nose rub, which I did. Harley, not wishing to be left out, came over and

I repeated the process. They then stood there looking, clearly wondering what I was doing.

He made no noise, just a slight scrabble behind me and I was whirling around in trepidation.

"Toby!" I whispered, once my blood pressure had gone back to near normal levels. "It's nice to meet you."

"Hi," he said gruffly, adding incongruously, "Um, thank you for being here."

Really, he had impeccable manners, Roberta would be proud. I made a mental note not to tell her just where and when I had come to that conclusion.

"How can I help?" I said, sounding ridiculous, as if I was at a meeting with prospective unit clients.

"Mum said you work with illegally trafficked species?"

"Yes, or actually I did." I knew where we were going but it still felt much too close to the truth to be comfortable.

"Can you get something I've found, back to where they belong?" He was cautious.

"I'd do my best," I tried to sound positive, but not too definitive.

The horses were watching us, each time we spoke they looked at the speaker, as if waiting politely for their turn in the conversation, but not wanting to interrupt as it would be rude. The moon came from behind the clouds and I could see him clearly where there had just been shadows before. My breath came at a gasp and he spun on a heel, checking the trees for danger.

"Sorry," I said, "I'm cold and there was a sharp, er, gust of wind," I finished lamely.

Toby looked so much like Pearl, with his dark eyes, skin colour and the even patrician features. Luke's first partner must be genetically direct. The expression on his face was very familiar as well, she had often used it when I was going on too much about nothing.

He spoke in a loud whisper. "You can come out now!"

Ash moved quietly from the treeline and sauntered over to join us. The horses were overcome with curiosity and delight in equal measure. "When did you pick me up?" he asked the teenager.

"Just after I reached the edge of the first field," Toby sounded apologetic.

"Good spot," Ash was genuinely impressed, which really helped.

I got back to the important things. "My toes are freezing and I can't feel my fingers. Can we move this along a bit?"

Toby was quiet, his face in the moonlight a myriad of youthful anxiety and indecision. He sighed. "This way." Taking us to the outer edge of the field opposite the cottage and away from the riverbank and treeline, he hopped over the fence and beckoned us onwards.

We walked silently onto part of what I'd identified as Shortacombe Common. The ground was rough and I tripped a few times, we hadn't gone very far when I heard the noise, a sort of chuffing.

Tucked away from prying eyes in amongst some prickly gorse bushes was a hide, a carefully built nursery of twigs and branches, full of soft haylage.

"I think they're some sort of species throwback, they look like Smilodon, you know, prehistoric, but they can't be, they're extinct." Toby was middle of the night helpful and informative.

The kittens were very young and cute, with short stout legs, round ears and a spotted coat like a snow leopard. The fact that they were Smilodon gracilis, the smaller of the species, and their upper canines hadn't yet developed, was something to be thankful for, but not much, they would be hunting soon. Native to North and South America and extinct for around ten thousand years in this now, they would make quick work of the flocks of sheep in the area once they had grown. Usually, they stayed with their mother for much longer than other big cats, but instinct can sometimes be stronger than learned behaviour.

Ash picked them up after putting gloves on and tucked one of them under each arm. They made the chuffing sound as if asking for help, disconcertingly they were calling to Toby. The teenager was showing signs of distress, so I marched him ahead and back to the cottage, while Ash put the kittens into a container that he had secreted close to the fence line between the cottage and the field.

I sat Toby down with a milky drink by the glowing embers of the fire. Badger had appeared from under the kitchen table, so Ash must have put him in the cottage on his way into the field following Toby.

He was very annoyed to have been left out of the proceedings, but as usual, forgiving. Toby stroked his ears and head in mutual comfort. Clearly, he had bonded with the kittens.

He sighed, much too sad a sound from a young person. Which is what he was, on the cusp of being older, but not yet. "Will you be able to help them?" His expression was as penetrating as Pearl's had always been when faced with the impossible.

"Yes, I really think I can." It would take a bit of effort, but I had done it before, of course not from back to forward and then further back, but I was already working out the process.

His relief was visceral, I wished I didn't have to say the next thing.

"It might be best if you didn't go into detail with your parents, I wouldn't want them to worry."

"Huh! I'm not going to tell them anything; I'd be grounded *forever*!" The look on his face made me laugh out loud.

I thought that Roberta would be well aware that something was going on, but maybe I could allay her fears without causing a problem. She struck me as the type of mum who only interfered if actual blood was spilt, and her children would grow into independent resourceful people because of it.

Ash came in and patted Toby on the shoulder in the male ritual of solidarity in adversity. I envied them the simplicity of the emotion.

I yawned and it became catching, farming life was mostly an early morning one and this was really late. Ash helped himself to hot chocolate and sat down next to me for a moment, he hadn't taken his coat off. Badger had wisely gone back to sleep as close as possible to what was left of the fire. He only opened one eye and then snorted with approval when I got up to put on more wood to burn so the flames caught again.

Toby was beginning to lose hold of the mug in his hand and his head was bobbing forward. "Come on lad, let's get you home," Ash said quietly. "I'll take the quad and bring it back before I walk along the river," he told me.

As they were going to the door I asked casually, "Toby, have you seen anyone around who doesn't belong to the area?"

"You mean the sort of person who could be trafficking endangered species?" he said, with far too much cynicism for someone his age.

"Yes, or really, just a new face?"

"Apart from you, no." He yawned again, this time it was a full body action. If he made it to school the next day it would be fuelled on willpower alone. Stopping in the doorway, he added, "You're weird, but in a good way."

Ash shrugged and they left, Badger stayed by the fire and hoped not to be noticed.

I made myself another cup of tea and went up to the bedroom, after the usual ablutions and some thinking, I got into bed. Badger was already curled up at the bottom, he opened one eye and, reassured that he wasn't going to be tipped off, went back to sleep, dreaming puppy dreams that made his paws and nose twitch. If Ash wanted his dog he would have to come back in the morning.

The sound of the quad bike filtered through my own night-time wanderings, but it didn't wake me. What did, was the connections my brain made.

I MUST HAVE GONE BACK to sleep because Badger alerted me to his own clean up requirements by licking my nose until I woke, and then pawing at the covers until I got up. It was early morning and full of dawn shadows, the mist from the river swirled around the field and garden making ghosts of the horses. I turned on the bedside light.

"*You* are *very* annoying!" I grumbled at him and he yipped his thanks at the compliment. Then ran downstairs, his stubby puppy tail sweeping as he went.

I followed him and unlocked the door; Ash was standing the other side. I gasped and stepped back abruptly, one hand making an involuntary fist and the other grabbing the nearest weapon, a boot, which I threw.

"Good reflexes!" Ash dodged the missile and came in bringing the cold with him. Badger, with a brief hello, left to do his business.

After hopping outside in the cold and retrieving the boot, I pointed at the kettle. Ash made the tea and I lit the fire.

"How much sleep have you had?" I looked at the clock, my circadian one didn't seem to work in this now and I missed my comm. It was seven.

"Er, about three hours, I needed to check some of the sheep." He made a full pot and drank two cups in quick succession.

"Was Toby able to get into the house undetected?" I was curious.

"He climbed in through a window at the back using some badly sited trellis." He grinned.

"Do you think she knows?" I poured myself a cup and put out the makings of breakfast.

"Oh yes!" He said, snorting with laughter.

I sat at the table and drank my tea. Ash was slathering butter on bread, followed by an impressive layer of marmalade.

I spoke quietly, "He doesn't stand out as new to the area, because he isn't, he's been here a while, possibly, like you, for years."

Ash dropped the bread on the floor the wrong side down, it splattered spectacularly.

I added, "And when those kittens are no longer around, it will confirm that we are aware of him, because he will know, to lessen the damage, we would send them forward to be returned back to their own now."

It was quiet for a moment. I could hear Badger scratching to come in, so I went over and opened the door.

Having retrieved the bread and made an effort to scrape up some of the mess, Ash pointed to the remainder and Badger obliged.

"So, we just rang the bell?" He sighed, looking really tired.

"If you like," it was a good analogy. "I can't understand why he doesn't stick out like a—"

"Smilodon?" Ash helpfully finished the sentence for me. "How did he get them here, if he's been stuck back in this now?" He looked at my face and leaned back in his chair. "He's not just getting information from forward; it's help too." He sounded desperate.

"Eagle-eye will have to be told in a separate communication. I might not like his decision making, but I trust him to sort it out."

I decided to take my tea and do the bathroom stuff as I was still in my pyjamas. When I came down, Ash was asleep with Badger by his side on the sofa. I tiptoed about, putting things away and tidying up, my connections scattering in different directions but coming back to the same conclusion.

"He would want to be close by, he gets an emotional charge from watching them," I spoke my thoughts.

"Is that your intuitive thinking process?" Ash hadn't opened his eyes. When I didn't reply he sat up and looked at the fire, not at me. "I haven't terminated anyone since I've been here."

I think my mouth dropped open; I was confused. "I thought we were getting this deviant and *returning* him to forward?"

Ash didn't speak. I wanted to kick something but the wood furniture looked resilient. "This is Eagle-eye again?"

"I sent the coded message on the dark web last night when I got in Ari, requesting that they open a three zero-point energy field link at exactly twenty-one hundred this now."

"Has it ever not been done when you asked?" I was curious.

"No." Ash was adamant which was reassuring, as it was meant to be. We both needed to know they were still there, and listening.

A part of me silently added, 'Until they are not.' But I shrugged it off as a stray anomalous thought, and not part of my connections.

"I need to do some looking around. I'm going with Roberta, in her other guise as Tippi-teethi, to see if I can find out anything."

"You don't think his arrogance will bring him to us?" Ash was stretching, he was so gangly he looked like he'd grown up under the low gravity dome on Ganymede. I smiled.

"What?" he said.

"Nothing. Are you going to check in on the kittens, or shall I?"

"Are you likely to bond with cute small furry creatures, or is it just velociraptors that you try and cuddle?"

"I did it *once!*" I tried to sound annoyed but I was laughing.

He snorted, "I'll see to them."

I sent a text message to Roberta, who seemed happy to have the company. She asked if I could get to the stables in half an hour as she needed to start early. I sent one of the yellow faces with a smile and hoped it meant what I thought it did. "These phones are addictive!" I grumbled. "I'm going to need a reset when I go forward, never mind squandering paper and fossil fuels, I can't believe they give devices that cause a deterioration in developmental abilities to *children,* I can feel it affecting my own cognitive skills by the second—"

"You wait until you see someone smoking actual tobacco!" Ash cut in on my complaining as he went through the front door.

"Wait, *what?*"

I could still hear the laugher as he made his way round the back of the cottage, over to where he had stashed the kittens in the hedge. I watched through the large windows in the living area. It was almost imperceptible, but I could hear the chuffing sound Toby had made to reassure them.

I was sarcastic, "Of course *you're* not bonding with the cute small furry things!"

THE JOURNEY through the village was becoming disconcertingly familiar, I waved to the same people and paused at the main road for several farm vehicles to pass by.

It was cold and clear with a frost on the ground and the beginning of the season for resting some of the fields; that's if you weren't wheat drilling them or ploughing in preparation for planting in the spring; then there was the harvesting of potato and sugar beet crops, bringing in the last of the winter feed to storage and bedding down cattle and sheep that didn't stay out. I knew from my childhood that winter for farmers was exhausting with dark, cold and often wet, early mornings and sometimes late evenings.

Ash had disappeared off with Badger, still laughing at me. Even the puppy looked amused, he wagged his tail and grinned until the desired effect was achieved and I hugged him.

Before I left, I took a photo of a contented Ernest who was gazing over the hedge, a puzzled expression on his face. Scratching his neck until his eyes started to roll with contentment, I explained carefully that the kittens would be gone by the evening. Satisfied, he went back to cropping at the grass with a completely disinterested Harley. I examined the field and tried to work out if they would need haylage soon.

My learned information didn't run to crop values and I couldn't remember from my own farming childhood what the levels of nutrition should be. Both of the horses had some hardy Exmoor DNA, but it was another question for Roberta.

The stables were quiet when I arrived and I parked the quad bike over to one side of the yard. A few of the inmates were shuffling and munching, their curious heads eventually coming over the stalls when they heard me enter. There didn't seem to be anyone else around. I could see the remains of the muck heap through the large barn doors at the end of the stables, it was still impressive and so was the view beyond.

"Hey, you're early, excellent!" Roberta said, coming up behind me. "Can you give me a hand to get the equipment into the car?" She held several implements that looked worryingly like something a giant would use to floss after a really chewy meal.

The tools were stored neatly in the office in labelled containers and the car was parked in the stable yard. It didn't take long to transfer it all across to the boot of the large utility vehicle.

"If you don't mind me asking, how much does all this apparatus cost?" I was curious.

"About ten thousand pounds and it's more to service than my car!" She grinned at my stunned expression. "Nothing too difficult today, just some basic maintenance."

The vehicle had two comfortable seats in the front and a grill between them and the back, which was all storage and no seating. Roberta drove like a woman who had the ability to see round corners.

"Toby says you don't have a television?"

"I don't," I said, after checking my information with what I hoped was not too much of a creepy look. It seemed to be a flat version of the story-vision I was used to. I added, "It was important to have a break from the real world." I glanced at the side of her face; at least she was now looking at the road.

"What else did Toby say?" I asked warily.

"That you helped him with some illegally trafficked, endangered animals and not to worry, because although you are *really* weird, his words not mine, you are very kind and good at your job."

I snorted; she had the interrogation skills of a unit professional. "Are you worried?"

"He's fourteen," she said simply, "so, yes."

Our arrival at the first farm was announced with a screech of tyres and an inspiring, sideways, mud induced, shimmy. A burly farmer leaned out of a nearby barn, his frown turned to a grin and he waved in recognition. I exhaled, as my eyes were beginning to blur from the slight lack of oxygen to the brain due to the breath holding.

"Roberta, is there anyone around here whose behaviour you think is, I don't know," I paused, hunting for a non-threatening but accurate description, I went with, "somewhat eccentric?"

Her expression was bemused. "It's Exmoor, that pretty much describes everyone!"

THE FARMER QUIPPED about Roberta's driving skills, which I thought was very brave of him. He introduced himself to me. "Martin Cooper, incomer to the moor, my family have only been here since the nineteen sixties." He was the same height as Roberta but muscular, with dark hair and eyes, he shook my hand and I told him my name. "Ari Bickerstaff, it's an unusual name, are you by any chance related to the family that runs a small seaweed farm on the north Cornwall coast?"

"I er," was all I could manage. My family were farming there, but not in this now. I tried to remember what my aunt Rosie had told me about our history, and only came up with the vaguest of memories, it was as if I was looking through clouds of dust. Fortunately, Martin was more interested in his own recollections.

"My dad grew up there, my grandad came further up country as there was land available, but he used to talk about his neighbours with great fondness. I hear they're running into trouble financially, it's a shame, because seaweed is such a good crop, animal feed, fertilizer, biomaterials," he was really enthusiastic, "never mind the fact that it can store carbon better than trees!"

I must have looked stunned because Roberta interrupted, "We need to see Wellington, Martin?"

"Of course!" Martin led us into the large barn where a variety of farm vehicles were stored. Bales of wrapped hay were stacked neatly and a collie sheep dog was snoozing on some old sacks.

There were three stalls down one side. Two horses peered over the doors and eyed me curiously, a very large bay with a white streak down its nose and a piebald with one blue eye and one brown. The third stall looked empty, but that was where we were headed.

"Bit of advice, as it's your first time, don't turn your back on him." Martin smiled cheerfully and then strode hastily towards the barn entrance. "I can't stand the rasp noise," he shuddered, "so text me if you need anything. Rodger and I are off to check the sheep."

"I'll just get my gear out of the car," Roberta raised her eyebrows as she watched him leave.

I looked over the stall door. A small, shaggy, golden-brown Shetland, with the most malevolent expression stared back at me, as if checking for weakness.

"Don't be fooled by his size," Roberta said, "he's my most difficult client."

"I believe you." I helped her set out her tools. "What's the plan here?"

"*Not* to get teeth marks on my bum this time," she huffed.

"Oh joy," I muttered.

ROBERTA STRAPPED a battery-powered electrical base unit around her waist and I went to fetch some water. There was a bucket on the floor with various bit of kit including a huge syringe. My role was handing her anything she pointed to.

Wellington already had a head collar on, which was gratifying, because when he saw the equine speculum, basically a mouth gag with expanding jaws, his face took on an aspect of challenge that was really quite worrying.

I watched as Roberta skilfully manoeuvred the speculum into place, it was done before Wellington could think of a plan. Oddly he didn't seem to mind it once she had fixed his mouth open. Kneeling down in what looked to be the most uncomfortable position if you weren't pregnant, never mind if you were, she began examining his back teeth with a bright head torch. I held his collar, ready to pick up the requested tools, and waited for signs of possible rebellion.

She put a mask over her nose and mouth and pointing at her face said, "tooth dust and debris." Then she used the huge syringe to clean out the detritus from his tongue and teeth and attached a tool to the base unit. Before I could ask, she added, "This is a float, and filing down the sharp edges or hooks and ramps on the teeth, is called floating."

The sound of the file made me wince, but oddly Wellington didn't seem to mind, in fact he rolled his eyes as if tasting something interesting.

Roberta kept up with the commentary pointing at various things in the bucket, which I handed her. "Eighteen years ago, farmers did this for themselves with a non-electric rasp, you pulled the tongue over on one side and did the teeth on the other."

I snorted, "Not that farmer!" Indicating the barn doors where Martin had been.

She leaned back and felt inside Wellington's mouth with her hand, I saw the gleam in his eye and tightened my hold on the head collar. Not that he could have done anything with the mouth gag in.

"You look and then feel with your hand too, and don't blindly work on a tooth," Roberta explained. I nodded; it made sense.

We paused between treatments and Roberta let the speculum down so Wellington could rest his jaw.

"Do you ever sedate them?" I asked curiously.

"A drooping head is very heavy," she shrugged. "And if I'm doing my job properly then I shouldn't need to. A tooth extraction is of course, very different, and a tongue infection. I would say what I see but there's no crossover with the vet who will do the actual diagnosis and operate if necessary."

We carried on after Roberta straightened herself for a moment. I wondered how far into the pregnancy she would work. As if reading my mind she said, "I'm going to try and keep going for as long as I can because we need the money and my clients need me, but my back is going to require a deep tissue massage when I get home!"

Wellington was all done and chewing his haylage when Martin came back into the barn. "Great

Tippi-teethi, let me know what I owe you?"

Roberta didn't comment on the title, but handed over a copy of the work done and used her phone to send him a bill which he paid while she was packing up her tools. It was impressively efficient.

The day got away from me in a sea of faces and farms, we stopped on the top of a hill with a view of the Welsh coastline in the misty distance, the wind was cold but the air felt wonderfully clear and there were patches of blue in between scudding clouds. Small scraps of frost clung to the deeper folds of the moor where the meagre warmth hadn't managed to penetrate.

A packed lunch appeared and a flask of strong tea with loads of sugar made its way down my dusty throat. We sat in comfortable silence for a while and I contemplated the fact that not a single person had stood out as interesting in the way I needed them to be.

Once again, as if hearing me speak, Roberta said quietly, "Exmoor is a good place to hide."

———

WE GOT BACK to the stables at four in the afternoon. Sitting in the car I considered my physical state. I was filthy, covered in straw, mud, dust and probably horse muck as the last 'client' hadn't been so amenable. The grumpy cob had given me a massive shove when Roberta had finished, showing his contempt at the awful treatment he'd received. Offering me a hand and hauling me up off the stable floor, the farmer was belatedly helpful. "Our Eddie's never liked the dentist."

The car was quiet for a moment. "Tea?" Roberta said eventually.

"Please," I managed.

We pulled off jackets and scarfs and divested ourselves of dirty boots in the utility room. Roberta washed her hands; I brushed my clothes dirtier with mine before scrubbing them and shook my hair upside down to remove some of the debris. Nothing but a hot shower was going to fix the problem.

The kitchen was tidy and clean, all the paperwork was somewhere else. A sleepy cat spread out on the sofa opened one eye and the two dogs, who hadn't even bothered to bark, didn't stir in their place by the range. It was quiet too.

"We have twenty minutes before a horde of hungry children come through that door for some low-level looting of anything food related," Roberta said wryly.

The tea and buttered fruit cake was the best tasting feast I could remember. "Who made this?" I asked when I could speak without a mouthful.

"Toby. He loves to bake, thank goodness!" Roberta acknowledged the kitchen deity with an appropriate gesture.

I heard the arguing just before the door sprung open, it was an assault attack of epic proportions. I have seen less forceful entries from a unit shock team.

"Hey!" Roberta yelled, "Boots *off*, guests in the house!"

Toby slung his footwear and a bulging backpack in the corner of the utility room and headed straight for the fridge. "Hi, Ari, when's supper mum, I had double maths today and geography, I'm starving!"

I wasn't sure if the two subjects together had caused the drop in his blood sugar, but he took an enormous trifle out of the fridge.

"Put that back *right* now, you can have a sandwich, supper will be at six as it always is, which gives you enough time to do some home-work!" Roberta rescued her pudding.

A small blonde girl stood in the doorway and examined me, much as the team psychologist did just before a departure. I would have recognised the face anywhere; it was as familiar to me as my own.

The unit had a holographic hall of fame for certain scientists, detailing their contributions, and her features hadn't changed much from a child to the woman. I felt the dots forming in my thoughts and linking up to an identifiable pattern.

"Abbigail," she pointed at herself. "Did you really help Toby with some trafficked, endangered species he found on the moor?"

"Have you been eavesdropping again?" Toby rolled his eyes and snorted with frustration.

"I wouldn't need to if you told me what was going on," Abbigail said reasonably, which seemed a valid point.

She put her shoes carefully on the shelf designated for them in the utility room and removed her coat, hanging it up precisely where it should be, then came over to me. "Toby says you're very smart, can you help me with my science project?" Behind her back both her mother and brother were shaking their heads in warning.

"I'd need to know the subject matter first," I prevaricated.

She plonked herself down next to me and fished around in a pack not much smaller than she was. I wondered at the damage it would be doing to her still-growing vertebrae and at the lack of common sense in an education system expecting young people to carry actual books around with them.

The next hour was taken up with watching a family unfold their busy day into early evening. Roberta started making supper. Luke arrived, cold and tired with more files of work, he took a lump of cake and some tea and left for a shower and his study, closely followed by Alfie who made himself a sandwich after saying, "Hi again," and also went upstairs to wash off the day. Toby set his own books out on the table and began writing, every now and then looking at Abbigail with an indulgent grin.

I pointed out suggestions in a stunningly advanced assignment on genetics, trying to avoid the pitfalls of what I knew and what I should know.

Eventually I asked, "Who suggested this as a topic?" thinking she would say one of her teachers.

"Nathen did," she said, correcting a tricky bit of coding.

"He's the kid's driver," Roberta explained, moving back to the table and doing something interesting with the ingredients for a vegetable stew. "And you should call him Mr Wingate, Abbigail."

Something about this set off an alarm in my head. "He picks up all the children from the farms around the area?"

Luke came back into the room and pointed upstairs to Roberta. "Go and have a bath, I'll finish supper." The fixings for the meal were passed seamlessly between them, with what looked like long practice. He carried on speaking and chopping. "Nathen's been taking them for the last two years, the previous driver disappeared without so much as a letter of resignation!"

I'll just bet he did, I thought.

My eyes returned to the page Abbigail was working on and I saw a small hieroglyph in the top corner, it was in a different hand, hers was childishly clear and precise, this was a scattered scrawl.

"Who did that?" I asked her, a bit too sharply.

She looked up at me, slightly apprehensive, "Nathen, he said it was for luck?" she explained.

I stood suddenly, making everyone stop what they were doing. "Sorry," I said, smiling, "I really need to go and get a shower, I seem to be wearing the inside of a mucky stable."

"Yeah, that happens when you go out with mum," Toby muttered.

"Toby!" Luke was trying not to laugh, so I did it for him.

"Can you come back and help me?" Abbigail looked serious.

"Abbigail!" Her father was equally exasperated with her.

"Only if it's okay with your mum and dad," I went for diplomatic.

"You'd be welcome to have a shower here and stay for supper if you would like?" Luke offered.

"*That* is a wonderful prospect, but I must get back; I have an appointment this evening and I can't be late." I headed out of the kitchen door. "Tell Roberta, thank you for today, it was very, *interesting*."

"Hah!" I heard Toby say, he added, "Bye Ari, see you soon!"

Abbigail waved at me. Then said to Toby, "she's probably off to help more animals?"

It was a stunning bit of prescience, something that in forward she would be well known for.

Luke put on his boots and coat and despite my protestations, saw me safely off on the quad bike and down the lane to the village. I shouted my thanks and heard his faint reply.

The dark was comforting, a sky full of early stars made a wonderful canopy overhead and I could hear the last of the evening tasks being done in the various farms I passed along the way. I ploughed through the river and up the other side. My cottage light was on in the kitchen, so I wasn't surprised to see Ash when I opened the door, though there was a disconcerting moment when we were both on our guard, just in case it *was* someone else.

I took off my dirty coat and hung it up, much as Abbigail had done, in the 'right' place, my boots followed. Badger came over from his warm nest by the lit fire and wagged a puppy tail, I leaned down and hugged him, he licked my face then looked disconcerted about the taste.

"Sorry, Badger, I'm covered in horse muck and dental debris," I explained.

"Do you want to eat first or shower?" Ash asked, he was toasting something and the smell from the cooker made my mouth water.

"It's the children's driver and it's not just them he's after. Think about it, he doesn't have to kill a local, well known and popular family who would be missed, just two people who can get them all through what happens next, and he's influencing Abbigail. He set a trap, we walked into it. He must know how the unit works intimately."

Ash stood completely still, a spoon poised and dripping dramatically over the pan of soup he was stirring, which bubbled dangerously.

"Shower first," I said, pointing upstairs.

"And another thing." I was clean, though it had taken a lot of soap and shampoo to remove the evidence of the day. Ash's grey eyes went from tired to wary as he put down the buttery knife. We were sitting at the kitchen table and I was gratefully eating hot soup, fresh bread and cheese. It tasted wonderful. Badger sat on my foot under the table in the hopes of leftovers, sighing theatrically every now and then to remind me.

"He must have actually been in the unit offices," I said eventually, full enough to share a lump of bread and butter with Badger.

Why?" Ash was leaning back in his chair.

"This." I handed him the scrap of paper that I had palmed from Abbigail's assignment. I am good at prestidigitation; working in a bar on Mars with tool pushers, it was amazing what you learned that became useful later in life. I showed him the hieroglyph. "Do you recognise it?" I asked him.

His face was expressionless, but being around people who are prone to violence means you see hidden emotion quickly, or suffer the consequences of not doing so.

"It's the sign above the entrance to the travel area," he said, adding "it roughly translates as 'time.'"

I had always thought it looked like a crudely drawn standard lamp, but I could appreciate the sentiment and I smiled, as it confirmed his own close connection to the unit not evident in the file I had read.

"We'd already come to the conclusion that he was getting help." Ash was really worried.

"Now I think it must be someone who's from the unit," I said simply, then whispered sadly, "and Eagle-eye knows."

We were quiet, Badger was still clearing up the mess he'd made under the table, his tongue rasping on the wood flooring. I reached down and stroked his soft head and got a buttery lick for my troubles.

"How long until the link opens?" I asked.

Ash looked at his watch and I remembered I was also wearing one. Half an hour. We cleared up the evening meal and I began putting on layers by the front door. Badger was waiting to be let out.

"Sorry puppy, not just yet," I explained, giving him a hug.

He huffed his annoyance then for some reason he was suddenly on high alert, ears pricked, a slight curl of his lips in a mini growl.

Ash turned off the lights and looked out of the window to the back field. I waited. He shook his head. The puppy listened. Ash shrugged, nothing. But he moved silently over to the kitchen, opened a drawer and took out a small stubby pistol and a magazine. My mouth dropped open; I was absolutely certain it hadn't been there before, as I had done a thorough search for anything interesting on two previous occasions. I really don't do guns, it's not that I can't, my training included every conceivable type of weapon and they hadn't changed that much from back to forward.

I observed Badger as he stood down his inner watch dog to disinterested puppy. Whatever it was had gone. Hopefully.

The ponies were up in the corner of the field and I took them treats; they also seemed to be a bit wary and shuffled about, keeping away from the area where the link would be made, which was helpful. Neither of them was keen to wear a head collar again but I put them on and added a lead rope to each, then loosely tied them to the fencing. They were both completely disgusted.

"Sorry," I whispered, "it won't take long." Ernest was unforgiving. Harley had found a smidgen of beech leaves still edible to occupy him.

I could feel the build-up of energy buzzing inside my head and I went over to where Ash was waiting with the box containing the kittens. He would have to remove them and push them through as the container would probably be rejected. I was confident that Daniel Roper would have set up a control field at the other end. They would be safe.

The spark of the first zero point was quickly followed by the other two and then the growing puddle of dark nothing. It stopped and my ears were finally able to hear the normal night noises again, like the steady rustle of the wind in the tops of the trees and the hurry of the water over stones in the river. The horses whinnied their bewilderment at the activity and began a nervous shuffle.

I helped Ash with the kittens, we both wore gloves and I gave the first one an encouraging shove, it disappeared through to forward, the other kitten was making a fuss, hissing, spitting and yowling, the noise made the two ponies look over in alarm.

Badger was barking inside the cottage which added to the level of collective apprehension; I leaned down ready to 'assist' the furious bundle of fur. Out of the corner of my eye I saw shadowy movement, something about it made my atavistic DNA respond in fear. I turned to see a huge shape bounding towards us. Instinctively I tossed in the kitten and threw myself at an astonished Ash, he fell with me on top of him, just as a fully grown female Smilodon launched herself at us. She went over and into the core flow to forward, just as the link closed.

WE LAY there in the cold, both in shock. The noise I had heard on my first night now made sense, it had been an actual large cat howling and not my problems with misplaced back, forward, memories. Both Ernest and Harley had pulled free and were huddled up close to the far boundary of the field.

Eventually, when Ash said nothing and didn't move for several minutes, I started to feel mildly uncomfortable about our relative positions and I sat up. Badger was still barking, but it wasn't a cautionary clamour, more a 'being left out of the fun' type of commotion.

"You're going to have to send a timed coded communication on the dark web to warn them," I said.

Ash became unusually garrulous. "Did you see its canine teeth? The size of railroad spikes!"

"How big is that?" I was inappropriately curious about the comparison as I staggered to my feet, still shaking with adrenaline.

"*Huge*!" Ash announced helpfully, pushing himself up. He sighed, "I can't do the message."

"Why not?" I waited until Ernest came over to me, rather than approaching the spooked pony. He blew equal parts snot, fear and resentment into my face. I patted him carefully and he eventually settled down a little, letting me scratch his neck.

"Something happens when we open the link more than once in the same exact here, it becomes now in both back and forward." He got up slowly.

I was stunned, it didn't make scientific sense. But then I had only ever been through the link to return trafficked animals. "I've always wondered why they kept it open for me instead of reopening it, when you think of the power required to make the zero-point energy fields."

It actually took an ocean of power, which was why it was situated inside a dome under one. I didn't bother to say that to Ash because he clearly knew a lot more about the unit than I had originally surmised.

"Then that also means there's no longer a time dilation field between this now and forward." I knew that this indicated something really worrying, but I couldn't make the connections. "And Eagle-eye would have known, so he must think it's worth the risk." Ash shrugged; it was very irritating.

We checked the ponies and removed their head collars and lead ropes, which I hooked over my arm as I watched Ash carefully examining the other side of the boundary fence with his head torch for clues as to the mother Smilodon's sudden appearance.

"Do you have any idea what you're looking for?" I asked wryly, I knew I didn't, even though Daniel Roper, who was going to be as mad as a hornet when we met again, had taught me the basics, because returning species to their rightful now came with its own set of hazards.

"Nope!" Ash replied.

I GOT ready for bed by taking a boiling hot bath, the pre-Smilodon quick shower having done nothing for my aches and pains, *or* the subsequent effect of the adrenaline spike on my nerve endings.

Ash left with a sleepy Badger tucked into his shoulder, the sound of his quad bike disappearing into the darkness made me feel suddenly lonely. Which was odd, as aloneness had been my default state for most of my life. Our brief 'post link' conversation had consisted of leaving the plans until the early morning. It felt as if we could do so and we were both really tired, Ash because he actually *was* running a moorland farm and working on several innovative projects, and I had been standing in draughty barns and stables holding the heads of reluctant horses all day.

A hot drink seemed a good idea and I puttered around in thick pyjamas and warm slippers, just using the small light over the stove, leaving the chiaroscuro dance on the floor from the moon and clouds through the windows, to lull me into calm. The kettle on the stove boiled and I got a mug from the cupboard and made a cup of tea.

The cottage was beginning to feel dangerously like home. Leaving would be difficult. I looked out into the quiet moonlit field and saw Ernest and Harley resting gently in the half sleep of watchful prey animals. Something, I thought wryly, I could identify with.

The phone pinged and I picked it up, expecting a message from Ash to say something helpful about the size of the big cat's teeth again.

It was from Toby. 'Please help me, come to the stables now.'

I knew he hadn't written it.

THE SCRAMBLE TO get dressed and round the back of the cottage to the quad bike in the middle of the night darkness, was accompanied by a level of swearing that would have seriously impressed the tool pushers in the main dome bar on Mars.

I messaged Ash as I left. His answer was almost immediate, 'wait for me!'

Texting while steering over the much deeper river and up a dark track was clearly not in my skill set, but the adrenaline was back in waves and though I wobbled about, several times missing the appropriate synchronisation of clutch changes and gears, I managed to send, 'already left.'

I kept up a constant whispered recrimination to myself, "How could I have misjudged the situation, he can't have felt that threatened by our progress, surely, the man had had years to plan, what had spooked him?" I just couldn't work it out.

There were still a few lights on in the houses and barns that I passed in the village, farming didn't stop because the day had ended for some of us. I drove across the main road, then turned off the engine and risked leaving the bike in the hedge. It wasn't as if he didn't know I was coming, but there was some sporadic traffic to cover my arrival and I wanted to see how close I could get.

I wished for a moment I had the gun Ash had taken from my kitchen drawer, but it wasn't there when I checked. Misha, Eagle-eye's mum, had taught me that going into a negotiation armed took something away from the possibility of a peaceful outcome. Though, to be accurate, the woman never went anywhere without her sonic stunner and at least one set of sedative spiked knuckles. What I was really hoping for was a compromise of some sort.

I crept up the back lane entrance towards the stables, hopped over the field gate to the left and cut across past the depleted muck heap. Standing quietly to one side of the bales of haylage heaped in vast stacks, I listened. The big doors in front of me were slightly ajar and a safety light in the stable office at the other end glowed dimly. Nervous whinnying noises from the few horses inside as they moved about restlessly, turned up my own sense of foreboding.

Nothing, no indication as to where this man might be, or Toby for that matter, and I didn't doubt that he was here, they both were. The sharp needle to the side of my neck was a big giveaway and a clear 'no' for the possibility of any negotiation.

I FELT the tickle of straw on my face and a steady murmur of a single voice. The change in my breathing must have alerted him to the fact that I was awake.

"You can sit up," he said calmly. The voice sounded disconcertingly familiar.

My head swam with a ferocious shimmy but I wasn't sick which was a bonus. The drug must have been quick acting or, I touched the side of my neck and there was another small lump and a spot of blood, an antidote had been administered.

"You were a chemist as I remember?" I said, looking at him. His appearance was totally different, I knew of people who had undergone some serious surgical alteration for a variety of reasons, but his process must have been genetic level and excruciating for it to be so extreme. And, I thought, it would definitely have added to his altered mental state. Because he was, completely unhinged.

He sat on a small bale of haylage, calmly threading a piece of harness through his fingers, tall like most of the forward population in comparison to this now, with bright blue eyes and wispy blonde hair. His hands were particularly beautiful, slim and supple like those of a pianist. He was dressed in the 'local farmer on a night check of the stock' outfit, thick shirt, waterproof jacket, warm trousers and boots.

I made myself more comfortable by moving back a little and leaning against the side of the empty stall we were in. It was tidy and clean, with fresh straw and the pre-prepared nutritional feed bucket waiting for its morning horse.

Toby was lying on the opposite side, he looked like a rag doll abandoned by a bored child, I watched for a moment until I saw his chest rise and fall and relief washed over me, making my eyes sting.

I sighed, "I remember Simon Wetheridge, what happened to him was awful." It sounded like a platitude, which it was. I hadn't really known him that well, he'd had a reputation for bad temper, arrogance and impatience. But no wonder Eagle-eye had flinched when I had mentioned his name a few days ago, he knew who was here.

"Where is Ash Grey?" He kept his voice low, but there was an edge of unreason that made my nerve endings prickle with a warning.

"Why the Smilodon kittens?" I was curious and deflecting.

"It would have triggered a nice warning alert on the unit system." He stood up suddenly making me flinch, something that caused a smile to cross his wax-like expression. "And it got your attention; the adult female was an accidental bonus!"

I wondered why the dogs weren't barking. Although we were apart from the farmhouse and the other side of the lane, they would have heard something and Roberta struck me as a person who checked on her horses at the least sign of trouble.

"Are they okay?" I managed to keep the tone of my voice even but I was ashamed of my underlying fear.

He pointed to Toby. "I came over to give Abbigail a book she had unfortunately left in my taxi, so of course they invited me to stay for dinner." He walked over to the boy and leaned down.

I shuffled as if I was about to stand up and he swung round coming back towards me. "So," I said, "you drugged them." He stopped.

"It's possible to synthesise quite an effective sedative from a combination of plants including deadly nightshade, they just grow all over the place in this now." His voice was disturbingly conversational, "I put it into the soup," then adding, with another abnormal grin, "Everyone went to bed *very* tired."

I tried not to show my feelings, and just nodded. "Did we cause this?" I pointed to Toby.

His expression was impossible to read, so much had been altered he was unable to move the facial muscles naturally, though they rippled creepily as if he was underwater pushing against a strong tide. It must have taken a monumental physical effort to appear normal.

"I needed the link to be the same now back and forward and it's done."

"*Why?*" I was hoping for an answer that would make sense of all this.

"Because I want to go home," he said simply. "Unlike you," he added with a rickety grin, "I can still do that."

I was puzzled and he laughed, it was an awful sound, squeaky and rasping. "You don't know?" He raised his voice a little, "You'd better come out here and tell her, Ash!"

Ash appeared from the shadows, he glanced in my direction, then at Toby and back at the man. He leaned casually in the stall doorway. I was hoping he was carrying around something more than an air of capable menace.

"May I introduce Bart Asquith," I said formally, "he was Simon Wetheridge's partner."

Ash tipped his fingers to his forehead.

The situation seemed ridiculous and weird in equal measure. I was used to levels of surreal; dealing with extinct species made for an interesting working day, but this was something else entirely.

"So, now what?" Ash said evenly.

"We go to the cottage she's living in; you contact the unit, they open a link and I go through," Bart was equally calm, he produced a nasty looking weapon and used it to indicate. "Move, so I can see you and turn around."

Ash obliged, stepping no more than a pace or two inside the stall, he lifted his jacket and emptied his pockets, nothing.

There was no doubt in my mind that Bart would try and kill both of us before he left this now and I was equally aware of his intentions once he arrived forward. The personnel standing nearest the link would be dead from whatever he decided to concoct to take with him. The man was nothing if not resourceful, the same 'useful' plant species existed in both nows, identifiable DNA for the core flow and therefore able to travel through. And whatever the resulting blip from our deaths, would follow as soon as the link closed.

"You're going for it belt and braces then!" I said dryly. "Why would we *ever* consent to doing that?"

Before I could blink, he pointed the wicked looking pistol and fired off a round so close to Toby's head that I saw his hair flutter. The weapon had a small silencer attached to it and the sound was muted and menacing.

"I will kill all of them," Bart said simply, "starting with him." His face was contorted with hatred, an expression it seemed he could manage.

The sense of fury was overpowering, I launched myself at him and so did Ash. The gun went off again. I felt a sharp sting in my left arm. Bart screamed his own rage and tried to fire another round, but the shovel that Ash had leaned on the outside of the doorway connected with his head, and there was a sickening thunk of meat on metal.

Sharp whinnying noises of fear pierced the momentary silence, the horses were upset and moving around in their distress at the smell of blood and cordite.

I pressed the wound on my arm which bled profusely. Ash was leaning down, checking for Bart's pulse. He stood up and shook his head. The body lay in the straw, limbs splayed at impossible angles. I picked up the gun. "What did he mean, when he said I can't go forward again?" I asked Ash in my most reasonable voice as he came towards me, hand outstretched to inspect the wound on my arm. And raising the gun, I fired.

WE STOOD STILL, frozen in place. Ash actually looked down at his own body to see if he had any damage before he turned round. Bart now had a bullet hole in his forehead to go with the massive dint in the back.

"The gene therapy he used to change his appearance, although effective, can cause a type of acromegaly and hyperkeratosis. The bones and skin thicken, which is why his facial expressions were so difficult for me to read and it's impossible to get an accurate pulse." I am nothing if not thorough. I spoke with no intonation in my voice. My hand shook and Ash, with great care, reached out and gently took the weapon from my clawed fingers. He removed the magazine, pulled the slide back then let it go forward, ejecting the chambered round, then unscrewed the silencer. Putting the round in the magazine, the gun went in one of his pockets, the magazine and silencer in the other.

I waited while he used a large and surprisingly clean hankie to tie over the bullet graze in my arm, which was still bleeding. I pointed towards the feed room. "Roberta has a medical kit in there." I stepped over Bart, left the stall and walked into the shadowed gloom of the stables.

"WHAT DO we do with the dead body?" I was examining Toby, he seemed to be sleeping peacefully, though technically he was drugged and his pupils when I gently lifted a lid were huge and dark. For a seriously psychotic personality, Bart was clearly a good chemist. But I turned the boy carefully onto his side and placed him in the recovery position anyway, just in case.

"We need to clean up this stall and dispose of it." Ash was going through Bart's pockets, removing his identification and wallet. "That means taking it on the quad bikes and burying it on the farm or out on the moor. What do you think?"

I snorted, "My knowledge in getting rid of human remains is sadly lacking a little something, like, for example, *experience!*" I was going through the second stage of shock and babbling and I could hear the note of suppressed hysteria in my voice. "But I *do* know the ground's frozen solid and predation can be an issue if the body is not deep enough." I stood up and looked out of the back of the double stable doors towards the newly formed muck heap. "I've got an idea."

Ash followed my gaze and eventually after careful thought, he shrugged his agreement. "It could work."

"It's heaving with microbes which generate a lot of heat, it should break down in a few weeks and be completely disintegrated into er, compost, by the time the muck's removed next autumn." I was getting lost in the science, literally.

Ash looked at me, his expression unreadable. He sighed, then came to check my vet wrap bandage which I had put over the top of the hankie to add some pressure. It was starting to sting, and I was getting so cold that my teeth chattered. For some reason he hugged me.

We went back to clearing up the mess. The straw had soaked up the blood and we put it in a wheelbarrow conveniently positioned by the back doors.

I began digging in the newly formed heap. The muck eventually gave way to a semi solid and very strong smelling gloop. I could feel the heat rising and was oddly grateful as it warmed me, and I soon found a layer of evil soup.

Ash wheeled the body over. He had stripped Bart of his clothes and temporarily re-covered most of him with the man's coat. In the shadowed light coming from the stables, I could see the changes in the bone structure of his legs caused by the genetic treatment, as they flopped up and down with the rhythm of the barrow's movement.

Ash removed the coat and heaved the body out and into the sludge. Bart slowly sank and disappeared under the hot black slurry, his white limbs flailing in an attempt to attract our attention for one last bitter remark.

I stood still, trying to find a place inside my head to hide this haunting memory, while Ash went back into the stable and began filling the area where the man had been with the blood-soaked straw.

"There didn't seem to be an appropriate moment to ask him about his accomplice," I spoke thoughtfully.

Ash looked bemused, as well he might. "*That* is Eagle-eye's problem now. But what about Toby?" His exhaustion showed on his face in the half-light coming through the stable doors.

"We could take him into the house, the issue is I don't know if Bart lured him out here or if he took the boy from his bed after drugging them all." I went into the stables and checked the stall we had been in. Toby was no longer lying in the recovery position, but curled into a ball like a wintering dormouse, his cheek pillowed on a hand. I backed out warily, pushing Ash in front of me, my finger on my lips when he went to ask a question.

"He's asleep," I whispered, "not unconscious."

After carefully and quietly examining the floor and walls for any sign of blood and our activities, we left via the muck heap. The safety light in the office was just enough to see by and my eyes had become accustomed to the gloom, as I studied the general shape of it and concluded that if you weren't looking for a difference, you wouldn't know.

I staggered down the lane to where the quad bike had been abandoned, waited while Ash started it, and got on behind him. It sounded loud in the darkness but as the farmers were often out to check for stock problems, we wouldn't rouse any curious sleepers.

He had left his own transport several fields away and run the remaining distance. It would have been impressive if I hadn't been so angry with him.

IT WAS STILL DARK when we got back to the cottage. Ash came in after me. He walked over to the kitchen area and removed a first aid kit from a cupboard. Unpacking the contents, he indicated that I should take off my coat and jumper.

"*Activated*, that was the word you used when I arrived." I peeled away the bandage and the hankie and then took off my jacket. The jumper was a little difficult as the dried blood had stuck it to my arm and I couldn't raise either of them to pull it over my head. Ash solved this by getting a pair of scissors out and cutting it off.

When I flinched, he said, "It was ruined anyway, you can't wear a jumper with a bullet hole." Ash was deliberately misconstruing my reaction. We both knew I wasn't bothered about the clothing.

He cleaned and glued the wound and put on a waterproof dressing.

"We need to talk," he said eventually, looking at my expression. His face seemed sad. "Can we do it tomorrow? Quite frankly I stink of blood and horse manure and so do you, I need a shower and some sleep."

I looked at him, then sighed. The traumatic flashes over what we had done and the kitchen first aid was making me feel dizzy and sick. I nodded.

Ash picked up the bloody evidence and put it into a rubbish bag. A small part of my brain registered with some disgust that it was obviously made of petroleum by-products. He went towards the door and turned as if he was about to say something, then changed his mind and left, taking the gory evidence with him.

I stood there listening to the noisy silence.

THE PONIES in the field were my first conscious thought, as the grey light of a cold morning slowly crept over me and I sat carefully up in bed. My arms and legs ached with a post drug and violent activity reaction and I had damp and tangled hair. A restless half-sleep full of questions, bursts of disordered feelings and the pain in my arm had made for a miserable night.

After showering and washing my hair again, I padded downstairs and made coffee and a breakfast of fruit, cheese and oatcakes. The view from the back window showed Ernest and Harley leaning over the fence looking curiously in. I picked up another jacket from the collection by the door and added my boots after inspecting them for signs of blood. They were covered in muck, so it was difficult to tell.

Sharing the oatcakes with the horses and leaning my face on thick manes while they munched gave me a little peace. I remembered doing the same thing when I was a child on the farm. Somehow, even in this now, it was still comforting.

WHEN ASH ARRIVED WITH BADGER, I was drinking my second coffee. The puppy was delighted to see me, he yelped until I picked him up and gave him a squeeze. It helped me to centre on something tangible, everything else seemed to be floating slightly. Ash looked dreadful, tired and drained. He had a large plastic file folder filled with paper pages in one hand, it made me wince on so many levels.

The breakfast things were still on the table and he began buttering an oatcake. "Sorry about last night, I'm out of practice."

I know my mouth dropped open. "I'm actually glad to hear that!" He looked uncomfortable which was somehow reassuring.

Ash slid the file towards me and I paused before I opened it, then began reading. In the background I could hear him making more coffee and adding a lot of hot milk and sugar to mine. He waited patiently while I felt my anger rise and fall and my hands shake with desperation as I turned the pages.

Eventually I stopped. Pointing to one section I said, "How do I have all this money?"

Ash seemed surprised at where I had decided to start the conversation. "It's a back forward investment thing." He sat down.

"What does NKR stand for?" I had worked it out, but I wanted to hear him say it.

"No known relatives," he whispered.

"So, I was taken from this now to forward and," I checked the page in front of me for the exact word, "*seeded* with a family?" He nodded. "Isn't that kidnapping?" I asked mildly. Something in my tone made him look wary, as well it might. "Hence the word *activated?*" I added.

Ash spoke after a suitable pause, "You know I didn't get a say."

"Is it about the grandfather paradox, we keep our forward by making this now happen the way they want it to?"

"With some of the observer effect, which is Schrodinger's cat, I think," he prevaricated.

"Schrodinger's grandfather then," I said dryly. He was going to laugh but my expression stopped him. I was furious, picking up my cup which was full of hot liquid I threw it at the floor. It smashed in a spectacular fountain of milky coffee, sending Badger under the table, whimpering with fear.

We were silent for a moment, then Ash said, with just a dash of irony, "You're taking this well." He stood up and began cleaning the mess, while I got my breathing under control and patted Badger who wasn't coming out from under the table.

"*I* was supposed to terminate him, not you, I'm sorry," he whispered.

"Why?" I was puzzled about the apology.

"Because it's what I do." The words were simple and said with a great deal of real regret.

"No, it isn't, you're a sheep farmer." I didn't know why I was being kind; I was still furious.

He seemed oddly grateful. "Thank you."

I sat for a while watching him as he tidied. After making me another cup of coffee, he said, "Just in case you feel you need to throw something again."

"Well, I guess there's not a teenager alive who doesn't think they've been brought up by the wrong family, only in my case, it was true." I drank the coffee instead of throwing it and Badger came out from under the table to sit by me in solidarity. I rubbed his ears for my own comfort, but he was happy to help. "Misha finding me in Mars main dome was no accident, I assume." I was talking to myself and adding things up, Ash just left me to it. "The extensive job training she did and the recommendation for the unit, it all makes sense now."

I tried not to cry but it felt like such a betrayal. "Did everyone know but me?"

Ash looked devastated. "Just Eagle-eye, it's handed down to every head of the unit, and for what it's worth, he tried to keep you there."

I couldn't stop the tears, they rolled down my face. Badger was distraught and clambered onto my lap, licking the drops as they fell. Ash wanted to come over to my side of the table, but he wisely stayed put. "Was Bart right, I can't go forward again?"

He was quiet for more than a moment. "Yes," he said simply.

The water closed over my head, but in there somewhere was a calm, I think I'd always had a sense that I didn't belong in forward. I sat back in my chair and Badger settled down, puppy long legs dangling one side and nose in the crook of my arm.

"Does anyone know why?" I was curious.

"Ash laughed, "Eagle-eye bet me that you would get to the science really fast!"

"How much?" I spoke sarcastically.

"Quite a lot if you consider the accumulated interest on the debt!" Ash felt able to be funny.

"I know from Daniel Roper that adult trafficked extinct species don't survive very long forward, which is why we identify exactly when they came from as soon as possible. I always understood there was a DNA issue, I think I thought it was easier to transport juvenile versions because they were small and therefore less trouble, but it must be that the very young have a unique embryonic stem cell profile the core flow can recognise."

"The physicist who talked to me about it said something about up quarks, down quarks, fermion particles and," he hunted for the words, "er, photons and gluons recognising their place in the universe."

I huffed, "Basically, I was able to go forward when I was a baby but as an adult my stem cells are less adaptive and therefore not acceptable."

Ash was back to the not amusing stuff. "What I don't understand is how Bart was able to stay here for so long, he's from forward? It's one of the questions Eagle-eye wanted an answer to."

"More confirmation that Eagle-eye knew exactly who was here." I glared at Ash.

"To be fair, I don't think he was sure, there were several possibilities, and it was along the lines of, 'If he is from forward, then find out how he's done it!'" Ash sounded reasonable; I still wasn't convinced.

"If it's genetic, how do the smugglers manage?" I paused, adding eventually, "*and* the tourists?"

"They take their chances because it's worth the risk and er, the statistics of a successful return through the core flow are, let's just say *grossly* exaggerated to the tourists."

I was stunned. Then quiet, as I thought through my unit experiences. It was true, I had never actually interviewed a returned sightseer who had been back to another now for more than a few hours. I let my mind wander to try and make the connections.

"This is what I think, not what I know, so you might want to start with that when you leave a message with the unit. Despite the fact that most of humanity has learned not to mess with its own DNA coding, he had obviously undergone radical and highly illegal genetic alteration to change his appearance. He must have added a scientifically questionable embryonic therapy using his own stem cells, which he would have had to continue in this now, because he thought that would get him back through the core flow and both clearly contributed to the paranoia and destabilisation!" For some reason my anger was simmering again which made Badger look up anxiously.

This time Ash did move, coming over to my side of the table and squatting down, his worried face almost on a level with mine. He took my hand. "I am very, *very* sorry."

I leaned my head down on his shoulder and all three of us stayed like that for a while.

BADGER and I were sitting by the lit fire and I had moved on to hot chocolate and biscuits, the open file next to me on the small sofa. Ash had taken the chair, his long legs stretched out, a hazard to the unwary.

"I can't believe Eagle-eye would take such a big risk in losing the protection of the time dilation field between back and forward, it's going to be so much more dangerous to have us running on the same now. Unless..." I thought about it while Ash let me. "What do you think the chances are that there are others?"

Ash raised his eyebrows. I swore in exasperation, he'd obviously worked it out before I had and the fact that we were both activated, was a lot of commitment for just one job.

"Why aren't you angry?"

Ash sighed. "My situation is not as complicated as yours, people like me are assessed and recruited for our, er, specialist abilities. I didn't have a family forward, or back for that matter." He moved on before I could speak. "*You* need to work out what you want in the here of this now."

"What's your plan?" I was curious.

"Well, introducing regenerative farming. I have the project of rewinding the rivers to finish, and another one on adding various appropriate fungi to the soil of the trees I'm planting to develop a wood wide web. Plus, the special breeds." He stopped and grinned at my expression of incredulity.

I sighed. "According to that file, I have no past history here, the culture and standards, all the scientific and environmental differences, it makes it difficult to find any connection."

"You could always travel," he said with a grin.

"Oh, very funny."

I began thinking about the seaweed farm in Cornwall that Martin Cooper had told me about, run by a family called Bickerstaff, which was in financial trouble. A possible investment plan began to form.

My phone pinged. "Perfect example, this thing is a nightmare of *epic* proportions!"

Checking it for a message, my nascent good mood dissipated. It was from Roberta, there was a photograph of the muck heap in the early morning light. And the question, 'Are my children safe?'

I showed it to Ash. "Do you think she's worked it out?" he asked me.

I rolled my eyes. Then, after a moment of silent agreement for what was going to be our actual purpose in the here of this now, I texted back, 'yes.'

FISH GIRL

*This short story began its life on a boiling hot night, in an upstairs bar somewhere in central London, at the before screening party for a film called **Chamber**. I was talking to the partner of the writer director. She expressed a drunken wish to write a screenplay about a girl bitten by a fish, and at the end her boyfriend had to let her go... that was it! I promised to do a treatment and as we were both, er, somewhat the worse for wear, no more was said. Having started this book of short stories I was looking through my collection of ideas; written on the back of a very dirty receipt for two large glasses of Merlot were the words, girl — fish — genetics.*

The song that runs endlessly in my head when I think of this story is, Don't Fear the Reaper, by Blue Oyster Cult. It was playing in the bar that night and when I thought of the cliff chase, I could hear it in the background.

LAURA

The water was warm on my skin, something of an illusion for the north-west coast of Wales even in the dog days of summer and without a wetsuit. I checked back towards the beach to see Charlie and Tom sitting close together, looking at the computer. Charlie was, as usual, here doing research, counting seal pups and we were visiting, again.

Tom and I live in London for most of the year, but for the three months in the autumn that Charlie is working on this vital annual project we go with him, and the previous December in the Antarctic summer when he was observing the young emperor penguins, and before that in Mongolia working on the Przewalski horses. As you can see, there is something of a pattern building here.

The three of us have been friends since university. I studied mediaeval history, Charlie marine biology and as far as I could tell, Tom played rugby. His father paid for a medical degree but I don't think he ever went to a class and he never graduated. The professor who was his tutor said Tom was the most intelligent and gifted failure he had ever met. Tom's dad is just grateful he stays out of gaol, though it has been something of a task for Charlie and me to keep it that way.

Tom is stocky, muscular, with olive skin, dark curly hair and black eyes, *very* good looking and unfortunately rich; or actually his family is, they put funds into his bank account and never see him.

His English dad is too busy making money for himself and other people, his American mum writes for an online news company and his sister does something for both governments. If it wasn't so sad it would be awful.

My folks run a farm; several hundred acres close to the moor in the south-west of the country. My dad works every day including Christmas because he loves it, and my mum loves him. My younger sister has the farming bug and was lambing sheep before she could walk properly. I am less inclined to get my hands anywhere near the rear of a sheep, cow, or chicken. Table talk at every meal was always something to do with herbage, the weather, or scrofula. The British Library where I do most of my contract work was usually a complete haven from all farm related topics. Though the last 9th century manuscript I translated, written by the monks in a monastery on Anglesey, had quite a lot of sheep references.

Charlie grew up in a small town in North Wales, his mum, Elsie, is the local GP, and her patch covers nearly all of the national park. In all the years I've known him, twelve to be exact, he's never mentioned a dad. Tall, slim and blonde, and very quiet around most people except Tom, he is highly regarded as an expert in several marine related species, most of which I have to look up, like *siphonophores*.

Exeter university was something of a shock for all of us and from day one we were the odd trio, thrown together by our lack of belonging. As the weeks went by, we found friendship in our collective peculiarity.

Charlie waved and I turned to look at him, he pointed, shouting something, then Tom was on his feet running towards the waves. I spun back to see what was getting them both excited, thinking seal pups, or a dolphin. A shiver of fear followed the dark shadow tracking towards me underwater, *fast*. I found myself trying to back away, half swimming half kicking, still facing the flickering shape. I could hear Charlie shouting and Tom splashing towards me. Too late. It grabbed my leg and I was dragged under.

Gasping, I took in a mouthful of seawater. I fought slippery skin and sharp teeth, pointlessly pushing it away. It came back and then back again, dragging me down towards the deeper, darker water. And then it was gone. I swam upwards, looking down at the curious shape. It turned and for a moment I thought I saw —

Tom grabbed me by the hair and earned himself a fist in the face which did nothing as we were both underwater and the pressure took all the power out of the punch.

I was helped by both of them, fussing and flailing each side of me, a look of combined horror on their faces.

The bite on my leg was bleeding but not profusely. Tom was trying to get a signal on his mobile and Charlie was pouring some stingy liquid from his medical kit into the wound. I hissed as it made contact.

"Stop panicking Tom, you're upsetting the women!" Charlie said, through clenched teeth. I snorted.

"What *was* that?" I asked him.

He answered carefully, "I thought it was a seal, what did you think it was?"

I tried to remember what I had seen, but it felt like a dream. I looked at my leg. "Tom! I don't need an ambulance!"

"Maybe some antibiotics and an analgesic?" Charlie suggested calmly. "Their bites can be really infectious."

Tom's voice came back down from stratospheric levels that only mice could hear, to something nearer normal. "Are you okay Larry?"

He only calls me that when he's really worried or done something wrong. I checked out the bite mark. Charlie was cleaning the blood away and it looked oddly less impressive than it had done. He inspected the wound again, his nose inches away from my calf.

"Hmm," he said.

The beach was empty except for a few birds who had settled back to looking for breakfast after the fuss had died down. I glanced up at the cliffs and saw the blurred figure of someone watching us. The person disappeared so quickly I thought they must have reassured themselves that we were all okay and gone back to whatever they had been doing.

"See, it's fine, don't worry. I'll get an appointment with the local GP when we get back to the cottage." Charlie grinned and it was Tom's turn to snort: the doctor in question was Charlie's mum.

"She doesn't like me," he whinged. The one person he hadn't been able to charm.

"It's not personal, she doesn't like anyone!" Charlie explained.

"She likes me," I said smugly.

"You're not just anyone." Charlie smiled.

We cleared up the debris of our early morning and the medical emergency and I staggered to my feet, really the pain had gone, but I felt strangely floaty as if the painkillers had been a bit too strong. The path up to the cliff top was steep and the sun was hot on my back. They were being helpful, and after I tripped over Tom's feet for the umpteenth time, I persuaded them to let me walk unaided. It was either that or one of us was going to end up going over the edge.

I was relieved to be back in the cottage. Both Charlie and Tom escorted me to the bathroom door, where I managed to persuade them that I could shower without help. I heard them in the kitchen making a second breakfast as I took off my swim shorts and top.

The shower was good and hot and I soaped and rinsed my hair. Standing under the water I closed my eyes and the shifting underwater shadow came back. I tried to remember what I had seen but the memory wouldn't coalesce. I realised the dressing had come off the wound and was floating in the bottom of the stall among the soapsuds. I examined it, there were small shiny particles stuck to the gel surface. My wound was almost completely healed, the ridges of the scarring slightly scaly under my fingers.

"WHAT DO YOU THINK?" I asked Charlie.

He had his nose once again right up close to my calf, my leg was propped awkwardly on a stool, and I sat at the kitchen table while Tom made toast and tea.

"Hmm." Charlie was worried.

In the half an hour since I had been in the shower, the scarring had spread. It looked like an old burn, silver and slightly raised. It was cold to the touch and I shivered as if someone had opened a door to winter.

"Tom, pass my bag," Charlie said, his voice calm.

"You're kidding me?" I was incredulous.

"I need to do some research." He saw my face. "I'll figure it out, Larry."

Great, now they were both calling me by my nickname.

Tom stood leaning on the counter by the sink, arms crossed, his face impassive. Turning towards the window, he seemed to be watching something on the cliff edge. "What's going on, Charlie?"

"Let me work on this," Charlie evaded the question. He got up and fetched the kit he usually carried around for his projects, as Tom hadn't moved away from the window. Glancing to where Tom was looking, he came back with the equipment himself and took out a small scalpel and a specimen jar.

The scrapings were rainbow coloured and shiny. Charlie went through to his laboratory and I decided to follow him. Picking up a coat from the stand by the front door, I pushed my arms in and wrapped it around me.

"Cold?" Tom asked me. I nodded. He gave up his position by the window and came over, folding me into him and rubbing my back, trying to warm me. "It's really hot out in the sun, why don't you go and sit on the veranda?"

Tom is taller than me, actually, everyone is, I am able to fit my head under his chin. He made the mistake of calling me pipsqueak when we first met, but a childhood of farm labour (it's cheap) made me very strong, and a brown belt in Krav Maga meant he only did it once.

Charlie's study is filled with amazing things in jars and up to date equipment for his research. I don't know which grant covers what, but it would be impressive in a laboratory, never mind a spare room in a cottage in Wales. In one corner is a huge seawater tank, with Stroppy the common octopus. He has a tendency to nocturnal excursions which have freaked me out on occasion. Charlie says he has a modified gill structure that can absorb oxygen from the air, and no, I don't really understand what that means.

Tom was back by the window in the kitchen and I could hear him talking on the phone, but not what he was saying.

"What do you think?" I asked Charlie.

"I have been at this exactly three minutes, I don't actually have a conclusion yet," he harrumphed.

Little things were scraped and mixed and whizzed into smaller plastic containers and put into bigger things and computer screens were tapped.

"But it's not the Nipah X strain?" Tom persisted, as he came into the study.

"No! I checked for that first." Charlie was exasperated but we were all relieved.

It had been more than thirty years since the first Covid pandemic which the world had survived, and twenty since the Nipah pandemic which we nearly hadn't. You would have thought that the first one would have warned us to prepare for the second. It didn't. I had been safe on the Exmoor farm, vaccinated and educated. Tom was at his family's country estate in Herefordshire running wild and Charlie was growing up without seeing his mum who worked with her team in the local hospital trying to save people. It was a desperate time, but we were all young and I mostly remembered reading under the trees and wandering the fields on my pony, Cherri.

There was an irritating scratching noise I didn't recognise. "Stroppy, stop that!" Charlie sounded exasperated, but kept concentrating on the dance of technology in front of him.

I turned round, the octopus was attached to the side of the tank by several tentacles, he held a small rock from the bottom in another one and was sliding it along the inside of the iridescent clear wall. It sounded like fingernails down a chalk board. I winced.

For a moment we seemed to be looking at each other and I heard a whisper of something inside my head, more a picture than a word. I went over and put my hand on the tank where his suckers were placed. Suddenly he jerked away, flinging the rock out of the top of the tank and scaring me backwards.

"Huh." Charlie was beside me. "He's never done that before."

I looked up at my friend, and he smiled suddenly, it was like the sun coming out. He put his arm around me and kissed the top of my head.

Charlie is extremely attractive, wise and kind; at university lots of interest, from many people, went, as far as I was aware, unrequited. One night at a boisterous rugby party, after a home win of epic proportions, an extremely drunk and belligerent prop forward with an overabundance of testosterone challenged Charlie. His face was right up close to my friend and red with beer fever, "So, what sex *are* you?"

Charlie replied calmly, "potato cod."

The drunk swayed on his feet for a moment, and because most of the rugby team had some sort of science degree, added, "Not trigger fish?"

"Other way round," Charlie said.

"A snog isn't out of the question then?" The drunk grinned.

I personally have never asked, that would be rude, but I did look up potato cod.

TOM and I were curled in bed together, my head on his chest. Wearing his winter pyjamas and an old cardigan, plus two hot water bottles, I was finally beginning to feel warm.

We were quiet but I could hear him thinking. All men think really loudly.

"What were you looking at this morning in the kitchen?"

Tom was evasive. "When?"

"You know very well *when*," I whispered, raising myself up a bit to look at him in the semi-dark of a summer night.

"I just thought I saw something."

"Something or someone?" I wasn't going to let it go.

Tom has another job, apart from the one where he goes into his father's firm in London for a day every now and then, and does nothing except have coffee and chat with the accountant who pays the money into his bank. I am sure he knows I know but we have never discussed it. I think he was recruited at university in his first year. He is frighteningly clever and has a certain flexibility towards right and wrong that would interest certain people.

"Someone," Tom said.

I listened to him breathing for a while. Neither of us could sleep.

———

WANDERING into the kitchen in the early morning I gradually became aware of a clicking sound. I made the coffee and drank two glasses of cold clear water, running the tap and letting my fingers play with the flow. It felt like silk.

The door to Charlie's study was slightly ajar and I pushed it open. He was sitting at the computer, his nose inches away, whispering to himself and drumming a steady beat with a pencil on the desk. The screen held a pattern of molecular structure that I recognised as part of a DNA sequence.

"What's that?" I asked.

He jumped. "Laura! I didn't know you were up."

"Have you been here *all* night?" I handed him my coffee cup and he gulped and winced, I like it with milk and sugar, he usually drinks his black.

"I'm checking the results again." He examined the coffee to see if it was going to get any blacker, shrugged and swilled it down, which was impressive, as it was really hot.

He swung around when the computer pinged and the screen re-established the wavering shape, then scrubbed his face and looked at me. "I'm going to send this to some work associates."

"I don't think that's a good idea." Tom was standing right behind me.

It was my turn to jump. I thumped him. "Don't do that!"

"You did it to me!" Charlie said.

"That's different!"

Tom handed me more coffee and drank his before speaking. We looked at each other. I could see that they were both worried. I felt oddly calm.

I sat down in the chair next to the desk and curled up, my knees under my chin. "I take it this is me?" I pointed to the spinning DNA strands and the structural formula. "What language is that?"

"Mine," Charlie answered, earning a snort from Tom. He came over to me and squatting down in front of me he got hold of my hand. I shuddered as my equanimity vanished, replaced by worry, something I could see reflected in his own face. "I need help with this," he added.

"I don't think other people should know what's happening," Tom said enigmatically.

"And what exactly *is* that?" I whispered.

"There is a group of us," Charlie stopped and ignoring my question, began again, "we are scattered all over the world, and we share information on the research that we do. I've never met some of them but we are all scientists."

"Some of whom work for governments," Tom was scathing.

"*I* don't." Charlie was emphatic. "We are privately funded, and most of the research goes to medicine and the environment." He shrugged. "My biggest grant comes from the legacy of a businesswoman, on the understanding that I share my findings with other scientists if it would *benefit humanity*," he said dryly.

"I still don't like it." Tom was adamant.

"I know, but I can't do this on my own," Charlie was equally blunt.

"Now I know how Stroppy feels," I snapped, "I *am* sitting here, and I'm asking, *what is happening?*"

"I can't be sure, but it seems to be," Charlie paused, hunting for an appropriate word and not finding one, "evolution."

My mouth dropped open. Tom looked at Charlie. "You've always wanted to say that, haven't you?"

"Little bit," Charlie nodded, finger and thumb slightly apart.

I SAT out on the veranda looking at a restless blue sea. The crofter cottage was down a narrow lane, which connected to a farm further inland. You couldn't get to a tarmacked road for several miles and although it had access rights through the farmland, people seldom came here. No one really knew where here was.

I leaned against the warm stone of the old wall behind me. Charlie had bought the place with the farmer's blessing, Huw Cummings had also helped with the renovations, because all farmers have to diversify or lose. And this one had picked the building trade as his other job. He and his son Bryn left milk, cheese and eggs at the door and along with Huw's wife Efa and Bryn's partner Ceri, they were the best neighbours you never saw.

The four-wheel drive car was tucked in close to the side of the building furthest away from the sea, which gave it a miniscule amount of protection from the corrosive salt air.

The cottage, sat sideways on to the coastline, so you could see the waves from nearly every window, consisted of one living room kitchen downstairs with the study at the back. Upstairs were two bedrooms; Charlie's had a small shower room attached and the guest bathroom had a large bath and separate shower. Rainwater was collected in a supersized tank, which was almost always full, because it's Wales and it rains a lot. The electricity came from photovoltaic tiles on the roof and a small, rarely used emergency generator.

Charlie had financed a community cell tower which must have cost a fortune, but came out of one of his grants. The locals were ecstatic and effusive, though all of them thought Huw was responsible. It was hidden in a small forest of trees a mile further inland. Charlie had decorated his house with white walls and wood floors and *hundreds* of books.

I *loved* being here.

I COULD HEAR them discussing the *situation* as it had now become, through the open study window. I sighed and got up. Charlie and Tom argue all the time, but only about who was able to touch their nose with their tongue and what was more important than rugby or science (nothing). *Never* about me.

"How bad is this going to get?" I asked quietly when there was a lull in the endless back and forth. Charlie shrugged. "I don't know."

"That in itself should tell you something, you know *everything,*" Tom countered completely without irony.

Stroppy was glued to the clear wall of his tank looking at me, he scratched with his favourite stone to get my attention, but when I walked over to him, he sped away in a cloud of inky fear.

"He's interested but frightened," Charlie explained, "and it really worries me."

"To be fair, that's how *I* felt when I met you," Tom said. I thumped him on the arm.

The computer pinged, and Charlie went over to examine the results of whatever he had been doing. "That was a friend of mine in China, she said she might have something that could slow the progress of the virus."

"Is it a virus?" I asked Charlie.

"For the purposes of this conversation," he indicated the computer, "Mei thinks it is."

Tom was grey with tiredness and apprehension. "Please tell me that was encrypted and untraceable?"

"Nothing is that," Charlie shook his head. "But the DNA profile I sent indicates a bonobo and the computer conversation we are having is on the dark web."

Tom looked at me. "*Not a word.*" I said. He smiled; an inappropriate tiny monkey joke unspoken.

"Is that legal?" I asked. Silence followed as the two faces contemplated an answer. "Fine."

A knock at the door had all of us jumping in an undignified manner. Charlie and I looked puzzled but Tom's expression was unreadable. He pointed to me and then to the corner of the room where the water tank made shadows on the wall. A small weapon I had *never* seen before appeared from somewhere around his ankle.

Charlie watched this with bemusement and then went through the study door, which was still ajar from my entrance earlier, and into the living room. "Hi Huw, how are you? Ceri you look wonderful. Please come in, would you like coffee?"

Tom made the gun disappear as quickly as it had arrived and we followed. I put a smile on my strained face and Tom held my arm. The fact that we were all still in an unattractive combination of sleep wear, did not go unnoticed by either, but went uncommented. Both of them had probably been up and dressed before dawn.

"Ceri, I had no idea, when are you due?" Tom asked her.

"Sometime in the winter. The little bug is running around in here at the moment, do you mind if I sit down?" She plonked herself at the kitchen table, depositing the eggs, cheese and milk, as well as some cake and late wild strawberries. Charlie got on with making drinks and finding biscuits.

I excused myself for a quick shower and something to wear that wasn't my dressing gown. The patch of scarring on my leg was larger, but smoother and not irritating. I ignored it.

When I came back downstairs, I could hear the conversation was about the local rugby team and the latest results, which were not good, abysmal in fact.

"So, if you could see your way to give them some advice," Huw was almost pleading, Tom looked bemused and a little pressured.

"Huw, how well do you think *advice* from someone who played for several English teams is going to go down in Wales?" Tom said diplomatically.

"I think things are so bad they would take it from the devil himself if they thought it would buy them a win!" Huw's accent had become more pronounced.

"Tactfully put," Ceri said into the silence that followed. She turned to me. "How are you, Laura?"

"I'm fine, I caught a bit too much sun yesterday, I have the chills today," I explained away my layers of warm clothing. Jeans, a merino wool top and a cardigan, everyone else was in shorts and t-shirts.

"Aah," she squeaked, "feel this!" She grabbed my hand and put it on her stomach.

The pulse of sudden movement and the sound of flickering shadows in my head made me try and pull my hand away, but she held it tight against her. It was an uneasy moment that only Charlie seemed aware of and his expression was, as usual, enigmatic to everyone except me. If Ceri noticed my discomfort, she covered it with new mother enjoyment of life within.

Huw turned the conversation back to the less than successful local rugby league team results and we all sighed. Tom gave in as I knew he would.

"I'll come and watch the next game with you, but I will need a disguise and you'll have to tell everyone I'm your long-lost nephew from Port Talbot, who was captured by the English at university and made to play for them!"

This was greeted with stunned incredulity by Huw and Ceri, Tom's humour being something of an acquired taste.

"That actually might work." Huw nodded slowly and narrowed his eyes.

The coffee was drunk, but not by Ceri who stuck to water, and all the biscuits were gone; for a change Tom was outeaten by her, which was impressive. I have always wanted to consume a whole packet of chocolate biscuits.

They left eventually. It felt odd, as if they wanted to ask something not sport related, but were apprehensive about doing so.

I went through to the study while Charlie and Tom cleared the debris of coffee and biscuit rugby strategy, even the tea cosy had been co-opted as the referee. The window was open to the sea sounds, it usually had a positive effect on Stroppy, but he was doing loops of the tank in a very disturbed fashion. I heard the whisper of my name on the breeze, and then the word, "agwerin." It was Ceri speaking in Welsh and she sounded worried, but also something that seemed to be excited.

Charlie came through and began checking his computer.

"What does agwerin mean?" I asked him.

He looked puzzled, "I think you mean y gwerin, it translates as 'the folk,' why?"

"Something Ceri said to Huw when they left." I sat in the chair by the desk and Charlie tapped keys. "More information from the dark web buddies?"

"We're not a club, we're work associates," Charlie was avoiding the question. "Are we going to address the pachyderm in the room?"

"Which one, the fact that I have never seen Huw and Ceri sat at your kitchen table in the ten years you've lived here, or where I seem to be developing a new virus?"

Charlie waved his hand around in the air mimicking a gun with two fingers and a thumb. "Ah," I said, "that one."

Tom walked into the study wiping a cup on a tea towel, he and Charlie were both very tidy, whereas I like to think of myself as the organised practical one. I remembered what was needed, Charlie agreed to whatever it was and Tom put it away. It worked well for all of us.

"What's all that about?" Tom indicated the dirt and grass track where two figures could be seen in the distance.

"I think they came to see me," I said, with the prescience that usually made Charlie nervous. He liked his science without any pre.

"Have you got anything?" Tom asked Charlie, who was studying the computer and muttering to himself.

"Maybe a breathing space," Charlie went over to the book shelves and began pulling various tomes, flicking pages for something. "I need to work on this, go and get some rest Laura." He disappeared into full geek mode in front of our eyes.

Tom shrugged. "Give me a list, I'll go shopping, the fridge is bare."

I settled down outside by the window to the study, listening to Charlie talking to himself, the computer and occasionally, Stroppy. And watching the waves for I don't know what. The sea birds dived for food and shrieked at each other. Every now and then I saw the curious head of a seal watching me back. I realised neither Charlie or I had asked Tom about the gun.

TOM

Tom took the small road onto a wider one and kept driving. He had intended to do the shopping in Abermaw but he just didn't stop. Panic and fear got him as far as Shrewsbury, by the time he got to Telford he knew where he was going and why. The north route around Birmingham was as usual stop, go, all the way to Northampton.

He stood by the side of the four-wheel drive car that belonged to Charlie and waited for the charge to finish. His phone beeped again. The message read, "getting worried!" Laura had tried ringing him twice but he hadn't answered. The new superfast, and therefore expensive, electric charging station flashed green at him after three minutes, and he removed the plug.

The motorway from Northampton took him straight into London and eventually he parked outside the flat in Soho Square. It was quiet and dark as he sat in the car for a while listening to the ticking of the engine and his thoughts. Exhausted but hyper, his hands shook with adrenaline.

The keypad was dirty from too many greasy fingers, but the hallway was clean and well lit. His flat door as he closed it gave him a false sense of security for a few moments. Right up until the man spoke, "We haven't heard anything for a while, so, thought it was time for a catch up."

Tom turned round. "What took you so long?"

The two men sitting on his sofa were middle aged and greyish, with uniform casual clothing and hair. Tom wondered how anyone could mistake them for anything other than what they were. The other man smiled. His accent was soft west coast American. "You haven't been to see your *dad in a while.*"

Tom speculated on how the co-operation between international government agencies had improved over the previous decade, and the fact that his handlers were from both sides of the Atlantic. Double the trouble.

"Why are you here?" Steve asked him. British, tall, fair and not his real name.

"Laura is ill and I came to get some of her things." Tom began checking the hall cupboard.

"What's wrong?" Dave sounded genuinely worried. Athletic, dark skinned and also not his real name.

"She has a really bad virus; Charlie is looking after her." He snorted quietly to himself; his face hidden behind the open cupboard door. Both men were extremely fond of Laura, and in the ten years since he had been 'recruited' they had developed quite strong feelings for her. Even to the point of commenting on the choice of hair colour when she had dyed it; Steve liked it, Dave not so much. They mostly praised everything about Laura and had both expressed their views as to why she stayed with him, something he wondered about himself, often.

"Please tell me she doesn't have the Nepah X variant?" Dave was almost whispering.

Tom shrugged. "We don't know, Charlie is working on it."

"Is there anything we can do to help?" Steve looked at Dave and then at Tom, they all knew that if she did have it, though it wasn't particularly infectious now, it was nearly always fatal. They were both devastated, Tom almost felt guilty.

"I trust Charlie, but if you could give me a break for a week or two, until I get this sorted out?"

"Sure Tom," Dave was shaking his head at Steve. They still couldn't see Tom's face which was a mixture of apprehension and determination. He realised that he had never actually lied to these two men before which was odd, considering that he lived a lie. He didn't include withholding information which he felt was a necessary dance around the truth. The only reason he had never deceived Laura was because she had been very careful about not asking any questions, he always wondered how much she had actually worked out. She was so much smarter than him, he thought, so it was probably all of it.

"If Charlie's doing the research, then she has the very best chance," Steve said, reassuring himself.

They really liked Laura but their respect for Charlie veered irritatingly towards hero status. How they felt about him, Tom didn't really know. But he was pretty sure it didn't include either of those feelings. He had perfected the art of appearing to be an ignorant buffoon, so well in fact over the years, that he'd come to believe it himself. That way if the intelligence on his father and his associates was not entirely accurate, they didn't blame the idiot giving it to them.

"That's an awful lot of clothes for a week," Dave said suspiciously.

Tom smiled disarmingly. "I have no idea what she'd like to have with her, you'd know better than me, what do you think I should take to make her comfortable?"

It worked. Dave and Steve began "helping" and ended up putting in most of the contents of the cupboard into the cases, arguing over each item. Tom gestured towards his own packing needs and they hardly noticed.

It was Steve who picked out her work books and backup files, tidying them into a cardboard container. While they were busy Tom went into the kitchen and on the pretext of clearing out the fridge, which Laura had already done before they left for Charlie's, he removed a small package containing their passport IDs and other illicitly gained essentials, secreting them under his shirt. He got the feeling it was going to be difficult to get back to normal after this, though what that was he wasn't sure any more.

The two men helped him load up the car with most of their personal things from the flat. Far more than he had intended to take. He looked around at what was left. Furniture that didn't belong to either him or Laura and several paintings and pieces of artwork his father had given him, which were probably stolen or a tax write-off. It was odd, but all the stuff that really mattered to him and Laura was already at Charlie's house. He wondered how that had happened and then realised he didn't care.

DAVE AND STEVE

The two agents waved him off much to the delight of a drunk who joined in, standing on the pavement next to them, until encouraged to move on.

"Do you think he was telling us the truth?" Steve asked Dave.

"He's been slow walking us from day one, so no," Dave said pragmatically. Steve nodded his agreement. "We follow," Dave added. They stopped waving as the car went round the corner.

TOM

The journey back was slower, as there was more traffic and Tom was really tired. He stopped twice, once for an hour of sleep and then again to phone Laura.

"I went to pick some things up from the flat," he explained when she answered. There was a long pause.

"Excellent idea," Laura said eventually. "I'll see you soon, be safe." She disconnected.

They had always kept their conversations short and to the point. Tom because he knew someone was listening and Laura, well, he had just assumed she didn't like to talk on the phone, but he was beginning to wonder if it wasn't about the fact that he kept their passport IDs in a butter container in the fridge.

He was so glad to see the turning to the sea cottage, his hands gripped the wheel with a sudden overwhelming emotion. It felt like home. Laura waved from the seat near the window to Charlie's study.

LAURA

The three of us stood there looking at our boxes of belongings, the view was pathetic and I said so. "Is this *it?*"

Tom nodded. "We actually have more here than we do there." He looked sad so I gave him a hug. "You're cold!"

"I am really glad you brought my winter clothes." I was, I didn't tell him the patch of abnormal skin, as we had begun calling it, had spread. And Charlie was looking concerned when he examined me. The expression was one rarely seen on his face, that and the fact that he'd called me Larry three times, meant I was worried.

"I think I should speak to my mum," I sighed. I needed to wait until the milking had finished. They had a variety of stock, including goats and they made cheese as well. My sister had introduced changes that had not just kept the farm going but made it profitable. Everything was 'bespoke' and sold on line or "at the gate." The bigger farms were still trying to supply the national need. Of course, they didn't have so many people to provide for post pandemic, and the subsidies were substantial. We still imported some food, but the country was a leading exporter of dairy products, and my sister wanted a slice of the specialist pie. I knew the cheese was sold at an astonishing price at the tables of French restaurants, something my dad was particularly proud of.

I picked up my computer and tapped keys, checking the inbox as I went, little holographic swirls of information swam towards me. I saw one from my contact at the museum with a list of attachments for new assignments. They looked interesting. Another unknown email address had a request for an urgent translation. It was a short manuscript and the money was excellent, I decided it would be a good distraction and accepted the request, the money pinged into my account satisfyingly quickly. It wasn't unusual for the museum to recommend me to other establishments, though they weren't always so lucrative. I also got requests from other less salubrious clients sometimes, and this looked as if it might be one of those.

Charlie and Tom caught up in the corner of the study, then Tom took our meagre belongings upstairs. I drank the coffee that Charlie made. "Is this the usual brand?"

"Yes, why?"

I shrugged, it tasted different. Not unpleasant, just altered somehow.

"What are you looking at?" Charlie was swirling his fingers irritatingly in the mediaeval manuscript's rather beautiful illustration in the top corner. Tom thundered down the stairs again, he always sounded like a herd of elephants. It was somehow comforting to hear him clattering around in the kitchen. Charlie went back to his own computer, he preferred his text to stay on the screen for the most part, but occasionally I saw the DNA strands and the chemical formulas dancing around as he moved the keys.

Two words caught my eye and I gasped.

Charlie was over in an instant. "What is it?" I pointed and he swore, his voice was strident which attracted Tom's attention, he came in from the kitchen where he had been making lunch.

"Laura?" Tom added his nervousness to the mix.

I pointed again. "Why is the spelling different, is it because of the middle English?" I asked Charlie.

"It's a Welsh thing," Charlie explained, "The g is pronounced when it's spoken."

Halfway down the first page were the words, y werin, the folk.

"WHERE DID THIS COME FROM?" Tom was almost angry with fear. None of us could understand the implications.

"Could it be a coincidence?" I asked hopefully. Both of them looked at me. "Okay," I said.

"Why didn't you stop it before they paid?" Tom was upset now.

"I thought it came through the museum," I explained. "It usually would have done. Besides I hadn't checked it then, and it might not be anything now!" I was getting frustrated.

"You're morphing into a *fish* of course it means something, everything does!"

Charlie interjected, "not a fish exactly, more like Stroppy."

"Not helping!" I turned on him.

Tom looked horrified, "What are you saying?"

"Come and sit down, let's deal with the manuscript first. Laura, how long will it take you to translate it?"

"Maybe another hour, it's only a page fragment from a palimpsest."

"Where does the client want the results sent to?" Charlie was calm.

I checked the details; it was non-returnable. "Huh." I tried the money trail, nothing. The payment had gone into my account but the sender was hidden. Clients did that sometimes if the documents were less than honestly come by, I tried not to do too many of those but the money was good and unless I recognised the manuscript as stolen, I usually just let it slide.

"And you're sure that's what Ceri said?" Tom pointed at the words on the computer.

I nodded; I was now.

"Laura, can you concentrate on this, while I do some more work? We can confer in an hour." Charlie looked at Tom.

"What do you want me to do?" Tom asked.

"Lunch." Charlie said.

I smiled at the expression on Tom's face, which had argument written all over it, then he sighed and left the study quietly. I heard him in the kitchen, chopping some poor vegetable over enthusiastically.

"Stroppy?" I asked Charlie in a whisper.

"Leave it with me, I'll explain more after I have spoken to Mei."

I sighed and went back to the detailed illumination in the corner of the manuscript. The miniature seemed to be a chimera, but not the one of mythology, in fact nothing I'd ever come across before. I was very sure that although the document was of significant historical importance it was never going to be shown to anyone by me. The figure was a finely clothed female but with long snake-like hair waving away from her head; her body where you could see it, was covered in fine pale scales, she was beautiful and sad at the same time. I felt a shudder of fear.

"Laura?" Charlie was always sensitive to my moods.

"I'm okay," I lied.

I read with half an ear for the whispered conversation over on the other side of the room. When I glanced at the tank which bubbled comfortingly along one wall, the light on the water reflected the image of flickering books. Stroppy was watching me intently, his tentacles waving around like the hair of the chimera.

Mei was working late, I could see some of the holograph, her own study space was comfortingly like Charlie's, but shadowed in evening colours. I heard her asking sharp questions, as if she knew she was only getting half the information. She sighed.

Eventually she said, "Charlie, we have worked together for nearly ten years, I hope I have never given you cause not to trust me?"

"It's a sensitive one Mei, I'm sorry if you feel I have been less than honest." He added some detail to the DNA results and something that looked like a chemical formula.

I heard her gasp. "You're sure?"

"I ran the tests three times," Charlie said.

There was quiet. I worked to finish the document and found comfort in the process. Mei and Charlie tapped keys at the same time and the scroll of detail moved around in a cylindrical spiral.

Eventually Mei said, "I think that's it." She looked at Charlie and held a hand up, he did the same, their fingers mixed in the holograph. It was so poignant that I stopped what I was doing to watch.

"I'm here if you need any more help, but be careful." Then she was gone.

"Does she know?" I asked Charlie.

"It was not possible to keep the human DNA from her, it differed enough for it to skew the test results. I have known her for a long time and I trust her."

He began setting up the laboratory apparatus for creating whatever was on the computer. I thought about the fact that he was able to do so. Everything, including equipment, was smaller and more efficient, probably as a result of the last pandemic; people had had to adapt and learn to work alone, sharing their findings and developments at a distance, particularly in science. And yet, we hadn't seemed to progress much where humanity was concerned.

Tom came into the study; his face was grey with exhaustion. "Lunch is served." He indicated with a small bow.

I found the food oddly comforting, Tom had made fish finger sandwiches with thick slices of buttered white bread and a large salad of nearly everything crunchy and colourful. It tasted interesting and oddly exotic.

We sat outside drinking coffee with varying degrees of milk and sugar, me a lot of both, Tom some milk and Charlie, black with no sugar. We were a trifecta of collective difference.

"So, let's talk." Tom went to get my notes and Charlie his. I sat on the bench waiting, looking out over the sea, sipping coffee and feeling oddly calm.

I held the computer pad and read aloud.

"On the day for St Eulalia, the day before ides—"

"Laura!" Tom interjected.

"Sorry, dates in the Middle Ages are usually marked by saints' days and Christian feasts and— oh never mind. It's the 12th February and King John is on the throne and has been for three years, so it's 1202. I think this comes from Penmon Priory, but I can't be sure without the whole document. There is mention of Rhodri ab Owain Gwynedd who was Lord of Anglesey around that time. But the dates don't quite match. Anyway, it refers to the House of Aberffraw and their responsibility to protect the folk. The manuscript is torn around this part but it seems to have been dictated to a monk who was from the monastery, he wrote it out in Latin, adding the rather fanciful illustration. It says that something, and this is the bit that is missing, but whatever it is, 'coming from the water will keep us safe through the darkness that sweeps the land,' quite what that means I don't know, but it's odd that a Christian monk would be so taken with what is clearly a mythical scare story, as opposed to an allegorical religious one."

Charlie was looking puzzled, as if trying to remember something important.

Tom spoke, "what does that have to do with Laura?"

"Everything I think," Charlie said.

I began to choke, the food I had eaten came up undigested and mixed with blood, splattering all over me and the floor, more blood dripped out of my nose and ears. I gasped for breath but it wouldn't come. I saw Tom panicking and his hands reached out to grab me before I fell. Charlie was running into the house.

CHARLIE

Fumbling with the tiny amount of immunotherapy activator that he had been able to synthesize in such a short time, Charlie grabbed a pressure hypodermic syringe and tried not to spill any. He checked the computer readings for the dosage and shut his ears to the sound of fear that Tom was making. He ran outside. Laura was lying on her side gasping for air. Tom was holding her in place while she fitted and thrashed her legs and arms. He was covered in her blood and vomit.

Charlie pulled at her trousers, exposing the skin of her upper thigh and pushed the hypodermic into her muscle; the liquid dispersed quickly. They waited. Laura's limbs stilled and she took a small breath in, then a bigger one, and another. Charlie felt as if he was breathing with her, and for her.

He added another two syringes of liquid. "Vasodilator, and an anti-inflammatory," he explained to Tom's unspoken question. They sat watching Laura struggle with the internal battle.

"You're back," he said, as her eyes focused on his face. She heaved once more, this time the vomit and blood ended up all over him.

"What now?" Tom asked Charlie anxiously.

Charlie sighed, Laura was asleep on the sofa in the living room, she wouldn't go upstairs to bed, he knew she was afraid to be alone. All the years of their relationship he had seen the myriad of shifting emotions that was part of the reason he loved her, but he had never seen her scared before. He tried for an answer, one that Tom would understand.

"I don't know, I've given her an activator that I synthesized from a section of Stroppy's RNA, bearing in mind the changes in her are at a genetic level—"

"Please explain to me how that is possible?" Tom was angry, something that Charlie understood was part of his coping mechanism for fear.

"Laura was bitten, and I don't know why, but it set off a reaction that acted like a retrovirus, every cell in her body was infiltrated with a DNA copy of its RNA genome at the most basic level, which is changing the genome of each cell—" Charlie looked at Tom's face. "It's rewriting the DNA instructions of her cells."

"What was in the first injection you gave her?" Tom asked him, in a whisper.

"I'm hoping it will slow down the progress, and give me more time," Charlie said quietly.

"Hoping?" Tom put his arm on Charlie's shoulder and they stood there for a moment.

"Hey, it works for me," Laura said, her eyes still firmly closed.

The three of them sat still, watching the evening light slide across the wood flooring. Tom went over to the kitchen and started preparing a meal of local fish and rice. He made it as bland as possible.

Charlie spoke quietly, "My father was studying the migration patterns of phytoplankton—"

"Your father!" Laura interjected.

He sighed, as Tom stopped what he was doing and leaned on the work counter between the living area and the kitchen, his mouth forming questions.

Charlie began again. "He was a famous geneticist, much older than my mum, I worked it out when I was a teenager from some of the things I found in her home office, and I looked him up when I was in uni. He died in the first wave of the Nipah virus. The work showed that global warming was pushing the cold-water species further north and the warm water species was moving into our local waters. Things were changing at a rapid rate. People were not listening. Then it happened and climate change didn't matter." He looked at their faces. Laura and Tom were thinking their own thoughts about why.

"How many people died? No one seems to know, probably more

than two billion in the last thirty years, but now the rate of decrease in the size of populations is also increasing. Yes, we are managing, most countries have a reasonable infrastructure, we went back to our profligate and destructive fuel and food ways, trade, economics, secret state groups, it's all there, except—" He stopped abruptly, wondering if they were both going to think he was ridiculous, a conspiracy theorist, of whom there were many, there was nothing like a pandemic to bring out the irrational in those looking for other explanations as to why their world had changed.

"Go on," Tom said, reading his mind in the way that made Charlie smile. "It's not as if we think you're off on the crazy train," he added helpfully, "more of a geek walkabout."

"We were experiencing species decline at a phenomenal rate before the Nipah pandemic. Extinction events were hitting essential groups, insects, wildlife, plants and the oceans, which were becoming acidic. My father was part of an international scientific alliance who were examining the levels of carbonate ions and the effect on calcareous plankton." He could see that he'd lost them a little. "CO_2 absorption increases cause hydrogen ions to increase, which then causes seawater to become more acidic and reduces carbonate ions." The faces were really blank now. "Okay, trust me, it's important, it affects the food web and the atmosphere."

They both nodded and there was a pause while everyone considered it.

"You're saying, that after a short reprieve caused by the pandemic, climate change and species decline are back?" Laura shuffled on the sofa, trying to find a more comfortable position.

"Yes." Charlie nodded.

"What is different now?" Tom asked with great perception.

"It's us this time," Charlie said, "we're the species that's in decline."

CHARLIE WENT BACK to his computer and tried to concentrate. The morning had slid carefully into afternoon. No one had eaten much lunch, including Tom, who usually had the appetite of a growing twelve-year-old, consuming anything and everything at all times.

Stroppy was gliding about in restless movements. Charlie went over to the seawater tank and tapped on the clear wall, Stroppy sped across and stuck himself on by two tentacles as if trying to hold hands. When Laura came in, he shot away in a cloud of disapproval and fear. She looked at Charlie.

"Is it me?"

"I think so," Charlie said, "I just don't know why."

The computer pinged and Mei's face appeared. She looked odd, the holograph of her head distorted for some reason. "Hey Charles, I was just checking in." It was as if they had not just spoken four hours ago.

"Mei, how are you this evening?" Charlie glanced at the time; it was late evening in Beijing. And Mei knew that his name wasn't an abbreviation of Charles. He followed her lead.

Her face was partly obscured by her hair. "Laura, how nice to meet you, how are you feeling now?"

Laura looked at Charlie and he made a slight shake of his head. "Good evening to you Mei, I'm fine, just a bit of a fever, nothing much else, thank you for asking."

"Charles, the work I did for you has been interesting, let me know if you need any more help."

"Of course, Mei. I have no new information on the bonobo, but when I get the latest from my contact in the DRC, I'll pass it on," he finished cheerfully.

"Thank you. Goodbye Charles." Mei sounded sad, and frightened. She disappeared in a wave of light.

"What was that?" Laura asked him, alarmed.

"A warning." Charlie though that there was a chance he would never speak to Mei again. "I think the dark web connection has been compromised."

"And what does that mean?" Tom had come in, hearing the tone but not the words.

"We're on our own." Charlie was trying to keep his fear under control, but he looked at the two people who meant everything to him and he couldn't help an involuntary shudder.

Stroppy was back stuck to the side of the seawater tank again, and this time he didn't shoot away when Laura went over to him. His tentacles caressed the clear wall, tapping gently in response to her face leaning on the cool surface.

DAVE AND STEVE

"Huh!" Dave looked at his phone.

He and Steve were driving down to the Welsh coast. They had stopped for lunch and a small snooze at a nice country pub and changed seats to share the driving. The sun was setting, and the sky was filled with gold and the deep blue of the countryside. Both men had called their families. They would be away for a few days. Steve's partner was in 'the business' so he was read in on most of the job details, Dave's wife was a busy barrister and really didn't have time to think, never mind worry over what his mid-level civil service job entailed.

"Is that about your daughter's football final?" Steve was honorary uncle to both of Dave's children.

"No, we're going to have to do a hostile pick up." Dave was stunned.

"They want us to bring Tom in, why?" Steve was sceptical, things had been slow but they were still getting plenty of useful intelligence on the business and associates.

"Not Tom." Dave was looking at him. "Laura."

LAURA

I tried to sleep but gave up after a few hours of restlessness. I was so cold; the shaking had stopped, but not the sense of internal disquiet. I could literally feel the changes. It was odd but there was an awareness of the inevitable about it, as if I'd already given up. And I wasn't so frightened.

Tom always slept as if he'd been knocked out with a hammer. It was irritating. I contemplated giving him a good thump for his complete inconsideration. But even in the half-light I could see the dark shadows under his eyes and the unusual frown of worry. His hand clutched something under the pillow. I pressed down lightly on the bump, it was metal, the shape obvious. I wondered where he had got it from, and how long he'd had it.

As I came quietly down the stairs, I could hear the tapping of computer keys and the soft hum of the mass spectrometer. Clearly Charlie hadn't gone to bed. I slipped into the study and watched him for a while. He muttered occasionally to Stroppy who was at the top of the seawater tank, flopped decoratively over the edge, testing the air with an inquisitive tentacle.

"How long is Stroppy able to breathe out of the water?"

Charlie didn't turn round or stop what he was doing, nor did he jump at the sound of my voice.

"It's more complicated than that, but the short answer is usually about thirty minutes. They have an organ called the pallial cavity and a modified gill structure.

"Usually?"

Charlie sighed, "Stroppy has been out of his tank for more than six hours, and no, I don't know why."

"So, I'm not the only one changing?" I tried to sound as if I was making a joke.

"My colleagues and I have been seeing various developments in several species." Charlie looked sad.

"I take it Mei was one of those doing the noticing?" Sitting down on the chair between the seawater tank and Charlie's desk, I curled up and tucked my feet underneath me. Stroppy watched with interest. "How blown are you, Charlie?"

"I've tried to contact seven of the nine people I work with on a regular basis, I haven't been able to reach any of them."

"What about the ones that you don't work with all the time?" I watched as Stroppy made his way down the side of the tank and across the study floor.

Charlie thought about it. "I put out a warning after I couldn't get a response from my associates. If they've got a sense of self preservation, they won't reply to anyone, not even me."

"Why now?" I asked. Charlie turned to face me; his expression was one of extreme worry. "I mean, what inspired the people who are interested to make a move?"

"I think I tipped them off," he said, his voice horrified. "It was me."

I shuddered. "Charlie, if these people have been watching you and your fellow scientists, it could have been any one of you, don't go there, if you lose it, so will I and then where will Tom be?"

Charlie snorted, then smiled. It was weak but welcome.

"There's no possibility one of you would betray the rest, is there?" I added, wiping the smile off his face.

"Only under extreme duress." Charlie went back to the keyboard and the holographic images of molecular results that spun in the air. "We all have our Achilles heel Laura, ask Tom."

"Ask Tom what?" He stood in the doorway of the study, this time the question and his sudden appearance made both Charlie and I jump guiltily. Clearly my hearing was not going to develop into a super-sense.

"Have you left any food out?" Charlie said, pointing to the trail of seawater across the floor and into the kitchen.

"Stroppy!" Tom yelled, "leave the fridge alone!" He departed abruptly and both Charlie and I sniggered as we listened to him trying to reason with the inquisitive cephalopod.

He arrived back into the study with Stroppy wrapped in a tea towel. Doing his best to escape, he tapped Tom's face gently with an indignant tentacle. "Oh, alright then." Tom gave in and put Stroppy down on the floor, where he promptly went back out of the study on his night time foraging quest.

"He's very smart," Tom said proudly.

"A little too much," Charlie commented.

Tom sighed, removed a stack of books from the chair by the window and put them on the floor, then as he went to sit down, he straightened up again. "I need a hot chocolate," He looked at me and I nodded. Charlie lifted a hand without turning away from his holographic screen.

I could hear Tom talking to Stroppy in the kitchen as if to a favourite child, while he banged cupboard doors and assembled the ingredients. It was always made with full cream milk and chocolate hazelnut spread, whisked up with cinnamon.

"Do you ever wish you had children, Laura?" Charlie's question was almost a whisper.

"I have never felt safe enough, the pandemic, the nomadic existence, and Tom's family thing—" I stopped abruptly as Tom came in with a full tray of hot drinks and homemade ginger biscuits. I didn't know when he'd made them, but he was always adding to a meal preparation with a cake or pudding for later. Stroppy followed him like a puppy promised treats.

Tom passed around the drinks and the biscuits. He had a small dish of freshly cooked anchovies and he handed them one by one to Stroppy who took them in a polite tentacle and transferred them carefully to his mouth, there was minimal slurping, though I could hear the click of his beak.

"Do you want one?" Tom asked me.

"No, thank you, the chocolate is hitting the spot for now," I said wryly.

"Just checking," he grinned.

"I don't think I can fix this," Charlie said. He slammed the computer making the holographic spiral of DNA spin alarmingly. "Not on my own."

I went over to him; his head was bent down in exhausted defeat. "If anyone can do this it's you, and if you can't, then it's not possible."

He held my hand for a moment, looking me in the eyes. I could see Tom watching, with the cobra of despair coiled around him.

A slight sound of something not of us caused Stroppy to sprint for his tank and the relative safety of the large rock cave in the murky bottom. His startled flight made for a comedic moment in a fountain of scattered fish food and a stolen biscuit. Tom leapt to his feet and ran out of the room tripping over the books he had moved. He seemed to be airborne for a long time before he hit the floor the other side of the door with a thunderous impact and an even louder swear word. Charlie knocked over his chocolate drink in a sticky tsunami, and it spread over the computer, dripping down his face and clothes. I stood there helpless for a second, then started to laugh, I couldn't stop.

Tom appeared in the doorway, his expression a picture of indignance, right up until he saw Charlie, then he too cracked. Stroppy crept out of his cave to see what all the noise was about, his tentacles describing his puzzlement.

We cleaned up as best we could, Charlie went back to the biochemistry and genetic formulas with a black coffee as a companion. I could see Tom outside; the dawn sky was beautiful so I joined him. He was examining something on the ground under the study window. I saw a footprint in the second before he erased it with his own foot and straightened up to smile at me. I didn't comment and he didn't explain. We just sat on the seat and watched the sky turn from deep dark blue to gold. Both of us listening to Charlie in the study, through the open window, tapping computer keys.

I had never asked Tom any questions, preferring not to have my suspicions confirmed, but I realised that most people, including his family and all the employees at his father's business, thought he was not too bright. I remembered the Tom I had met all those years ago in the first days of university, he was clever and quick. I became aware of the thought that keeping up the appearance of stupidity must be exhausting. Flashes of the old Tom surfaced sometimes, disappointingly fleeting and more infrequent of late; maybe he had been doing it for so long even he believed it. Like an agent kept undercover past the point of safety. I shuddered.

"What are you frightened of Tom?" I asked him, our faces close enough for me to see the faint shadows of clouds flickering across his dark eyes.

"You mean apart from my girlfriend turning into a fish?" he said dryly.

"Not a *fish*!" Charlie interjected loudly through the open window. He sounded high on adrenalin, exhaustion and coffee fumes.

I sighed. "For three people who are so close we do seem to keep a lot of secrets."

Tom nodded sadly. Charlie's computer was silent for a moment while we contemplated our friendship.

CHARLIE

Charlie could feel his fingers freezing on the keyboard. The challenge for change. It was Laura who was the catalyst, the one who kept them together, their relationship glue. Always full of good ideas; he wouldn't have specialised if she hadn't suggested it, or gone on to do studies in the Antarctic or Mongolia. She had found the cottage on one of his seal research trips, when they had been living in the cramped camper van, and persuaded the Cummings family to sell it to him, emphasising his family ties to the area and the importance of his work.

He heard a stifled cry, then Tom's anguish, and he ran.

They carried Laura between then to the sofa in the living area and placed her carefully down. Tom tucked a blanket around her, the day was warm but she felt cold to the touch. She was impossibly still. He checked her breathing using his watch, less than ten per minute; the respirations were far too slow.

"Charlie?"

"I think we should put her in the tank." Charlie went back into the study and looked at his chemical calculations spiralling out of the connected computer and mass spectrometer.

"Let me get this straight, you want me to throw the love of my life into a seawater tank?" Tom sounded desperate and hopeful instead of the more understandable, incredulous. He stood in the doorway, glancing back at Laura and then at Charlie.

"I was thinking more of lowering her in gently," Charlie explained, checking his computer for the hundredth time and finding the same results.

"Are you sure?"

"No, yes, I think so," Charlie was still looking at the computer and not at Tom. "I've done this calculation a thousand times and I keep getting the same result. Laura's gaseous exchange is more like Stroppy's now, she needs the sea water."

"If you're wrong, she'll drown," Tom whispered.

"If we don't try this, Laura will stop breathing. She's not getting enough oxygen." Charlie moved towards Tom and held his shoulders, their faces close as brothers, or lovers, the for always moment of trust passing between them. Tom nodded.

They both turned to look at Laura and then back at the very large, rather high, seawater tank. "Huh!" Tom said.

After much discussion, in which an astonished Stroppy seemed to be contributing, Charlie decided that they would both get into the tank with her. He stripped off and put on his swim shorts, Tom went upstairs and got changed. Charlie knew he was putting the gun, that he now wore permanently strapped to his ankle, somewhere close by. He realised they were going to have to have a discussion about it, but without Laura he didn't know how to start.

Having examined their options once again, Charlie went to fetch the stepladder from the kitchen cupboard, it was three steps higher than the ground. If they both lifted her up, then one of them got into the tank while the other one held her, it was possible.

"Are we going to undress her?" Tom asked him.

Charlie looked at him in utter disbelief. "If she comes round and finds herself completely starkers in Stroppy's seawater tank, I do not fancy our chances of getting out of here alive!"

"I just thought, it would help her to, I don't know, breathe better," Tom explained.

"She's not respirating through her skin!" Charlie was beginning to laugh. He couldn't help it.

"What's so funny?" The voice from the doorway made both of them leap into the air, with a combination of guilt and surprise.

Laura was clinging to the doorframe, her face pale and her breathing rapid and shallow. Her lips were a shocking navy blue.

"Why are you both in your swim shorts?" Laura made it to the chair by the tank with Charlie's help.

"You have to get into the seawater tank," Charlie said gently. "It will help you."

"Are you sure?" Laura gulped for air.

He nodded. Tom hadn't moved from his spot on the stepladder. He seemed paralysed with worry.

Charlie held out his hand and Laura took it; they looked like dancers about to take to the floor.

"Wait," Laura said. She stripped off her jeans and jumper and was left standing in her sports bra and knickers. She held out her other hand to Tom.

The entry into the tank would have gone better if Laura hadn't lost consciousness again right at the point when she was half in. Tom lowered himself into the water, trying not to let too much of it slosh over the edge, but as Charlie helped her, she fell, swamping Tom and pushing him under. Stroppy shot into his cave in fury at the invasion of his private space, and a tidal wave swept over the edge of the tank into the study.

Charlie realised he had missed something. "Displacement," he gasped through a mouthful of tank water that had hit him square in the face. He reached for Tom. "Let her go."

"I can't," Tom was panicking, more water was sloshing over the edges.

"If you want to save her, you must!" Charlie was insistent.

Laura was oddly buoyant, bobbing just under the surface with her feet off the bottom. Stroppy stuck his head out of his cave and the look he gave them both was one of complete incredulity. Charlie helped Tom out and the water went back down to safer levels. He checked the feed and opened the outside valve which released more seawater into the tank from the one topped up outside.

Laura looked peaceful, her eyes were closed and her lips were returning to a normal colour.

"What now?" Tom asked Charlie, his face close to the clear barrier, watching Laura.

"We wait. And er, clean up the study floor," Charlie said.

———

THEY GOT mops and cloths from the kitchen and began wiping. A small sound made both of them look up, the farm dog was observing them from the open doorway. Charlie went down on one knee on the soggy floor and the dog came over to him, wagging his tail.

"Hey Raq, what are you doing here?" Charlie laughed when the dog licked his salty face. "Just what I need, more water!"

"He came with me," Ceri said, from the kitchen.

Tom looked horrified. He tried to shield the sight of Laura by standing in front of the tank, an all but useless move.

Charlie got to his feet. He wasn't really surprised, in fact things were beginning to make sense.

Ceri strode arrogantly into the study and looked at Laura. "It's progressed fast, are you still giving her the immunotherapy drugs?"

Charlie nodded. "An activator. Are you saying I should stop?"

"If you want her to live," Ceri was blunt.

"What the hell are you two talking about?" Tom was incandescent with fear and rage, and he looked completely ridiculous in red swim shorts, still holding a mop and bucket.

"We are of the folk," Ceri said simply. She looked at Charlie. "You don't seem surprised?"

"My nain told me about some of the myths, when I was a child. Granny," he explained to Tom, who had put down the mop and bucket and was alarming Raq by getting too close to Ceri. "I suppose you're a direct descendant of some mystical princess—"

"Don't be daft, this is biology not woo-woo shit!" Ceri was scathing.

Charlie sighed and sat down on the soggy chair by the tank, glancing at Laura and wishing she was here to defuse the situation, he really missed her. "She's right about the evolutionary biology," he said.

"I was born this way, but—"

"You decided to give evolution a little push by infecting Laura!" Tom was letting his fury take over.

"We were dying out and so are you!" Ceri shouted. Raq got between her and Tom and by sheer force of personality, combined with wet border collie furry love, they both stopped and took a step back.

"He's very excitable," she said eventually to Charlie, "that must be his American side?"

Charlie contemplated his computer and got a small hypodermic out of the drawer. He pulled up a solution from one of the many vials stacked in the fridge by the mass spectrometer.

"Are you sure?" Tom asked him.

"No, but we can't keep her suspended between one thing and another." Charlie's heart was full of sadness and longing for other days. He stepped on the ladder by the seawater tank and leaned in to inject Laura. She didn't react, just bobbed under the surface. He felt broken.

"You've got a problem," Ceri said.

"My girlfriend's turning into a fish, you mean?" Tom said sarcastically. He had retrieved his work tools and was swabbing the wooden floor viciously.

"Not a fish!" Charlie and Ceri said at the same time.

"What is it?" Charlie asked her, focusing on something that wasn't breaking his heart.

"There are some strangers just arrived in the village and they've been seen in the forest." She added, "a man and a woman, both Asian, and another two men," She looked at Tom, "those I think you know."

Charlie glanced at Tom; he couldn't feel any sadder. Tom's face was a picture of 'chickens coming home to roost'. He wished that they'd had a chance to talk, the three of them, and dispel some of the secrets that had been growing, like invasive species.

"The two Asian people are posing as research scientists and have asked for your whereabouts Charlie, but no one is telling them. The other two haven't spoken to anyone and look as if they know exactly where you are." Ceri pointed to Raq. "I will leave him with you."

"Don't tell me, the dog as well?" Tom was still in sarcasm mode.

Ceri looked puzzled, then exasperated. "He barks." Tom still didn't understand. "At strangers," she added.

"Ah," Tom got it.

Charlie laughed out loud.

There was silence for a moment. Raq went over to the seawater tank and put his nose on the clear surface.

"How is that thing not sinking through the floor, it must weigh enough?" Ceri asked.

"The tank itself is not made of glass, for a start," Charlie explained, glad to be taking about something practical. "It's a type of bio-plastic, which is why it's slightly iridescent."

"Seaweed agar based—" Ceri went over to stand by Raq.

"Give me a break," Tom interrupted. "I have questions."

"I'm sure you do, but I don't trust you, you sold out your family!" Ceri was sharp.

Charlie thought things couldn't get any worse, he was afraid Tom was now going to explode and stood between them, much like Raq had.

"It was either her or them, and I chose Laura," Tom whispered.

Charlie held his arm and squeezed gently, trying to give his friend something to hold onto as the person he usually reached for was unavailable.

Ceri tapped the tank and watched for Laura's reaction. Her face rippled in the water as the clouds crossed the sun through the window. "Some people's DNA speaks loudly to them," She speculated.

Charlie snorted in derision, "in my experience there is a large section of the human race that doesn't listen!"

"I will keep the incomers away from you for as long as possible, the rest..." she waved her hand towards Laura, "will have to run its course."

"Will she be the same?" Tom asked hopefully.

Charlie's heart felt the pain of the truth but he couldn't speak the words.

"No," Ceri was blunt again. "But as you can see, I still live in this world." She stretched her back and the curve of her large baby bump strained against her loose dungarees.

"With all due respect, Ceri, you have no idea the effect this will have on Laura." Charlie was equally plain. "Why did you do it?"

Ceri looked as lost as Tom, for a moment they were bookends of sadness. "As I said, both our species are dying out, and this seemed to be our best chance for survival. The combination of genes might help us, or at least that's what your father said before he died."

If it was remotely possible for the room to have slipped out of time and frozen the four people in it, this is how it would have appeared, Charlie thought. Even Raq was still, his face a picture of doggy concern.

Ceri left as abruptly as she had arrived and Raq stretched out by the tank, keeping watch over Laura and the study door in turn.

"Well?" Tom said to Charlie.

"I don't know." He looked at Tom's face. "What?" He sighed with exasperation. "Sometimes I just don't!"

"Okay, it's just not three words I usually hear you say."

The floor was mopped as best they could manage. The wood had been treated with a proofing material for just the situation of the tank spillage, so it didn't take it too long to dry. But Charlie fetched a dehumidifier from the storage room and set it up. Raq watched with interest as they worked and got up every now and then to comfort one or other of the two men. Charlie saw Tom gripping Raq's coat in his fingers and the dog responding with licks and yips of support.

"This is what I've got," Charlie said, sitting at the kitchen table. Tom was making them something to eat from the contents of the freezer. He had to look at the clock to remember what time it actually was. Sleep had not interrupted his frantic research and his circadian rhythm was out by several hours. Tom's efforts at cooking were desultory at best, he'd ground to a halt like an unwound clockwork toy.

Charlie carried on, "Evolutionary survival skills are built into our genes, we adapt with what we pick up along the way, viruses make up about eight percent, because we found them useful. Epigenetics change how your body reads a DNA sequence."

"Evolutionary survival?" Tom resumed the food preparation.

"Higher ground," Charlie explained. "It's an advantage in adaption." He watched as Tom processed the information.

"Natural selection?" Tom said.

"Yes." Charlie sat quietly as Tom put something on a plate for him and tried not to weep with pity for himself and the friend he loved, when he saw Tom set out a plate for Laura without realising it. And then bend with grief when he did. They both looked at the food and each other, picked the plates up and went into the study.

The tank was bubbling comfortingly and Laura looked peaceful, suspended in the seawater, her feet inches from the bottom and her head under the water. Her hair floated around her like seaweed. Stroppy was out of his hidey-hole and wandering restlessly around, in an unusual daytime perambulation. He didn't seem to mind Laura being there, occasionally he would tap her with an enquiring tentacle on the leg or arm and was content with the unquantifiable response.

Charlie tried to eat but he was so tired that his jaw wouldn't connect around the food. He was afraid of choking himself so he abandoned the attempt and put the vegetable frittata down, barely touched. Tom, he noticed, had finished his. Without realising it Charlie found himself asleep and dreaming.

The waves rolled into the shore with that calming rush of ozone. He could feel sand between his toes and the sun was warm on his bare back. It was a memory from his childhood, on a beach further up the coast. He could hear his mother shouting not to go too near the rocks, he turned to her and signalled, that yes, he had heard. She waved back and then picked up a large medical journal. His mum was always studying in his memories.

He saw the children playing in the waves really close to the rocks and went to warn them. Something about the two made him stop for a second and watch. They had no fear and seemed to be daring each other to take greater chances. The boy, probably around his own age, got onto a rock with remarkable agility and then dived into the water. Charlie was horrified, he waited, then ran, he was so far away that it took him several minutes to get to the shore. The little girl was laughing as the boy came up beside her. He had been down so long Charlie was sure he had drowned. The little girl saw him and was immediately wary. Charlie stopped and smiled, hoping to make friends. The boy didn't but she grinned back, then put her finger to her lips in an age-old gesture. Another moment and the two of them were gone beneath the waves. He looked for them but there was no trace. When he walked back to his mother and told her, she said he must have imagined it. He didn't understand why she insisted he repeat the words several times.

Tom was shaking him. "Charlie, have some tea. I made biscuits."

Charlie managed a groggy reply, "Ergh, sorry I just couldn't stay awake." He sat up, clutching his neck which was still chair back shaped and difficult to rearrange and took the tea and several biscuits. He dunked, realising how hungry he was. When Tom had made them, he didn't know, but they were ginger, chocolate chip and delicious.

"Are we going to discuss the Asian scientists?" Tom asked him.

"What about the two secret service men?" Charlie countered. Tom's expression was blank. "I thought not," he added.

He remembered the dream children and his mother's insistence that he had imagined it. "Have you ever heard of neurolinguistic programming?"

Tom shook his head, puzzled at the change of subject.

"I think my mum is really good at it." Charlie sighed with frustration.

"If we ever get out of this, maybe you'd better ask her?" Tom suggested, dryly.

Charlie went to his computer and began checking information. Then went to the tank, and getting on the step ladder he leaned over to take Laura's pulse; it was slow and steady. "Pass me that hypo, will you," he asked Tom.

"What are you doing?"

"I need a bit more blood to verify the DNA developments and I'm going to rig up a pulse oximeter, which quite frankly I should have done hours ago. I'm playing catch up, and I can't help feeling that Ceri could have done more sooner, but I imagine, 'I've infected your friend and I don't know if it will kill her,' is not a conversation you can have easily." Charlie was really angry for the first time in a long while. It was exhausting, he wondered how Tom managed it.

"Do you think it was just her then?" Tom was helping him by reaching for things Charlie pointed at.

"No," Charlie sighed.

"And the elephant in the room?" Tom asked him.

"Which one would that be?" Charlie laughed. "Laura in a seawater tank, MI5, or Chinese organised crime?"

"I was thinking the bit about your dad actually," Tom said.

"Oh, *that* elephant."

"And it's MI5 *and* the FBI," Tom added sadly.

Charlie was stunned, he couldn't imagine how it was possible that they could be in any more trouble. "I suppose it says something for

American and British interdepartmental relationships?" he joked weakly, sitting down suddenly on the top of the stepladder.

"Your dad?" Tom persisted as he handed Charlie his tea and another biscuit.

"I don't know, I confirmed the death certificate on line, but as you know these things can be hacked, either way he disappeared. I did notice the research he was doing was carried on by someone until four years ago."

"Are you saying your dad was still alive all that time?" Tom whispered, horrified.

Charlie shrugged, dunked the biscuit and tried to think, he felt tired and ill, his eyes and his heart ached in unison. "She's right you know," he said, through a mouthful of soggy ginger bits.

"About what?" Tom was tidying up; he examined the books to see if they were dry and then put them back on the shelves. The chair he moved to the sunny spot and put the cushion, which had received most of the damage, out of the open window and onto the seat. He examined the dehumidifier and poured the contents into the plant pot in the corner. Most of the spilled tank water was in the bucket which he lifted and took into the kitchen to empty.

Charlie watched; this was their pattern. It was ineffective without Laura though; they were two legs of a three-legged stool.

"Species diversity, or the lack thereof, it's more of a threat than climate change, something else my dad was working on, clearly for a lot longer than I realised. He had, it seems, spent quite a lot of time in the Amazon."

Tom was back with his eyes on the tank and Laura. He nodded. "Understandable, it has the most diversity on the planet."

Charlie grinned, that was the thing about Tom he loved the most, he still had the ability to surprise, even after all he'd been through.

"I do listen," Tom said, as if reading Charlie's thoughts. "You know, I can understand why he might have faked his own death."

"To protect the research and his family," Charlie said, his voice sounding bitter, "I think I set off this last chain of events with Mei. How could I have been so stupid?"

"I don't think that your level of stupidity is anything we have to worry about," Tom said, sarcastically. "Me, on the other hand—"

"I know the rest of the world was fooled by the change in you, but Laura and I weren't," Charlie said. He felt apprehensive speaking the words out loud, as if he had broken an unwritten pact.

"Why didn't you say anything?" Tom asked him.

"We thought, or rather I did, that if you were doing it, you must have had a good reason." Charlie shrugged. "And when it came to secrets, well, we all seem to have more than our fair share."

"What secrets do you think Laura has?" Tom sounded puzzled.

"I think," Charlie turned to look at Laura, "that when it comes to hiding things, she'd probably outdo us both." He wasn't sure but he thought that he could see the traces of a smile turning up at the corners of her mouth. Either that or her breathing was improving exponentially.

"What does *that* mean?" Tom sounded frustrated.

"Laura has been keeping our secrets for years." Charlie sighed, putting his hand on the tank. He watched as her arm moved in slow motion and the fingers reached out to the other side of the surface. He heard Tom's sharp intake of breath as she mirrored his hand with hers.

"She can hear us!" Tom's voice broke with emotion.

"Of course, she's not unconscious." Charlie felt that this somehow made it worse, he couldn't imagine being under the water and not being able to communicate. However good a swimmer she was, it looked anything but right to see her respirating in the tank.

Something that didn't fit in with the normal noises of the sea outside the window and the offshore winds made him look round. So did Tom, who had also picked up the sound. Charlie checked his equipment, the mass spectrometer was humming, but that was part of the usual.

Raq stood up suddenly, his fur on end and the low resonance of his throaty whine caught both of them by surprise. If it wasn't so disturbing Charlie would have laughed. He could tell by Tom's expression that he had forgotten Raq was there. The dog clearly had a gift for blending in with the furniture, something, Charlie thought, which must come in handy on dark cold rainy nights when he didn't want to sleep outside.

Charlie got to his feet slowly and quietly and made his way towards the seaward window. Suddenly Raq growled open mouthed and launched himself at Charlie who dropped instinctively to the floor. The dog sailed over him and out of the open window, a hail of furious barking followed, and then a disturbingly sudden silence.

After a moment of frozen disquiet, Charlie crawled towards the window and peeked carefully out from one side. "Where is the gun?"

"In the bedroom," Tom sounded frustrated. He made his way to the door on hands and knees and checked the living room kitchen area much as Charlie had done, with an incongruously well-trained level of caution. He carried on and scampered up the stairs, seconds later Charlie heard him thundering down them. The kitchen door was opened with barely a sound, just a slight waft of sea salt on the draught.

"Nothing," Tom said in a whisper.

"Here either." Charlie was puzzled.

Suddenly another furious outbreak of barking was followed by a scuffle and the sound of running. Moments later Raq returned as he had left, through the open window, only this time he held a piece of bloodstained material in his mouth. He dropped it at Charlie's feet and sat down. The dog's expression held a canis lupus memory of triumph. He clearly expected praise.

Charlie patted and hugged him, effusive and gushing. The dog looked satisfied and then proceeded to shake himself. Dust, lots of hair and the residue of the seawater overflow he had been lying in covered both men and most of the newly cleaned floor.

After making sure his efforts were truly appreciated, Raq went over to the tank, checked on Laura and Stroppy and then lay down to await his next mission.

"Yeah, sure, that dog hasn't had any upgrades!" Tom muttered.

"Do you just have the one?" Charlie pointed to the gun. He was unnerved, the piece of bloody material clutched in his hand.

"Sadly yes," Tom said, "I really didn't plan on needing more fire power." He began clearing up again.

Charlie went over to the work bench and started to examine the fresh blood. He scraped a tiny sterile brush over it and snapped the end off in a test tube. After capping the lid on, it went into the mass spectrometer. He began tapping keys which steadied his hands and his mind.

"What do you hope to find?" Tom patted him on the shoulder.

"Information." Charlie's voice was clipped, he knew he sounded frightened and he hated himself for feeling so vulnerable.

Raq looked up and whined again, this time it was a sign of recognition.

The same draught of air indicated someone opening the kitchen door quietly. "Charlie, Tom?" Ceri whispered.

"In here," Charlie replied at normal volume.

"Sorry about that, she got past us." Ceri had a shotgun broken over her shoulder. Its muzzle faced away from them. "I brought you this." The gun was held out to Charlie. "Your dad said you know how to use it."

"Did he now?" Tom was sarcastic. "Do I get one of those?"

"You've got your own." Ceri was pointing to whatever Tom held behind his back. "An old Sig Sauer P938, if I remember correctly. You really should find somewhere else to leave it other than your sock drawer, when you go swimming." Her cheeks dimpled as she grinned. "Six plus one, Parabellum cartridge, I hope you have a spare magazine or two," she added.

"Yeah, not in the sock drawer though," Tom drawled as he smiled back at her.

Charlie tried not to roll his eyes at the bonding ritual of two cosmic sized egos. He also ignored the remark about his father.

Raq was wagging his tail, but hadn't moved from his post by the tank. Charlie watched him as his gaze went from one to the other, then he looked at Charlie, a doggy expression of exasperation at humankind seemed to pass between them. Charlie walked over to him and rubbed his head, Raq's rough tongue rasped across his hand. Suddenly he sat up making Charlie rear back on his heels.

"What is it Raq?" Charlie looked towards the window where evening was beginning to express itself in colours of orange and gold.

He felt as if the day had got away from him. He glanced at Laura, her eyes were open and she was focused on Raq.

The dog was completely still, watching the window. Ceri took the shotgun from the chair where she had stowed it and closed the chamber with a slight click. Raq huffed an almost bark and then settled himself down again. "That was odd," Ceri said.

Tom pointed towards the living area and then went through the study and quietly out of the kitchen door. Ceri put her fingers to her lips and walked over to the window.

Charlie shrugged, he believed Raq, whatever had happened was now over.

DAVE AND STEVE

"What did you do that for?" Dave, whispered, incredulous.

"She was running away from the house with the farm dog snapping at her heels, and we know they're Chinese freelancers." Steve was also whispering as he checked his weapon and twisted the silencer off the barrel.

"I don't mean you shouldn't have shot her; I would have liked to question her first!" Dave sounded exasperated.

"Oh, right, okay, well, there's the other one, he's bound to be here somewhere." Steve placated his partner.

The body had dropped further ahead in the trees. They went forward, carefully checking for movement. Quietly, their well-trained footfalls were hardly noticed by the birds or a busy fox, out on an early reconnaissance mission of its own. However, someone *was* watching them. The two men came to stand by the body of the young woman. She was lying face down, her blood seeping into the carpet of moss and lichen. The bullet had penetrated the spinal cord at a high level.

"Nice shot," Dave said pragmatically, having considered things from all angles for a moment.

"Thank you, I find this new firearm has excellent accuracy at a reasonable distance." Steve was equally practical.

They took it in turns to conceal her with loose foliage and checked around once again for any sign of her partner. "If he was here, he's not now." Dave was rubbing soil and leaves from his hands and clothes, while Steve kept cover.

"Anything on her?" Steve asked Dave.

"This." He showed Steve a slim short weapon, they both admired it before Dave put it away for further examination later. "No identification," he added.

The two men made their way on stealth mode to the cottage, the immediate surrounding area was windy cliffs and bracken, with bushes or a few low growth trees, which meant very little cover, except the undulating terrain where a practised combatant could merge into the shape of the land.

Dave pointed to the open study window and he and Steve slid over to take a sneak peek. They could see Charlie, who was squatting down by Raq, and Ceri, talking to Charlie. The dog huffed, sitting up suddenly and looking at the two men. In the tank, Laura's eyes opened and focused on them. He and Steve darted back, headed for a small area of low bushes and slid down on their fronts to watch. They saw Tom looking around, handgun held down at his side. Steve gestured to Dave, raising his eyebrows in a 'Where has the gun come from?' gesture, and Dave nodded back.

They relaxed a little when Tom returned to the cottage and Ceri's face disappeared from the study window. "Well, it's not the Nepah X virus," Steve drawled sarcastically, his American accent suddenly becoming more evident.

"Do you think anyone is going to tell us what is going on?" Dave said with some frustration, turning on his back and looking at the sky.

"Just as well you've been making friends with that dog for the last three years," Steve said. "Though it wouldn't stop you cutting its throat," he added quietly. Dave nodded his agreement. Even Dave's wife thought there was a little 'something' about him. It usually came out, she told Steve, when they were playing Scrabble.

"What now?" Steve said.

"We wait until dark," Dave said.

"Oh, because the sight of Laura floating in a gigantic fish tank with her eyes open staring right at us, wasn't creepy enough in the daylight?" Steve asked. Dave shrugged, which was not easy to do lying down, but he managed it.

The man watching them shook his head, his expression was a combination of sadness, anger and eventually resignation. He gave a wry nod of almost agreement, and moved stealthy away.

TOM

Tom made himself comfortable on the sofa in the living area, and for ten minutes he closed his eyes. His gun was tucked carefully under a cushion with a full magazine, the safety catch on. It was not in his hand, so less chance of shooting Charlie or a table lamp by mistake in an exhausted fug, easily accessible but not dangerous.

He sighed and wondered when had his life become such a mess, then answered himself: the moment his father had decided the Russian mob would be good business partners. The second the two secret service men had walked in through the front door of his student flat he knew life would never be about his medical career. He'd tried to keep it going, finishing all the exams with good pass rates, but the last two years of practical placements got away from him. His father was delighted that the family 'firm' was chosen instead of the sinking healthcare service. He had refused the threats and blackmail and only agreed when they showed him the film of Laura. It was appalling, and had made him rage with frustration and despair. He wondered if she even knew or had any memory of it. He was trapped.

Evening crept quietly, and they talked of making plans, the three of them. Ceri was interrupted by a video call from Huw. "The partner of the Asian woman has been looking for her, she seems to have disappeared, he was in the woods at the back of the cottage. Then I lost him, he's good, be careful. I haven't seen Tom's friends."

"They're not my friends!" Tom was suddenly furious; he couldn't hold ten years of blackmail and coercion in for a second longer.

"I'm sorry," Huw was contrite, "poor choice of words, whatever it is they have, we'll help you to fix it."

Tom was stunned, enough that he could feel a sensation that had been evading him for some time, hope. Ceri did something odd, she came over and gave him a hug. Her baby got in a well-placed kick, and he laughed for the first time in what felt like forever.

"She likes me!" He said, pointing at her bump, which was still moving around.

"Don't get too up yourself, she does that when I'm hungry." Ceri went to the tank and patted the clear wall. "Not long now, Laura."

Tom looked at Charlie who was hiding behind his eyes, something he usually did when the pieces didn't fit, Tom's hope suddenly became ephemeral. He could feel it disappearing over the horizon somewhere close to where the sun was setting on the sea.

Ceri pointed at Raq. "Guard!" Raq barked once in acknowledgement. "I've got to go and check on the sheep and put the chickens in their hut, the foxes will be licking their chops otherwise! Shout if you need us or send Raq." She left the shotgun behind, securely broken open and tucked into the study chair.

"What is it?" Tom asked Charlie when he was sure Ceri had actually gone. Charlie was silent. "You could learn a thing or two from the dog," Tom muttered, "like answering a question."

Charlie went over to his work area and began checking the different equipment for test results on the blood. Tom watched as a small spiral of holographic information began swirling out of the computer. Charlie gasped. His face turned the colour of the really old parchments Laura said were her favourite to work on.

"Charlie?" Tom put his arm on his friend's shoulder and eased his stiff body into the chair. Charlie folded in grief and Tom held him close. He'd never seen such raw pain, except maybe when he'd looked into the mirror after watching the surveillance tapes on Laura. "What is it?"

"The blood, it's Mei's," Charlie whispered.

CHARLIE

He couldn't get his breath; he knew it was freaking Tom out

133

because the expression on his friend's face suggested as much. For both their sakes and Laura's he had to control the panic.

"I don't know what to do." Charlie's brain was a fog of despair.

If anything, Tom was confused. "I've never heard you say that!"

For some reason they both looked at Laura, whose eyes were open and focused, she seemed to be amused. Charlie began to snigger, he couldn't help it, the stress, fear and sadness manifested itself in a bubble of humour so inappropriate it came out as a snort of laughter. "Come on, I must have said it once or twice?"

Tom thought about it carefully, making Charlie laugh again. "No," Tom shook his head, "not once, in twelve years." He was beginning to grin. They both looked at Laura for approval, she smiled a watery smile.

"Tom," Charlie tried to explain his reservations, "I need you to understand, I don't trust Ceri and Huw, they are too sure this is the right thing to do. And remember, they infected her in the first place."

"I will never forget that," Tom growled.

"Do you know anything about plankton; it was one of the species my dad was working on?" Charlie shifted the findings about Mei reluctantly to one side.

"Single cell microscopic organisms, er, microalgae?"

Charlie was cross with himself for falling into the trap of Tom's false trail of stupidity. "Exactly, usually divided into two groups, phytoplankton and zooplankton. But," Charlie moved some information around on his computer and another swirl of holographic information appeared. "This is mixoplankton. It's the middle ground between processing light for energy and consumption."

"I'm not sure where you're going with this?"

Charlie sighed, "neither am I really. I think there's something about species divergence and reconvergence in there, and It's just that I feel we're at the mixoplankton phase."

Tom went over to sit by Laura. Raq lifted his head and licked Tom's hand in a demonstration of support. He began stroking the matted fur and the dog settled down again.

Laura's eyes were closed, thought it seemed to Charlie as if she was listening. He tried again. "There was a study several years ago on collective neuroscience, the experience of being on the same wavelength, synchronised around the auditory and visual areas of the brain and the more complex higher order brain functions."

"Are you saying that we're connected?" Tom was gratifyingly quick to understand, he pointed at the three of them in turn, himself last.

"Yes." Charlie nodded. "I did some tests when we were first together. I couldn't figure out our close compatibility, considering our backgrounds and experiences, never mind the genetics, it didn't make sense."

"How like-minded are we exactly?" Tom got it immediately.

"So much so, that it won't just be Laura; to a certain extent, they will have us too," Charlie said, finally realising what was bothering him.

"There was me thinking it was friendship," Tom snorted.

The sound of an incoming message pinged and Charlie went to a drawer in his desk by the saltwater tank and unlocked it. That he had a secured computer inside, didn't seem to surprise anyone in the room, even the dog, who just huffed his irritation. Charlie checked the details and tried not to feel too relieved, though he wasn't sure why.

"What now?" Tom asked him. He pointed at the shotgun in the other chair.

"No, it's from Mei, at least she's not too badly hurt. We need to meet her away from the cottage, apparently, it's being watched by two men."

"I think I might know who they are," Tom said dryly. "It will be dark soon, how about I go out, head for the village and circle back through the woods?"

"They might split up, one watch the building and the other follow you?" Charlie was trying to think of everything, but the lack of sleep and the stress were making it difficult.

"They're stitched at the hip." Tom shrugged. "It won't take them long to work out that they lost me and they will be back, but it should buy us some time."

Charlie was quiet for a moment, he looked at Laura, her eyes were on Tom and she seemed really sad. "It's worth a try." He sent a coded message hoping that it wasn't another trap. He could feel the unanswered questions tapping at the door to his consciousness.

"I told her to give you thirty minutes to get them away." Charlie looked at Tom who nodded and stood thinking for a second. He picked up the shotgun and checked the barrel, snapping it shut. Then he handed Charlie his pistol.

"Just point and shoot, the safety's off." Tom walked into the living area and took the car keys from the bowl by the door. As he left the house, he shouted very loudly, doing a good impression of an angry drunk. "You can't stop me, I'm going into the village and if I see them, I'll use this!"

Charlie leaned back in his chair and grinned. It just might work.

DAVE AND STEVE

"You have got to be kidding me!" Dave whispered loudly as he and Steve scrambled to their feet, hoping to avoid a local incident where someone got shot, other than when they were doing the shooting of course.

They both ran. By the time they reached their vehicle, which was parked off the dirt track near the woods, Tom's car was disappearing round the bend towards the farm road, wavering in an alarming fashion, the lights bobbing up and down as he hit the bumps at speed.

"He won't need to shoot anyone; his driving is lethal enough!" Steve pulled away leaving a spray of soil fanning into the air and the decidedly un-stealthy sound of squealing tires.

"In all the time we've known him I've never seen him drunk, or out of control." Dave was holding onto the dashboard.

"Everyone has their breaking point," Steve said sadly, "I guess seeing the love of your life in a fish tank will do that to you."

Dave tried to look as if he knew how that would feel but he couldn't manage it. The love of your life part, not the someone in a fish tank bit, *that* he could imagine.

CHARLIE

He waited for a moment and then went over to the tank. "Stroppy!" The little octopus crept warily out of his cave and came over to see Charlie. They regarded each other seriously and with respect. "Look after Laura." He didn't really think that the creature could actually understand him, but it felt good to ask. Stroppy confounded him by going to Laura and after contemplating the possibilities, he settled himself around her left foot, like a cat.

"Raq," Charlie said, the dog sat up, "guard them!" The dog barked once, all but rolled his eyes, and settled down again with his head facing the open study door and the seaward window, his gaze flickering from one to the other.

Charlie spoke to Laura, who was looking at him with what he usually described as her mother face, something akin to indulgent exasperation. He knew because he'd seen it on his own mum who used it when he was intending to utilise the kitchen crockery for his latest biology experiment.

"I'm going to speak to Mei, I don't want to leave you alone, but if necessary—" he stopped abruptly and pointed to the pistol which he had left on the desk next to the tank. The thoughts about the sudden and disturbing increase of weaponry in his life bounced around in his brain. She nodded, then put her hand on the transparent wall between them, he covered it with his own in a gesture of friendship. It was odd, he felt that it was more a thing Tom would do, he and Laura were usually about words; somehow the lines between them were blurring.

Charlie made the connection with his computer and tapped a few keys, the holographic images spun out in front of him. He swore in frustration, something that Tom was also inclined towards. There was no time, he would have to leave it until after he saw Mei.

He took the small first aid kit from the desk drawer because he didn't know how bad the bite was going to be. "I hope you didn't do too much damage Raq?" The dog looked faintly guilty and his eyebrows porched above his eyes in a slightly pleading way. Charlie ruffled the fur on his head in forgiveness.

Waving at Laura, he went to the window on the other side of the study; sliding it up and leaning out he looked carefully around. The back of the house faced the woods, the message from Mei had just said by the tree line. It was evening dark, with the stars becoming full in the sky and he could hear the steady rush of the sea on the sandy shore in the bay below. There was no sign of anyone.

Charlie was used to a certain level of stealth as creeping up on wildlife was an occupational hazard full of varying degrees of achievement, or the lack thereof. He made it to the trees and rested against a trunk. His night vision was good, but the light from the cottage was casting irritating shadows, it looked to his tired mind as if the gorse bushes were moving.

A rustle of dead leaves and the whispered swear word made him snort. Tom was back. "Here," he said quietly.

They waited.

The sounds were not of someone who was keeping a low profile. A few irritated Chinese words and the odd noise of exasperation made it clear the person was in fact doing the opposite.

Tom rugby tackled him before Charlie could say anything, in a move that would have impressed the fans at Cardiff Arms Park, Charlie thought wryly.

"Oof!" The man said.

"Hi Chao," Charlie reached down to help him up.

"Sorry," Tom was contrite, "I thought you might be, er, you know, a skilled ninja, or something," he finished lamely.

"Firstly, I'm Chinese not Japanese and I know it's a bit of a struggle, but despite the fact that I *am* Chinese, I'm actually one of the good guys."

"He works with Mei," Charlie explained.

"Sorry, again," Tom said, trying to look it but failing because he was grinning. "Why were you making so much noise?"

"That!" Chao pointed at the shotgun Tom was holding. He began brushing dead foliage from his very nice clothes. Charlie helped by picking a few bits from the man's hair.

"Not to be a downer, but we have about fifteen minutes before Dave and Steve discover that I'm not drunk and shooting up the village pub!"

Charlie wondered if the proximity to danger and all the stress had made Tom revert to his university days. If the language choices and the rugby tackle were any indication, it would be yes, he thought wryly.

"How did you get here so fast?" Tom asked, with false casualness.

"She called me, I have money and we weren't in China." Chao answered, omitting the real explanation. He pointed at his city clothes and shoes. "We left in a hurry."

"Where is Mei?" Charlie whispered.

"Over there," Chao said sadly. He pointed to the path into the woods.

Charlie's heart squeezed in his chest; he couldn't understand. "Where?" he asked urgently.

Chao looked at him in the half light of the torches that he and Tom were both holding, their hands pointing to the ground to help them keep their night vision. The expression on the man's face as he regarded Charlie was one of pity. Charlie realised he didn't want to understand, because if he did then Mei wouldn't be helping him with his research, or laughing at him over his regularly mangled Mandarin, and there would be no more times when they just sat in silence working together but apart.

For a moment he was swimming, the water salty and pleasing, his eyes slightly unfocused through the transparent wall of the tank. A sharp tap on the shoulder brought him back to the swaying trees and rustling shadows.

"What was that?" Tom said in panic. "I just saw the tank in the study, from the inside!"

"You too?" Charlie was intrigued for a second. He added sadly, "What happened to Mei?"

"Your friends shot her, in the back, and buried her under the leaves." Chao was blunt and furious. He shook with suppressed rage. "I followed her, she told me to stay in the village while she went to talk to you, but I couldn't. I was too far away to help her," he sighed. "I watched while they covered her, they were matter of fact about it," Chao sounded as disgusted as Charlie felt. "I observed them when they went to the house, they were standing by the window and both of them were really freaked out by what they saw." He sniffed. "Serves them right!"

"I take it Mei has told you what's happened to Laura?" Charlie asked Chao. He glanced at Tom who was uncharacteristically quiet.

"Yes, we worked on a formula together, she said she couldn't send it, we had to bring it. I've been on a plane and in a car for what seems like forever." Chao shook his head, he looked exhausted.

"Where is the formula?" Charlie felt hopeful for the first time in days.

"She had to carry the basic structure herself," Chao said sadly.

"Did the two men take it?" Charlie was worried, then puzzled.

"I mean it was in her," Chao repeated, "there was no other way to keep it safe," he said.

Charlie suddenly understood. "She injected herself with it?" he whispered.

"She's dead, I couldn't get to her quickly enough, it's gone." Chao was bereft.

"I don't understand." Tom was trying to keep track.

"We need a fresh blood sample," Chao explained.

"We've got one," Charlie said, "I already started running it." He went on, "The dog bit her."

"You have a dog," Chao said, "and it attacked her?"

"It's a long story," Tom started to head towards the cottage. "And they are *not* my friends, they're my blackmailers."

Charlie was frozen, watching the shadows by the building, they seemed to be growing. He hissed a word at Chao and Tom, "Wait!" Chao heard, Tom didn't.

"Sorry," Chao gasped and returned the rugby tackle. They tumbled to the ground, Chao putting his hand over Tom's mouth before he could swear.

Charlie though it was undignified and slightly unnecessary but he agreed that perhaps it was owed, and anyway it was effective.

The two shadows were moving towards the window to the study. He paused as they slipped into the cottage and then he ran as quietly as possible. He could hear Tom and Chao scrambling to their feet and following.

LAURA

I could see Tom's watchers peering in the window, the water and an odd weight on my ankle seemed to be holding me back. I looked down for a second, Stroppy was clinging to my left foot. I opened my mouth to ask him to move and choked. A bright think picture came into my vision. It wasn't very complementary, 'Close your mouth, open your mind' and something that looked suspiciously like 'stupid' was added after a pause.

The two men disappeared from view and I struggled with my jelly limbs and the increasing weight of my body in the air as I climbed out. Charlie had thoughtfully left the step ladder next to the tank, which meant there wasn't an undignified scramble over the top and no longish drop onto the floor. There were puddles of water around me and I wobbled. But I inhaled deeply, it tasted delicious and felt light and easy.

I patted Raq, whose low-level growl was threatening to become a full-blown barking fit. He looked at me and stopped, waiting for instructions. "Raq, go and find Ceri," I mouthed, pointing at the seaward window. He scrambled up and jumped, clearing the sill like a horse at an easy fence.

I could hear a whispered conversation, though they must have been very quiet, my hearing was obviously affected, sound waves travel faster under water due to its density, how it would make things louder for me in air I didn't know, I was hoping Charlie would explain it all.

Picking up the pistol I crept towards the door, the lights were on low in the kitchen, a small fire in the grate gave of an illusion of cosiness that was in direct opposition to how I felt. The tank lights illuminated the study as well as a lamp on the desk, but there were plenty of shadows to hide in. I watched as Stroppy followed me down the side of his home and onto the stepladder and then the floor, his exit, I thought wryly, was a great deal more elegant than mine. I saw a flash of amusement from the little creature. The reflection of the rippling through the lights seemed to give the room the interesting sensation of being underwater, which I found oddly comforting.

The men had come to a decision, and I now needed a distraction to give Charlie and Tom a chance to get back to me. Hopefully one not involving me shooting anybody.

Stroppy came up with it.

I lifted the little 'puss to my shoulder and then he crept gently over. We stood very still.

Looking through Stroppy's eyes, I saw as the men climbed in the window at the back of the house and into the study. They were arguing, in voices barely a whisper, it sounded as if this was something that they had perfected over the years. Though I had never spent any time with them, I recognised their faces from the occasional encounter, usually disguised as workmates of Tom's. Dave and Steve.

I waited, in a shadowy corner between the half-light of the study doorway and the dark window facing the sea. They cleared the room, but for some reason didn't see me. Both of them stood looking into the tank, as if wondering whether I was hiding under a rock, or had developed invisibility, which would have been useful. I pondered. Stroppy was an octopus and clearly able to change his skin surface to camouflage himself, something else to discuss with Charlie.

The men turned slowly, checking the room with that sixth sense we all have written in our DNA. They both saw me at the same time and as Dave brought up his weapon, Steve swore, taking a step back that was impeded by the tank being behind him, knocking into Dave, who also cursed.

Stroppy was covering my face, his tentacles, the ones not clinging onto me, were waving around in a somewhat theatrical fashion.

"What the—!" Steve shouted.

I raised my arm, pointing with an accusatory finger and began walking towards them, the hand behind my back holding the pistol, safety off, barrel down.

I heard Dave shriek; he came at me having cleared his weapon from the tangle with Steve. Stroppy was obviously enjoying the effect.

"Dave don't, it's Laura!"

We held back as Steve grabbed Dave's arm, then Stroppy let loose the secret weapon. The syphon that he uses for swimming and er, waste, spouted a fountain of black ink. I knew it contained tyrosinase, so the effect was instantly irritating. Both men were shouting and rubbing their faces, which only made it worse. I ducked as Dave's gun went off. The shot went wide and hit the bookshelf. Paper flew into the air like snowflakes on the wind. Charlie was going to be *furious*.

I grinned; I couldn't help it. Stroppy had moved so that I could see with my own eyes and I skidded through the doorway into the living area and ducked down behind the kitchen counter. I could hear Tom and Charlie shouting as they came in through the front door. I stayed where I was until they went past me.

The noise from the other room ceased and I guessed that Dave and Steve were escaping out of the study window. The fact that they couldn't see very well would make it hazardous. The shotgun that Ceri had given Tom blasted out a deafening note. And rounds fired back meant that Tom had missed.

"Where's Laura?" Charlie shouted in a panic.

"I'm here," I said calmly. Rising up from behind the kitchen counter and going towards the study doorway, I peered in.

The three of them looked at me with that expression of puzzled amazement that men have been giving us since we kept the fire going and the predators away while they were out having fun chasing mammoths.

"This is my girlfriend, who is turning into a fish," Tom said to Chao.

"Not a *fish!*" Charlie and I said together.

"Hi, I'm Laura." I held out a hand to the good-looking Asian man.

"Chao." He shook it and then studied the transfer carefully. "Ink?"

I pointed to Stroppy on my shoulder, who was sulking as the fun had stopped.

"Ah." Chao tried to wipe the residue from his fingers onto his clothes.

That doesn't work and the fragrance is partially digested fish. The expensive cashmere wool trousers were going to need dry-cleaning, I thought. I didn't say anything, but Stroppy was proud of the continuing demonstration of his efforts.

"Has you tongue started to fall out yet?" Chao asked me, "I saw an amazing horror film at FrightNight where—" he looked at my expression, "okay never mind."

"Are we going after them?" Tom said cheerfully. He came over and patted me on the back, squeezing me against him for a moment. "You're all soggy!"

"I've been in the saltwater tank!"

"Yes," Charlie said. "I don't think we have a choice. But first I need to check the antidote that Mei sent me." He went over to his equipment area and began tapping computer keys. The holographic images must have made sense to him because he smiled and said quietly, with a combination of sadness and admiration, "Mei, you're a genius."

Chao nodded his agreement.

"Why am I going to do this?" I asked.

"Informed consent." Charlie was adamant. "This will be your decision, not Ceri, or my dad, and not some unacceptable act of forced genetic manipulation."

"Very commendable!" The voice from the doorway had us all jumping in surprise, unwisely as both Tom *and* Chao, who had managed to pick up the discarded handgun, were armed. Ceri came further into the room followed by Huw and a very superior looking Raq, whose scruffy tail was wagging so fast it caused a breeze, I congratulated him on his skills.

"Why are you back?" Tom asked her and then Huw.

"The gunshots were a bit worrying, so we came to help," Huw was placatory.

Ceri just looked furious. "What are you *doing*?" She pointed at the holograph of the genetic answer to my problem. "She needs to complete the process!"

"I am actually standing here," I said quietly.

"Your father did this research!" Ceri wasn't giving up as she confronted Charlie.

"My father was *wrong*," Charlie emphasised the last word so carefully, I could virtually see it in italics.

There was silence while we all digested this life-shattering piece of evidence. I had never heard him say anything about his dad, that he clearly *knew* about him was now evident, but this was something else.

I sighed, "he's right, Ceri."

"About what?" her voice was sharp.

"Everything," I said simply.

We all contemplated the following; I was just about vertical, dripping a combination of seawater and smelly octopus' ink, Stroppy was clinging onto my shoulder and waving a tentacle at Huw, who was doing his best to calm a furious, very pregnant Ceri, Charlie was standing in front of his computer and science equipment, grunting verbal thoughts, and Tom was trying to work out who he was angrier with. Chao was just being enigmatic, something I thought he achieved at an almost professional level.

"I'm going to shower, and yes, I can see the irony of that, but I'm covered in smelly ink and my hair is crusted with salt." I turned to go.

"The hydrogen peroxide is under the sink," Charlie said, not looking round. "For the ink," he explained, also without turning away from his computer. "Mix it with soap," he added.

I handed the little 'puss over to a willing Huw, who put him back into the seawater tank and I left the room.

I heard Tom saying, "Do you think Dave and Steve will have gone?"

Charlie replied, "They'll stay close by, they want Laura."

"What about who is giving them orders?" Chao asked.

"I'm guessing, but I've always thought they had some autonomy over their actions, and won't establish contact until they have a result," Tom answered him. "And, if I've learned one thing from dear old dad and corporate hell, it's that you don't report your failures."

I found the bottle of hydrogen peroxide and some washing up liquid, mixed them and commenced scrubbing the ink from my fingers and neck with cold water and the solution. Then got into a shower in which you could have boiled carrots.

As I came down the stairs, I could hear the strained conversation about gene therapy and a bubble, phage, delivery system. It sounded dire.

"Well?" I asked, as I walked through the study door. They were all sitting, which was an improvement. Several more guns had appeared like malevolent weeds in a peaceful garden. I sighed, planting myself on the floor next to the tank, between a curled up Stroppy, who was tucked into his watery hidey-hole on the other side, sleeping like a child, and the oddly horsey fragrant, but very pleased to see me, Raq.

"How are you feeling?" Ceri was leaning against a well-placed cushion in the chair by the sea-facing window. The two very low lights shadowed all the faces of the people in the room.

"As if wherever it is I'm *not*, in or out of the seawater, I need to *be*," it sounded better inside my head, but she nodded her understanding.

"It's how we all feel, most of the time." She rested her hand on a shotgun and her eyes glanced out towards the sound of the waves. She pointed out of the window, then at her own ear. We all paused and listened.

I could hear men's voices. It was obvious that it was only Ceri and I who were able to, I wondered about Huw, but he shook his head when she looked at him. I couldn't, however, understand what the two men were talking about.

"It's one of the perks," Ceri explained, "orca ears."

Tom opened his mouth.

"—One word about my size and I *will* shoot you!"

"I *was* going to ask what they were saying." He spoke with great dignity, but no one actually believed him.

"Nothing much, they can't see very well and the smell on their clothes is disgusting, they're not exactly whispering." She shrugged.

"I guess that's how it feels when your lunch fights back," Chao said. Nobody laughed. "Wow, tough crowd," he muttered.

"Stroppy is a friend," I explained solemnly.

"Whose idea was it to, you know," Huw asked, waving his hand in front of his face.

"Stroppy's, he thought bioluminescent eyes, but we settled for the creepy tentacle look and the ink splatter."

"You can talk to him?" Charlie spoke up from the computer without looking over at me. He sounded Intrigued.

"Not words exactly, he thinks in pictures." I saw Huw and Ceri exchange glances.

Ceri did some more, out of the window, orca listening. She huffed, "your pal Dave is something of a psycho."

"There's a lot of it going around," Tom was sharp.

"If you two don't sort it out, I'm going to have to do it for you!" When I use my mother voice, people generally listen. They did, and although Tom looked suitably contrite, Ceri had a sullen look which didn't bode well for future negotiations. I saw Huw grin and smother the smile with a large grubby hand.

I thought for a second. "Why do you think that?"

"What?" Ceri was slow to catch up.

"He's a psycho?" I reminded her. She had our complete attention.

"Oh, right, he's trying to talk Steve into storming into the cottage and shooting everyone, except Laura. And I'm not sure he would care too much if you were hit. He doesn't think they need to bring anyone in alive. Steve, on the other hand, would like you to be unharmed, he's not that bothered about the rest of us."

We were all stunned. I'm not sure why, I didn't know much about them, just what I had worked out over the years, when I thought they were employed by Tom's dad. It's probably a well-known fact that psychopathy and big business are not exactly mutually exclusive.

"Delightful," Chao said, "I'm just so pleased to be here!"

"Why *are* you here?" Ceri demanded belligerently.

"Mei was my friend and work colleague and she asked me to come," Chao said with gravity.

Charlie shook his head and was still for a moment of grief, then went back to the calculations.

"Why did all this happen, Tom?" I pointed to outside and the men we couldn't see.

"Because of you," he said simply.

If it was the answer, it wasn't the one I was expecting. "Er?"

"This," he held up his phone. "They were going to put it out there, and send it to your family, I assumed you'd been drugged, I'm so sorry." He paused, then added, "After a while, when I wanted to tell you, it became about my father and the people he was in business with. They said you would be in danger too." His eyes filled with ten years of frustration and sadness.

I could hear the panting and grunting before I got across the room, but he turned it away so only I could see it. I was stunned and furious and a bit puzzled, as it looked as if the entire rugby team was there. "Tom, you've seen me naked, *a lot*, how could you *possibly* think this was me?"

His jaw dropped. Ceri, who had sidled up and taken a good look sniggered, "that's a double D at least, girlfriend here is a single C at the most."

Charlie added his own previous knowledge, "Not as much as that."

"How do *you* know!?" Tom spluttered.

"We shared a cabin in the Antarctic for three months!" Charlie went back to the computer.

"Why didn't you say?" I asked him gently.

"It felt like something we shouldn't talk about," he finished simply.

"I *don't* understand you people, you *really* need to learn to communicate!" Chao shook his head.

"And that isn't Edwards, either," Charlie added, turning his head at an angle and squinting at the screen.

I took another look. "Are you sure?" I was now wondering if the unrequited interest hadn't been requited.

"Potato cod, remember?" Charlie said.

"Now *that* I do get!" Chao smiled.

Tom was starting to develop a resemblance to a piece of just dug up, highly unstable, world war two ordnance. He seemed to be struggling to breathe. "I'm going to kill them," he whispered.

"You can't," I said, "not yet anyway."

"So, what are we to do?" Tom asked me. Much to the puzzlement of both Ceri and Huw, not Charlie though, and oddly Chao had a decided lack of surprise at the direction of the question.

"Charlie, how long will it take for you to sort out the cure?"

"It's done," he said firmly.

Ceri was beside herself. "Please, we need this!" She inadvertently patted her baby bump.

"What do you think will happen if I carry on?" I asked Charlie, trying to ignore the obvious distress from the woman.

"According to Mei, you'll die, and I have no reason to doubt her." Charlie sounded worried.

"Ceri, can I survive out there in the sea at this level of progress?"

She looked hopeful, then puzzled. "Yes, why?"

"How long before what's happening becomes detrimental to my health?" I asked Charlie.

"*Laura!*" Tom used his warning voice. I moved my hands in a downward, placatory gesture.

"Maybe another ten or twelve hours, then you really must start." Charlie was adamant.

"What's happening?" Ceri asked. Huw was glancing from one to the other of us trying to keep up and not let his worry for his daughter-in-law show too much.

"I've got an idea," I said.

Tom laughed, exasperated, "of course you have!"

"Charlie," I said, "how do you feel about the carpet in the living room?"

DAVE AND STEVE

"What the—"

"These people are mad!" Steve interrupted Dave. "Is that a body in the carpet?"

"A bit old fashioned, but effective for blood loss and biological fluids," Dave said thoughtfully.

Not for the first time, or even the three hundred and first, Steve was aware of his partners total lack of real emotions.

"Who do you— damn, it's Laura!" Steve wiped his face; the ink was still there and reeked of old fish. He sighed.

"Why are you so sure it's her?" Dave was puzzled.

"That's Charlie at one end and Tom at the other," Steve explained.

"What about the farmer and his daughter-in-law?" Dave checked his gun, ready to rise from their meagre hiding place in amongst the gorse.

"Wait!" Steve held his arm.

Ceri and Huw came out of the cottage and began walking up the lane towards the farm. "I really thought it was going to work, I didn't know she would die." Ceri sounded genuinely sad. Huw patted her on the shoulder.

"What do you think happened?" Dave asked Steve.

"No idea mate, but Laura was floating in a seawater tank and the last time we saw her she had tentacles growing out of her face. So, nothing good!"

"What did they want her for?" Dave was full of questions. "The breathing underwater or the octopus face?"

"Well above my pay grade, and yours," Steve was processing. He made a decision. "We won't call it in yet, we'll follow them and recover the body, then tidy up."

"What about those two?" Dave pointed in the direction of the receding shadows on the farm lane.

"Later," Steve said ominously.

They both nodded their agreement of the plan and began sliding along in the appropriate half crouch method of covert pursuit. Neither of the men noticed the shadow on the dark path following behind. They never would have believed anyone would dare. It had been a while since somebody had been strong enough to challenge them, and they were sure of themselves, their position, and their power.

Moving as swiftly as they could after the staggering figures, who were going as fast as was possible with the heavy awkward bundle, around the cliff edge and down the path, the sand and gorse impeding their effort. Dave and Steve couldn't hear what they were saying, which was probably just as well. One of them, Steve thought it was Tom, had a head torch which cast weird bobbing lights on the shadows, giving everything a momentary shape, like dancers in a nightclub. And the half-moon behind clouds described an eerie chiaroscuro.

CHARLIE

He wasn't sure this plan of Laura's was going to work, it seemed to rely on the naivety of two men who had never appeared to him gullible in any way, the effect of the unusual situation they were all in, and darkness, where the incomprehensible was always easier to believe.

They were bickering again, in whispers, Laura's voice muffled by the carpet.

"Hurry up, I can't breathe!" She sounded really uncomfortable.

"*Seriously*. You've been in a seawater tank for hours, use your gills or something!" Tom was gasping with effort.

Charlie felt obliged to intervene with the inevitable, "Not a fish!" Though he didn't think either of them heard him.

"Have you put on weight?" Tom added, unhelpfully.

"Stop grumbling and get on with it!" Laura hissed with exasperation.

Charlie knew they were squabbling because of the fear, if he'd had any spare lung capacity, he would have joined in. The urge to look behind him was becoming pathological.

They made it to the beach and ran along the tide line to reach an area of sand where there was a dangerous drop off into deep water, caused by an eddy around some rocks. Ceri had assured them Laura would be fine. Charlie felt that trusting her came with baggage, and she would always have her own agenda.

The plan had been discussed carefully but too quickly to really work out the kinks, and the men following them were seasoned operatives. He was sweating and the carpet-wrapped Laura was slipping from his hands, she hit the packed wet sand hard and he heard her swear. Tom grabbed at it and pulled to loosen its folds.

They waited until the sensation of people closing in was overwhelming, then he and Tom clambered onto the rocky outcrop which looked benign in the daylight, until you realised that there was deep water on the seaward side. Lifting the heavy carpet with Laura inside they swung, letting go on the highest trajectory and flinging her as far into the sea as they could.

Charlie leaned over, his legs giving way, a movement which he realised with horror had saved his life, as a shot all but missed him, save a scrape of sleeve material and some burning, bleeding skin. He began running again over the hazardous rocks. Tom was in front and climbing down closer to the water. Another shot seemed to have hit him and Charlie screamed his name as Tom fell into the turbulent sea. He could hear the crack and see rounds of light leave guns, and then, as the two agency men found themselves under fire from Ceri and Huw on the cliffs, Charlie followed Tom into the black water.

It was so cold, and he was disorientated. The urge to inhale against the freezing water made him realise how much trouble he was in, panic bubbled to the surface with his last lungful. Someone's hands grabbed him and a mouth clamped over his, breathing into him. There was a slight spicy note of air on his tongue and a blurry ghost face close in the dark water, fingers tapping him on the cheek. He held the hand that gripped his and they moved swiftly through the current into calmer waters.

He surfaced on the instigation of the person helping, and knew alone he would have drowned. It wasn't Laura, he could tell by the feel of the mouth on his. The moonlight was quiet on the lazy waves. They were in a small hidden inlet further round the bay, and a place of relative security, as it was inaccessible by the cliff path or the shore at high tide.

They sat on the beach, gasping and bleeding, Tom's wound was now spreading dark droplets on his wet clothes and a small smear on the packed sand.

"Well, you're full of surprises!" Laura said to a grinning Chao, as she tried to put pressure on Tom's bleeding shoulder. Tom swore.

"I didn't think there was any chance you would be able to rescue both of them if it went wrong." Chao was practical. He handed over a perfectly folded white handkerchief. Laura squeezed out the seawater before flattening and clamping it over the wound. Tom swore again, loudly.

Ceri and Huw arrived via a near-invisible fissure in the rocks below the looming cliffs. Charlie was sure it had been used for more than the private swimming that had been suggested, he could see the shadows of the past walking with them. Smuggling and the secret landing of people in a dim and distant past filled with intrigue and dissent. It was Wales, the country of warriors and longbowmen, if they weren't fighting each other, then they were fighting someone else.

"You can hear your dulcet tones from a mile away Tom, just as well they've gone," Ceri said. Sitting down suddenly, she added, "I'm exhausted, you're going to have to help me up, I'm like a whale."

"I got shot," Tom said, in a somewhat aggrieved manner.

"Of course you did," Ceri sighed with exasperation.

Charlie looked at them, they were all tired, not just Ceri, the post fear malaise was creeping through his cold limbs and making his brain fuzzy with unnecessary thoughts. Laura was propping up a slumped Tom, his shocked face white in the half-moonlight. Huw leaned down, holding his side as if he had run a long way. Charlie couldn't remember when he had last slept at all, never mind in a bed. Chao, irritatingly, looked as if he had just stepped off the set of a fashion programme, minus the shoes. Ceri's expression was speculating, and worryingly acquisitive, he waited.

"You're one of the y gwerin then?" She asked Chao.

"We don't call it that, but yes. How do you think Mei found the cure so quickly?" he countered.

Charlie was puzzled. "You didn't know?"

Ceri shook her head, irritated. "We don't have a handshake!"

"Speak for yourself!" Chao was laughing. "She's right, Mei told me what was going on here. We've been friends for years, since we were children, she knows about me, and I trust her." He looked sad. "Trusted her," he corrected himself.

Charlie could hear the unspoken words. Chao didn't know any of them, and had kept his own secret to himself, until he couldn't. He leaned forward and took Chao's hand because he also recognised their shared heartbreak. "Thank you," he said simply.

They were all quiet, listening to the sound of the waves and the odd noise of slipping sand which made comforting sense of the night somehow.

"We must get back to the house so I can start the drug regimen for Laura and sort out Tom's shoulder." He staggered to his feet, the world was spinning out of control again, and he needed to find something to focus on.

Pulling Ceri up took both him and Chao. Tom was in too much pain to comment, though Charlie was reassured that there was some remark he was storing up for later. He realised that he could actually see the expression on their faces; it was getting light.

A thought filtered through the exhaustion. "What are we going to do about Dave and Steve?"

LAURA

All of us staggered up the cliff path and into the cottage, to be greeted by an effusive Raq, who followed me as I went to get the medical pack from the study. It was an impressive collection because Charlie said his mum worried, and that manifested itself in a top of the range trauma kit. I cleaned and sterilised the wound on Tom's shoulder, the projectile was a tiny piece of nastiness buried deep in the muscle. Charlie took over after the anaesthetic spray. Tom was practically transparent with shock afterwards. And the language!

We sat in the dawn light as the sun came up behind the house and turned the waves into golden wings. It was my favourite time of the day. That early morning moment where life is full of possibilities.

Ceri was looking at her phone. Her face was a combination of disgust and resignation.

"Dave and Steve?" Tom asked, echoing Charlie's question of earlier.

Ceri held out her phone and turned on the recording. "This was overheard by a friend of ours—"

"Parabolic microphone?" Charlie interjected helpfully.

Ceri shrugged and grinned. "He usually refers to it as his ears, but yes, he did record it on a device for those of us who do not have the necessary upgrades!"

Tom snorted, he sounded full of bravado but I knew him well and I could hear the worry. "Play it then."

It was Steve's voice, "... delta sierra reporting, we're coming back in for an update, my partner is wounded, but it's been field dressed and he's fine for now. The target is down, I repeat, down, and the asset is missing. There are several other persons in play but not considered interesting for the purposes of this transmission. Over."

A voice no one recognised replied, "Understood, out."

There was silence for a moment. Then Charlie said, "What do we do now, how long have we got before they come after us again?"

Ceri looked at her dad and he nodded. "It's being taken care of."

DAVE AND STEVE

The car had reached the turning to Dolgellau before either of them spoke. "Do you believe they're all dead?" Steve asked Dave.

"Laura, certainly, I think that her body floating in a tank and the octopus face was something that Charlie might have done, why I don't know. Tom probably is, I'm sure I winged him and that water's cold. Charlie," he shrugged, "it could be a follow up assignment, or someone else's problem." Dave was matter of fact; he didn't really care. They'd had a good run with this asset, but he was ready to move on now, and his side was beginning to hurt where some of the bits of shot were buried too deep to remove and the pain relief was beginning to wear off.

Steve grunted, he was much more invested in Tom and Laura and not entirely convinced that he knew the real story, he vowed to look into it even if he was sent elsewhere. Right after a well-earned rest from this task, and he really needed a break from Dave. He pondered the big unanswered question in a whisper almost to himself, "So, who was shooting at us?"

The tractor was coming up the dirt road fast, no lights, no warning. It hit.

"Shi—!" Dave said.

The car turned over and smashed into a drystone wall.

There was a momentary unnatural stillness and just the steady sound of the wind in the trees. Then a huge explosion of fire.

LAURA

I was making breakfast, Charlie had just come down from his shower and Tom was stretched out on the sofa with Raq, by the now lit fire. It wasn't cold but he was clearly still in shock, his eyes were closed and he was listening. Ceri and Huw were helping themselves to tomato sauce and salt for the eggs and Chao had changed into some of Charlie's clothes, he managed to make them look expensive. His white shirt was open at the neck and tight to his torso displaying very impressive musculature, and it was attracting some undisguised admiration from Ceri. Huw hid his exasperation not at all.

Charlie had synthesised a formula and given me the first dose. I felt wobbly but nothing seemed as if it had changed. I still wanted to get into the seawater tank and rest for a while.

"How does it work?" Huw asked him.

"Well, basically it's just a reverse copy of the same retrovirus structure, encased in a bubble delivery system, targeting the RNA at a cellular level and changing the genome of each cell."

There was a short pause, then I heard Tom snort, "Now you know what I have to put up with!"

Chao was bursting with questions but he exercised superhuman control and just went with, "Impressive, Charlie."

"It will take time Larry," Charlie whispered, leaning over me and helping himself to toast and butter. There was the nickname again, I started to worry. He sat down next to Ceri just as her phone pinged. She looked at it and winced.

"Well?" Charlie asked calmly.

"It's done," she said with finality.

I really wanted to pretend I didn't know what that meant.

"What about their tracking devices, are they enabled?" Charlie said.

"No one's done that since the techno meltdown in 2033," Ceri said with satisfaction. We all nodded, and shuddered at the same time.

"Can you get rid of the bodies?" Chao asked her.

"Yes," she said simply.

"It would have been *really* nice if you'd had to think about it for a second!" Tom snapped grumpily from the other side of the sofa.

"Do you know who sent me the palimpsest translation work on y gwerin?" I asked Ceri. "It came just after..." I mimed a bite with my fingers on my leg.

She seemed surprised and looked at Huw. He sighed, "Probably your mum, Charlie. I think Elsie was trying to give you some, er, advice."

Charlie was going blue in the face, so I banged him on the back until he stopped choking. "She *knows?*" he managed eventually.

"She's a local Welsh lass Charlie, of course she does," Huw sounded amused.

"Good grief," Tom's voice whispered theatrically, still semi-prone, eyes closed.

There was some eating and drinking and eventually Tom came from his place by the fire and sat with us, he looked awful. I buttered toast for him and poured tea. Raq, who was nicely warmed on both sides, followed him in the hope of his own breakfast. I slathered bread for him too, and he said thank you with his tail, unlike Tom who just grunted.

"Are we really the same?" Ceri asked Chao hopefully.

"We've evolved differently, but yes."

"What does that mean?" Tom mumbled; he knows I don't like him talking with a mouthful.

"It's a type of species divergence, like high altitude oxygenation of the tissues." Chao looked at our blank faces. "People who live in the Andes and the Himalayas have evolved to do the same thing differently."

Tom snorted, "You sound exactly like Charlie!"

"Thank you!" Chao spoke completely without irony, his lovely face flushed with pleasure.

"Do you think there is any hope for us?" Ceri said sadly.

"Of course," Chao was surprised. "Ceri, *we* are at the reconvergence stage, the mixoplankton, we can live in both worlds."

"That was part of the research my dad was working on," Charlie said cautiously. "Were you and Mei studying species development too?"

"Yes, it helped that I was one of the test subjects." Chao was matter of fact. He pointed at Ceri and then himself and swept his hand in my direction. "*We* can help you change things for the better," he emphasised the word.

I could feel myself sweating as all eyes turned to me.

"No!" Tom said emphatically, "Larry's done enough."

I sighed. "What do you need?"

Chao looked at Charlie who was studying his toast as if he'd developed pareidolia. He swooshed the melted butter with a knife, keeping the image, if there was one, to himself. "Can you get hold of a hand-held MRI scanner for me?"

"Yes," Ceri said.

"*Again*, please pause before replying!" Tom rolled his eyes.

"I can do most of the genetic research here with Chao's help, I just need to document the changes as they happen." He made it sound so simple; we all knew that it wasn't.

There was a moment for reflection before I asked, "Where is Mei now?"

"Someone took her out of the woods while we were on the beach and she was cremated. I have this for the seventh day, I thought maybe we could put it on the cottage door?" Ceri was respectful, holding out a red plaque with Mei's name on it to Chao. He looked stunned, then bowed his head.

"I'm sorry," she added, "it's not much, but we couldn't wait."

"It's more than I expected, thank you," Chao said, with great dignity.

We finished our breakfast in almost silence and I began to clear up, Tom went back to the sofa with Raq, who had decided he needed canine company. They made a nest out of cushions and blankets.

"Don't get used to it, dog," Huw said, "it's back to work tomorrow!"

I looked at the expression on the face of the furry one, then Tom, and somehow doubted it.

I could hear Charlie and Chao talking in the study and went to listen, they were tapping keys and comparing notes on computers. Ceri followed me.

"If you think about it, all of us process vitamin D through sunlight, if I can tweak the DNA—"

"I see where you're going with this! Chao interrupted him. Ceri was grinning at the two men who were full of hope and possibilities.

I turned to her, as a thought picture suddenly appeared in my mind. Stroppy was watching me from the seawater tank.

"Who bit me, Ceri?" I sounded sharp, and everything went quiet. "Because it wasn't you."

Huw suddenly appeared in the doorway and Tom and Raq sat up on the sofa, both on full alert.

"Clever girl," Ceri said, smiling and patting her bump. "It was Bryn."

Huw's son Bryn, Ceri's partner.

"Where is he?" I asked, "I haven't seen him for a while."

"Out there, he prefers it now." She sounded sad.

"We didn't know what he was going to do," Huw explained.

I glanced at Ceri. Huw might not have, but she certainly did from the guilty expression inexpertly hidden.

"How did you work it out?" Ceri was curious. I pointed at Stroppy.

"You're still linked?" Charlie was surprised.

"I think it makes sense," Chao said, "two intelligent beings capable of higher thinking, connected."

"There are lots of creatures in the sea more intelligent than us," Huw said simply.

"If you ever want to know about your dad, just ask me Charlie," Ceri paused at the door, "or you could ask your mum." I could hear Huw scolding her as they left through the kitchen.

Charlie was silent and still. We waited. Nothing. He pointed at the DNA holograph, Chao began tapping keys, and the world moved on again.

"Come on, fish girl." Tom was staggering over to me followed by an exasperated Raq. "Let's go for a walk." He could barely move but we made it outside to the seat under the study window.

"*Seriously,* I wish you'd come up with a non-fish analogy!" Charlie had the last word.

A CONVERSATION WITH 'LAST RESORT'

THE FILM SCRIPT

I WROTE *this as a short story but a friend of mine suggested I turn it into a film script. It was supposed to be something that I would submit to FrightFest to start a new branch of my writing career, which is another 'long story!' I don't want it to disappear, because for a writer, writing is hard enough. It has to be out there somewhere living its life.*

The music I associate with this is, Looking for Space, by John Denver. Because at some point, we all gaze up at a dark star filled sky and wonder who we are.

A WOMAN IS SITTING at a console. We can see her face over the top. She's tapping holographic keys and talking to a holographic head. She sighs as the image fades. We can't hear what she is saying. As she turns in her seat to acknowledge the young man who has entered through a clear shimmering barrier, we can see an implant on the left side of her face, just under the skin; in the background there are hundreds of other people in similar work areas.

Yi da

Hey Pen!

Pen Darrow

Yi da!
They tap fists and hug.

Pen Darrow

How was the shift?
He is setting up his station as she is collecting her personal items. The handover is casual.

Yi da

Really, I don't know where to start!
She runs her fingers through her hair in frustration, collects herself and begins.

Yi da

Okay, there's a potential pirate attack going on somewhere out on the edge of Callisto territorial space. I've had two conversations with the captain of the freighter Empress of Elara. He's putting off the inevitable if you ask me.
Pen Darrow is sitting in the chair she has vacated and is tapping the holo

computer keys on the holographic console whilst glancing at her and nodding that he is listening.

Yi da

The privacy screens went down seven times in the night!
Pen Darrow has stopped what he is doing and turned in his chair to look at her.

Pen Darrow

You have got to be kidding me?

Yi da

One minute it was peace as usual and then I'm listening to two hundred other people all trying to hear their clients over the racket of us talking to our clients... if you see what I mean?

Pen Darrow

Seven times! What was going on?
She shrugs.

Yi da

No one knows...
She lowers her voice to a whisper.
The Ithizar techs were going crazy!
He shakes his head with a stunned expression on his face, then turns back to the console in front of him.

Pen Darrow

Mutters. I'll just bet they were.

Normal voice. Okay. What else have you got?
She is quiet for a moment so he looks up at her again.

Yi da

Two or three hang-ups...

Pen Darrow

What did the locator say?

Yi da

That's the odd bit... I couldn't get a location.
*Pen is looking at her again. He leans his chin on a fist and his face is full of
incredulity.*

Pen Darrow

Maybe it's part of the same problem?
Yi da glances over her shoulder as if to be careful.

Yi da

Possibly...
*Pen nods and is holding his fingers over the same implant on the side of his
face that she has, ready to start work. But Yi da is still standing there. He raises
his eyebrows and she winces.*

Pen Darrow

He speaks quietly, slightly worried. What?

Yi da

Ms Marianna Score...
*Pen Darrow lowers his fingers away from the implant on the side of his face
and looks at her for a moment, she winces again in sympathy. He leans forward
and bangs his forehead gently against the desk in front of him.*

Pen Darrow

Muffled. How many times?
*Yi da pats his shoulder in understanding. She is trying very hard to hide a
smile.*

Yi da

Just five calls, but she won't deal with me, she only wants to talk
to you.

Pen Darrow

I was having such a good day. I managed to get some real coffee.
The pilot on the transport ship actually smiled at me this trip...
*There is more shoulder patting. He sits up, gets his act together, drinks a
mouthful of coffee and grins wryly at Yi da.*

Pen Darrow

Go home, get some sleep. I've got it. I mean how bad can it be?

Yi da

I think Montgomery is missing again...
*Pen Darrow shakes his head in exasperation and waves her away. She
smiles at him and gives him one last pat on the shoulder. Then she walks through
the shimmering privacy barrier. It is silent for a second or two as Pen Darrow*

taps the console and connects himself with the control board by pressing the implant. Immediately several holographic flashing lights appear in front of his face and he checks each one, tapping a key to connect.

Pen Darrow

Location and Recovery, how can I help?
A holograph of a man's head appears, he is stressed and there is blood trickling down his chin from a head wound.

Captain James Carter

This is Captain Carter of the Empress of Elara. We are now under attack. I am raising the request level to critical and life threatening.
Pen taps keys quickly on the console in front of him while he speaks.

Pen Darrow

Calmly. I have your location, Captain Carter. Are you officially requesting assistance?

Captain James Carter

Wearily. I am officially requesting your assistance.

Pen Darrow

Any casualties?

Captain James Carter

We have three injured and there are at least seven dead pirates.
Pen is still tapping keys and checking the list of holographic information over to one side at the same time as speaking.

Pen Darrow

Good for you captain! Can you hold out for a support team? I will have one to you within nineteen minutes, your time frame.

Captain James Carter

We can't keep this up much longer; it's a fuel freighter. We have civilian techs on board and passengers.

Pen Darrow

Do your best; I'll get the team to you as fast as I can.
There is the sound of firing and the captain turns his head to see something.

Captain James Carter

I have to go!
The holo of his head swirls into a pinpoint and disappears. Pen is calling up another image. This time it's a woman with short hair and a stern smile.

Pen Darrow

Major Garner, you've got the code one? The freighter has been boarded! I am opening a jump point for you to the east of your current position; the co-ordinates should be coming through now. You will be under fire immediately. I am going to drop you from your jump point directly into space, so, full combat rebreather kit.

Major Grace Garner

She snorts with laughter. Is that even legal?
Pen makes a face and waves his hand side to side to indicate 'maybe not' while he works.

Major Grace Garner

Understood. We're at the jump co-ordinates now. Do you have any information on numbers?

Pen Darrow

I've got nothing, but it's pirates, so expect the worst, Grace.

Major Grace Garner

Grins at him. See you later kid.
Shouts to her team. Come on you ugly lot, do you want to live forever?
In the background we can here the faint reply 'No boss!' As the holo swirls away.
It is quiet for a second or two. Pen looks puzzled for a moment then dismisses whatever it is with a shrug; he sips some coffee and resets his console. Adding information to the report, he grimaces and his lips move silently as he thinks about what to put down. (It's going to be an imaginative report!) Satisfied, he taps another blinking red light.

Pen Darrow

Location and Recovery, how can I help?

Ms Marianna Score

About bloody time, Penwith Darrow!
Pen freezes the holo image and sighs to himself.

Pen Darrow

Shaking his head, muttering. I don't know why I didn't just shoot an albatross this morning and get it over with.

He reinstates the holo. The older lady has long hair in two neat plats and her face is angry.

Ms Marianna Score

Did you just put me on hold, Penwith?

Pen Darrow

No Ms Marianna. We've been having trouble with the computer links this last planet rotation.
Dryly. I hear you've been honing your people skills this morning?
Her face is doubtful and her eyes are narrowed. She snorts, ignoring his remark.

Ms Marianna Score

Snappily. Montgomery is missing again.

Pen Darrow

Said not unkindly. Ms Marianna, this is costing you a fortune in location and recovery fees, wouldn't local law enforcement be more... appropriate?

Ms Marianna Score

I'll decide what I do with my money Penwith Darrow! Now, get me that nice Major Garner, she found him in no time at all last month.

Pen Darrow

Diplomatically. Major Garner is off planet at the moment. As soon as she's free though I'll ask her to come and check on you.

Ms Marianna Score

Hisses. You just make sure you do! Or I'll be speaking to your boss, kid.

She breaks the connection before he can. He sits back in his seat, puzzled again for a moment. He shakes his head and taps the console with the report information and then hits a lighted key for the next client.

Pen Darrow

Location and Recovery, how can I help?

The voice is a man's, deep and full. An older man, weary. There is no holo, just a voice.

Harry Wickwire

You're not easy to get hold of kid...

Pen Darrow

Who is this?

Pen Darrow is tapping keys. He is puzzled.

Pen Darrow

I can't seem to get your location; can you give me co-ordinates? How can I help?

Harry Wickwire

No point in trying to get a lock on me, I'm off the grid. And I intend to stay that way.

Pen Darrow

Are you okay sir, how can I help?

Harry Wickwire

Well, I'm almost out of air, and I lost ship's gravity when I took
that last hit.
Said dryly. But other than that, I'm fine.

Pen Darrow

He is worried and sounds slightly stressed. Let me help! I can't do
anything without co-ordinates. I can get someone to you, are you
suffering from hypoxia, do you have any emergency air? What about
injuries?

Harry Wickwire

Out here they call you 'last resort.'
Pen looks around, slightly anxious for a second.

Pen Darrow

Sir...

Harry Wickwire

It's Harry Wickwire. Call me Wicks, kid.

Pen Darrow

I'm Pen Darrow, but you must know that, unless your screen is
down, do you even have light, Wicks?

Harry Wickwire

No light, no heating, I'm not sure which is going to get me first, the cold or the lack of air. Either way it's going to be interesting.

Pen Darrow

Why won't you let me help you? I'm sure I could get a team to you in time!

Harry Wickwire

By jumping them into space next to the ship? Gutsy move kid. But not exactly by the book.
Pen looks carefully over his shoulder.

Pen Darrow

Whispered. How do you know I did that?

Harry Wickwire

I've been monitoring you for a while, kid.
Pen is really worried now, he checks his console lights and taps keys. His face is puzzled again and he leans forward as if to confirm what he is seeing.

Harry Wickwire

They can't hear us. I've put a little bug into the system.
Pen sits back in his chair; he thinks for a moment, then nods gently to himself.

Harry Wickwire

Dryly. Look kid, I really don't have time for a dramatic pause this long!

Pen Darrow

Sarcastically. I was going for substance not longevity!

He sighs. It was you, wasn't it? All the hang-ups and the problem with the privacy screens. You set this up, so they will think it's just more of the same if they check.

Harry Wickwire

The 'blue skins' don't have much imagination.
Pen winces at the political incorrectness of the remark.

Pen Darrow

Warily. What is this about?

Harry Wickwire

There's a lot I need to tell you kid, so you need to listen. Your grandfather—
Pen cuts in, apprehensive.

Pen Darrow

My grandfather died in a mining accident out in the Kuiper belt.

Harry Wickwire

No kid he didn't... I'm sorry, I thought we'd have more time, but, well, they found me. Sadly. Your grandfather, my friend, was very much alive until last week.
Pen Darrow is stunned and angry he leans forward to cut the connection.

Pen Darrow

Coldly. I don't believe you. He wouldn't have done that to me.

Harry Wickwire

Please listen!
Wickwire's voice is getting weaker and stressed, his breathing is laboured.

Harry Wickwire

He told me to tell you... he said to say... remember the Bays Hill Road. Now, I have no idea what that means, but he said you would understand.
Pen Darrow leans back in his chair and his face fills with one emotion after another. His eyes are full of pain and he closes them for a moment.

Pen Darrow

After my parents died, I went off the rails a bit, I would have been caught too if my grandfather hadn't found me, he came and got me and took me home with him. No-one ever knew about it.
There is silence, except for the laboured breathing of Wickwire.

Harry Wickwire

Softly. I'm sorry to rush you kid, but the air in here is getting pretty thin.
Pen Darrow leans towards the console.

Pen Darrow

Quietly. What do you want me to do?

Harry Wickwire

Quietly. I need you to get out of there. All the answers are here.

Pen Darrow

To a broken ship on the edge of nowhere, for who knows what reason? It's not much of a story!

Harry Wickwire

You work for Last Resort, a company set up by the Ithizar. You 'assist' people in dire need and then take half of what they own for that help.
Said with urgency. Aren't you looking for something... more?

Pen Darrow

We do help people!

Harry Wickwire

You work for the Ithizar, kid. They don't do anything for nothing.

Pen Darrow

They gave us the Jump technology, it opened up space, I live on Earth and commute to Mars and I'm on Phobos right now!

Harry Wickwire

I know where Last Resort has their base of operations kid. But the Ithizar own you... they own all of us...
Wickwire's breathing becomes laboured and Pen leans towards the voice.

Pen Darrow

Are you okay, can you get to any spare oxygen tanks?
There is no answer. Pen gets worried. He taps keys and tries to check details that he can't access. He swears under his breath.

Harry Wickwire

I'm still here kid, I got a tank from the medical bay, its half full.
Pen sighs with relief.

Pen Darrow

Is there really nothing I can do Wicks?

Harry Wickwire

Not about me, but there is something. I need you to trust me. When you get the next call, go along with it...

Pen Darrow

I'm not sure if I believe any of this, but the fact that two of my 'frequent fliers' both referred to me as 'kid' today...
He snorts and shakes his head.

Harry Wickwire

Yeah, that was just an idea of mine to give you a false sense of security.
Sarcastically. It's a trick I learned from the 'blue skins.'

Pen Darrow

Dryly. So, they're good for something then?

Harry Wickwire

I know, you know, that things are not right kid, you've been aware of it for a long time. You questioned your parent's death and you got into trouble for that. Your grandfather was trying to keep away from you but he said it was obvious that if he didn't do something, you were going to end up dead, so he came to get you. But the longer he stayed the more danger you were in, so—

Pen Darrow

Sadly. He faked his death.

Harry Wickwire

I'm so sorry, kid.
There is silence for a moment as Pen contemplates the possibilities. We can hear the noise of Wickwire's laboured breathing.

Harry Wickwire

I hate to rush you kid. I know this is a lot to take in but—
Pen interrupts him again, shaking his head at the frustration of the situation.

Pen Darrow

You're running out of time—
Harry Wickwire interrupts him.

Harry Wickwire

Not me kid...
Dryly. Well, yes me, but you're the one who's out of time. The 'blue skins' are through the first firewall. Damn, but they're good; I paid a geek a fortune in black diamonds for that bit of hacking.

Pen Darrow

Sharp. Just exactly what do you mean?

Harry Wickwire

Well, they have been monitoring you for a while, pretty much since they knew you existed.
Amused. How do you think you got the job with Last Resort?

Pen Darrow

Worried. I don't understand?

Harry Wickwire

Exasperated. Take a look at that thing on the side of your face, kid. do you think it turns off the minute your shift is over?
Pen puts his head down and rubs his face, he raises it back up and without moving it, his eyes slide over to the side and an expression, first puzzlement and sadness, then one of pure hatred crosses his face.

Harry Wickwire

Gently. Be careful kid, get it together. I can see you. I also see a 'blue skin' heading your way. Nothing serious yet, but she's going to notice the expression on your face it you don't wipe it off immediately!
Pen's face becomes neutral and professional.

Pen Darrow

I thought you said your screen was down?

Harry Wickwire

No, you said that, I just didn't confirm it. I can see you and them...
she's moved on.
Frustrated. But kid, they will be coming for you soon and I can't do
a damn thing about it from here!

Pen Darrow

Why? I haven't done anything!

Harry Wickwire

We lost something, or rather someone, then the 'blue skins' found
us, me and your grandfather that is. We were always careful; no one
person has all the pieces, but your grandfather was always vulnerable
because of...
Pen Darrow points at himself and then snorts in frustration.

Pen Darrow

Wicks, I'm on Phobos, there's nowhere to run to!

Harry Wickwire

It's in hand kid. When it happens, you'll know.
He gasps.

Pen Darrow

Wicks?
There is no answer.

Pen Darrow

Wicks ... Please?

Harry Wickwire

Sorry kid, I'm just about done here.
Kindly. It's up to you now, a lot of people are counting on you...

Pen Darrow

Panic. Oh great. Fantastic. What does that mean? For last words, they're a bit cryptic!

Harry Wickwire

It means, kid. That you need to: Get. A. Grip!
He laughs and then is silent. There is complete silence.
Pen Darrow leans back in his chair. He takes in a deep a breath, as if he hasn't done so in a while. He taps keys and looks at the lighted holo readings and his face is puzzled. A red light on the console blinks and he taps the side of his face.

Ms Marianna Score

Shrill. So much for your help, Penwith Darrow! You are useless.
Loud. Well, I've fixed that!

Pen Darrow

Ms Marianna—

Ms Marianna Score

Very Loud. Don't you Ms Marianna me, Penwith Darrow, my Montgomery is still missing and you are personally going to come back here and find him!

Pen Darrow

I err... um...

Ms Marianna Score

Snorts. I know people and I had you suspended. It's your own fault, you should have been better at your job.
Pen is looking shell-shocked. But he gets it together and glancing over his shoulder for a second, he turns back to the holo head and tries to look contrite.

Pen Darrow

Quietly. I will do my very best to find Montgomery for you, Ms Marianna.

Ms Marianna Score

Angrily. Leave now. That nice Major Grace Garner will be here, just as soon as she can get away from that blasted freighter captain, stupid man!
Pen looks astonished.

Pen Darrow

She will be? I mean, yes, of course she will!

Ms Marianna Score

Nastily. Get. Moving.
She cuts the connection.
Pen goes into his shutdown routine as a young man comes through the privacy screen. He smiles at Pen with embarrassment. Then he checks to see if anyone is watching.

Parker

I'm sorry Pen. For what it's worth, I thought opening a jump point next to that freighter was a gutsy move. Don't sweat it, you'll be back after the enquiry and Grace will support you. It saved a lot of lives, that has to count for something, right?

Pen Darrow looks around him as he vacates his desk, as if storing the memories. He taps fists with Parker.

Pen Darrow

Wryly. Let's hope so.

Pen leaves through the privacy screen as the scene fades on Parker setting up.

LOVALOTT INTERSOLAR REMOVALS

I HAVE LONG WANTED to write this story after listening to two friends who ran a removals firm. Unfortunately, most of the things they told me are unprintable and unbelievable!

The music I hear when I see the ships of my imagination moving through the endless dark is, Dream a Little Dream of Me, by The Mamas & the Papas.

SUNDAY

An advertisement came up on my computer feed at exactly the same time as the latest, and may I say rather grumpy, reminder for my five annual voluntary days. It seemed like fate, or just convenient. I really didn't want to go on an expedition through the solarnet for something that I could do without thinking too much, *or* damaging myself. I was also required to be working locally.

The link actually started with the words, 'voluntary days approved,' and the official logo was prominent in one corner of the hologram swimming in front of me, which was a big attraction. I knew someone who had actually done all the work before finding out it wasn't affiliated. He had to start all over again. It was a mess; he only just avoided a substantial fine and a three-week penalty of additional time. The global government took 'staying in touch with real world issues' very seriously. It had to be within a geographical catchment area, this was in the small town on the coast near to where I lived, so it was really local. Some people applied for off Earth status, but it wasn't usually granted. As I travelled a lot for my work, I really didn't mind.

Tapping the 'yes' key that I was interested, and including my biography, got an almost instant reply, 'Can you start tomorrow morning?' That was it, no Ms Veryan, or would you like to meet so we can check each other out for weird stuff. I looked at the company title more carefully. Lovalott Solar Removals, which I thought was an interesting choice of name. But as far as I could ascertain from the solarnet, that was what they did, move people and their things. The job description read, 'office work.' How difficult could it be? I confirmed my availability and the computer holograph pinged its approval. I was all set.

I transmitted a short holo-text to my boss. He didn't reply immediately, but it was close. The gist being, what was he supposed to do at the alliance mining conference without me? I sent another one telling him that we would both be in trouble if I didn't complete the days. He grumbled, and trust me the man could put that over in a very few words, but we knew it was not avoidable. As he was already on his way to Demos for the meeting, I then despatched, by secure relay on the deep space network, all the relevant documents I knew he wouldn't read, and a brief overview, which he would.

My assistant, Rowell Finnan, who was smarter than me and my boss put together, got the next message. He replied with a holographic smiley of his actual face which was weird and creepy, and a large yellow and red cartoon of two thumbs up, also not quite right. I don't do emojis, of *anything*, but Finn's young and has a life outside the office.

I looked at my wardrobe full of work clothes and then looked in the mirror. My hair was a single colour, because it was frowned upon in government departments to look in the least bit interesting. It was long and dark because I couldn't be bothered to change it in the mornings before work, I also don't alter my brown eye colour. I am tall, which my boss doesn't like because I look over the top of his head, though he finds it useful when he can't see someone coming towards him that he wants to avoid. I have the usual permanent makeup, but not too much and no facial tattoos, as once again the department is not keen. They put out a holo-memo on a regular basis with reminders of what we can't do. It's understandable, security is difficult enough without having to program in every possible variation. We can have cosmetic changes for medical reasons but not just because we find looking at ourselves unacceptable. Most of the people I grew up with have had to send me new identity holos. One friend, who quite frankly I think needs a psychological assessment, has sent me five in the last fifteen years GMT. I mean, what's *that* about? I sighed, I'm clever, well paid, but boring.

MONDAY

I booked a local shuttle vehicle to the coast town. I love where I live, it's moorland and therefore isolated, but very beautiful.

Finn has been to visit me once, he'd thanked me, but as far as he was concerned, 'there was too much distance before you could see anything other than trees and grass, stuff was alarmingly green (fields) or very blue (the sea) and not in a good way, the birds were noisy, the changing weather made him nervous and there were animals just walking around *everywhere*.' I suppose it's understandable as he grew up in a city dome on Mars. They do red, dusty, and have a tenuous relationship with fur or feathers; what they *don't* do is outside.

The shuttle vehicle picked me up early; my house is on the hill between the coast and the farmland that borders the moor. I have farmers for neighbours, so most of them had been up for hours. Sheep and cattle were enjoying the early spring sunshine that promised some warmth. It had been a long cold winter, with nearly two months of snow and freezing salt-filled winds.

Programming the address code into the vehicle screen, I waved at the man in the tractor as it trundled past. My closest farmer still went out into the fields himself and delivered extra feed, but some of the younger ones had artificial intelligence bots. Mark Welling, who owned the land, said you needed to see the animals to actually find out what was going on. His partner Samuel said he just liked being close to the land and he didn't like AI telling him what to do.

The town had survived many changes over hundreds of years, a busy fishing village, holiday destination for the rich, and eventually the not so wealthy; during the bad times it had curled in on itself and hunkered down. Folk looked after each other as best they could and it shrank like most places, with very few surviving, it had been full of empty houses and streets. I've seen the pictures in the museum. But it was busy now and the nearby transport hub made it prosperous. It also meant I could live in the country and get to any of the main cities in a matter of minutes, the longest part of my journey was usually still the commute from my house to the hub. It had kept its name, unlike a lot of places, a colourful old sign still proudly displayed, Minehead.

The vehicle stopped at a building in the storage area close to the embarkation point, part of the industrial complex by the sea. I couldn't remember if I had passed it on previous occasions but as I was often working on my computer, I must have missed it.

I remembered to pay using my personal code rather than the work one and hopped out smartly, the vehicle already making moving on noises to encourage me. I was with Mark when it came to AI.

I opened the door to the office. Chaos.

"No, your hand *hasn't arrived* yet!" She paused momentarily as the holo head swore loudly and imaginatively. "Well, you shouldn't have stuck it into the *jump field*!" The holo began to grumble inaudibly and she interrupted him again. "Stop whinging, next time use the part you think with!" She slapped at the console, cutting off his reply. "And we all know it wouldn't be the bit between your ears," she muttered.

I cleared my throat. "I'm here to help."

"You're here because you people need to stay in touch with the real world and it's mandatory," she said tartly, then sighed. "Sorry, *that man* is wired to the moon, he was messing with the jump drive, *don't* ask me why, and left his hand behind."

"Left it behind?" I repeated.

"Yes. They're going to reattach it when it arrives." She was shuffling information discs and checked the floor for the ones that were filed there in an untidy heap.

"When does it?" I asked. "Arrive I mean?" I was trying for a reality moment.

"In two days, GMT, apparently."

My mouth dropped open.

"Are you okay?" Her question clearly indicated concern for my inability to form a coherent sentence.

"Just catching up." I came in and shut the door.

She had the kind of attractiveness that made you look and then look again. I could imagine people tripping over invisible cracks in the road and bumping into furniture while she was around. Unusually short for the present times, more my grandmother's height, and hair and eyes still one colour like mine, but a rich gold brown. There was a small, beautifully done facial tattoo of a butterfly on one cheek. Her clothes, unlike my basic trousers and top, were fashionable and expensive.

"LOVEDAY ENYS," she held out her hand in an old-fashioned gesture. I shook it.

"Rosalee Veryan." We stood there solemnly for a moment. "Why did you offer me the days?" I knew the answer, it was in the names, but I wondered if she would say.

"You look like your grandmother." She grinned.

It's not actually true and wasn't the response I was expecting, in fact it was as disarming as the severed hand, if you can forgive the inappropriate pun. I managed, "Myttin da."

Her smile widened. "I don't speak it well, but I knew you did as soon as I saw your biography."

"How do you know my grandmother?" I sat down after removing the mountain of unstable information discs and odd unidentifiable articles from the only other office chair, one of which looked like a very old sandwich.

"I don't." Loveday was short. "Your grandmother and mine were both part of the second generation 'educated' at the same time."

I gaped again; it was odd for me to feel so unprepared. I didn't really know anyone in the town, only usually coming in for supplies and an occasional walk along the beach.

The holo line beeped and she answered it with a cheerful, "Hey Taylor, everything okay?" The holographic image was of a man looking exasperated. His hair was close cropped and very curly, almost reddish with the hazel eyes that usually matched and a pale space worker skin colour. He had the requisite spacer tattoos, identifying him as a qualified freighter pilot on his neck and an ID on one side of his brow. I could see the inside of the transporter with its busy blinking lights and the darkness of space in the front view.

"You've *got* to help," he said quietly.

I was instantly on alert, looking for an indication of air breach or attack, ready to contact emergency location and recovery.

"She's doing it again." His voice, though reasonably calm, went up at least an octave, though I'm no judge of musical scales.

"Now Tay, take a moment, it's just BoBo. He hasn't settled in, once he does, so will she," Loveday was placatory, and calming.

I stopped looking for floating objects and oxygen deprivation and tried not to smile.

"You weren't there the last time or the time before that," he sounded frustrated. "She won't leave me alone, it's the seventh call in two hours and, " he added with finality, "I'm not dealing with her or that *cat*!" He cut the connection. I recognised the expression on his face, it was the one my dad had when my mum asked him to tidy his workshop.

I had *so* many questions.

"Ms Winwright has moved twenty times in the last ten years, to every planet and moon in the system, including the ice worlds, though that only lasted for three weeks. She could have bought the asteroid belt with what she's spent on transfer costs, we've had to do it because she won't let anyone else near her things. If we refuse, her best friend, who is the governor of Mars main dome, sends us a thinly veiled threat, although I think he's just glad she's not moving there, *again*. BoBo the monster is clever, with a slightly sadistic sense of humour, and well above normal domestic earth size. Myrtle Winwright can terrify a roomful of security shock troops, don't *ever* let her back you into a corner!" Loveday took a well needed breath.

"Well, under those circumstances I thought he was very calm."

"Actually, that's what Taylor having a strop looks like, I've seen him deal with a micro meteor strike with less emotion!"

I just couldn't help myself. "Her cat is called *BoBo*?"

"WHERE DO you need me to start?" My fingers were twitching with the desire to tidy. I was not disappointed.

"Arlo looks after this office; I'm usually based in Moon main dome," Loveday paused and gazed around with a somewhat stunned expression. "I had *no* idea; it really needs sorting out." She added, "I've read that's what you do."

I thought I'd file that one away with the visible mess for later consideration. "Is Arlo?" I held my hand up and swiped it at the wrist with my other one.

She looked at me with amusement and eventually nodded. "Tact-fully put."

"Have you worked together long?" I tried to cover for my inappropriate humour.

"You could say that, he's my brother." She grinned as I winced. We surveyed the office together, her with dismay and me with the light of a challenge. "I love him to bits, but he's, well, his own person."

"Yep, I have that much misunderstood trait myself!" I announced.

The incoming holo line buzzed, and she sighed. I pointed towards the tiny utility room that I could see through a door currently propped open with what looked like a dead plant. She nodded and answered the call.

It was a small kitchen and living area, with a bathroom off to one side. There was a surprising number of cleaning items, though on closer examination they were all unused.

I tidied, a *lot*, and cleaned, chucking mounds of unidentifiable items straight into the recycler unit, which looked as if it had never been turned on, then started on the current filing system. It seemed to have a heavy emphasis on proximity to the main desk, presumably meaning that the move was getting nearer the closer it was. Loveday answered the constant stream of holo calls. From what I could hear and see, which was everything, as people didn't hold back, I think I had the better end of the bargain.

As far as I could understand, it was appointments to either view the property moving from, via computer link or in person, location, size, how many rooms, pets, family members travelling, packing required, exchange of contracts dates, port inspections, details and viewing of the property moving to, location, size... unpacking if required, and so on. I was exhausted listening to her. And really, the emotional *state* of some of the people. Most of them were near to a meltdown, real end of the tether stuff. I heard her talk several away from the proverbial cliff edge.

There was a moment's pause around the close of the day. "Whatever you're paying yourself, it's not enough," I said, as I watered the not quite dead plant I had rescued and put it on the now visible other desk in the office. The accompanying wobbly chair had a loose screw underneath so I upended it, using the multitool that was a present from my mum, and which I always kept with me.

Loveday looked around. "Thank you."

"Do you want some hot chocolate, the café up the street does an impressive selection?"

We both grabbed backpacks, her designer, mine utility, and put on another layer as the wind from the sea was chilly with a fret just bringing in salty moist air. The calls kept coming, but she transferred them to a digital assistant, who answered the basics and booked another appointment with Loveday for either a holo conversation or additional visits. I could hear the murmur of constant conversation and the odd angry response when they recognised that they weren't talking to a person. Nothing much changed, we still liked real human contact. Which was odd considering what had happened to the Earth.

THE CAFÉ OWNER was looking me up and down. He was a big man with dark hair and eyes and a slight spacer shuffle when he walked. I realised that I hadn't checked in the bathroom mirror before I left the office, I could see the effect the day had had on my clothes which were filthy. The self-cleaning nano fibre would allow me to shake out most of the dirt, which I did, and he politely ignored the cloud of dust that was forming around me as it settled on the spotless flooring. He seemed to be focused on my hair, so I ran my fingers through it and was a bit disconcerted to see several unidentifiable bits of detritus fall out. He exercised commendable self-control and pretended not to notice.

"Two double hot chocolates with clotted cream and four of those, please!" Loveday was really going for it.

We sat down at a table and both sighed with relief as the cups arrived. I took a large gulp and inhaled the amazing smell. My legs ached and my fingers were sore. Loveday was silent, her voice completely used up. It was an oddly comfortable quiet between us.

"Are you going to ask me about them?" I said eventually.

"I was, but I thought I'd give it a few days." She smiled.

"Where does the business name come from?" I ate a cake. It was full of local fresh cream and honey adding a layer of stickiness to my fingers, which I remembered I hadn't washed before we left. I shrugged inwardly, my immunotherapy treatment for multiple travel destinations would probably cover anything lurking in the office.

Loveday pushed a tab on her phone. A holograph of the company heading appeared, and I examined it. Even without the enhancements, my pattern recognition abilities are pretty sharp.

"Lov, Loveday, Alo, Arlo, and T for Taylor, what about the second T?" I asked.

"Taylor Trucker!" She laughed, and so did I.

"His family name is *Trucker*?"

"Actually, it's Tucker, but everyone calls him TT, so," she finished with a shrug.

"How do you decide which team does what?" I picked up another cake.

"If I like them, they get the good-looking ones with the muscles and If I don't, it's my brother."

I spluttered all over the table, the owner sighed and brought a cloth and more cakes. He waited until I had finished coughing before he wiped the surface, then offered me the very clean cloth for my very dirty hands. I did as I was bid, as he looked as if he was going to do it for me.

Loveday was still laughing, and several of the other customers glanced at us and smiled. My phone buzzed, ruining the moment of companionship. My boss.

His voice was the opposite of Taylor's, panic, stress, over the top emotional reaction. *Delightful*. The holograph was a wide angle of the conference room on Demos. There were people moving around and 'I'm at an important meeting' faces were everywhere.

"Finn's gone walkabout!" It was shouted, so the racist remark didn't just make me cringe, there were interested parties on both sides of the holo call. Loveday was studying her hot chocolate as if an important message had been hidden under the cream.

"Are you sure he's not just seeing his mum?" I asked calmly, hoping my reasonableness would have an effect. Sadly, it was not to be.

"He's turned native on me and I haven't seen him since this morning!" My boss was if anything louder and shriller.

I sighed. The racism was pointedly Mars related and about to cause an international incident. "Mr Betts, please moderate your tone!" I applied the appropriate voice modulation. "What *exactly* is the problem, Ethan?" I waited for him to calm down. The use of his family name, which reminded him of his father, of whom he is quite fond, followed by the given name his mother chose, a rather intimidating woman, usually works.

He sat down and sighed, "I really need you to be here by this evening Rosa."

I looked at him for a moment. "I'm on my way." I cut the connection.

"I'll get you a car and book you in for the next hub lift." Loveday was already pinging the local firm.

"Thank you, I need to pick up my travel bag from the house, and wash, so give me an hour."

She nodded and we left the café. I paid the bill using my phone and the holo code displayed by the counter, the owner handed me a sealed cup with hot chocolate in it and some boxed cakes.

"For the journey, it sounds as if you're going to need them." He was smiling gently in sympathy.

"Thank you, Janos," Loveday said, as he handed her a cup to go as well.

We both got into the waiting vehicle and I tapped my destination code in. I swear the damn thing sighed with "make your mind up" exasperation.

"I'll be back by tomorrow morning," I assured her. It was part of the voluntary days contract and I didn't want to get fined, or worse. "Mars is in the night sky at the moment so we have clear line of sight and I can use my government ID."

"I've always wanted to see inside your home," she said by way of not answering. "Your dad designed it, didn't he?"

I wasn't going to ask her how she knew. Minehead was a small town and my folks had been based here all their lives. My mum had been born on the farm she was now living in with my dad and where I had grown up. It was closer to the moor, but not more than a few fields away from where my house was. Most of the coastal villages hadn't survived the difficult times and the diaspora, and the people who remained were aware of their neighbours.

We got out and Loveday paused to look at the view. It was worth it, fields and trees, sheep and cows, the Exmoor ponies down in the valley. A sea eagle watching from a (sturdy) branch of the nearby big oak, and a small flock of meadow pipits swirling in the evening sky in preparation for the coming night.

I opened the door and moved aside to let her go in ahead of me. She stopped abruptly, looked down and removed her shoes. My dad's floor has that effect on everyone.

Meryasek, my dad, is an architect, but he also makes things and he built the house. The wood floor was from reclaimed church pews, subtle colour changes flowed around the one-story building into each area. I'd had a house warming party for a few locals, everyone removed their shoes at the front door and clung precariously to the edges of the main room as if we'd all been put into a house-size centrifuge.

While Loveday stared at the floor and then the view through the window wall, I stepped into the bedroom off the living-room and stripped, heading for the bathroom and the fastest walk through in the shower.

"You could use the sonic wash?" Loveday shouted.

"I need hot water," I yelled back. I turned on the warm air for a quick dry and grabbed useful work clothes and my travel bag, which was always packed.

The sitting area and the kitchen were lit by the evening sun from the back windows, the front of the house faces south east and it catches the best of the sunrises. You can just see the coast from the bedroom area. The reinforced glass walls can be switched to look opaque from the outside for privacy inside, but I can't say I have ever bothered in the living area. My neighbours are usually the cows and sheep and they've never looked the least bit interested. There is plenty of wood and brick in the walls elsewhere in the house for stability, but the one you can see through makes it special. I sighed, it would have been nice to light the fire and read a book while toasting my toes. Instead, I was going to be on a lightspeed commercial flight to Demos. Oh joy.

"Ready?" Loveday asked me.

I held up my travel bag in response.

The autonomous vehicle had that air of impatience that drivers always have about the people who they are waiting for. I wondered who had programmed it. This time Loveday tapped in the code and we set off for the hub through the early spring evening.

It was busy as usual, lots of comings and goings, the meeting up of family or friends, those who worked there and some who just liked watching people travelling somewhere.

The lift off area was small by international standards, but for all that, Minehead hub punched well above its weight.

I turned to say goodbye to Loveday, only to see her collecting her own travel bag from an interesting character with a very expensive, extremely colourful, luminescent, prosthetic hand. He waved it at me. He was unusually dressed and looked a lot like Loveday, with just the one small ID tattoo on the side of his temple. "I understand I'm not going to be able to find anything when I get back?" It clearly wasn't a joke.

"I, er—"

Loveday gave him a shove and interjected, "Go home, I can't *believe* you got that choice, it's like looking at an out-of-control rainbow and it's giving me a headache!"

"Hey, Hijinx has this version!" Arlo looked insulted.

"Exactly!" Loveday said tartly.

He waved again and wandered off, oddly several people asked for his holo autograph, and he obliged, using the neon writing feature on the fingers. They looked delighted as it appeared in the air above their phones.

Loveday sighed, but there was a great deal of fondness in the exasperation.

"I didn't realise he was *that* Arlo, exactly how high is his IQ?"

"Over three hundred," she said wincing, as he bumped into the still closed hub doors. Someone kindly opened them for him but he didn't notice, it looked as if he was thinking.

"It's not easy being a genius," I said.

"Or growing up with one," she replied dryly.

WE SETTLED INTO OUR SEATS, bags stowed and drinks served. The take-off was smooth and the complete lack of inertia always impressed me no matter how many times I did it. We went from evening blue to black space in a matter of minutes. And the vertical trajectory meant that the liquid did no more than ripple in the cups. I have been on bumpy rides, but they were usually weather related and therefore confined to the troposphere. The ship settled into the curve of the planet below and for a moment Loveday and I were in silent admiration of the view from the window.

"We will be setting up for light speed in just a tick folks, stay seated throughout the trip, unless you have a problem with your inner ear and vomiting, in which case speak to your friendly cabin crew!"

"Why is she so *jolly*?" Loveday asked me.

"They go on a training course," I said sarcastically.

She snorted, accepting another drink from the 'friendly cabin crew' who was rolling his eyes at the continued dialogue of the pilot. Flight time would be a quarter of a GMT hour due to the close proximity of the two planets, and therefore no slinging around the sun was required.

Loveday looked at me. I sighed, where to begin. "What do you know?"

"They call themselves the tremenysi, which in Cornish means travellers, and their appearance is different to some people. I've never met any of them, but my great-grandmother was one of the first children to be 'educated,' along with yours, and my brother was one of the last. He doesn't talk about it and I don't ask."

"They're probably polyploidal—"

"I thought that was only plants?" she interrupted, then seeing the expression on my face, grinned. "Sorry, go on."

"As you're aware, the chromosome sets in a human are usually diploid, though half of all known plants are polyploidal, as are some reptiles, insects, amphibians and invertebrates. And no, I don't know exactly how many they have, but we think more than seven sets."

Her mouth was open to ask something but I went on, "I don't know why they speak a form of Cornish, but it could be that it's related to Breton and Welsh, in which case it's probably about a people, time and place, as in the Celts prior to the Roman conquest. Yes, they have been here before, well, it probably wasn't just here. I think they went wherever they saw astronomical interest. Ancient Greece, maybe the Egyptians, the megalithic builders, and the druids, and no, I don't have any evidence, it's purely a personal view."

She tried for another question but I carried on, "I've met one of them on several occasions. He's called Partechi. He looks male, mature and very, very tall. He does not look human; I use the term *he* because he does. His appearance is probably close to or exactly how he looks, because I'm not bothered, but I think they tone it down to those they worry will freak out or find it unacceptable. They are unfailingly polite and very intelligent." I stopped. We both paused, me because I was out of breath and Loveday because she thought I hadn't finished. She was right.

"I think it's clear they have faster than light travel, because it would have taken them forever to get here from anywhere else and no, I don't know where that is, but despite the endless conspiracy theories, I'm absolutely sure they didn't come from here in the future. I imagine they haven't given us the science for FTL travel yet because as they keep saying, 'we are not ready' to be further out, though I think that actually means there is *something* out there we are not ready *for*, which I find a bit disturbing, and why do you want to know all this?"

"Because one of them has contacted me and asked if we could move them," Loveday said calmly."

I stared, eventually managing, "Huh," which is the universal sound for complete incomprehension.

WE WERE BOTH QUIET. I looked out of the window, thought a bit and sighed. It meant something, I just couldn't work out what. Loveday was doing her own assessing, gazing into the remoteness of space. It explained, of course, the sudden and unsolicited offer of voluntary days on my computer.

The dark was full of the lights of ships in all sizes and shapes, and the stars of out there were in the distance. I could see a large cargo freighter preparing to depart in the queue before us and at least two commercial passenger flights behind us. The other hubs were just as busy, with craft on their way to planets and moons. The freighter was probably heading to the asteroid belt.

"Just waiting for a slot before we depart. It's a busy evening, anyone needing to use the facilities go now, I'll give you plenty of warning so you can arrange your clothes. Please don't wander about without them appropriately assembled, it upsets the delicate nerves of our wonderful cabin crew!"

"Seriously, *what* is wrong with the pilot?" Loveday asked me.

"One too many flights around the sun?" I said helpfully.

"One too many somethings," I heard the attendant mutter. He saw me noticing and grinned.

"Speaking of which, would you like to try these?" I asked Loveday. "We've had a long day already and this will keep you awake." I offered her the container of small, dark brown capsules.

"What are they?" She pushed them with a suspicious finger.

"*Very* strong liquid chocolate with quick absorption nanobots," I explained. Before I could warn her, she had picked up and swallowed two. "Oh, er, they're actually very effective, one would have been enough."

"Thanks for the timely warning!" Loveday exclaimed.

"*Now* you know why the captain is so damn jolly!" The attendant quipped with another grin.

I took a capsule and washed it down with the more normal version from the travel cup. The attendant said, "Is that from the café on the high street?" I nodded. "Janos is my cousin; I'm Andras Farkas."

"Rosalee, and this is Loveday." We all shook hands. The young man was smartly dressed with the usual ID tattoo on his temple and another spacer one that denoted further qualifications. He looked just like his cousin.

"Cabin crew, ready for light speed," the captain announced suddenly.

He darted off in a hurry, encouraging people to return to their seats, one or two I noticed were, as previously advised, tidying themselves up.

Light speed engines are silent, there is no woosh or noticeable movement, just the sudden sensation of your middle ear trying to remember which way is up. I watched as the stars flashed and the lights disappeared.

"I don't think I'll ever get used to it," Loveday said to me.

"How much have you done?"

"I go to our moon on a regular basis as I usually work from there, Mars once a month, Jupiter's and Saturn's moons three or four times a GMT year, I haven't been to the ice planets for a while."

"And I thought I travelled a lot!" I laughed.

"It's part of the business, plus I meet Taylor sometimes when he can't get back for a while."

"How well does that work?" I asked curiously.

"We do better when we're not on the same planet all the time, we both like our space," she explained without a trace of irony.

"Loveday, did the tremenysi contact you about hiring me for the voluntary days?"

She hesitated. I must have looked disappointed, because she quickly spoke, "I was taking calls for new clients after Arlo had his, er, little accident. It was just a holo-text transmission from a private sender, it said your name and details and the fact that you were running late on applying. As the coded message came from a traveller, I just sent the advert into the system. You were the only reply. I recognised your name and I know your biography from Arlo and my grandmother. A few moments after you accepted, the holo pinged again and I got another request for removal and relocation from the same private sender."

I thought about this. "Arlo knows about me?"

"Yes, though when I asked him how he did, he wouldn't reply."

"I've never met your brother. I've heard of him, of course, his ideas are impressive." I stopped. She looked at me enquiringly so I carried on. "Why do you think he won't talk about his education with the travellers? Do you think he was unhappy and wanted to come home?" I had never heard of anyone feeling like that. Most of the 'educated' had very good memories of their time in learning.

"I think the problem is he was *very* happy, and he *didn't* want to come home," she explained sadly. "You have to understand, Arlo never fitted in anywhere except with them."

We sat in silence again for a few moments. I drank the last of my hot chocolate and Andras came over. "Just checking your eyes aren't rolling up into your head yet!" He grinned at Loveday. I rolled mine.

"I hope the captain isn't experiencing any side effects?" she asked him.

"Na, Captain Nutwell's got the constitution of a woolly mammoth!" He wandered off to check on a passenger who was displaying light speed induced pre-vomiting symptoms.

"Mammoth?" Loveday said. "Interesting analogy."

"He's studying adaptive evolution. I just looked him up, apparently, they have a very remarkable immune system and he's part of the latest de-extinction project."

Loveday appeared thoughtful. "I know we were circling the drain when they arrived this time. I just wonder what is the long term," she paused searching for a word, and chose, "plan."

I sighed, lowering my voice. "We were dying, my grandmother said the endless pandemics wiped out a huge number of people, and society was breaking down. Neither you nor I know what it was like to live in a solar system without them. We wouldn't be out here. The 'educated' came back really clever, they worked out a way to remove the microplastics from the oceans. Food security, insect biodiversity, amphibian preservation. It's not as if the travellers just came in and did it for us, they gave us the ability to do it ourselves. Didn't Arlo advise on the AMOC, that thing about the Atlantic currents, that no one understands but we desperately need?"

"I know, I know, and yes he did," Loveday was contemplative not angry, her voice was no more than a whisper, "what do you think the *something* out there' is that they're protecting us from?" she asked, quoting my own hasty words back to me.

"Exactly how far out does Taylor get?"

"Is the prescience part of your enhancement?"

"No, that's all me," I said.

"He was past the ice planets near Pluto and Orcus in the Kuiper belt for a while, looking into a possibility for one of our clients—"

"Why would *anyone* want to live out in the Kuiper belt?" I exclaimed, a bit too loudly for a quiet conversation.

"It wasn't about a place to live, more, er, a business proposition," Loveday explained.

"Ah," I said. "My boss is interested in the minerals on a particular area of asteroids near Haumea, though transporting it is going to be expensive."

"Ask me, I'll give you a good quote!" she said dryly.

I snorted. Mining contracts were strictly controlled. Great, now I was punning in my own head, maybe *I'd* overdone the chocolate.

"What was that?" Loveday asked me, gesturing at my expression.

"An unspoken thought about drilling regulations being a mining-field!"

She crossed her eyes.

"We are due to arrive in two minutes," the pilot announced, "cabin crew, please do the safety checks."

The 'cabin crew' which consisted of just Andras, did his visual checks of the passengers and the stowed luggage. He tossed our cups into the onboard microbe recycler and we put our work phones away just in case of a loss of cabin atmosphere, which Andras explained to another passenger, was held at nine tenths of Earth gravity. No one wanted a black eye from flying possessions heading towards a breach. I've never been in anything that lost pressure, but I've seen the safety holo's and it's not pretty. "Most accidents happened when ships dropped out of light speed," I heard him say, unwisely I thought, to the same person. The man was obviously nervous and sometimes the truth is overrated.

"It's just a precaution," Loveday explained kindly, after Andras had rushed off to complete his tasks. "We both do this trip a lot," she added. He seemed grateful. His face was a nasty shade of green so I was hoping for a smooth exit.

We dropped suddenly out and the sky became red as we circled close to the planet. I could see we were closing in fast on the Demos hub. The clear dome city was visible and getting nearer. After light speed everything seemed to be moving at an unacceptable rate. Sadly, the poor man opposite lost his battle with nausea. Andras was quick with the bio vacuum. I hoped they were paying him a good salary. I wouldn't have wanted the job.

I CLEARED entry before Loveday and waited for her. My ID means most doors are opened quickly, which is one of the perks of the department. Actually, it's probably the only one. She joined me, her bag had been checked and the contents were rumpled and sticking out of the hastily refastened top.

"I have no idea what they expected to find!" Loveday was exasperated.

"I imagine going through your underwear is reward enough for some folk," I said with a grin.

"You're joking?" She looked horrified. I started walking to the exit. "You *are* joking?" I heard her say.

A man was waiting for her on the other side, he literally enveloped her in an embrace. She came up to his armpit. The rest of the body matched the holo call I had seen of him, he looked like a friendly bear.

"Taylor," he said reaching out a large and somewhat grease-stained hand to me in a once again old-fashioned gesture. I shook it. He hadn't let her go. They looked at each other, him down, her way up, there was a lot of affection and respect between them. "I've booked somewhere for Loveday and me to stay the night; are you open for a meal and a drink later?" he asked.

I was surprised. "I need to check in with my boss, but I can send you a message once I work out what the problem is."

Loveday gave me a hug. "If we miss each other tonight, I'll meet you here for the first shuttle home."

I nodded. They walked away chatting about clients, the transporter engines and Arlo. It was easy and uncomplicated, as if they fitted into each other's memories.

I wished for a moment that I had easy and uncomplicated ones, memories I mean.

No one met me. I made my way to the conference centre in a vehicle. The dome was evening quiet. They don't have as many plants or birds on Demos as they do in other domes elsewhere, and when you look up the sky is mostly red with Mars. I always feel lacking by the time I get home, as if I haven't had enough green and blue. There is also an 'aroma' to dome living, most people are too polite to mention it, but it's there, a sort of plastic, fried air smell.

And then there's the constant hum. I find it gets into my bones after a while and gives me a headache. Finn has, however, filled me in on the dire effects of what would happen if it went silent. The lack of breathable air would be the immediate problem, right before being sucked into space. I find the very thought makes me long for the skies of home and a really deep breath of Exmoor evening. Finn loves dome life; he says he can't sleep without the hum and has to replicate it on his sound system.

I showed my pass at the door to the conference room and a guard I recognised spoke quietly, "He's over there, and we're *all* very grateful you've arrived."

"How bad was the meltdown, Walter?" I asked in a whisper.

"About a level three on a scale of one to five." He grinned. I patted him on the shoulder in sympathy. My boss can make life very difficult for those trying to do their jobs.

"Mr Betts," I said calmly.

He turned round at the sound of my voice. "What took you so long? I've been waiting here without the proper information; Finn is nowhere to be found—"

"Finn took a leave of absence for a day to see his mum, which you approved. I sent all the information, to him *and* to you before I went on my compulsory voluntary days, and it has taken me less than two hours GMT to get here." I spoke in a monotone and very quietly so only he could hear me. "So, Ethan, what's really going on?"

My boss is medium height and thin, he was born on the Earth's moon before they had proper gravity, and he has the pale reflective grey eyes, dark skin and hair common to the moon settlers. I am *very* fond of him. And as I am guardian to his two children, I like to think the feeling is reciprocated. I also know him really well.

He leaned in, his face changed to the slightly wily expression I recognised. "The governor of Mars main dome is playing games with the contract and I don't know why."

I must have looked puzzled; it was a box ticking exercise. Earth and Mars each had half the proceeds from mining the asteroid belt, it had been set up thirty years ago GMT and blocking it didn't do either of the signees any good; no one would get anything. The grumpy boss, Finn's absence and the lack of information were him stalling for time waiting for me to arrive.

"What the heck?" I muttered.

"Quite so," he said.

The conference room was fairly empty, just a few staffing assistants like me and the three main mining representatives, my boss from the global government, the governor of Mars main dome and the mining consortium agent who was looking very tired. She's usually based at the dome on Ceres and covers the operations on Vesta, Pallas and Hygiea, as well as the inter space activity on the smaller asteroids. We speak regularly and get on well, I have always admired her because she never loses her temper in the face of ego driven impossible behaviour. Right now though, it was looking fifty-fifty as to whether she would keep it. I went over to get a cup of coffee and drowned it in milk and sugar, Walter Dean the security guard was watching me and winced. He likes his black and very strong. I made him a cup and he grinned his thanks then gulped the scalding liquid down. All the guards were ex intersolar marine corp. The collective ability to swallow boiling coffee was one of their superpowers. The other was hearing stuff without being noticed.

"What's the buzz, Walter?" I whispered. We were standing between the entrance doors and the self-service coffee counter, and his eyes glanced from person to person constantly checking. He could subdue an ice planet miner with two fingers, so I knew not to mess with him. I also respect his take on just about anything.

"Governor Mwangi is trying to er, impress on the people of Mars main dome that he is doing a good job."

I was confused. "I thought he *was?*"

"He is." Walter shrugged.

"Who said he wasn't?"

"The person who is *after* his job." The guard nodded carefully in the direction of the staffer who was sitting down looking exasperated at the stupidity of the people doing the contract negotiation.

I closed my eyes and tried for the calming blue and green of home. It had been a long day and the effects of the chocolate stimulant were wearing off.

My boss raised his eyebrows and his grey eyes glittered; it could be off-putting for some folk, though I have always thought they were interesting. I nodded and walked over to the staffer and smiled down. The words came out of my mouth before I realised that they were in my head, apologies were going to have to be said, eventually.

"Do you know Myrtle Winwright?" I whispered to her.

She snorted, not even bothering to look at me but busying herself with pointless holo forms, "Do I ever, that woman nearly got me fired, I'd rather deal with a pandemic!"

As millions of people had died during the last one, I tried to resist the temptation of telling her smugly turned back that the remark was not just inappropriate but appalling. And I was also starting to develop a heathy regard for Ms Winwright's perspicacity.

"I happen to know she's planning on returning to Mars main dome, *with* BoBo."

She froze and finally actually looked at me. I checked my finger-nails and removed a tiny bit of office dirt from one. "If you get off your behind and fix the problem you've caused, I will endeavour to persuade her to stay where she is."

"How do I know you're telling the truth?" The nascent signs of worry manifested in a wobbly sneer.

I sighed and tapped a key on my phone. Loveday answered, the usually perfect hair on her holo head looking a little rumpled. Before she could say anything, I spoke, "This is Loveday Enys from Lovalott Intersolar. Can you just confirm for this staffer that Ms Winwright has asked you for help with moving back to Mars main dome?"

Loveday didn't blink. "Absolutely; I have already given her the quote."

"Thank you." I disconnected. The staffer looked sick. She glanced from me to her boss and back again. I leaned down. "Fix it!"

I watched as she went over to the governor and talked quietly to him, he was resistant at first but she was persuasive and to give her credit, which I did, reluctantly, it was done with no fuss or demonstration of power and influence. I saw Ethan not noticing, as was most of the room.

Walter smiled at me as I made myself a cup of really strong chocolate. "Thank you, my partner's birthday is tomorrow and I had to tell her I was going to miss it."

We both looked up at the clear ceiling of the conference room to the dome and Mars beyond. Demos is a tiny moon and the dome sits mostly planet side, but if you want to see space you don't have to go far.

"Do you like working here, Walter?"

"I love it, it's always interesting, speaking of which, *incoming*!" He moved away as the staffer walked stiffly to the conference room door and went through, just as Finn tumbled in.

"What's the problem? I thought everything was going well, otherwise I wouldn't have left!" Finn came straight up to me and took the cup from my hands, downing it. He had obviously been asleep and he must have dressed in a hurry, his usual smart clothes were askew. "Ugh! What is that?"

I waited. My boss approached governor Mwangi and they began to talk, they were joined by Anna Schneider, the consortium agent and eventually they all sat down. I made coffee and took the tray of very superior snacks over to the table. Holo contracts were signed and everyone sighed with relief.

"Thank you, Rosalee," my boss said. He added, "You know my assistant," to the governor.

"I do, if you're ever looking for a new posting please come and see me." Governor Mwangi grinned. He's been trying to poach me for years. Ethan Betts scowled.

"I'm not, but Finn is looking to transfer back to Mars, and he comes highly recommended by both of us." As this was news to my boss *and* Finn, they both did a very good impression of not looking surprised.

"I would be delighted to talk to you about that, let's have a conversation in Mars main dome tomorrow." The governor picked up his computer and left after speaking briefly to Walter.

"Well, you've spun your usual magic," Stella said, adding with just the right touch of acid, as she gathered her own personal and work items, "*What* did you say to that staffer?"

"Something I'm going to need to apologise for tomorrow," I answered wryly.

"And *when* exactly did you decide Finn needed a transfer?" My boss was equally sharp.

"Look at him Ethan, he loves it here, he hates being based on Earth *and* he misses his mum!"

Finn was laughing with Walter and he seemed to be stronger, not quite so bowed under by, I don't know, gravity, unfiltered air, the horizon.

It must be *exhausting*, being right all the time!" Anna said as she hurried out, no doubt to get some sleep before going back to Ceres. My boss snorted.

It is, I thought.

I NEVER USUALLY REST IN a dome, I keep listening for silence and even if I use a sound system of the waves on the shore or a thunderstorm, I'm still waiting for the terrifying quiet of no air.

My boss went off to spend what was left of the evening with some buddies from his military past, and no doubt there would be alcohol and lots of tall tales. I just wanted to find somewhere to lay my head for a few hours until the first shuttle back home. Walter came to the rescue of course, that man has more connections than the deep space network. In quick time I was in a small pleasant hotel, with a view of Mars not space, and the most comfortable floating mattress. I took a boiling hot bath, which was something of a luxury on a satellite moon.

Most people use the sonic shower, but I felt I needed to make up for the earlier walk-through sprinkling. And oddly for me I actually slept well.

TUESDAY

Breakfast was a large, very sweet, milky coffee on the way to the hub.

I took my seat on the transport, looking around for Loveday. A few bleary faces sat in quiet contemplation of the early morning commute. I shrugged, I could open up the office, but the finer points of removals were still a mystery. The doors were closing.

"Wow, impressive timing!" The cabin crew on this occasion, consisted of a small blonde woman, who was displaying a high level of respect as Loveday slid through the automatic doors, which hissed their disapproval in trying not to squash her.

She threw herself into the seat and grabbed the cup of coffee I was holding. Sighing with relief, she downed it in one.

"Well, hello to you too!" I said, laughing. "I was looking forward to that."

"I'll buy you one from the café as soon as we land." Loveday closed her eyes and was instantly asleep.

"Must have been a busy night," the shiny, attractive blonde said with a grin. "I'm Maja, Janos is my cousin."

"Well, of course he is," I replied. "Are there any more of you?"

"Good morning! This is your captain speaking, cabin crew get ready for departure. And please be nice to Maja, she's a no vomit zone!"

I pointed upwards as if that signified the direction of the person attached to the voice, which it didn't. "Is *that* Captain Nutwell, again?"

"Yep, she's working on her ships master's licence, only three hundred more GMT hours to go!"

I heard Loveday mutter, "Oh good."

The engines whined a little and the shuttle took off in a neat curve away from the moon Demos while Maja was still doing her visual checks on the passengers. She didn't seem to mind, though she rolled her eyes at me as she eventually sat down. Most of the people were frequent flyers and were fine without the advice or help.

As I watched the receding moon and the red gold of Mars disappear behind us, I could see the sun's rays reflecting off the surface of the living domes on the planet and the orbital satellites which were part of the deep space communication complex. It looked like a dance of light, as if Mars had its own guardian stars in the darkness.

I wondered if Walter had made it home for his partner's birthday. He had said he was hitching a ride on a freighter leaving in the early hours, so he could make her breakfast in bed before she went to work. I hoped his marine training had included the finer points of toast and marmalade and not just a self-heating scran pack.

The captain cheerfully announced light speed and Maja did a quick cabin check. Once again, she had barely any time to sit before the steady whoosh and the do-se-do of the middle ear set in. I could see the veterans clearing their dizziness without breaking their concentration or conversation. I always equalised using the close your mouth, hold your nose and blow gently method, which worked just as well underwater as it did in space. Loveday performed the task without opening her eyes.

THE SHUTTLE CAME out of light speed at the exact point we had left the previous evening and without a bump or shake. It was perfect. I applauded, and several of the other passengers smiled and joined in, it was an unusual moment of companionship in amongst mildly jaded complacency.

Watching as the planet crept up in the window, the ring of satellites was similar to the ones around Mars. I could just see the old debris net strung out beyond the trailing lights, it still caught up the odd hammer and screw from past space mishaps. Most of the other junk had been collected and repurposed. Nothing was wasted. The north pole station came in to view as we manoeuvred towards the space lane that covered the hubs in the northern hemisphere. And then down into airways.

They still kept to the pre-established required levels and distances once you joined the upper atmosphere.

The town was early morning quiet as we disembarked. I left Loveday yawning her way to the office and sped up to my house. Throwing my travel bag in the bedroom, I changed rapidly and grabbed a pair of boots. For a moment I looked out of the windows at the sunrise and contemplated the green and blue with a deep breath of moor air.

The café was full of people waiting for a takeaway breakfast or eating. I was surprised to have two cups of hot chocolate thrust into my hands before I'd even had a chance to order. A large box of something interesting was added with a grin. Loveday had been busy. Janos just waved the payment away and got on with the next, somewhat desperate looking, customer. I left in a cloud of chocolate fumes and admiration for his whole, extended, hard-working, clever family.

Loveday was deep in conversation with a holographic head when I arrived. "Hey Rosalee," Taylor smiled at me, suspended above the computer console.

"Hey yourself," I waved back at him.

"I hear you blackmailed that nasty staffer with Myrtle Winwright to successfully close the mining re-contracting agreement? I'm seriously impressed!" He seemed thrilled.

I froze, Loveday looked at me. "Er, well, I *was* going to explain about that this morning," I put the cup of chocolate on her desk and shrugged winningly. As an afterthought I said to Tayor, "Could we maybe keep that to ourselves?"

"Are you *kidding* me, Walter told me before I dropped him off at north pole station, I should think half the solar system knows by now!" He was enjoying himself.

I sat down at the other desk and leaning forward, banged my forehead gently on the surface. Ethan Betts was well experienced at *not* knowing exactly how I achieved his goals, but this was going to be difficult to ignore. And from the look on Loveday's face, she wasn't too impressed either.

"You know, it's very disconcerting to watch a holo head do that?" Taylor said, still laughing.

I sighed, "Okay, it wasn't my finest moment but I was winging it, it worked *and*, I didn't like her, she's—"

"Nasty?" Loveday interjected helpfully.

"Yes!" Taylor and I said in harmony.

"Anna thought it was priceless," he added.

"How does *she* know?" I shouted.

"I told you, *Walter* and half the solar system?" Taylor explained, with barely concealed delight.

There was always this thing with freighter folk and gossip. I wondered, and not for the first time, if it was being out there in the big dark that made the small, back here stuff more interesting, because if ever I needed to know what the buzz was, they were always first on my list.

I heard a light speed alarm. Taylor's smiling face turned away for a moment and all we could see was his short curly hair. He looked back to Loveday and waved, the rainbow of colours swirled and I watched as she held her own hand into the holographic image of his. It felt as if I was intruding on something very personal, so I checked the bottom of my chocolate cup for interesting dregs.

"Where is Taylor off to next?" I asked.

"Ganymede, it's a short hop today, it should only take him fifty minutes GMT. He's going to unload, which will take *all* of a GMT day, and then stay overnight and he'll be back tomorrow morning." Loveday was already reaching for the list of appointments that had pinged up in a holo-message from the overnight digital assistant call centre.

"Does he park the freighter at Moon main dome?" I was curious, no one brought them to the surface, it was too expensive and awkward, all loads were shuttled up to the bigger transport.

"North pole station." Loveday looked at me, her face was a myriad of unexpressed feelings, mainly anxiety.

"I'm sorry, I was desperate and tired and it was the first thought that came into my head. I shouldn't have used something I heard here to sort out my problem." I felt it was probably too late considering the outcome, but worth saying anyway.

She looked puzzled then laughed. "From what I gather it was the right move, I'm not bothered about it!"

"What *is* worrying you then?" I got up and put our empty cups into the recycler. The office was clean and tidy still, so Arlo hadn't made a night time foray to re-establish his territory.

"This." She pointed to a communication that had come in after hours.

It wasn't on the digital assistant messaging service list, and had bypassed all the security protocols. There were very few details but they consisted of a destination point, the weights, measured in Earth gravity, and the dimensions of various containers.

"Where *is* that?" I couldn't it work out; the three-dimensional grid reference didn't seem familiar.

She ran up the solar system holo-map and tapped in the coordinates.

"Er," was all I could manage.

THE POSITION, highlighted by the holo-map with a helpful red arrow, was somewhere on the outer edge of the Kuiper belt. I couldn't see anything there; the nearest possible dwarf planet was Orcus and its moon Vanth. But due to the planet's rather odd orbit of the sun, it was difficult to tell.

"What does that mean?" Loveday asked me, indicating the information on the image.

"I don't really comprehend the dynamics of perihelion and aphelion, you'd need an astrophysicist for that, as I understand, it's the distance from the sun, as in the closest and furthest away."

"Okay," Loveday snorted then looked speculative, "so, what we're saying is a destination point somewhere on the edge of the Kuiper belt."

"Do you think this has anything to do with that, er, business proposition Taylor was looking into out there?"

Loveday glanced up at me. "There's that home grown prescience you were demonstrating yesterday."

"I'll take that as a yes, then," I muttered.

"Do you—"

The door burst open and Arlo exploded into the office. Anything Loveday was about to say was lost in the dramatic entrance.

"It's here, *just* arrived! I thought I was going to have to wait another day." He frowned. "My calculations are going to need tweaking." He drifted out of the here and now for a moment. "I think I've got it." His face brightened.

"What's here?" I asked, stunned.

"My hand, of course," he said, exasperated.

"It's going to be one of *those* days," Loveday sighed.

"WAIT, *WHAT* DID YOU JUST SAY?" Loveday was sharp, it took me a second to catch up. "Please tell me you didn't *deliberately* put your hand into the light speed jump field!"

Arlo looked puzzled. "It was necessary for my computation."

"You don't think that was a tiny bit... *inconvenient?*" Loveday was sarcastic.

"Don't be silly, "Arlo replied seriously, "it's not as if I used my foot!" He left as abruptly as he had appeared.

What is he calculating and why, I thought, but didn't get a chance to say anything out loud.

Loveday was pressing her forehead into the palms of her hands. "Can you imagine growing up with that every day?"

"Actually no. I'm an only child. Would more hot chocolate help?"

Loveday sighed, "I'm floating on fumes as it is, I think I'd just better get on with the client list."

"Give me the easy ones, I'm sure I can manage, and if I can't, then you're right here!"

The morning disappeared in a flood of quotes, appointments, contracts, setting out conditions, the exchange dates, storage of excess possessions (and there were lots of those), animals, some of which could not be transported unless accompanied by their owners and a few that should absolutely *not* be going anywhere off the planet. I tried to reason with a man who wanted to bribe me so he could take a tiger cub with him to Titan main dome. Loveday grabbed the holo call and threatened him with the international rangers and protected species act, he cut the connection abruptly.

"*He* won't be getting his deposit back!" She was furious and tapped in the details, sending it off to the appropriate authorities with a slap of satisfaction on the last key.

"Does that ever happen?" I was incredulous.

"Sadly yes, there is still a trade in illegal animals, and some people will try because the money is so good."

I didn't have time to express my horror as the lines just kept ringing, I went for the next on the list.

"Good morning young lady!" A holo face that I recognised from the files appeared. Loveday leaned back out of sight. "Don't think I don't know you're there, Ms Enys!"

"How can I help you, Ms Winwright?" I asked, in my best placatory voice.

"Well, you could stop using me to threaten Martin's assistant!"

I must have looked puzzled because she continued.

"Governor Mwangi, is an ex-pupil of mine, he was a *very* clever little boy." She seemed proud.

I was still reeling from him being called a little boy, or even the thought that he ever actually was one, the governor is nearly as tall as the average traveller. I could see Loveday trying to get my attention by waving her arms around and indicating that I should get to the point and wind the conversation up as quickly as possible, presumably without committing the business to any more moves and hopefully minus bloodshed (probably mine).

"I am sorry for using your name, and please be assured that no one at this firm had any prior knowledge of my action or was in any way complicit—"

"Oh, dry up, that silly selfish girl had it coming, it was time someone sorted her out!"

There was a stunned silence for a moment, then I tried for something more prosaic. "What can we do for you today?" Out of the corner of my eye I saw Loveday miming strangling herself in frustration.

"I wanted to speak to Arlo, have you seen him?" The holo head regarded me with the expression that most teachers have perfected over the years, the type who never have problems with unruly pupils.

"He was here earlier this morning, but I don't know where he is now," I said, adding helpfully, "his hand arrived, and he's very excited.

"Did it?" Ms Winwright was surprised. "The calculations must have been out by a factor of—" she snorted and cut the connection.

"Do you know what that's about?" I asked, really intrigued.

Loveday was quiet, her facial expression back to the worry of the morning message. "I have this feeling, it's as if there's a storm coming."

"About the 'spooky move' job?" I made my fingers wiggle in an appropriate fashion.

"It could just be someone wanting to live off the grid?" she pondered hopefully.

It was my turn to snort, "it's hard to put it down to that when everyone *not* in a main dome is pretty much doing grid free living anyway!"

She sighed, her face working through the various levels of apprehension of sensing something, but not knowing what.

"Calculations?" I asked.

"Um," Loveday was confused.

"Ms Winwright and Arlo, their mathematical collaboration, do you have any idea what they're both doing?"

She shook her head slowly.

"But they clearly know each other?"

"I think they met because he's moved her twice." She shrugged.

"Really Loveday, you need to ask more questions!" I laughed, but the sense of disquiet was beginning to creep up on me as well, like the sea fret that hung around on my early morning runs.

We took a short break over lunch and went out. The calls were still coming in, apparently people don't stop to eat when they are moving.

The café on the high street was crowded, but Loveday had phoned in our order and Janos handed it over with more hot chocolate and a busy smile. Without discussion, we walked along the front and found a spot on the beach between the breakwater and the seawall. The wind was cold but the spring sunshine held a trace of warmth, and we were both wrapped up with the necessary layers required for living on the moorland by the sea.

I unpacked; Loveday was watching the waves as though the answers were there if she listened carefully. I'm familiar with the feeling, I do the same with the trees on the moor.

Lunch was cheese and herb rolls twisted into decorative shapes and a thick mushroom soup. I dunked and ate hungrily. Loveday sighed.

"Did you find what you were looking for?" I pointed out to sea.

"I have always loved the sense of distance, and the sound." She turned towards me. "Don't eat it all, I'm starving!"

We shared the soup, the momentary peace and the sticky honey cakes. A curious dog came over and her owner followed.

"Hey Rosalee, Loveday, it's nice to see you. How are you both, I hear you're doing your voluntary days at the removal firm?"

"Nice to see you too Raji, and your furry darling!" I patted the small scruffy terrier who was looking hopefully at the remainder of our lunch.

"Sheriff Jones," Loveday said warily.

Raji sighed, "it's Arlo, he walked in and out of the hub without registering again, and he left the container with his hand in the bathroom. I took it to the local hospital, they said it was fine, still in suspension fluid. But it really freaked out the woman who found it, could you..." she ran out of words, I didn't blame her; I think my mouth had dropped open.

"I'll sort it out," Loveday sounded resigned.

Raji smiled as she and her dog, now full of cheese roll, left to continue their walk. "Don't call me sheriff, I knew you when you wanted to be a princess!"

"I was three, I thought it was a job with nice clothes!" Loveday shouted after her.

"You went to school with Raji?" I was intrigued.

"She was team captain of everything, even then," Loveday said wryly and with great affection.

The receding figure was throwing impressively aimed driftwood into the waves for the happy dog to retrieve. I watched until they disappeared around the curve of the beach.

Raji had been voted into the post unopposed for several years, she covered the moor and several towns inland and along the coastline. It was a big patch, but her team were well trained and consisted of the sea patrol and rescue, the local rangers and technical specialists. We had very little trouble, or so I'd believed.

I thought about the call in the morning and the tiger cub. I read the transgression reports for my boss and informed him when it encroached on his jurisdiction, which was hardly ever. The high-level crime generally occurred around the big city hubs, and usually consisted of corruption. It could be violent but the international rangers dealt with it. This casual introduction into the callous movement of protected species was disturbing.

"The man this morning," I said.

Loveday didn't need to ask which one. "He's being picked up, I checked before we left the office. The cub is in protective care."

"Will there be any comeback for you, he must know you reported him?"

"Have you seen the size of Tay!" Loveday snorted. "Plus, we have Raji, why do you think she came to find me?"

"I thought it was," I waved my hand around in explanation.

"That too," Loveday said, exasperated. Getting to her feet, she leaned forward and pulled me up. "Don't worry about it, the travellers are always on our side."

"They can't fix everything," I muttered to myself, dusting off sand, bits of sea grass and wild valerian. It was something my grandmother said, *a lot*. We were well past due a holo call, but the days slipped by so fast, and it was always me who forgot.

LOVEDAY WENT TO THE HOSPITAL, to check on the 'hand situation' as it had now become. I answered the general enquiries and tried to deal with the endless questions about how to move, when there was availability, and the paperwork needed. I filled out forms, sent off quotes and placated those current clients who needed to speak to Loveday about their actual relocation.

I found myself commiserating on the 'misplacement' of some human ashes belonging to the mover who was taking her husband with her, as he had always wanted to live in Ganymede main dome. I promised to speak to Loveday as soon as she got back so they could be reunited (the client and her husband's ashes, not her and Loveday).

I was just leaning back in the chair and holding my aching head when she returned, accompanied by a now complete Arlo. He showed me the clear gel casing around the severed connection. I know I couldn't really, but my imagination thought I could see the nanobots working their little spidery programming on the tissue of the bones, nerves and skin. I shuddered. The fact that I used them on a daily basis for all sorts of things from house plumbing maintenance to a more efficient absorption of a chocolate high, doesn't mean that I like the idea.

"I'm going to miss my rainbow holo-hand—" Arlo interrupted himself, "has Myrtle called me?"

Not being on first name terms with Ms Winwright it took me a moment to catch up.

Loveday was quicker. "Yes, what are you up to?"

Arlo looked hurt. "I'm insulted!" He stormed off, slamming the door to the kitchen, then realising his mistake yanked it open and did the same thing with the office door to the street. The question seemed to float on the air, unanswered before it dissipated. I saw several people approach him, he showed them his hand and they high fived him in return. Loveday winced. She was right, it was barely healed and in danger of needing reconnecting.

"Well," I said.

"I need a drink and a bath and a really long sleep." Loveday was still watching her brother wandering down towards the beach, he had clearly forgotten where he was going. She sighed. "I'd better go, can you lock up for me?"

"Sure, I'll set the digital assistant answer system." I clicked a few holo-keys and the calls, which were still coming in, transferred across. "My dad does that."

"What?" Loveday was collecting her very nice coat and extremely expensive handbag.

"Deflect, when he doesn't want to answer a question," I said.

"Is he as good at it though?" she muttered.

I had to admit, Arlo was in a class of his own.

GRANDMOTHER ELOWEN LIVES in a small house in the middle of the moor, she said the quiet spoke to her and she could get on with her writing. She is well known for her vast tomes about science in the language of maths and physics that most people, including me, can't understand. Her latest books document our history with the travellers. I had never met my grandfather and as far as I'm aware my mum hadn't either.

I don't really know my great-grandmother Auryn very well, she spends her time out in the solar system and only comes back to Earth for conferences. Her relationship with the tremenysi has been described, by my dad, as 'integrated,' and with her family as 'unconventional.' She had been one of the first group of children 'educated' by the travellers.

My mum, grandmother and great grandmother are all tall with blonde hair and green eyes, they look remarkably alike. I asked once and I was told great-grandmother used parthenogenesis, helped of course, using genetic development from the travellers. By the time my mother came along the laws of the land had been enshrined to favour the female line, and she could inherit the farm without a problem.

I wish I hadn't been so curious when my mum explained that she had been conceived with one set of genes from each donor... the old-fashioned way, believe me, you do *not* want to have that image in your head when talking to your grandmother. I, apparently, am a genetic anomaly, my mum, Beryan says there's plenty of interesting unattached DNA from her side to go around, my dad, Meryasek says I look like his family. I don't. He is a big man and has black eyes and black hair, his skin is light brown, and he looks like the Breton people the

Cornish are connected to by their love of the sea and the very similar language.

His mother and grandparents still run a fishing fleet of three boats and he was working the nets as soon as he could hop over the gunwale unaided. I love the sea; it just doesn't love me back.

My house was quiet and comforting, I shut the front door and slid off my shoes. The sofa facing the moor beckoned but I did the right thing and showered and sorted out my travel bag for the next emergency journey, because there was always going to be one.

By the time I sunk into the cushions to make a call it was late evening and the sun had set. I could see shadow sheep under the trees and hear the wind from the moor rising to battle the barely visible fret from the sea. There was moisture on the windows and a chill in the air; I got up again and lit the fire.

My grandmother answered immediately. "Rosalee," she said, smiling.

"Elowen," I spoke, my smile echoing hers. She is beautiful and looks younger than me, I haven't had any anti-ageing treatment yet, so my hair has the odd grey strand and my face a few wrinkles.

"I hear you blackmailed a staffer on Demos using Myrtle Winwright, excellent form!"

I gaped. "How do you know that?"

"I have my sources!" She laughed.

"How are the voluntary days going?" Elowen was not just a head, she had decided to go full holo screen and I could see her wandering around the living area of her house, eventually sitting down next to her own fire which was lit against the early spring cold of the moor. We were each other's three-dimensional connection. I'm also not keen on the holo head thing, I think it looks weird.

"What do you want to ask me Rosalee?" Elowen said gently when the silence had stretched. I could hear the fires crackling at both houses in unison in the quiet of the evening. Just a lone owl calling, though I couldn't work out if it was outside her window or mine.

"Tell me about when the travellers arrived," I asked eventually.

She sighed, "why do you want to know this now?"

"Because things are happening and I feel, *uninformed,*" I struggled with the right word, but that one would do.

Elowen laughed, "it was inevitable that you and Loveday would meet eventually, and we needed you to talk."

"So, there was a plan." I said warily, adding as an afterthought, "And who, exactly, is *we?*"

"It's really more of a pattern," she said, with her mathematical face, not answering the question.

I tried again. "Are you the person making these decisions?"

The lights in her living room were low and I could see the shadows of the trees in the moonlight beyond the windows wavering in the wind, which was increasing. Looking out to my own view the same moon cast similar shapes on the fields, the lonely owl called a hollow cry again in my fields and not her part of the moorland. I love where I live, but it felt as if my most precious things hung in a precarious balance.

"What do you want to know?" Elowen asked me into the quiet.

"I *think* I'll recognise whatever it is when I hear it," I mused.

"That enhanced perception is a pain!" She sniffed theatrically.

"Everyone should have it," I replied waspishly. I have never had my DNA messed with (as far as I know) the training came with all other stuff, non-verbal communication, neurolinguistics and a degree in business psychology.

"It must be exhausting?" she said, using some fairly effective sensitivity of her own.

It was. I always needed a lot of quiet and aloneness to get over spending time with demanding people, who were inevitably making the usually nominally challenging decisions, difficult. It can be incomprehensible to some folk who get their energy being in crowds. 'Radiators and drains' they call it in psychology, though it uses a more professional sounding terminology. It was my turn to be reflective.

Elowen began, "Auryn said, that the before times were awful, the last pandemic had followed a mess of several wars over resources. She remembered being so hungry and cold all the time, no child went to school, people were fighting over what was left, and her own mother had died of starvation.

When the tremenysi came no one was able to do anything anyway, so, if it had been—" she stopped abruptly, paused, changed the direction of her words and then went on, "the possibility of your children being safe, fed and warm was a promise they made, the fact that they would be 'educated' as well," again she stopped. "There was a disparity in diversity numbers at first, let's face it, if you have a Celtic parent, they don't care if you have to go to Proxima Centauri and back, as long as you come home with a qualification in every 'ology!'"

We both laughed, I have two Cornish grandmothers in my life, they are *very* ambitious for their offspring and *all* the following generations, so I know this to be true.

She continued, "Other people caught up eventually and were grateful when the children came back happy, healthy and really, really, *bright*."

"Did the travellers interfere much in the politics at the time?" I was fishing, but I didn't know for what.

She sighed again, "you mean the disappeared?"

"I don't think I did, but we could start with that!"

"You must have heard about it, or read something?" Elowen was stalling or deflecting me.

"I wouldn't be good at my job if I hadn't studied the past." I got up and made myself a hot drink of milk and cinnamon. I added some of the honey biscuits that Janos had made to my tray. The holo image followed me around the kitchen and back to the sofa.

"There were still some very bad people around then, those that had survived the pandemics, they lived in closed communities and stored food and medical supplies for themselves."

My mouth dropped open, which was very embarrassing as I was still chewing a biscuit. I spluttered crumbs. "I thought those stories were *apocryphal?*"

She laughed. "If Beryan had seen you do that you'd be in trouble!"

"Don't tell her!" I sniffed. "People *actually* disappeared?"

"Some of them," she answered, "others were allowed to, er, adjust."

I thought about that for a second or two, we had programmes for recidivists and there was the possibility for genetic alteration for anyone who displayed malignant tendencies towards narcissism and psychopathy. I knew that decision was made by a committee of doctors and psychologists, but I didn't know enough about it to make an informed opinion on its effectiveness. For everything else, and there was other stuff, we had the sheriffs, rangers and marines. County and city, country and solar.

My grandmother tapped in some information and a globe of the Earth appeared, spinning slowly. I was puzzled. Nothing looked quite right. For a start the north polar icecap and the Antarctic were tiny.

"What's this? I felt really worried, hopefully it wasn't a prediction of the future.

"It's our planet before the tremenysi came." Elowen was sad.

I looked carefully, tapping on sections and for a while we were quiet, her because she wanted me to concentrate, me because I was stunned.

You can integrate the holo images, though I have always found it creepy, someone near you but not there. For a minute or two it was as if Elowen sat next to me on my sofa. We both needed the proximity.

The image ran through the changes to permafrost and species decline, and the slowing down of the earth's spin due to polar ice melt. I watched as the elephants died and the trees were decimated. Oceans became acidic and destroyed the ecological balance. The wars over resources were terrible, but the pandemic that followed I couldn't watch, I turned away. Tears streamed down my face.

"They thought we were worth saving," Elowen whispered.

"After looking at all this, I'm not so sure!" I was blunt. And angry.

"I have lived in a world where we have DNA banks for flora and fauna, horizontal food production, massive wildlife reserves, biodiversity, and the diaspora to the rest of the solar system," she paused, contemplating her words.

"*Why* did they help us?" I just couldn't see it.

"Art, music, literature, imagination and humour, I would think." Elowen grinned.

I let out the breath I didn't realise I was holding. "Are we better for them being here, shouldn't we have saved ourselves?"

"I don't think we could, but they gave us the autonomy to make our own decisions and the chance to change and most people took it."

"But some didn't?" I asked.

"No," she said quietly.

I looked out to the dark shadows and the fields on my doorstep. Mark Welling and his partner Sam had a licence to farm, as did my parents through my mother's hereditary claim. The sheep and cows were bred for species protection and the meat from their DNA was grown on the farm and packed off to the markets, never having been a live animal. I didn't eat it myself but lots of people preferred to do so.

"We're not perfect," Elowen said. "There is still plenty of bad to go around, but we're better than we were and we've spread to out there."

I looked at her, back in her own house and on her side of the hologram again. "Are you saying that there's balance?"

"Yes, exactly." She looked pleased.

The diaspora to the other planets and moons in the solar system was spinning out on the image of the Earth in front of me. I had seen it in school but this was more detailed. The space stations and the hubs; the energy net collecting and transferring power to the planet through a series of storage devices. Dome building was based on a transparent graphene, incredibly strong and durable which was invented by one of the first of those 'educated.'

It was somehow comforting to see the names of the scientists and engineers, as I watched the development unfolding with the GMT readings showing next to it.

I turned to her. "What about the politics?"

"Well, they did suggest putting women in charge for a change." I must have looked confused because she laughed. "Never mind, it's something that you wouldn't understand even if I told you."

She hunted for a simple version of what must have been a stunningly complicated process. In the end she went with, "Yes, they did interfere."

I waited for more but there wasn't any.

She sighed, "really they had no choice, the possibility for just going back to what we had done before was too ingrained, and we wouldn't have survived."

I waited for the holo to swirl into a rainbow of light before I cried. For some reason the long ago had really affected me, a hundred and fifty years of GMT didn't seem to have diminished the enormity of death and destruction. It wasn't the fury of tears, more the silent slow grief of loss for something I never knew.

WEDNESDAY

"Don't tell me how to deal with this!" Loveday blasted out as I came through the door. I took a step back and she waved me in with the hand that the face on the end of the holo call couldn't see. A man with the chastened expression of the recently aware looked back.

"Of course, Ms Enys, I would never do any such thing, we at the Minehead hub have always held your experience in these matters in the highest regard. I will await—"

Loveday cut the connection using a word that would have put her on the thinking step for some considerable time if my mum had heard it.

"Let me guess," I said, closing my eyes for a moment and pretending to process with my finger on my temple, "Arlo?"

"He went into the computer systems room this morning and said he had some new calculations to work on and they left him to it." I raised my eyebrows in encouragement for her to continue, though I had an idea of what was coming. "He set up the light speed parameters and stuck his hand back into the jump field."

"The same hand?" I asked.

"*Yes!*" She shouted, "what does it matter *which* hand it was?"

"Well," I said placatingly, "he can still use the luminescent prosthetic hand."

"That's what *he* said!" Loveday was beyond exasperated.

I grinned. "You know Hijinx has that version?"

She was thinking of shouting again but despite her best efforts, Loveday's face cracked into a smile and then laughter.

"How can I help?" I said eventually after we had both sobered up.

"I just need a bit of normal, and you're already doing it." Loveday began sending messages and setting up appointments. I made the coffee.

"Do you want to try and advise a current client with an actual relocation date today?" she asked me in between slurps of hot liquid and holo-key tapping.

I thought about it, they always seem to be fraught with danger when I watched her do them, people in the process of moving lose their ability to be rational on any level. "Sure, why not, how bad could it be?" I smiled at her look of incredulity.

I checked the file and the details swirled out in steady neat lines of information and diagrams. A family moving to Ganymede main dome for work purposes. Two adults and one child. I clicked on the forms I needed to fill out and then on the connection to the current home.

As soon as my face appeared and I opened my mouth to speak, the young man began asking questions, or actually spraying them in my general direction. It was like being bombarded by a hostile committee at an interview for a job I didn't want. His voice was well above what would be considered healthy on the stress level scale.

I tried again, "Could you—" he continued as if I hadn't spoken. "We can—" nope, the man was beyond reason. I cut the connection. Turning to a grinning Loveday I said, "Any suggestions?"

"Actually, I thought that went *really* well!"

I laughed, "I'm not giving up, that was round one!"

"Go for it, girl!"

The door bounced off its hinges and Taylor barged in, he grinned at me and kissed the top of Loveday's head in a move that they had obviously perfected over the years. Hot chocolate and cakes spilled out of his hands and over the table in a sticky waterfall of delightful smells.

"I'm amazed you're still here; the previous voluntary days bod didn't last for more than four hours GMT!"

"*Taylor*!" Loveday shrieked.

"What?" He looked at her, really puzzled, a large fist around one of Janos's cakes and a cup of steaming liquid in the other. He slurped and offered me a cup, which I was delighted to accept.

"Could you *be* more tactless?"

"She's been dealing with our client group *and* met Arlo's new hand; I think we are well past tactful!" Taylor was matter of fact.

I nodded my agreement. Loveday raised her eyes upwards and muttered a string of Cornish words that sounded vaguely rude.

Taylor had the feline grace of the spacer about him, as if he walked on tiptoe in less than Earth gravity all the time; the brief encounter we'd had on Demos hub hadn't given me more than the passing impression of his true size. He handed Loveday her hot chocolate and a cake as if she were royalty and she took it with the same smile I had seen before, love by name and nature.

The holo calls were backing up. Red lights flashed and beeped in irritation at being ignored for seconds.

I sighed. Slugging back thick powerful sweet liquid and straightening my shoulders I made the connection with the client again. Before he had a chance to speak, I plunged verbally in with a steady stream of information, using a placatory and soothing tone. A small aspect of my psychology training had been learning to negotiate with perceived dangerous or challenging behaviour, it was coming in handy.

As I drew to a close on the last form for immigration a hand appeared in the corner of the holo, with the universal sign of thumbs up, followed by the smiling face of one of the most beautiful androgys I had ever seen. They made an interesting couple. I signed off.

"Wow," Taylor said, "love really is blind!"

"It's not *that* blind," Loveday said, "it's probably wealth or access."

"How come *you* can be tactless but I can't?" Taylor said, frustrated.

"Those are just the rules," Loveday shrugged, tapping holo-keys and eating a cake in an impressively ambidextrous way.

"*Seriously,* you two!" I tried not to laugh, it was true, he had been slightly less than an averagely good-looking young man and genetic androgyny did tend towards the best physicality of both sexes.

I spent the rest of the morning answering calls and filling out holo forms. The client response didn't change, every single one of them required high levels of psychological technique. I was exhausted and wilting by lunchtime. Loveday looked like an expensive bunch of fresh flowers.

Taylor was lounging back in the new spare office chair and reading a book. His body language suggested that he was waiting for something.

I sat back in my own seat and watched for a second. Loveday's face changed and Taylor sat up without having seemingly noticed. They really did have a connection.

"It's here," she said.

"What is?" I asked, bemused.

"The details of the tremenysi request," Taylor explained.

It took me a moment to catch up, he had moved to stand next to Loveday and they were both reading the written holo transmission. I couldn't see it but the expressions on their faces were identically bemused.

"You have got to be kidding me?" Taylor said.

"What do they want you to do?" I whispered, as if someone was listening in. Loveday turned the holo around so I could see it. In the absence of any useful words a sharp intake of breath would have to do.

"WELL, I GUESS I'M GOING," Taylor said. "Have we got the personal details?"

"They're encoded," Loveday was looking at me.

"For whom?" I asked, though I thought I knew the answer.

She pointed at me and I nodded.

"Now we know why you're here." Taylor grinned. He didn't seem very bothered, or actually that surprised.

I took the holo from Loveday and input my personal DNA imprint, using my finger pressure on the keyboard. It connected but took a few moments to recognise me, then the holo linked to another server, coming from somewhere behind Earth's moon. As soon as I saw the identification code, I knew who it was.

He didn't change his looks for Taylor and Loveday, which impressed me and neither of them were the least bit concerned, something I also found impressive. Full on tremenysi can rattle some folk.

The door suddenly swung open behind me and I instinctively

covered the holo image with my body, reaching for the end transmission key.

"Hi Partechi!" Arlo was smiling in delight. I moved as the acknowledgement went both ways. Partechi's greeting was formal and dignified. "It is good to see you Arlo Enys."

Loveday and Taylor were looking from one to the other of them in an approximation of an audience at a very fast tennis match.

I heard Taylor mutter, "This just keeps getting better."

And Loveday reply, "Are we the only people here who don't know what's going on?"

I felt it was important for the facts to be clear, so I added, "Nope, that would be me too!"

Partechi didn't explain anything. He gave Loveday a list of container dimensions and the pick-up point, which was slightly too close to Venus for Taylor's liking, judging from the expression on his face.

Loveday took notes and everyone nodded and smiled. Even Arlo, who was wearing the oddest collection of clothing, some of which might have been sleep attire and the sort of boots that were usually used for working on the outside of vehicles in space, they made a disturbing ripping sound as he moved around, as if trying to stick to the floor.

Finally, Partechi spoke directly to me, "Rosalee Veryan, I would be grateful if you would accompany me on this..." he struggled to find a suitable word.

"Relocation?" I said helpfully.

He thought for a moment then nodded. "I have already discussed these adjusted voluntary days with your boss and he is willing to acquiesce."

I would have liked to have been the proverbial fly on the wall for *that* conversation. Ethan Betts had never, to my knowledge, done any serious acquiescing in his life!

Partechi cut the connection with a solemn, "Thank you and goodbye."

Arlo was contemplating the rainbow effects of his holo hand and wafting calculations around in the air. He smiled at me, looking for a moment very like his sister, who was actually scowling at him.

"How do you know that particular tremenyas?"

Arlo paused, and the complicated figures began to blink and fade. He looked puzzled. "Partechi taught me physics when I was being 'educated'." He went back to the floating calculations which sprang back into full colour and began to move around again.

There was a sudden loud ringing and we all jumped except Arlo, who looked delighted. "That's my hand, I got it right this time!"

He swung out of the door in the direction of the hub, leaving the three of us staring at the place where he had been. There was a faint outline of the work he had been doing which drifted into a smoky haze and was gone.

Taylor grinned. "This should be interesting."

"I'm not sure that's the way *I* would describe it," I said, really worried.

"Me either!" Loveday spoke with feeling, "Though I don't know which bothers me most, that," she pointed in the direction Arlo had left, "or this," her gaze was towards the empty space where the holo of Partechi had been.

"Why isn't he using a tremenysi transport ship? Unless," I paused.

"What?" Loveday whispered.

"He isn't planning on coming back," I said, real fear making its way into my heart.

"Tay, what did you see out there, that has them so rattled?" Loveday asked him.

He sighed, "I don't know, sometimes when you're looking into deep space, you can get a little crazy."

"Like being in the desert or on the sea, a sort of slightly apprehensive endlessness?" I said, wondering if it felt the same, as I had travelled a lot in both of those places, but not much in space.

"Exactly." Taylor was thinking. He came to some conclusion because he added, "It was just some anomalous readings and, well, a *feeling*." He looked down at his feet and then back at us. "Whatever it is, it's coming our way."

Loveday was horrified. "Oh, that's just wonderful, *very* dramatic!

"And not creepy at *all*!" I added.

"I NEED to eat some real food and get some sleep in my own bed," I announced after several hours of sending out quotes and taking details.

"Me too," Loveday yawned.

Taylor had left to go and find Arlo, which hopefully meant we might have a few more answers, thought it really felt as if it would just end in more questions. We had food delivered to the office and worked through whatever lunchtime was usually designated. I didn't mind, it kept me from thinking about whatever it was I didn't know, which seemed to be everything.

My boss holo-called me, whinging about several pretend problems. He seemed worried and puzzled and I couldn't enlighten him. He ended the call on a more serious note by saying, "please be careful." It was oddly endearing. Though he added, "I don't have the time or the inclination to train up anyone else." Which wasn't.

I locked up as Loveday was falling asleep in her cold coffee and I pushed her out of the door and into Taylor's waiting hug. They wandered down the road, heading for a meal, which I had no doubt she would sleep through too. Their house was on the edge of the town and was one of the older properties, it had managed to survive the changes and the subsequent biodegrading removal of the many empty unwanted buildings, using microbes that had been developed by an 'educated' scientist. My father, when he passed by, had always admired the sympathetic upgrades.

I took a shuttle car back to my home and sighed with relief as I closed the door and took off my shoes. The bath was filling while I made an herbal tea from the mix my grandmother Elowen had given me for just this occasion. It smelt of warmth and flowers, I didn't ask what was in it.

The sun had set on the fields and I lit the fire for comfort, not because it was cold. All the fears I had avoided during the day flooded back into my head. I went into the kitchen and found a bowl of vegetable and cheese bake in my fridge. My mum regularly came by and restocked it, for which I was forever grateful. I heated it and went back to the fire, ignoring the kitchen table.

Food is a great leveller; you can be brave when you're full of home-made cooking, particularly when it's prepared with love.

I fell asleep looking out at the moor in the moonlight, curled up in my bed. I dreamt of the cold distance of space and a whirl of stars. Something was chasing me and no matter what I did, I couldn't get away. Every time I looked behind me I couldn't see anything; I just knew it was there.

THURSDAY

I woke in the pale dawn, feeling as if I was being watched.

The window had been turned to both ways, and as I rolled over in fear a small curious sheep, its face pressed against the glass wall, jumped back in alarm. I nearly fell out of bed. My heart thumping, I untangled myself from the downie and sat up.

We looked at each other for a moment and then it wandered off to find something more interesting to observe. Sheep seem to do that a lot, and when it comes to people watching they are clearly very good at it.

I did the usual bathroom stuff and wandered into the kitchen to drink water and make breakfast. The holo rang and I sighed. It was Thursday, my fourth voluntary day. It was supposed to make you recon-nect with 'real' life outside the business of government, and I felt as if the world had changed and reality along with it.

It was my boss. "How are things going?" He was eating breakfast with his children; the two boys were at that stage where they inhaled food and you could actually see them growing. I waved, they hardly paused but I got smiley faces decorated with what looked like oats, fruit and yoghurt. Ethan picked a piece of blueberry out of the youngest one's hair.

"What's on the agenda at the removals firm today?" He looked straight at me. The holo heads of his children were framing his in a picture of domesticity and contentment.

I heard his partner saying, "Stop bothering Rosalee and get off to work yourself."

For some reason that I didn't understand I just smiled and muttered my agreement with her comment. It was the look on his face, or rather the complete lack of it. I have been taught to read micro-expressions and I was sure I detected a flash of emotion that might have been apprehension. I waved again and cut the connection.

I was pondering the sense of something else not right when the door chimed, I tapped the security screen in the kitchen. Loveday was standing there and her face was turned away checking the shuttle, now empty, going down the drive. My heart plummeted, as if a roller-coaster had been surgically implanted around it.

I opened up the old-fashioned way, by turning the handle, and stood there waiting.

"We got another holo call." She walked through the door and shut it firmly behind her. "Or actually Arlo did and he woke me up at three this morning."

"I'll make coffee," I said, because I really didn't want to hear what came next.

"I DON'T UNDERSTAND."

"Partechi said you have the *means* to get to a secure location for an illicit, unregistered, space to surface shuttle, take-off." Loveday was watching me carefully.

"I'm still not sure—"

"You've got a vehicle your dad restored that's illegal and therefore not connected to the information grid!"

Her impatience was getting the better of her and if I had been woken at three in the morning by Arlo, I would probably be in the same head state. She looked, however, as fresh as a spring flower. Her clothes were designer, naturally sourced and clearly bespoke, the matching handbag probably cost more than my first apartment.

I sighed. "It's this way."

"*Finally!*" Loveday spluttered coffee and wiped the spots from the table with a sleeve. She saw my expression and grinned. "It's nanofibre material."

In one of the out buildings, I swept the cover from the vehicle in a 'ta, da' move and waited for her approval.

Loveday was more stunned than impressed. "Your dad did this?" She looked in through the window of the ancient car. "How does it work?"

"Well, it's sort of a fuel-based engine, dad converted it."

"Isn't that dangerous?" Loveday opened the door and sat inside; she puzzled over the steering wheel.

I made the universal gesture of 'maybe' with my hand, and shrugged to underline the response.

"Does your mum know about this?"

I tried to look innocent. If my mum had known she would have been horrified and forbidden any further interaction with it. As she didn't, my dad had taught me to drive it when I was eight and tall enough to reach the pedals.

"I take it you know how to make it go?" Loveday was sceptical. I nodded. She snorted. "Your dad needs therapy!"

My mum would have agreed with her and to be fair I did too. He'd dragged it up off the bottom of the sea after a day out fishing, spent a fortune on the restoration, which took years, and if he'd been found driving it around the outer edges of the farm, there was the distinct probability of a hefty fine, never mind the possible reprogramming. However, it was just something that brought back good memories and when he had asked me to 'take care' of it, I'd agreed.

"How does Partechi know this is here?"

"Arlo told him," Loveday said, which didn't really answer the question.

I went back into the house and grabbed my travel bag, adding a few essentials, as in chocolate bars and the calming tea my grandmother had given me. For some reason I thought I was going to need both.

Loveday was sitting in the car on the driver's side, consulting a large paper map.

"Where on the planet did you get *that*?" I had never seen one before, it looked old enough to be from the museum and probably inaccurate for the current times.

"Raji." Loveday was struggling with the thing, it seemed to have a life of its own.

"Why am I not surprised that she's involved," I muttered.

Getting hold of the map I straightened it out and folded it carefully, with the larger part of the moor displayed in the middle.

"Hey!" Loveday complained, "It's not fair, your arms are longer."

I waved her over to the passenger seat. She was puzzled at first, but shuffled across, negotiating the gear stick with care.

"Where are we heading?" I asked.

Loveday consulted some slightly smudged figures written on the palm of her hand in what looked to be non-permanent eye makeup, and then scrutinised the map. "Here," she said eventually.

I looked, 'here' seemed to be nowhere in particular, but I shrugged and using an actual key started the engine. It chugged into life immediately, my dad always did a weekly maintenance check, or at least that's what *he* called it. More of a jolly around the tiny farm roads, completely ignored by Mark *and* the sheep. I sighed, thinking it was probably the worst kept secret in the south-west and I was really beginning to have my doubts about my mum *not* knowing.

Loveday had her hands over her ears. Wincing, she shouted, "Is it going to do that all the time?"

I KEPT to the edge of the farm and used the well-worn trails that farmers had made with horses and tractors over the many hundreds of years. The sheep watched with studied disinterest, which made me wonder how often my dad was racing around the old ways in the vehicle. It handled the bumps and ruts with great dignity.

Loveday was less than impressed and gripped the seat with white fingers, though she'd stopped shrieking every time I changed gear. I snorted with suppressed laughter as the wheels left the ground on a rather more defined ridge.

"You're enjoying this a little too much," she said, accusingly.

"So are you!" I could see her slight grin, and thought Taylor was going to have to find room for their own illicit vehicle. I wondered if my dad could find another one.

The spot on the map was a part of the moor down in one of the valleys. The car had a feature that locked the wheels forward and I slowed down, feeling the tyres grip in the mud. I could see a small space to surface craft close by the river, its stubby vertical take-off wings in the landed position. Taylor was doing a pre-take off visual inspection on the outside of the vessel and he looked up as we arrived.

I got out having 'parked' and did some checks of my own. Hand-brake on, engine off.

Loveday looked at me. "What are you doing?"

"It doesn't turn itself off and the wheels aren't automatically secured."

She seemed slightly horrified and then intrigued. Taylor opened the door for her and said, with indulgent exasperation, "*No*, we can't have a highly illegal, very expensive, polluting, antique car!" I studied his face carefully and then made a mental note to ask my dad.

They hugged. It was the desperate kind and my own apprehension found a new level. Arlo stuck his head out of the door of the craft, spoiling the moment. His tousled hair was several shades of crispy and seemed to be smoking at the ends.

"What have you done *now*?" Loveday broke away from the embrace and stomped over to her brother, smacking his head in several places. He cringed. "Keep still, you're on fire!" Even I thought she was a little too enthusiastic about putting it out.

"I'm just singed, stop it!" He gave her a brotherly hug and then a shove. She turned and glared accusingly at Taylor.

"Don't look at me, I don't have any control over him!" Taylor went back to finishing his space to surface vehicle checks. He spoke quietly to me, "we leave in ten, GMT."

I suddenly realised Loveday wasn't coming with us.

THE LITTLE CRAFT was smooth in the vertical ascent as it left the ground behind. Taylor sat in the pilot seat, his careful hands tapping computer keys as he watched the holo readouts and didn't look out of the front view. Arlo was sitting next to him. The console was open, and a disconcerting amount of internal bio-gel wiring was spilling out into his lap. I was sure the biological component of the system was pulsing in complaint, and though I only had a passing knowledge of how it worked, I was also sure there was a manual somewhere that advised in the strongest language possible, *not* to do what he was doing. He muttered continuously to himself with the occasional glance at Taylor, but also avoided the window.

I watched Loveday standing by the car, looking up. I had given her a hug. "Take care of them?" She was calm and smiled at me. "Apparently I need to stay here and cover for you." Her expression was the best hidden emotion I'd ever seen.

"You'll have to drive *it* back to the house," I said, pointing, with my own smile fixed in place.

"Sure," she shrugged, "how difficult could it be?"

We began to laugh and Taylor leaned out of the craft, he didn't say anything but their look was a lifetime of love and understanding. I walked over and in through the doorway and it hissed closed behind me.

The seat was cradling me into a slightly tipped back position and the horizon came up, then the blue and the black, and we slipped sideways. I am not usually space sick, but I was this time, spectacularly.

"Sorry, sorry!" Arlo apologised to me, "I haven't perfected it yet.

"You might have told me," I said weakly.

"Would it have made a difference?" he asked me curiously.

"No," I said.

"Well then!" He snapped, crossly.

"There's a bio vac in the unit to your left." Taylor spoke, he sounded sad and worried. I cleaned myself and my clothes, then used it on the floor beside my seat. Taylor tapped a key and the cabin flushed with fresh air which was a great improvement. He shook his head, like a cat caught in a rainstorm, and using the seat controls he swivelled round. "Agh! That doesn't get any better."

"Good to know." I took one of the lemon flavoured sweets he offered me.

The freighter was parked in orbit away from any of the usual designated areas at north pole station and 'dark' no lights, no pinging, I wondered how long it would go unnoticed. We docked inside the main storage area of the ship, using the computer, though I had no doubt that Taylor could have done it manually with just as much skill. Arlo was still messing with his mess and didn't notice or care.

Taylor tapped a few keys and the outer doors closed on the view of the blue planet. I felt the panic rising and as we moved out of the small craft I noticed a decided lessening of gravity, which was a bit disconcerting. Taylor saw me gripping a hand rail. "I can't light up the internal systems until we're ready to go, we'd appear on someone's screen down there like a Christmas tree."

I nodded, something sad inside me growing into a sigh and the loss and longing for home.

Arlo was rubbing his hands together, looking excited. We were on the bridge of the freighter which was comfortable, but compact, with lots of useful areas for different roles and several seats with a spectacular view of the stars.

"What now?" I asked.

"I do a larger and more impressive version of what I did to the space to surface vehicle!" He began pulling at the control units and grabbing gel wiring.

Taylor looked at the burgeoning disaster area and said quietly, "The things we do for love."

WE SIDESLIPPED AGAIN. Arlo warned me and I gripped the seat and closed my eyes, it didn't make any difference, in fact I think it was worse. I held onto my dignity though.

"See," Arlo said, "much better!"

I wondered briefly how this faster than lightspeed travel was going to affect the human circadian rhythm which was welded into our DNA, and why we had plus or minus GMT all over the solar system.

I heard Taylor muttering, but he shook his head a few times, and got on with the docking manoeuvre. None of the freighter pilots I had ever met liked doing this so close to Venus, which has a retrograde rotation that takes longer than the planet's trip around the sun. It does really odd things to the computer readings on most ships, and the current state of the systems due to Arlo's input was making everything more difficult. I stayed strapped in my seat and thought about the sound of the wind in the trees, the smell of spring rain on grass and the curiosity of sheep and cows. I was just getting to the joy of the Exmoor ponies coming up to the gate for a possible morning treat if they saw me, when Taylor swore.

"Arlo, did you touch the stabilisers?" His face had a slightly greasy sheen and his hands moved over the holo console trying to balance the now slippery freighter. Flashing lights were followed by a siren.

"Yes, of *course* I did, otherwise I can't set the new system up!"

"Well, *I* can't dock this ship without them, so if you could let me have control back right now, that would be good!" Taylor was gritting his teeth.

Arlo looked out of the front view. I followed his gaze, a tremenysi habitat ship was getting very large. "Oh, dear!" He went over to the mess on the floor and fiddled with several bio-gel wires, talking to himself. "This one I think... no, maybe this one—"

"*Arlo!*" Taylor and I shouted at the same time.

"That's it!" Arlo looked pleased.

Taylor did some spectacularly fast adjustments and manually docked, with about three seconds to spare.

There was quiet for quite a while. Arlo because he was admiring his handiwork, and Taylor and I because we were incapable of speech.

THE AIRLOCK HISSED. It's a noise I have never been able to get used to, because it means that somewhere close by, there is no air *to* hiss. I stood a little shakily, as the after effects of the sideslip and the adrenalin rush of the docking were still very recent. Taylor seemed calm for a man who had just saved us all from impacting with the other ship and probably Venus. Arlo was excited to see his 'old friends.' I didn't have enough time to process the word but that's what he had said, plural not singular. The now securely connected hull doors opened.

Three figures appeared out of the gloom, one very, very tall and thin, one slim and short and one round and furry.

Taylor swore again.

BoBo's puffed-up fur made him look even larger, and he was huge to start with. His back arched and a close-mouthed whine developed into an ominous-sounding growl.

I knew it was the infamous creature, because Ms Winwright said, "Stop that this *instant* BoBo, the lovely Taylor is only here to help!"

The person referred to was looking stunned. I couldn't blame him, for my part I was feeling slightly hysterical. Arlo had no qualms however and threw himself at Partechi, hugging him around the middle as he couldn't reach any higher.

I sighed and stepped in between Taylor and BoBo before the fur flew. Taylor's, not BoBo's.

"Were you tracked?" Partechi asked Arlo, who still had his arms around his friend.

"No!" Arlo's reply was muffled by the returned embrace, but adamant.

Taylor spoke far too calmly, something my dad did when he'd reached boiling point, "I don't think we have long before we start looking interesting on the deep space network, so if we could get on with the why we're here and what's happening next, I for one would be grateful."

BoBo stalked past him and Ms Winwright followed, carrying a small bag. Partechi disentangled himself from Arlo and we drifted back onto the bridge area. Partechi gave Taylor some details which he tapped into the computer and the freighter bots began moving storage boxes into the hold. I watched for a while but I don't like them, they look too much like spiders, lots of arms and legs and a bit creepy when they climb the walls and floor. I'd had a moment several years ago when one had surprised me while I was sitting in a small space to surface vehicle it was loading. When I jumped nervously, the bot *scuttled* away. I still shudder at the memory.

It was done in minutes. I saw Partechi give one last glance towards his home. It's never easy to interpret the expressions of the travellers, their faces are smooth, no eyebrows or head hair and the dark eyes with no sclera can be disconcerting. But I have worked with them all my adult life and I know longing and sadness when I see it. I felt the wash of fear and he turned to me as if I had spoken. I don't know why people think they look scary; I could discern nothing but kindness, intelligence and understanding.

Arlo was fussing with the innards of the ship's systems and Taylor was gritting his teeth, again.

"Please tell me you helped him with this?" I asked Partechi.

"We cannot break the rules." He smiled happily, the gappy open mouth grin making his face seem more human, something I think they had developed to connect with us early on.

I was suddenly worried. Arlo snorted. BoBo was curled up in Taylor's seat, exuding a challenge with his narrow-eyed tabby face. He washed a strategic paw with stunningly long claws fully extended. "What rules?" I muttered.

"We cannot interfere," Partechi explained. Taylor rolled his eyes.

"What do you mean, did Arlo do this on his *own*?" I was horrified. Arlo glanced up at me from the tangle of gel wires and looked hurt.

"I am reasonably satisfied with his calculations." I was going to interrupt but he continued, "If, however, you see me exiting through the nearest airlock at speed, then follow!" A sound like stepping on crunchy, dry autumn leaves came out of his mouth, I realised he was laughing. Arlo smiled in appreciation and it was as if they had a moment more like family than friendship.

"This *is* faster than light travel we are talking about?" Taylor was keeping an eye on the cat while trying not to trip over the mess on the floor and running the systems checks. I felt *really* sorry for him.

"Well of course it is, young man!" Ms Winwright was sharp, she was sitting in the seat next to BoBo and her hand rested on the glossy fur of his curved body as if for comfort. "We can't be all day," she finished with a snap.

"Myrtle," Arlo said, gently chiding her, without looking up from what he was doing. I was surprised at his tone; it was as if teacher and pupil had changed places somewhere along the journey of their relationship.

"Sorry," she sighed.

I was beginning to have an inkling of the cost some of us were going to pay for this, whatever *this* was. My fear began to spark thoughts and connections. Which is what I do because it helps with the stuff that makes for poor decision making.

"Ms Winwright," I asked, trying for careful words, "the reason that you have been moving around the solar system every three months or thereabouts, I assume has something to do with whatever's coming our way?"

I paused to listen to the answer. She just nodded and her hand gripped BoBo's fur so tightly that he stopped washing. "Sorry, old friend," she said quietly and stroked his head. "I was one of many, trying to find out just how much infiltration there was among the different settlements."

Taylor suddenly looked up from what he was doing. "And exactly how much *was* that, Myrtle?"

"More than we'd like," she said sadly. "People will agree for different reasons, but it was mostly greed and ignorance." Her sad expression turned to one of anger.

A dawning awareness and the memory of the last conversation I'd had with my boss came to my mind. I swallowed and tried not to let the tears fall on my tired face, wondering who exactly knew what. Taylor was standing completely still, and for a moment, his face betrayed a rolling screen of conflicting emotions, then he went back to the ship's systems checks. I glanced at Arlo who was enjoying the challenge of making impossible calculations into actual reality, and over to Partechi whose imperceptible shake of his head I almost missed.

The ship was finally ready and no one spoke, all I could hear was the steady purr of BoBo above the hum of the life support. Both were oddly reassuring.

As Taylor input the destination co-ordinates Partechi gave him, I saw the traveller reach out and pat Myrtle gently on the shoulder. They made a strange pair, but it felt as if that's what they were; I realised there was a possibility I was going to have to rethink my physiological assessment on the compatibility of our species.

Partechi adjusted his space suit to enable him to fit into the much too small seat more comfortably. I usually saw the travellers dressed in similar clothes to the ones we wore, just much, much larger. His long legs stuck out into inconvenient areas. He held a hand out to Myrtle and she took it.

Light takes approximately eight point three minutes to travel from the sun to the Earth, the distance of which is defined as one astronomical unit, it's about fifty AUs to the outer edge of the Kuiper Belt and would normally be more than a four-hour trip. We couldn't do that because everyone and his auntie would know where and who we were. I understood with my brain that we were probably heading for Orchus and its solitary moon Vanth at faster than light speed, it's just my body couldn't catch up. I gripped my seat and held my breath. Arlo whooped, Taylor tapped two holo-keys and we sideslipped, again.

Yep, still awful.

BOBO WAS HOWLING, at least I hoped it was him and not me. I waited for 'upright' to become available. I was really pleased when I opened my eyes and wasn't *actually* sick this time. Arlo was out of his seat, checking the rigged bio-gel wiring. Taylor had the 'close to' manoeuvres to deal with, and we were *very* close to Vanth. A small deep space living unit was orbiting in synchronisation with Orchus and the moon. I watched as Taylor did some magic with the docking procedures. We were attached and moving in harmony before I got my balance back.

"Well, that was excellent!" Myrtle Winright was being jolly, as if we had just arrived for a holiday in Mars main dome, instead of the edge of the solar system, using a conjectural, superluminal method of travel that contradicted the special theory of relativity, and had only previously been tested on the disappearing hand of a genius. I for one, was tired of the pretence, *and* the uncertainty.

"Arlo, how did we actually *do* faster than light?" I spoke to his back; he was looking at something through the bridge front view. I knew the 'window' was made of the same material as the rest of the hull, but it always made me nervous that you could see through it. For some reason it now appeared to be blurry. I wondered for a horrified moment, if it had been damaged in the sideslip.

"I made a traversable wormhole," he said, without turning around. No boasting, no excitement.

I followed the line of his gaze and realised the distorted effect through the bridge view was moving.

"What does that look like to you?" Myrtle asked me quietly.

"Chaos," I shivered, "it looks as if someone is boiling the stars.

Taylor had joined us. Partechi, who was standing the other side of Arlo, nodded his agreement.

There was a suitable silence, and it lasted a long time for four people and a cat who, it seemed to me, were somewhat running out of it, time I mean.

I turned to the tremenyas. "Why are we out here?"

"When they scan, they will see me," he said simply.

"Will that help?" Taylor asked.

"It is possible," Partechi was irritatingly enigmatic.

Taylor was incredulous, "is that *all* you've got—"

"Don't do that Par it's not useful!" Myrtle interrupted him, she turned to look at Taylor and me.

Arlo was working on setting up another sideslip, and he didn't seem to be the slightest bit interested in what she had to say, suggesting that he had already heard it before.

"We, um, now share some things in common with the travellers, most of us have cross species genetics." Myrtle saw the expression on my face, messing with our DNA is a highly regulated concern. She added, "It should keep them away."

"But, will it *work*?" I sounded desperate even to my own ears.

"Probably," Partechi said, "they don't like us, we can't be consumed."

"*Par!*" Myrtle shouted. Arlo snorted with what felt like, under the circumstances, inappropriate laughter.

Taylor's face was a mixture of incredulity and apprehension. But he got on with programming the bots to move boxes. I could see the habitat's inside on the holo screens, it looked spacious and ergonomically pleasing, as if my dad had designed it. I paused for a moment and peered closer.

Partechi disrupted my train of thought, "we are ninety five percent bacteria cells and twenty percent virus genes, you are fifty six percent and eight." I looked at him, then back out of the bridge view. "They find us too contaminated," he added helpfully.

"So," Taylor muttered from the seat by the holo screen, "racist microbes."

Myrtle smiled, as if pleased by a difficult pupil. "*Exactly!*"

I looked at the cloud coming towards us and then back at Partechi and Myrtle. "*That's* what you're banking on, *them* finding us *indigestible!*"

Taylor shook his head, incredulous. He glanced at me, I shrugged.

"There are others like us," Myrtle said, sadly. "Spread around the outer edge of the Kuiper Belt."

"How did you get everyone out here?" Taylor asked, a second before I did.

"We've been working on this for some time," Myrtle clarified. "We used the cover of potential mining operations mostly."

I gasped, "my boss?" She nodded. I slipped into one of the seats and leaned forward, trying to relieve the nausea that swamped me. The relief was a cool hand on my neck and Myrtle shushing me like a child with colic.

"You've gone a funny colour," Arlo said, looking at me when I finally sat upright.

"Grey, you mean? I always feel somewhat colourless around you lot, Loveday is practically a bird of paradise!"

Arlo was puzzled, "Loveday is a deep sea-green, and you're usually mauve, but you look a little splodgy at the moment." He went back to his tangle of wiring.

"Is that an aura thing?" I asked him.

He looked horrified as only a scientist could. Myrtle answered, as I had managed to render him speechless. "No, it's a synaesthesia thing," she explained. "Quite a few of the 'educated' have it. Mine is sound and mathematics, I literally hear numbers."

For the umpteenth time in my life, I felt cheated. My senses could have done with an upgrade or two.

"Mauve?" I said to Arlo. He grinned at me and nodded, not fully making a connection with my question as he was focused on his calculations. Something about being a colour was comforting.

Partechi was in the habitat pointing out to the bots the places he wanted his things to be put, he tapped out instructions on a handheld device and compacted the empty boxes to go back into the hold of the freighter. It was finished fairly quickly. The old books he liked and his collections of shells were spread around as if he had been here for some time. I was puzzled. He looked over to me, once again it was as if I had spoken. "It needs to appear well established. They are not stupid, just very focused."

I nodded my understanding and tried not to glance out of the view port at 'they.'

Myrtle was stroking BoBo in his chair. I studied the expression on her face and realised what was making her feel that way, the cat sensed something too and had his head tucked under his paws as if trying to put off the inevitable pain. I felt like joining him.

Taylor looked apprehensive as only a man can when the room is full of incomprehensible emotions swamping him. He glanced from one person to another trying not to be pulled in. Arlo was seemingly oblivious.

IT WAS TIME TO GO. I had for a moment thought I would be staying, that we all would. I felt a complete coward to be leaving, with that awful emotional paradox of relief, closely followed by guilt.

Arlo explained how the sideslip would work to a patient Taylor. "Just press this set of holo-keys, I've set it up—"

"Small one," Partechi interrupted him. Arlo stopped and looked up at him. And I thought my heart would break.

"No!" Arlo shouted, like a child who wants to come along on the greatest adventure and is denied. I was really glad for a moment that Loveday wasn't with us.

"You have so much more to do," the traveller said simply.

Taylor had turned away and was studying the holo console as if the most important message was in front of his eyes instead of the 'ready for instruction' screen.

Myrtle tapped him on the shoulder and pointed to BoBo sitting in the seat so tightly curled you could see neither head nor tail. Taylor nodded and she patted his face, as if memorising his features with her fingers for future reference. I think *that* was the point my heart *actually* broke.

Partechi and Myrtle hugged me briefly and walked into the habitat. Arlo was still arguing, I shushed him because their faces were so full of pain.

"I don't understand, why can't I stay? He looked at Taylor and me for an answer as the door closed on the two, one very, very tall and thin, the other small and slim, holding hands.

We moved carefully away from the unit, Taylor set up the previous coordinates for the orbit around Venus and I sat down in the chair next to BoBo. Putting out a tentative hand I stroked the rich tabby fur. He was silent and still. I'm not an empath but I had been trained to develop my empathetic abilities and I could feel the loss radiating from him in waves.

Arlo was still pacing with frustrated puzzlement. Taylor pointed to a seat; his expression stony. Arlo sat. His own stunned comprehension clicked in just as we sideslipped.

No one spoke. I released my grip on the cat, who had not moved.

"Did you know?" Arlo asked me, his voice scrapy with unshed tears.

"Not until Partechi said that the travellers couldn't be 'consumed'," I whispered.

"But *surely* that means they will be safe?" Arlo was hopeful.

Taylor said, "They will all have to be *tasted* to find out what the tremenysi have done." His head was down and he spoke to the floor.

BoBo howled.

I DON'T KNOW how we got home. Well, I know we travelled by sideslip to a dark area of the freighter long stay section in north pole station, where we disembarked with the space to surface vehicle Taylor had put in the hold, still not pinging any lights or identification. If he got caught, they would not only revoke his licence but he would serve time in a reprogramming facility.

We landed in the same place on the moor, three hours GMT later than we had departed. It was disorientating and unsettlingly too short a time. Loveday leaned on the car, like a long-ago speed racer, completely at home with her polluting illegal engine. The sun was high in the clear early spring sky, streaky clouds filled the blue and I could hear the moor ponies moving quietly through the scrubby trees, looking for somewhere familiar to find the best grass.

Arlo hadn't spoken or even glanced up during our docking and transfer to the vehicle. I clutched BoBo in my arms for the walk across the cargo deck, no mean feat as he was heavy. He just curled against me and buried his head in my shoulder. When I tried to put him on his own seat for the trip to the surface, he dug in the very long claws and I quicky relented. We stayed cuddled together for the journey. I didn't mind, it was furry comfort.

Loveday looked at our faces. "What happened?" she whispered.

Taylor gave a brief explanation, "Bigoted microbes are trying to take over the solar system, astonishingly brave travellers and people, who have both illegally changed their DNA, are dotted around the Kuiper belt, trying to stop them."

I couldn't fault the accuracy but I thought the brevity was a little challenging. From the expression on Loveday's face however, Taylor's method of imparting information was nothing new to her. She got it. She reached out, and he folded himself down into her hug. It lasted far longer than a moment of greeting, more a reciprocal solace.

Arlo just stood to one side, alone in every sense and comfortless. My hand reached out to his, which wasn't easy, and I think my face must have been red with effort as I balanced BoBo on one hip. Arlo eventually noticed me and then, much to the surprise of both of us, he took the offering. I squeezed his fingers for a second, then let go, recognising his uneasiness with emotional gestures that he didn't control.

We crowded into the car. Loveday drove, or performed a somewhat distant interpretation of the word. I was going to have to speak to my dad about second gear, which I think we left on the moor.

I waited until they were all in the house and sitting in various states of shocked silence before I put BoBo down slowly and gently on the end of my bed. He curled up into a tight ball and hid his furry face. Hurt and loss buried within every curve of his sinewy body.

My travel bag was back by the door, not having been opened on the brief journey. I took out the calming brew my grandmother Elowen had given me and going into the kitchen, I poured boiling water over the fragrant leaves in a large teapot. Cups and chocolate biscuits went onto a tray.

The living area was silent; I put the tray down and waited the requisite three minutes for it to infuse as instructed. Handing the cups around, my hands weren't the only ones shaking.

"What now?" Loveday asked.

"I don't know," Taylor said eventually, then he looked at me.

"I'm still trying to catch up on who knew. My boss for sure. Arlo?"

He sighed, and put his empty cup down, which was impressive, as I thought it was still too hot to drink. Rubbing the newly reattached hand, he just shook his head.

I watched for a moment then spoke, "Let me tell you what I think; there must have been awareness of 'their' existence since the travellers first arrived, your great-grandmother, and mine too, were of the first original group who would have been asked to keep a watch on the people who had, er, potential for causing trouble. Anyone who had been part of the 'educated' programme would have been told of the situation and *all of them* recruited into saving the solar system using different particular skills." I stopped and sniffed theatrically, "Clearly not *everyone* was told *everything*."

Arlo looked so sad that I added, "I would think that compartmentalising was a strategy to keep the information and those involved safe." He nodded and sighed, a sound that had his sister looking at him with concern.

"I don't wish to sound self-absorbed; I understand Loveday and Taylor." I paused, and tried to explain myself, "But do you have any idea why they wanted me there?"

Arlo seemed frustrated. He said, "You just demonstrated *it*. You can put things together other people can't work out, into words for them to understand." Loveday nodded her agreement and Arlo added incongruously, "*And* you're mauve around the edges." He poured himself another cup of scalding tea and drank it. I checked to see if it made his eyes water; it didn't.

"Mauve?" Loveday asked me.

"Apparently, you're a deep sea-green," I said. She seemed oddly pleased.

Taylor interrupted the possibility of wandering down the la-la lane of Arlo's synaesthesia. "Are we going to sit here and do *nothing*?" He was quiet but angry.

We all looked at him. "Rosalee, do *you* think what they are doing will work?" he asked.

They turned to look at me. I thought about it for more than a few minutes while they waited. I stood up and went to the window, counting sheep in the fields while I processed the information, the variables and the numbers. All the conversations I'd had ran through my mind, my grandmother Elowen, the many interactions with the travellers over the years. Even the last visit to the meeting on Demos with my boss. It all added up to a picture in my head. One that seemed to centre on the few numbers of people in the Kuiper belt. Eventually I sat down.

"No," I said. "It won't."

There was a stunned silence. "Care to explain?" Arlo was sarcastic *and* frightened, an interesting combination.

"As I understand from the little information I've been told, and what I saw, the entity, and let's start calling it that, 'they' gives them too much power, and 'it' just sounds like an implausible story: the entity consists of an intelligent life form, possibly a heterotroph, from the look of it."

Loveday held up a hand, I went on, "It means an organism that cannot produce its own food, it gets it's nutrition from other forms of organic carbon, as opposed to an autotroph, such as a plant or algae." I stopped, Arlo was looking insultingly impressed and Loveday was horrified.

"*I'm* the other organic carbon life form?" she asked me.

"What can we do?" Taylor was, as ever, the practical one.

I thought again, and they waited while I did. "Arlo, how many scientists can you get in touch with immediately?"

He grinned. "*All* of them!"

"How—" I interrupted myself, "never mind, I might ask you by what means that is possible after this, if there is an 'after this.' Tell them we need to get out there, why we do and give them the sideslip calculations—"

"*Sideslip?*" It was his turn to interject.

"It's the way I feel when it happens," I explained.

"I like it." He nodded his approval. "We'll go with that."

"Taylor, what about the freighter and transport pilots? We've got to get there."

"Pretty much the same, we have a dark web connection that's piggybacked on the deep space network, we use it for, er, off the books information."

I raised my eyes to the ceiling. "I work for the government and at some point, I'm going to wish I didn't know that!"

He shrugged and began opening up his computer and tapping holo-keys, as did Arlo.

"I can contact just about everyone who had moved home or business in the last sixty years," Loveday said helpfully.

"Don't tell me, you've also got a highly prohibited link used for illicit housing stuff?" I said, with shaky irony.

Loveday looked insulted. "Don't be silly, we're a removal and storage firm, we just keep good records!" She added quietly, "And I use Tay's web connection if I need to."

I sighed. "I'll speak to my boss and ask for an emergency internal memo to go out to all staff."

"How long have we got, Arlo?" Taylor asked him.

"Six hours GMT at the most." Arlo was concentrating on his screen, so he didn't see his sister shudder.

"Can I ask," Loveday said, "the people who didn't want this to go ahead, the ones who made a deal, can they stop us?"

"They could," I continued, "but probably not without exposing themselves."

"So, it doesn't matter?" she tried for clarification.

"Not now, if the entity hasn't been picked up on the deep space network yet, it will be soon."

"All the secrets are out," Taylor said, not looking up from his holo screen. His face was grim, "Well, most of them anyway," he muttered, and I thought I wouldn't want to be someone he found out had been making a pact with whatever was coming our way.

Loveday nodded, all three of them were working on gathering the information and distributing it to the necessary people. "You know, my great-grandmother told me, before the pandemic, people had social media, you could literally find out anything about anyone, and it was how they disseminated this sort of stuff."

"I thought that was a myth?" I was puzzled, "how did they get past the privacy laws?"

"There weren't any," Taylor interjected.

It took me no more than a few minutes to contact my boss and about three for him to send the words, 'It's done,' back to me. Followed by, 'I'm on my way.'

I answered that one immediately, with just, 'Please don't, you have children!'

He replied, 'It's *because* I have, that I need to do this.'

We gathered, in the outer ring of the Kuiper belt, the few vessels of the space rangers and marines, and millions of little ships. From every planet and moon, space station and asteroid. I could see the blinking lights on the holo screen and was surprised to see that several of the tremenysi exploration craft had joined us too.

Our freighter, piloted by Taylor, arrived back at the deep space living unit two hours after we had departed, which left me and just about everyone else with an uncomfortable time problem as well as breaking the laws of physics; literally, criminally and scientifically. Someone was going to be in trouble, actually several someone's.

"So," Loveday said to me after a pause when we all looked at each other, "how do you feel your voluntary days have gone?"

"I'm sure I'm about to achieve the absolute pinnacle of 'staying in touch with real world issues'." I tried not to let my voice shake. Through the front view of the bridge the oily cloud of the entity seemed to be really close.

The door to the unit opened and an absolutely furious Myrtle hurtled through, followed by an equally disgruntled Partechi.

"What were you *thinking?*" she shrieked.

At that moment a furry tabby missile flew out of a seat and hurled himself at her, if Partechi hadn't been standing behind her she would have landed on her back. I think I wasn't the only one who was disappointed that it didn't happen.

"Oh no, not BoBo too!" She was distraught.

"I couldn't leave him behind," I said. Her face turned to fury. "No, I mean it, he wouldn't let me, and as I'm sure you know, he can be very persuasive!"

Taylor held up his bandaged arm and I rolled up my trouser leg to let her see my own scars. Myrtle looked at Loveday.

"No chance!" She snorted, "He can travel *exactly* where he wants as far as I'm concerned."

The furry monster looked satisfied with his actions to date. Myrtle was scolding him for his behaviour but she did it while holding on too tight and her tears fell on his twitching fur.

Partechi sighed, "This is your blessing and your curse, it is why they find you interesting," he added quietly, "much as we do." The wording felt slightly sinister considering the circumstances, no one wants to be *that* attractive.

I asked Partechi, "Why are there other travellers here, I thought you weren't supposed to interfere in our problems?"

"I think that ship has sailed," Myrtle said grimly and with no sign of irony.

"This is about species extinction," Partechi added.

"Yours or ours?" I asked with a prescience I didn't feel was probably relevant.

"We have decided to take a stand," the traveller said quietly.

"Is that going to be allowed?" Loveday spoke, her voice shaking.

"We're about to find out," Partechi shrugged, sounding more like my dad than I would have thought possible.

I had a sudden realisation that I hadn't spoken to them, just left a message telling them not to worry, which was a ridiculous thing to say, as they would know exactly what was going on. Because somewhere out there was my grandmother Elowen, with my great-grandmother Auryn. And from what little I'd heard of the conversation, Loveday's parents were on the same ship. Elestren, her mother, had been adamant despite the combined best efforts of Taylor and Arlo to stop them, which I thought was interesting, as Loveday didn't even try.

"Waste of breath," she'd said when I asked.

Taylor was working hard, the sweat beaded on his face. So many vessels all breaking through into close quarters after the sideslip, caused some unfortunate collisions. But considering they had all had to follow the 'Arlo protocol' of hauling out the innards of their ships systems and jury rigging something based on theoretical physics, things were not too bad.

The coils of the entity were getting closer, they *slithered* towards us, which I'm positive was not really possible in the vacuum of space. For some reason the most curious tentacle was coming straight for the freighter, and we were still attached to the living unit.

Taylor shouted, "Stand away, I'm going to release the connection, just in case—" he didn't finish, but no one wanted him to complete the sentence anyway.

I held my breath, then let it out and my heartbeat was fierce in my chest. Several of the ships were being approached. The entity came faster and faster, until the front view of the bridge was full of a writhing pulsing mass. Little sparks of hopeless light flashed and were brutally extinguished.

Suddenly it was inside the ship, curling around us, circling, threatening, squashing me, pushing at my brain, paralysing my thoughts, then into my mouth, choking me. I saw Taylor with his arms around Loveday trying to shield her, and Partechi holding Myrtle's hand, they both had their eyes closed and were standing together. I screamed with no sound, BoBo howled and Arlo swore.

A ROUGH TONGUE was licking my face. I grumbled and it stopped, then started again. I opened my eyes and wished I hadn't. A huge tabby head with a gaping mouth looked down on me.

"BoBo!" I grabbed the cat and hugged him, for a moment he didn't seem to mind then he growled, reminding me of acceptable boundaries. "Sorry, furry boy," I whispered, "I'm just *so* pleased to see you."

Leaning up on one elbow I looked around, as actual sitting was not possible. My head spun with the worst drowning nightmare I have ever remembered. Colours and flashes of desperate feelings, unknown incomprehensible faces, and pain, flooded back to me, making me gasp.

I watched as one by one my friends were spat out of the receding greasy pulsing cloud, as I had been. They lay around like broken dolls thrown by a giant bad-tempered child. Partechi was first, then Myrtle and Arlo, and lastly and eventually, after a gut-wrenching pause, Loveday and Taylor.

Suddenly the entity was gone. No longer in the ship, in the bridge view, or the space around the Kuiper belt. Nowhere.

It was quiet. I managed to get to my feet, staggering over to the kitchen section I found water bottles and distributed them. BoBo meowed, and I splashed some fluid into a cup and held it out to him. He lapped gratefully while I swallowed the rest. My throat was dry and sore and I felt assaulted. It was awful. Nothing Partechi warned us about would make me understand what had just happened.

Loveday was sitting up. Tayor, amazingly, had made it over to the main holo screen and was calling other ships and vessels for a situation report.

"Why didn't they absorb us?" I asked Partechi, when I could speak. "I'm assuming that was what being 'tasted' feels like."

"I think, as am I, you are most *distasteful* to them now!" Partechi grinned.

"Are you saying we gave them indigestion?" Loveday's voice croaked.

"More like food poisoning!" Myrtle sat up and BoBo rubbed his nose on her face in greeting.

"Ha!" Arlo was still lying down, his voice sounded painful, but gratified, "so, we were 'vomited'?"

"Arlo!" Loveday, Myrtle and I said at the same time, Taylor just snorted without looking away from the endless sitreps coming in.

Arlo got to his feet and wobbled his way over to help Taylor. He sighed when he saw the lights of the other vessels winking away to the various planets and moons. He looked back at me. "They *really* didn't like you."

"Why?" I was puzzled, it seemed to me I had been in that slimy darkness for hours but from the GMT clock on the holo screen it had been less than three minutes.

"I think it was because you're mauve," Arlo said enigmatically, going back to sorting out the ship's innards ready for a sideslip.

"Right, okay," I whispered after a pause, when nothing more was forthcoming. I looked at Loveday, she shrugged, but Partechi and Myrtle were exchanging silent glances full of information, in that irritating way of some couples who have been together for a long time. My mum and dad did a similar routine and it drove me crazy.

I moved to a seat and lowered my stiff and aching body gratefully down. Loveday passed me another bottle of water on her way back from the kitchen area.

"Your DNA profile appears to Arlo as mauve," Myrtle said, with puzzled speculation. I suddenly felt nervous.

"Mine's a deep sea-green," Loveday announced proudly.

"Exactly!" Arlo said, still not looking up from his task.

"Hmm," Partechi muttered, he and Myrtle were both looking at me, much as a scientist would examine the contents of a petri dish after a tricky experiment.

I shrugged it off, as one more question I was going to have to deal with in the early hours of the mornings I hadn't expected to be awake for, ever again.

We left, another winking light in the vast space of the Kuiper belt.

Arlo joked about the fact that the journey back home was 'un*event*ful, *relativity*' speaking, then fell about laughing.

"*Really*, you just had to go there?" Loveday said, with hidden affection.

"I have one about Heisenberg's uncertainty principal?" he offered hopefully, but there were no takers.

We'd had a quiet moment during the sideslip, then the constant barrage of questions and requests began. Taylor put an overview of the situation out on the highly illegal system that he had with his other pilots and added my list, Arlo's scientist one and the contacts Partechi and Myrtle gave him. Loveday insisted he add hers, though I wasn't sure if it was just because she was feeling left out. I speculated about the significance of an emergency information signal from Lovealott Intersolar Removals and thought it would probably work for me.

Partechi and Myrtle decided they would pick up a connection in north pole station, as they were going to travel the old-fashioned way back to his habitat ship in Venus's orbit. Before they went, we all stood in the storage area of the loading bay, by our space to surface vehicle.

BoBo came over to me and tapped me with a paw, I knelt down, he put his nose on mine and rubbed it firmly.

Myrtle gasped, "You are honoured!" It did feel significant.

I hugged her and Partechi again, this time without the desperation. Then Loveday did the same, and Arlo and eventually Taylor, though I noticed none of them got even so much as an acknowledgement from BoBo.

FRIDAY

I didn't sleep. Even if I had wanted to, there were holo calls throughout the night. I answered the questions from the security teams, the global government representatives and the solar alliance, which included several tremenysi, and deflected the ones from people who didn't have the governmental clearance. Most of the scientists were asking about things I didn't understand and I referred them on to Arlo.

It wasn't easy, but I managed to get a sneaky look at the lists of the ships and the 'missing.' It was a relief to realise that the people I loved and respected were not on it, though there were names that surprised me and some, sadly, that didn't, a certain Mars main dome staffer for instance.

It went quiet at three in the morning GMT and I made tea and watched the sun come up.

The office was locked but I had a key code and I opened up, the digital assistant was still fielding calls so I left it like that and drank my hot chocolate. Janos had also been exhausted and his face was bruised when I went in to order drinks and cake in the café that morning. He asked me nothing, but nodded and smiled when I enquired about his family. I knew from accessing the highly secret lists that they had all been in the Kuiper belt on different small ships.

Loveday looked awful.

"Where's Taylor?" I asked, handing her a travel cup.

"Checking the freighter, he went up in the first shuttle this morning."

We sat in silence.

A small insistent beeping made us both look at an incoming holo; it had Partechi's secure ID. I answered it. He and Myrtle were in the habitat ship near Venus. I could see the planet through the huge living area windows.

"How are you both? Oh dear, you don't need to reply, I can see for myself." Myrtle was smiling. They were both full size. I wondered, in the part of my brain still functioning, if someone had told them about my acute dislike for head-only holo's. Partechi was making breakfast. "It's a private communication," she added, helpfully, "I know you will have questions."

Loveday spoke tentatively, "Do you think it took the people who had made a deal?"

Partechi shrugged.

"Will it be back?" Her voice shook.

He didn't seem to know, and oddly looked at me. I sighed, "I think it took those it could, but there are others it left here and it will find a way to come back."

"Great," Loveday was petrified.

"But," I said, "there will be time to sort something out."

"We have to go back to our previous *arrangement* for now, do you understand?" Partechi explained carefully. I nodded. Their images swirled into the rainbow and we were quiet for a moment.

"What did they mean by that?"

"Wait for it," I said, as I turned off the digital assistant from the call centre.

The public lines beeped and I answered the first one; a holo head appeared. Myrtle Winwright.

"Ah, Ms Enys, "she addressed a puzzled Loveday, and continued, "I can't stay here any longer. I need you to move me to Mars main dome *immediately* and get that young man of yours to pick BoBo up first thing!"

"Myrtle—"

"That's *Ms Winwright* to you!" She disconnected.

Loveday looked sad. "Is this where we are?" she said.

"For now." I patted her hand. "Try not to worry too much, things are happening."

The backed up holo calls blinked at us, but she sat there ignoring them and looking at the sea through the office windows.

"What are you thinking?" I asked eventually, when the silence stretched out.

Loveday wasn't letting it go. "This entity, you think it's probably heterotrophic, it consumes other sources of organic carbon?" I had a horrid feeling I knew where she was going with this. "Well," she added, "what is it that makes *us* any different?"

I thought about what I had felt in that bleak suffocating darkness, the complete lack of anything *interesting*.

"Everything," I said.

THE TIME TRAVEL TREE

I THOUGHT of this short story when I was travelling in Mongolia. Where backpackers and travellers stop to rest there is always a Travel Tree. Oddly there are still places out on the edge without much of a phone signal and people always want to leave something of themselves behind; something tangible. Usually, it's meaningful words about places seen, or things to do; sometimes a small piece of coloured ribbon or string. Often it is all of those things. Mostly these notice boards are in an understanding hotel at the lower end of the price range! Once, in a place far away from anywhere, it was an actual tree...

The song that I associate with this story is, Africa, by TOTO. Mainly because I sang it to my guide and my horse all the way through the north-west, and much like the Welsh all Mongolians love to sing. I have no idea what the horse thought of it!

MY TRAVELS HAVE TAKEN me past the tree several times now. Each time I've checked to see if there's a message for me. But there is nothing. Where are you, my friend? I am so worried.

I HAVE the time travel gene. Many, many years ago, they discovered that DRD4-7R was linked to curiosity and restlessness. The next genetic breakthrough which happened long before I was born gave science the chance to look a little deeper. Watson and Crick would have done backflips, though *I* have always been a Rosalind Franklin fan. It turned out that I was literally one in a million, or one in several hundred thousand anyway.

There was a scientist slightly before my own time called Dr Alice Dubrecht who was head of the team studying time genetics, she was asked about the variant and answered, "We just reproduce differently now," which I thought was a very practical response. The people in charge paying the bills were unsurprisingly not that impressed and cancelled the funding for her non-profit organisation. She set up on her own with the abundance of available private finance; the global government were of course furious.

Her company was called AD Genetics, but most people called them the time genies and Dr Dubrecht encouraged it. We had a less cute name: time pirates. They were as vicious as the global government when it came to looking for us and *much* better at finding us.

I was very young when I began to travel; it was either that or I would have had to go to work for the global government. There wasn't actually anything of a choice and if you didn't want to be part of the official system then you had to run. My parents were devastated; I was an excited thirteen-year-old, who knew precisely nothing about my own time or any other, but I was one of the lucky ones. And it really *was* luck; because there is no combination of arrogance and ignorance quite like that of a teenager and at that point in my life, I had an over-abundance of both.

As a runner I was fortunate enough to get help from the other seasoned travellers and in my turn, I have helped other time runners.

Once when I was still young and stupid, I had been caught out by a young man; a tracker. They, the global government, have never been known to give up too easily when they wanted something that was considered to be priceless. I had left him in mediaeval England in 1348 without his time fetish or his multi-drug nasal spray. I don't know how long the bubonic plague took to find him and I really don't care. If he had taken me back, I would have been bound; which basically meant being blind and deaf and left in a tank of amniotic fluid, still conscious, able to think and feel but unable to move, merely existing, forever tied to someone time gene-less and assisting them in travelling safely up and down the timeline. My genetic coding tapped, like the gallbladder of an endangered animal, until I went crazy. I was very aware that I probably killed two people that day, the tracker and his tank-mate.

My given name is Gallimora, which was my grandmother's name. Sadly, she had been picked up in one of the shameful pogroms that litter human history and I never met her.

Friends have always called me Galli or occasionally Doc, which was something of a joke because my family name is Poole, so my initials are GP. In past times it was an abbreviation for a general practitioner, which was someone who had trained as a doctor and served the local community. I have met a few on my travels, but no one in my own time would recognise the term.

These people have an odd time-related sense of humour. Over the years I developed fairly good skills in patching up the usual wear and tear of time travel. But I don't know if that was because people kept shouting for a doc or the fact that I have always been quite interested in a variety of scientific subjects, including medical science.

I am tall for history, but despite that and my warm skin tone and dark eyes, I can pass in the past.

Tolly had arrived just after I did, he is a few years older than me and extremely clever, his family somehow managed to keep him with them for longer by masking his skills and staying off the grid. His ancestors were nomadic and their lands crossed the Steppes from Mongolia to Russia where the old boundaries were, before the big wars.

He has bright, grey-blue eyes that slant slightly at the corners, black hair and is short, stocky and very strong. The looks and strength he told me he'd inherited from his dad along with the dominant time travel gene.

I once saw him ride a destrier that had lost its knight in an ambush; we were right in the middle of the first English civil war. King Stephen's army was on the hillside with a distinct advantage over Empress Matilda's. Tolly has the full genetic coding of his family's warrior history behind him.

It petrified me because the horse was huge, armoured, covered in blood and wild with fear, and I'd never stolen one before. It calmed down and stood trembling while he talked to it in a language that wouldn't be heard in England until Edward Longshanks negotiated with the Mongols over getting Jerusalem back from the Turkish Empire.

Tolly had ridden that horse through his time tunnel and into the bedroom of the rich man who'd ordered it. Using my own, I followed him instead of returning to safety, but only because I wanted to see the face of this particular idiot with too much money. It was odd, the tired, bedridden elderly man looked at that horse with love and the horse knew it and went over to him, nose in his hand in an instant. We left, but I have often wondered how they got it out of the house, as since then I have learned, from other equine related thefts, that horses will go up stairs, but don't like going down them.

WE STEAL THINGS.

Requests appeared on the time travel tree. Put there by other travellers who had made a journey back and forward with something that they had stolen. A contract usually generated another one; if it was not from the same person then it would be from someone they knew. Because word of mouth was usually so much safer for everyone, and it was as dangerous to take a contract as it was to make one.

The global government was not keen on private citizens keeping them out of a very lucrative loop; though they hadn't had much success in shutting down Dr Dubrecht either. She did her business under the auspices of research, which seemed to afford her some protection, as big pharmaceutical companies wield quite a lot of hidden power and influence. And though I, nor anyone I knew, had ever seen her, I have learned to be afraid.

Some travellers kept all the contracts they made for themselves, but we all have our specialities and mine is books.

I have always loved them; even when I was a very young child, I could be found under a tree in the garden of my family house, hiding from the adults, living in my imagination. There is and always will be, real time travel in the words of a book.

I HAD a big contract to fulfil and I wanted Tolly to help me, because I trusted him. He is good at watching my back and he could be absolutely silent while creeping around. When stealing books, you generally need to be quick and very, very quiet.

TIME WOULDN'T LET you take just anything. I eventually learned this important fact, because I have been attempting to get hold of the Empress Matilda's crown for ten years now. It should have gone down in the Wash in 1216, but as hard as I have tried, I can't *keep* my hands on it. Oh, I can *get* my hands on it but it disappears in the tunnel; which means that it didn't go down along the causeway when the baggage train forded across the mouth of the Wellstream. I'm going to have to try again, it's still an open contract and I've never been good with failure.

I am working on a new theory; King John stayed at Swineshead Abbey after the disaster on the sands, and he and his retinue then moved to Newark-on-Trent. He died on the night of the nineteenth of October. It had to have gone missing then and not with the baggage train which was swamped by the incoming tide, sinking in the mud of the Wash with all those horses, wagon drivers and soldiers.

Tolly usually rolls his eyes at this point as I always have a new theory.

THERE WERE OTHER RULES. You couldn't go forward in time past your own current present. You could go back in time to the past and come forward again to the future, just not your own personal future, and time passed at the same rate whenever you were, so there was no arriving back at the present before you left, or just after. Also, no breaking the grandfather paradox was allowed. Nor it seemed could you pay someone else to kill your grandfather. And there are some place/times that you simply are not allowed to go, like your own past. Time was always aware; it tolerated us like the irritating little mice that we were, nibbling away at the skirting boards of the universe.

THE SANCTUARY CONCOURSE WAS BUSY. Most of us live in and around the main area. It looks much like a train station from more than two centuries ago. I had it on good authority from my traveller mentor that it is authentic. He, Osric, said they still had trains when he was a child, though I had never seen one when I was growing up. The trains are all in the station and the new time runners live in dormitories in the carriages. They are mostly children because not many people get to adulthood without being found out.

I passed a small group with a teacher showing them how to lean on their fetish to help to fix their thoughts to the tunnels. Every now and then a child would pop out of view and then back in again, usually with a mixture of wonder and alarm on their faces. This was how I had learned.

The carriages are on tracks that end in the opaque glass walls of the sanctuary station and at designated intervals, someone starts up the engine at each end. I have no idea why, but the children love it.

I lived in the carriages for several years until I found my own place of safety. Many of the seasoned travellers still stay there, as they can usually have a car to themselves and all of them are well designed, comfortable and private with the concourse close by.

There are also lots of apartments above the shops and offices where several of my friends live, but it's expensive so you can only afford them if you have made a great deal of money on contracts. I have saved enough over the years to buy an apartment but I couldn't settle so close to other people now, and I don't want anyone to wonder how much I have earned with my own contracts. It doesn't pay to advertise your wealth. I think the proximity problem must be a city or country-side feeling, and also, when you feel at home is where you need to live.

OUR COLLECTIVE STORY tells us that the very first time traveller was a homeless man living in the train station. He had built the sanctuary to look this way because it made him feel safe; and little by little he stole things. Though I am not sure how you steal a train. I took an old car once and that was difficult enough. It was a nineteen fifty-eight Austin Healey Frogeye Sprite, I had to drive it into a tunnel and I nearly got squashed. I feel fairly sure a train would need tracks to go anywhere.

Most of the story is probably allegorical but it made for a good yarn and we who have no real past of our own need a history. I do know his statue stands next to the one of a small brown bear who, weirdly, is wearing a raincoat, hat and boots. I have *no idea* what that's about. I have often wondered what the sanctuary would have looked like if it had been a croupier at a casino who first travelled.

I WENT in to one of the many shops on the concourse that sold food. Lots of the younger children binge on junk when they arrive, mainly because for most of them it was the first time they had been able to make their own decisions about anything. I had done it myself, but as I got older, I began to appreciate something with a higher nutritional value. I find myself running a lot and it helps if you're not out of breath in less than a minute.

I smiled at Albert as he passed me my favourite hot chocolate. He always makes the drink just how I like it, thick enough to stand a spoon upright in it and strong enough to make my head spin. I offered the virtual currency credit number on my wrist, but he shook his head; I get beverages free because Albert has a collection, of *plastic*. That would be the highly illegal contraband that *doesn't* contain digesting microbes and isn't made of mandatory biodegradable material. I have no idea why time allows me to, but I bring him things I find in different places on my travels.

The last reconnaissance trip I took for a contract, I brought back a tiny toy troll for him. It had red hair and was wearing a costume that looked similar to a ballet dancer's tutu. I thought it was awful but he cried when I handed it over and his expressive hands caressed the impossible nylon hair as if it was the rarest silk.

I had bargained fiercely with an eight-year-old for it in a small English village and I didn't get the better end of the deal.

The little girl had been sitting on the wall near the house I was watching, where there was a very extensive collection of books inside, in an old library that was due to go up in flames the next evening. A horrendous loss that I was hoping to do something about, for a profit of course, though some of them would probably end up in my private collection. I have an expensive obsession with Copernicus and Galileo.

If either Albert or I were ever found out it could mean permanent exile from the sanctuary and if *anyone* knew about the boxed roll of plastic food wrapping that I had acquired for him, I think exile would be the least of our problems.

Albert is Sámi and I'm very sure his name isn't Albert, but you can call yourself what you like in this place of safety, and some of us are running away from more than the global government. He is one of our stay puts, which means, apart from the initial journey through the tunnels, he doesn't travel much. He picks up his stock from next to the time travel tree where it is sent through another tunnel from the present by someone that he never meets, and the financial transaction is done on the dark web with the usual virtual currency.

He is also in an on-again, off-again relationship with Tolly. Albert is fed up with me asking him if he has heard from my friend, so I just raised my eyebrows and he shook his head. I can see by the expression on his wonderfully sculpted face that I am not the only one who is worried.

Albert's cat Juno came over and rubbed her sinuous tabby body around my legs asking to be picked up for a cuddle. I was about to oblige her when I saw the medic who runs the emergency section beckoning me over. Rachel, which is also not the name she was born with, is intelligent, dark haired and stunningly beautiful. She's exactly how you would imagine a storybook Indian princess would look, because she is. Though sadly not the fairy tale part, which is why she had made it to the sanctuary, instead of her skills being *utilised* by her own family; something that she told me when we were both very drunk one night. It wasn't just the global government that exploited the talented, innocent and vulnerable.

She'd managed to train as a doctor by going into hospitals in the near past which is very dangerous for us; pretending to be a medical student studying alongside the others and going out on emergency calls with the air, sea and land ambulance services. She had a lot of help from several of the other travellers with successfully hiding her real identity.

Fortunately, we have people with skills. We need to stay one step ahead because the global government is accelerating its efforts on finding us and bringing us in. For our own good, of course.

Rachel looked at me, then at the group of arrivals, all small children she was shepherding towards the medical centre; her eyes slid expressively towards an adorable little boy. He was pale-skinned and his face was watchful, but oddly blank and emotionless at the same time. I nodded my head that yes, she was right to be wary of him.

The other thing that stood out was the general age of these children. The new time runners were definitely getting younger. A trend that was worrying not just Rachel and me, but most of the experienced travellers.

I DECIDED to try one more visit to the time travel tree before I went home. The area that was designated the in and out for time tunnel arrivals and departures was over on platform nine. And woe betide anyone coming and going anywhere else. Apart from the fact that it was considered *very* bad manners, it is also extremely dangerous as you could kill or injure a person if you opened a tunnel on top of them. Younger travellers spent a great deal of their lessons learning what the rules were and why we had them.

There was one more thing that I have come to understand. As you got older and more experienced it was sometimes possible to be able to shorten your tunnel. This is not a skill that can be learned or taught. It just happens to some of us. My own time tunnel is usually no more than an arch. It isn't a secret but it's not something we go about advertising and the general consensus is that the global government are not aware that this can happen. Or if they do know, they don't have anyone who can do it. There are distinct advantages to a short tunnel. It makes getting away quicker and it's easier to keep open. There are stories that you hear the younger travellers telling each other of someone lost in their own time tunnel. Running forever from the past and getting nowhere. I used to have nightmares about it, I still do sometimes. I don't think it's true, but it feels as if it could be.

I HEARD another time tunnel connecting before I was able to see the tree clearly. I stepped forward through the arch that was my tunnel as it solidified and then took a few paces back after it evaporated into a small hazy cloud, which looked like the warm breath of a swimmer surfacing into freezing cold air.

It was dark for a moment, then I could see a spectral, slightly eery, shape running towards me. He was staggering and clutching at his side. My instincts were to open another tunnel and get out of there. But something about the figure looked familiar and in the next second I realised who it was; then I saw the other two people chasing him, which I had thought was impossible.

Leaning into the tunnel as far as I could and reaching out a hand, I grabbed his when he was close enough and pulled so that we fell over together as his tunnel collapsed behind him. The sounds of the screams filled the air for a moment, then the silence emptied the noise from the tree room. "Hey Galli," he said, as he fainted.

I LIFTED TOLLY CAREFULLY over onto one side. He was heavy, and he groaned as I moved him. Checking the wound site, I could see it was projectile damage and bleeding, and I pushed a wad of material from his del against it and prepared to open my own tunnel to get him back to the sanctuary. His eyes opened.

"No," he said clearly.

"Why not?" I was puzzled, wondering if he had a head injury.

He looked at me with clear blue certainty and I waited. "Because of this." He pulled a small object out of his pocket pouch which he used in the absence of any actual pockets, and passed it to me. His fingers were bloody so it took a moment. "Do you recognise it?" he asked.

It wasn't easy as one of my hands was still applying direct pressure to the wound, but I realised it was a small stone horse, nicely carved, a fetish. It had been a while since I'd seen it, but eventually my mouth dropped open and I said a really rude word.

Tolly snorted in Mongolian, "If my mother had heard that, you would have got your mouth washed out with soap!"

"If *my* mum had heard it, she'd have used a brush!"

I turned it carefully around, yes, I was sure it was the same one. I had taken it from the tracker I had left in 1348.

"Where did you get this?" I spoke in a whisper.

"Who did you give it to?" Tolly asked me without answering my question.

WE SAT on the floor by the time travel tree as I checked out Tolly's wound again. It was still bleeding quite aggressively.

"I need to get you to the medic," I said, my voice shaking. Because something had changed, there was now a fundamental shift in the way things were.

"Galli, *who* did you give it to?" Tolly winced as I pushed the thick warm fabric against the wound again.

"One of the elders." I paused. "Travis."

Tolly nodded as if this made sense to him.

Our sanctuary was guided by a group who were nominated by us. They were older, more experienced, wise, and they kept us safe. We had been part of the process for Travis's nomination. I found myself struggling with conflicted thoughts.

"Can you fix this?" Tolly asked me.

"Not here," I said, exasperated. There was a rumble of noise to our left in one of the caves that surrounded the tree. Someone was coming through. I made a decision. "Are you able to stand?"

He held out his hand and I helped him get to his knees and then eventually his feet. He was sweating with pain and breathless. I opened a tunnel and we walked the few steps until he staggered into a room and the arch behind us dissipated quietly.

Tolly looked around swaying slightly, then smiled. "Very nice," he said, as he slid to the floor of my home.

I CLEANED the damage while Tolly was still very slightly unconscious. I couldn't move him as he weighed twice what I did, so he stayed where he fell, on the incredibly rare seventeenth-century tapestry wall hanging that I used as a carpet. I wasn't too bothered about the blood he was dripping, as there were several other similar, but now faint, stains. It was a non-book item I'd rescued from the house of a cavalier who, at that point in time, was on the wrong side of the English Civil War.

There was no actual projectile or exit wound. The loss of blood and the shock he was so clearly suffering from worried me, but he was strong. I sprayed it with an antibacterial which was a derivative of sphagnum moss, packed the damaged area with the dried version of the same moss we usually used in my time, and then covered it with a thick layer of clear repair sealant and a pressure dressing.

His eyes fluttered open. "Finished?" He asked me. I nodded, leaning back against a chair. My hands were smeared in his blood and sticky with antibacterial powder and bits of sealant. I decided to wait until my legs had stopped shaking before I went into the bathroom to wash. "Good, that was awful," he muttered.

"For me too," I said dryly.

He glanced around from the vantage point of the living area. "How many books are there here?"

"I don't think you should count books; it diminishes them." I got up and went to the downstairs bathroom which was through a door to one side of the kitchen. The small utility area had another door to the outside and one to the shower room. I washed my hands and wiped my sweaty face, checking for blood spatter in the mirror. There was a large splodge on the jumper I wore. I pulled it off and ran the cold tap into the plugged sink, then pressed the stained bit gently into the water and left it to soak.

"Do you know how difficult it is to get blood out of merino wool?"

"No, but I imagine you're going to tell me." Tolly had moved to a chair, his head was back against a cushion and he was leaning awkwardly, trying not to fold in the middle. His eyes were closed.

"I didn't expect this." He waved an eloquent hand around referring to the house. "When are we?"

I hesitated, not only had I brought someone to my personal place of safety but giving out an actual time would be the second of the three pinpoints for a return.

He opened his eyes. "I'm sorry. I shouldn't have asked that."

The silence stretched out for a moment or two, then I made another decision. "It's just after the second global flu pandemic and we are in England, the south-west to be exact."

Tolly looked as stunned as someone who had just been shot could do. "Thank you for trusting me," he said.

I began making tea. My house is an old bothie, it's really one big room, with the kitchen at one end and the living area at the other, divided by a long work surface, which has cupboards on the kitchen side and on the other, a small oblong table with two chairs.

A narrow open stairway on the left of the kitchen goes up to a balcony bedroom which overlooks the living area. There is a large bathroom beyond the bedroom. Another door on the other side of the kitchen opens into a storage area, and it balances out the one to the utility room and back entrance. There are double glass doors onto a patio on one side of the living area and a large wood burning stove in the centre of the end wall opposite the kitchen. It's not small and crowded though it sounds as if it is, and there is plenty of light. I'm not messy, but every vertical surface and any available space has book shelves; including the other side of the fixed kitchen island so that I can reach them when I sit at the table.

There was a loud knock at the back door in the utility room and a cheerful voice called out, "Hey Galli, post!"

Tolly cringed into his chair, rearranging his del carefully to hide the blood. I put my finger to my lips to warn him. "English only, no common tongue!" Then shouted, "I'm in here Tom, come on through."

The postman was dressed in shorts and a red fleece jacket, he smiled as he came in and dropped the post on the kitchen worktop. He is as tall and slim as Tolly is short and stocky, with the obligatory, healthy, out in all weathers, red-cheeked glow, to match his jacket. It was still quite cold outside as winter had turned to spring, but as I understood, the posties had a competition in the autumn to see who gave up the shorts first. Tom was of course winning, by not having given them up at all.

"Tea?" I asked him.

"I can't stop, I'm behind today. Oh." He saw Tolly who was trying, and failing, to look inconspicuous. "Hi?"

"Tom, this is my friend Tolly."

They eyed each other with real interest. Tom has an appropriate regional accent for the area and the time. He is kindness itself, looking after the people on his round, me being one of them. He immediately noticed the new patch of blood on the carpet but said nothing.

"Maddie has been up already this morning and mucked out the horses, she took Barney out for a long ride. Bessie went along on the leading rein, she said she thought you might be back. It must have been a short buying trip this time, where were you, Europe?"

I grunted and he nodded that this confirmed he was right. "Did you find anything interesting?"

"An original Copernicus at an auction sale in Amsterdam!" It had actually been from a house that was just about to be sacked in the English Civil War, and the same place I'd acquired the carpet, but in another room and on a different, carefully timed, trip.

"Cool!" Tom was impressed. "Oh, before I forget, Maddie says that Bessie needs her hooves trimming."

"I'll phone the farrier this morning."

Tom waved at Tolly. "Nice to meet you."

"Make some time for tea tomorrow, I'll show you the book." I said, as he hustled out of my kitchen on a mission to be agreeable to everyone.

"Only if you have cake!" He shouted as he banged the door closed.

There was total silence.

"*Bessie needs her hooves trimming?*" Tolly said eventually, his face suffused with incredulity.

"PAINKILLERS WITH YOUR TEA?" I asked Tolly after a suitable pause.

"Yes please," he replied.

The unspoken was not so much the elephant in the room, more of an entire herd.

TOLLY STAGGERED over to the kitchen and with gentle, respectful fingers, picked up the post. He gasped rather loudly, "This is actual paper!" Then grabbed at his side and I made him sit down at the table while he contemplated the inappropriate attitude to trees.

"Would you prefer our time's version of analgesia or the ones they have here?"

Tolly regarded me with that, I'm thinking, look. "Why would you be allowed bring our medical treatment through a tunnel?"

"Because everything we have there, would be viable here, it just hasn't been reinvented yet, it's used for different purposes, or no one has seen the possibilities. This whole area of the moor is covered in several species of sphagnum moss and bearded lichen, which was used in the First World War as a very effective antibacterial and for packing wounds as a coagulant, people have just forgotten." I indicated his own damage. "And they still have antibiotics here based on mould penicillin, in a few decades they won't be able to use them, the various bacteria will have adjusted."

Tolly looked puzzled for a second. "There isn't any phage treatment?"

"Not quite, it won't be long before it's available, but it is still being researched and tested."

I put his tea down next to him and sat in the other chair at the table. The small essential medical pack was scattered over the surface where I'd left it when I grabbed the necessary items for the wound. Tom, the postie, had looked carefully at it and then at me to see if I needed his help. When he saw the slight shake of my head, he had relaxed.

Tolly indicated that he would prefer his usual dose of pain relief. I reached for the spray and gave it to him; he puffed the inhalation in two great gulps of breath and his face relaxed in a few moments after the blockers entered his system through the lining of his mouth, nose and upper respiratory tract.

I took the small carved stone horse out of the pocket of my trousers, because some of us do actually have them, and put it on the table. I tapped it with a finger. "Are you going to tell me about this?"

Tolly sat back in his chair and his body tension eased with relief over the lack of pain and the feeling of temporary safety that my house gave everyone who had ever walked through the door, including me.

"I went home to help my mum and sister with the cashmere herd, the goats are scattered quite far from the ger camp, and my uncle is supposed to be watching them. He didn't return one evening for his supper. So, I went out to look for him." He paused.

"You've never really been interested in the time travel stuff, have you?" I speculated.

"I just want to be connected to the land where I grew up, and breed my Takhi horses, even if it does mean that I also have to look after my mother's smelly goats!"

He sounded so sad that for a moment my eyes filled with tears, because I have never felt a part of anything, including my own family; then I looked around and the being alone feeling dissipated. Sometimes you just have to find your own time and place.

"You understand now, don't you?" Tolly asked me with his hand on my face. He patted my cheek gently and leaned back in his chair again.

"As I came closer to the goat herd, I felt a strange sense of foreboding, I got off Brun and went the rest of the way on foot. Brun is very good at staying quiet, he stood very still, as if he also knew something was not right. I was creeping closer to the fire where I thought my uncle was. I had been thinking that maybe he was worried about a wolf, we have them roaming around in the winter, they're always after the foals and the goats, and in the spring everything is hungry. Occasionally a man will get hurt, though it is unusual. I saw my uncle sitting there, and I nearly called out in relief at finding him safe." He paused again, lost in his thoughts of home.

"What made you keep silent?" I asked.

He shrugged. "I don't know, all these years of being hunted by government trackers and the pirates, I think it changes you."

I got up and boiled more water for a fresh pot of tea. Tolly snorted when I clicked a switch for electricity and the kettle rumbled into life. I fished around in the cupboard for the homemade ginger biscuits I knew Maddie would have brought when she checked the house.

After carefully examining the tea cosy, he spoke, sounding bemused, "There is a wool hat on your teapot decorated with knitted mice."

"It was a present from a friend," I explained defensively. "Please continue."

"The fire was really bright and I could see shadows moving in the trees that didn't make sense to my eyes."

I have a healthy respect for Tolly's visual acuity. It's kept me out of trouble, as have all his other senses, so I nodded in understanding.

"I waited, and eventually I heard a whisper on the wind through the branches, then three men came out of hiding and walked over to my uncle. They hit him really hard, he fell over on his side and lay still."

Tolly was quiet. His face took on the bearing of a warrior, a trait that he usually kept hidden behind a fairly benign exterior. I never doubted it was there, but some people had made the mistake of thinking he was weak, because he didn't generally fight back immediately when confronted.

"What happened?" My mouth was dry.

"I waited; they went to sleep around the fire. One of them got up to relieve himself, I cut his throat. The other two." He shrugged. "They didn't wake up."

"And then?" I asked, as he examined his hands and remained silent for the number of minutes that most people would find uncomfortable and fill with words that didn't matter.

"My uncle was dead, either he had died after the first attack and they used him as bait to see if I would come out, or he died while I held on for a better moment."

I didn't say anything, we've all waited too long for one of those. I have a list inside my own head that I can see in my dreams. It was the way we had learned to live our lives.

"Did you buy this?" Tolly asked me, looking around at the house.

"It was Osric's, he left it to me in his will."

Tolly looked puzzled.

"He's my great uncle, as far as anyone here is concerned, and he lived here for thirty years or thereabouts. He was a much-loved eccentric and people still stop me in the village to tell their favourite Osric stories."

Tolly's mouth had dropped open, it made me smile.

"I really don't know what to say about that!" Tolly grinned and I was glad to see he was still able to.

His expression changed and he went back to the narrative. "I made a tunnel, hoping to lead whoever it was away from my family, but I've never developed the ability for an arch and as I was halfway through another three men came out of hiding and followed me."

"How did they get into your tunnel, Tolly?"

I must have sounded dubious. I've seen people from the past try and enter, but time won't let them. Even people from your own present are not able to. If you don't have the gene you can't travel in a tunnel. Time, however, didn't seem to mind us helping ourselves to horses, or any other animal for that matter. Though there seemed to be a grey area around extinct species. And I had always thought, like the destrier, that they would have died in their own time's immediate future, before we could bring them with us.

Global government trackers relied on their tank-mates to create a tunnel and a fetish to stay linked to it. The pirates were more likely to have a dominant gene and a fetish, I had never heard of them using tank-mates and they were not, to my knowledge, skilled at tunnel making, otherwise they would have been better at stealing stuff and finding us. Either way they both had to use their own tunnels.

Tolly waited until my brain caught up with my mouth. "Are you saying you think one of them was an experienced *traveller?*"

He picked up the fetish and held it in front of me. "I took this from the tracker who was holding it when we fought in my tunnel. I didn't see the others close up, one shot at me with some sort of laser weapon as I was running away from them."

"Tolly, when you and I travel we usually go through my arch or we meet at a designated time-spot. But we both have the dominant form of the gene and we have worked together for years, and even then, I can feel a pushback from time. It's as if I'm wading through deep water. How does a tracker with a tank-mate, or a pirate with the dominant gene, even *with* a traveller, get into *your* tunnel?"

He waited again and watched me while I worked it out. I sighed. "You can take people through your own tunnel without time's resistance?"

"You have the ability to shorten yours to an arch, mine lets me bring *anyone*, even the time gene-less. Albert has visited my family and my mother and sisters have been to see her ancestors."

"Wait, what?" I know I must have looked like I was having a

medical emergency, but my breathing suddenly became very difficult and I gasped.

"Just put your head down for a second or two." Tolly was calm but he had a grin on his face. I did as he suggested, took some long slow breaths and leaned over with my head between my knees.

I spoke, my voice muffled, "If anyone finds out—"

Tolly interjected, exasperated, "They already have, look at me!"

The door to the utility room swung slowly open and Tolly went on full alert. I waved a hand around in the air concentrating on my breathing and trying to process the situation. "It's Wilf."

A very large tabby cat wandered in and stopped short; he really is a drama queen when it comes to strangers, but after a quick sniff, he identified Tolly as someone acceptable and hopped onto the table, taking advantage of my recovery pose to help himself to a biscuit.

I sat up. "Tolly, meet Wilf."

Tolly reached forward and stroked the thick fur until Wilf purred and head-butted his hand and he obligingly scratched under the furry chin. The cat shimmered for a moment and Tolly could clearly feel it.

"When does Wilf come from?"

"The house where I acquired that carpet," I pointed to the one he had been lying on. "The odd thing is I don't think Wilf died in the fire, and I'm not sure he doesn't travel by himself, it's really interesting."

"Nothing surprises me now," he said. "We are so careful not to tell anything to anyone that we don't seem to have any real comprehension of our own or other people's potential."

"Tolly, I had no idea. I keep to myself, it's what we were taught to do to stay safe."

"Someone knows." Tolly sounded angry and what was worse, frightened. "They are aware of our abilities and they're selling them to the highest bidder."

I sat up. "Travis?"

Tolly shook his head. "I suspect he's probably a victim."

I thought back to the time I had seen Travis and told him about the incident. I couldn't remember anything of relevance after I'd shown him the fetish and explained what I had done. He hadn't seemed too bothered about it, so I'd parked the memory in the place where I kept my, 'don't dwell on this too much' thoughts.

"Do you think the person chasing you was the one I left in 1348?"

"I never actually saw the tracker at the time it happened Galli, I only know what you told me back then, but I suppose it could have been."

We sat for a while in silence except for the cat's purr. Wilf had settled himself close to Tolly who clearly understood the rules and was stroking the cat into a contented torpor.

"How are you feeling?" I asked.

"Is that me or the cat?" Tolly snorted. "I'm out of pain and the bleeding has stopped. I couldn't run for my life right now, so please don't upset anyone."

I was incredulous. "It wasn't me who chased the book burners of Florence at Savonarola's party night, yelling rude words in Italian. It took weeks for my eyebrows to grow back *and* I had to get my hair cut because one plait was completely burned off!"

"We got all those paintings though, you rescued several tomes that I think I can actually see on that shelf over there; and, the first rule of book stealing, don't stop to *read* the books!"

Tolly was clearly off topic.

"Have you been doing this all on your own?" I tried not to, but I must have sounded hurt.

"I couldn't trust anyone but that wasn't why I didn't tell you; It was because I didn't want you to be in danger, and now you are. I brought all this straight to your place of safety." Tolly's bitterness was evident in his voice."

"I would have done it anyway," I whispered.

"I know." He smiled sadly.

WHEN TOLLY HAD EATEN ALL the biscuits, and drunk four more cups of tea, gloopy with honey, which he adores almost as much as my cat does, we struggled to get him upstairs for a shower. After the first attempt we opted for the very small downstairs bathroom in the utility area. He was slightly incredulous about the wet room, his family usually skin brushed and sweated, and the facilities at the sanctuary were nearly all light related anti-microbial steaming. I had, however, become used to hot water on my skin and I'd grown to love the feeling.

Wilf waited politely at the door to the bathroom. I have friend status so I stayed while Tolly stripped, and tried not to gasp with horror at the sight of his bruises, which covered most of his naked body. He had taken a massive beating.

"They really wanted you dead," I whispered.

"I think nearly dead would have done it. Can you get the blood out of this?" He handed me his del.

"What is it made of?"

"Yak hair with some cashmere." Tolly grinned hopefully.

"I'm going to soak it in the bath upstairs, then I can put it in the washing machine."

He looked puzzled.

"More water related stuff." I indicated the shower.

"It's very wasteful." He tutted.

"One thing they have a lot of on Exmoor is rain, there's a reason it's so green!"

I ran up the stairs and went through the bedroom into the bathroom. It had a shower in one corner and a large free-standing bath in the middle. The water flush loo and a basin were against the end wall. Out of necessity, there were book shelves in here too, though I put them as far away from the shower as possible. The larger of the two windows looked down towards the small valley, which meant that I could lie in the bath and admire the view at the same time.

The cold water tap filled the bottom of the bath quickly. I dunked the thick wraparound garment and then pushed the bubbles out as it swirled blood into the water. There was a tiny burnt hole on one side of the material, which would need darning. I checked the wide-woven sash but it seemed to have escaped the blood and damage.

Tolly had given me a del made by his mum after the first few jobs we had done together. I used it as a dressing gown as it was warm and comforting on cold Exmoor evenings.

His aversion to stealing along the timeline meant that most of the contracts he did that paid real money were the ones I asked him to do. Apart from the destrier of course, I hadn't seen him for ages after that business, so it must have kept them going for months.

I could hear that the water was still running in the shower downstairs, which was accompanied by a tuneful Mongolian warrior song. He'd clearly got over his disapproval about the wastage.

Wilf appeared as if by his own time tunnel and wrapped himself around my legs. I sat on the floor next to the bath and we had a cuddle and a conversation, which consisted of him telling me in cat speak just exactly how hungry he was, and me saying how worried I was.

I drifted through to the bedroom with Wilf still complaining. The main window looked in the same direction as the bathroom and there was a smaller one on the wall behind the bed from which I could see the stables and the fields beyond.

Barney was cropping grass in his usual contented fashion, but Bessie watched me through the gate, her intense stare engendering a feeling of guilt. She made Barney look like a destrier himself, she was so small. At twelve point two hands he was average size for an Exmoor, strong and sturdy. Bessie was a small miniature Shetland and could easily walk under Barney's tummy, something that she did when she was frustrated with his lack of attention. It always worked.

I ambled down the stairs and into the store room, breathing in my home to reacquaint myself. The shelves were stacked with food, mostly in tins, and a variety of necessary items like loo rolls and wind-up lamps. I had boxes of my own spare clothing and a few that had once belonged to Osric, and I fished around for something Tolly could wear.

The singing had stopped as I wandered into the utility room. Tolly was sitting on the chair conveniently placed by the shower room. My friend looked very tired and was wrapped in two towels, one covering the bruises and dressing. He was gazing out of the back door which he'd opened, letting in the rather sharp early spring air.

"Here, try these." I handed him a thick warm shirt and some underwear and what Osric referred to as his walking trousers, the locally acceptable uniform for the moor, which were windproof and water resistant, according to the label.

"Osric's?" Tolly went into the bathroom to dress; it seemed strange as I'd seen him naked and covered in blood, but now inexplicably, clean and bare was less than appropriate.

He leaned out as he was dressing and pointed. "I didn't want to upset the young lady."

The teenager standing on the step, in front of the doorway with her mouth open, and an unfiltered look of the deepest admiration, was Maddie. I hadn't noticed her walking over to the house from the stables. She was carrying horse tack over her shoulder and a basket of fresh food.

"Come in," I said, smiling at her.

Tolly emerged fully dressed and Maddie was sweetly unable to hide her feelings of disappointment.

He sat down in the chair to put his boots on and I slid a pair of baggy suede slippers in his direction with a sideways motion of my foot. They were an old pair of Osric's; it didn't seem right to give away his personal belongings as I couldn't help feeling he would need them again one day soon. There was still a space where he had been and it gave me odd comfort to see them.

"Try these instead."

He pulled them on with a satisfied grunt.

We all followed the grumbling Wilf through to the kitchen and more tea was made. Maddie folded long legs under the table and put her chilled red hands around the cup.

"Cold ride out this morning?" I asked.

"There are bits of me that haven't thawed yet, I did see snowdrops and a few daffodil shoots coming up. Dad says we'll have wintery showers before the week is out."

Tolly was puzzled by the fulsome report, but I nodded in satisfaction. All conversations on the moor started with the weather, it dictated everything that could be achieved, in the way of school runs, food shopping, access to work, and every decision that the farmers needed to make; it caused my brain to sigh with contentment. I hardly ever missed my childhood home for a variety of reasons, but I always felt a longing for this time and place.

AFTER EXTENSIVE UPDATES on the horses, the cat, her father Tom the postie, and brief but informative journalistic level cover on most of the people in the village, something that Tolly was inappropriately interested in, Maddie said she would be coming up in the morning and asked, "Would you like more homemade biscuits?"

To which Tolly replied in the affirmative. I felt slightly surplus to requirements.

As she was going out of the kitchen door, Maddie pointed to the tack hooked over the chair she had just launched herself out of with her usual youthful exuberance. "It's worn in several places; you don't need a new bit but I'll try and get a headpiece and reins online."

"Thanks," I shouted to her disappearing back. The utility room door slammed shut on her cheerful reply.

"Why do the very young never close a door quietly?" I asked Tolly.

"Don't ask me, I live in a ger, door slamming is not an option, though my sisters still manage to make an exit somehow, and by the way I consider myself to be youthful!"

I looked at him. Neither of us had ever had the luxury of being a teenager.

"What are you saying, are we in danger, is the sanctuary? And if so, what do we do about it?" I picked up the teapot and realised that I was shaking.

"Yes, yes, and I don't really know." Tolly's face was back to its usual inscrutable expression.

I sat down again and put my head in my trembling hands.

"Galli, do you know when Osric is?" Tolly asked me, his voice somehow middle of the night scary, despite the early spring sunshine through the windows.

He used the word when and not where, which gave another dimension to our, off the timeline grid, lives. That the three rules of space and one rule of time applied to everything, was somehow reassuring to me. Tolly, however, looked anything but comforted.

"We need help Galli, and I don't know what to do. Osric is our best bet."

I hesitated and he saw it, his face was sad for a second and then resigned. I sighed, "He's in a monastery building up the road."

"When?" Tolly was relentless.

"1330," I said eventually and with great reluctance.

"Can you go and see him?"

"It's a *monastery* building!"

Tolly's expression was one of complete incomprehension.

"In *1330*!" I sighed with exasperation. "Come with me."

I got up and went into the store room. Tolly followed, his footsteps on the wood flooring were quiet and his breathing was even. I reflected that someone in this present time who had been shot a few hours ago would have been really struggling and probably sedated.

We stood together among my neat organised shelving. All the stores were in different sections according to their type, as in, food, clothing and emergency equipment. Tolly examined a few items.

"Did time allow you to bring this?" He looked surprised. The power supply unit had been designed so that it connected to the photovoltaic cells in the roof tiles, it was small and could have run the whole house for a year.

"I think it's like the medical stuff, already technically possible just not invented yet. The roof tiles are not exactly readily available either, but Osric had them made and installed."

I pivoted one of the blocks of shelving towards me and pressed six numbers into a lighted keypad. A section of wall moved silently into another, leaving a low and narrow opening.

Tolly looked at me and then back at the dark passage. I moved in front of him and as I walked forward the lights came on, they were dim and close to the floor but you could see where you were going.

The short passage tilted gently downwards and as we walked the sound of falling water became louder. I opened another sliding door with the same code.

A large space carved out of the rock by a long-ago river had been upgraded into a cosy but functional room. At one end was a wall of computerised screens which I turned on, they showed various areas of the buildings and the land around the house. At the other end of the room was a waterfall; it shimmered and glittered as the light from the valley shone through the water droplets. In between was a tiny kitchen area on one side and a sofa-bed on the other. Tucked out of sight was an equally small bathroom. Centrally, a desk was covered in books and scientific instruments from various ages, past, present and time-acceptable future.

Tolly went over to the waterfall. He reached out, much as I had done when I first saw it, but his hand made contact with the security barrier, and the jelly-like substance just gave a bit then went back to being impenetrable.

"Osric lived here when he first arrived, then he went about setting up a permanent backstory cover so he could stay. Once he'd renovated the bothie, he used this as his research area."

"What exactly was he working on?" Tolly asked dryly, as he touched the books, picking up each one and examining it for clues.

"The genetics of us," I said. A silence filled with falling water followed.

"Huh?" Tolly usually used the common tongue, but when speaking in English only, I realised he had in my place of safety time, a Scottish accent, something to do with his dad I was guessing; it made me snort with suppressed laughter. He added "How's that going?"

"I think he had a breakthrough the last time I was here." I pointed at the holographic screen after tapping on the computer keys. A dance of DNA swirled around, base pair sequences, strands and alleles. I knew this as they were conveniently labelled and not because I really understood what I was looking at. I pointed at two alleles that were highlighted, then tapped a few more keys and the holograph dived deeper into the atomic level. The highlighted areas took up the dance. "Every gene has two alleles, one from each donor, and the character-istic or genetic propensity is contributed to by more than one allele." I had learned the basics from Osric. "This is what makes us different."

We both looked at the chemicals and formulas with interest.

"You have no idea what that means do you?" Tolly asked me.

I shook my head. "Nope."

"Where does he think this will take him?" Tolly looked appre-hensive.

"You'd have to ask Osric that." I shrugged.

Tolly scowled. "What happens if the government, or probably worse, the pirates, get hold of the findings?"

"He's working with just two samples, mine and his. It's not exactly frontline research!" I felt defensive. Osric and I had been having the same conversation the last time we'd spoken. "Anyway, AD Genetics are not likely to come looking in this time *or* the fourteenth century."

Tolly was still worried. Eventually he said, "What now?"

I took a small piece of parchment and wrote a single rune on it in the appropriate ink with the carefully cut feather nib. Time would just bounce back modern paper and biro. It was not that keen on the words 'phone home' either, so we had come up with an acceptable set of runes for different messages.

The tunnel was small and carefully executed so that it could be dissolved in a second if necessary. I attached a smooth stone to weight it down and then as the arch materialised, I tossed the parchment through and closed it quickly.

Tolly was astonished and held his hands up as if asking for an explanation.

"Now we wait." I smiled.

"WHAT'S TAKING SO LONG?" Tolly said impatiently.

"I think it's the time of day that he sees people who are sick or injured. He's not allowed to use anything that isn't time appropriate, but he can set bones and treat infections with naturally occurring plants." I thought for a moment. "Also, they sing a lot."

Tolly nodded, slightly puzzled about the medicinal rules but, as a Mongolian, he understood the singing. He went back to pacing, then winced and looking around, sat down on the sofa-bed. He checked the covering on his wound.

"Have you ever wondered why we heal so quickly?" I asked him.

"I just assumed it was part of the time travel genetics." He pointed at the kitchen area.

"Is there anything to eat there?"

"I don't think everyone who travels recovers fast." I said, getting up from the chair at the table and opening cupboard doors. I made a reasonable snack out of tinned soup and some oatcakes with butter.

"Let me see," I said, as Tolly came over to the table. I checked the wound and removed the protective pressure padding. It was already granulating new tissue and completely dry under the repair sealant.

"Leave this off for now." I put the dirty dressing into a microbial digester that powered the cave dwelling. Once again Osric's design.

"What do *you* think then?" Tolly asked me, going back to a topic that was obviously on both our minds, not the being chased by unknown pirates but the DNA one.

"Look at this," I said, tapping more keys on the holographic screen. Two separate DNA profiles came up, there were clear differences in several areas.

"Is that you and Osric?" Tolly was eating soup and crunching oatcakes sticky with butter. He wiped his fingers on Osric's shirt. I winced.

"No, it's me and me."

Tolly stopped chewing. "How is that possible?" He whispered.

Osric spoke, making both of us jump, "I think time changes us."

I clutched my heart in a theatrical gesture, as it really felt as if it had jumped into my mouth. "Osric!" I went over to him and gave him a hug.

He was a great big man, firm and muscular with almost shaved grey hair and bright green eyes. If I had believed in therianthropy, Osric would have been able to shapeshift into a bear.

He went over to the large metal fire pit, which was balanced on a stand between the waterfall and the table, picked up a prosaic flint striker and lit the composite that looked and smelled remarkably like wood.

"I always feel that a fire makes this place cosy."

Somehow Osric filled the barren cave with his size, and it soon warmed, though it was probably the psychological feeling a fire gives us, the sense of safety we all carry in our memories from Palaeolithic times.

"Think epigenetics," Osric said.

It took me a moment to catch up and I could see by the expression on his face that Tolly was, unusually, processing at a slower rate.

Osric waited.

"Heritable phenotype changes that do not involve alterations in the DNA sequence?" I said smugly.

"You read that from my notes, didn't you?" Osric was dryly amused.

"Yes." I said, pointing at the holographic computer screen.

"'Interesting." Tolly had his thoughtful face on. "Epi means over or around, doesn't it?"

"It usually involves gene activity, yes." Osric was serious. "The effects can be cellular and physiological, but it's clear that it is coming from an external environmental factor, and not normal development."

It was completely quiet for several minutes. I realised that Osric's tunnel, like mine only an archway in depth, was still open. I could see a room which mirrored the one we were in. There were a few large scruffy tomes scattered on a table, rolled parchments and scientific instruments, crude, but clearly put together so as not to worry time too much. The books made my fingers itch to examine them.

Osric saw the direction of my gaze.

"No, you cannot *borrow* them," he said.

I smiled my most innocent smile and Osric sighed, but it was the proud sigh of a teacher for a difficult pupil. He had taken me on as his protégé when I first arrived at the sanctuary and trained me in the necessary survival skills. He'd encouraged a nascent interest in books to develop into a business that would provide me with a good living and would do what he most wanted, which was to save important works from the past for the future. That I had *saved* some of the books for my own collection he treated with parental indulgence.

"Tell me why I'm here instead of sitting with Oswith, the black-smith's wife, while she tries to give her useless husband yet another child?"

After processing that information with interest, Tolly spoke, "They lured my uncle into a trap and then killed him. I was chased through my own land by what I assumed were government trackers. When I was leading them away from my family's winter farm I made a tunnel, and they followed me into it. There were three of them. One caught up to me and we fought. I took this from him in the struggle." He put the small horse fetish down on the table. "When I killed him and ran the rest of the way to the exit at the travel tree, I was shot with a laser weapon."

I carried on, "I brought him here."

Momentarily still with apprehension, Osric eventually picked up the carved horse. "Is this the one you gave to Travis?"

"Yes," I answered simply.

"Did it seem they knew exactly where your family lives?" Osric looked at Tolly.

"I think so, but no one has ever gone after any of us like that before, it just doesn't make sense!" Tolly was frightened too. "I always thought if they hurt any of the time travellers' families then *no one* would go to work for them."

"That possibly still applies to the global government, I'm not sure it is the same for the AD Genetics pirates, and indeed Alice Dubrecht. I am beginning to wonder if they may have a different agenda." Osric sighed. "Things are changing, it's always been an unwritten rule that connected the people who could walk through time. The government has tracked us and left our families alone, but I don't think we can count on that any longer and I think in this case they were pirates."

"And I've just left my mother and sisters unprotected!" Tolly was white with fury and guilt.

"Why would anyone use a fetish belonging to another person?" I asked Osric, who was still holding the carved horse and turning it in his fingers.

"We travellers usually don't need to carry a fetish after training, but for a *very* few, this can be a memory map of journeys."

Tolly spoke quietly, "Is it more of the same time related genetic changes?" Osric nodded.

My mouth was dry with fear. "Would that apply to all fetishes?"

Osric shrugged. "The answer is, I just don't know."

"Tolly," I said, "where is your fetish?"

He replied sadly, "I left it with Albert. He wanted to copy it for someone who asked him for an eagle like mine."

I made a mental note to check in my bedroom side table for the mouse with a book in its hand, that Osric had made for me.

"Do you think Albert gave my fetish away?" Tolly was devastated.

"I think he was asked to make an eagle so that he would borrow yours and then whoever it was, took it to track you." Osric sounded resigned.

We sat in silence for a long moment.

"Were the men alive when you closed the tunnel?" Osric asked.

"Yes, I could see the other two running, but surely, they were lost when it collapsed?"

I was puzzled. I didn't think anyone really knew what happened when a tunnel disappeared, because to my knowledge, no one had ever been found or returned from the experience to talk about it.

"As we understand it, they are probably gone," Osric said.

"*Probably?*" Tolly whispered.

"Tolly, you have the ability to take time gene-less people into your tunnel, don't look at me like that, yes, I know about your own epige-netic development. Someone out there now knows what you can do. It would make life easier for those people who want to travel but don't have the gene and can't make a tunnel of their own. Think! No tank-mate or fetish required and as for the pirates, well, it would be a very useful and lucrative addition to their skill set."

Tolly's mouth had dropped open, he looked at me.

"Hey, I didn't tell him, because I didn't know until this morning that you could!" I was insulted. "I brought you to my place of safety *and* I let you use my downstairs shower!"

"Sorry." Tolly was instantly contrite. "I'm scared."

"Well, that makes three of us," Osric said.

"There's no possibility they could have gone back out through the tunnel entrance?" I asked.

Osric held his hands up in the air and with one above the other, palms facing slightly apart, he brought them together in a clap. I winced. It was graphic, but descriptive.

"Thank goodness for that," Tolly whispered.

"WHAT NOW?" I was pacing. Osric had been quiet for a while, in full deliberating mode. Tolly was stretched out in the chair by the fire. It was peaceful and the waterfall sounded like rain on the windows of a winter's night. I got closer to the tunnel arch that led into the room in 1330, curious about the books and what was on the other side of the locked door that I could just see the edge of.

"Gallimora!" Osric was not loud but I stopped still and it woke Tolly. Realising that it was just me in trouble as usual, he settled himself back into a more comfortable position.

"Stay away, please, in case I have to close it in a hurry."

"Why are you keeping it there?" I was intrigued, because I knew how much energy it took to open a tunnel, and to hold it.

"I asked brother Matthew to shout through the door if Oswith was in any difficulty. I can hear him and he is used to me locking it when I am working with dangerous herbs."

Tolly snorted. "The good brother must be a little short on observational skills."

"He has plenty of admirable abilities, including ignoring things he knows might turn out to be a problem!" Osric said dryly.

"I'm with brother Matthew, I find that strategy usually works for me," I muttered.

Nothing much was said again while we all contemplated the difficulties of what to do for the best.

"Well, we have no choice. We go to the sanctuary and see what we can find out about Travis. Then I think we will have to pay AD Genetics a little visit and remind them of the unwritten rule of time travellers."

"You mess with us we mess with you?" Tolly asked.

"Exactly."

"How are we going to do that?" The reply to my question was interrupted by a panicked staccato on the door through the time tunnel.

"Give me a moment!" Osric shouted, using modern English. Brother Matthew clearly ignored more than the goings on inside the herb room.

Osric turned to both of us as he got up, shaking his robes and walking through the smoky arch. "I won't be long; this baby is her fifth and the last one came out so fast I nearly fumbled the catch."

Tolly was pragmatic. As someone who delivered a variety of furry creatures each spring, he was well versed in the mechanics. I was surprised. Osric had played rugby along with Tom the postie for the local team and he was well known for never missing anything that was thrown his way.

He swept the door open, leaving the arch out of the line of sight, and I could hear the almost recognisable Middle English being spoken in the corridor. It was difficult to adjust, but I got the gist, which was something along the lines of, 'You really need to come *right now*!'

Osric waved a hand and the arch dissipated in a cloud of herb scented smoke, leaving Tolly and I to study the space where he had been and the plan he had suggested.

"This is going to involve running and shooting, isn't it?" Tolly said sadly.

I nodded. It would seem highly likely that there would be lots of both.

WE WENT BACK to the main house and I set about making tea again. I wasn't sure how quickly the baby would be born but Osric would let us know. Tolly was very quiet.

I was about to pour the hot water when I heard the door click open in the storage area. Osric came into the kitchen.

"You are kidding me?" I must have appeared as incredulous as I sounded because he laughed.

"I only just got there in time, mother and baby boy are doing fine, and as the little chap has four older sisters, his father is getting drunk in fourteenth century style."

We all looked at each other.

"Are we really doing this?" Tolly asked.

"I don't see that we have a choice." I sighed, then asked Osric. "Do you think it could work?"

"It will for now," he said ominously. "Things are changing. The stakes are higher and everyone wants what time can give them."

I shuddered. My life had never been simple, but it nearly always made sense and there were rules of a sort.

"Okay." Tolly got to his feet. "Show me what you have in the way of weapons."

I tried to look innocent. I don't usually carry anything when I travel, mostly I rely on stealth, sneaking around and running away. Tolly, however, wasn't buying it and Osric already knew where I kept my stash as it had been his. I pointed to the storage area.

We trooped in through the doorway and I went over to the shelving under the window. Pushing aside boxes of cleaning essentials I tapped the lighted keys of yet another security pad. A small door slid across. Inside were some very effective laser guns. And one or two explosive devices. Tolly whistled.

"It's important to be prepared." I shrugged. Osric nodded in sombre accord and Tolly shook his head at the two of us in disbelief.

"We go to the sanctuary first and come back here to pick up the, er, equipment?" He asked.

I looked at Osric, who concurred.

"I don't want to leave from here and go directly to our time, I can't take a chance on my security staying uncompromised. We have to travel to AD Genetics through the tree room." It would make things more complicated but I was adamant.

Tolly picked up one of the laser guns. "This is similar to what was used by the men chasing me, how is time letting you bring them through?"

"I didn't, I had them made here," Osric said. "The technology is available now but the design is not, I got a friend of Tom's to put them together for me."

I snorted at the description, the man who had delivered them was an ex-military associate of Tom the postie. And a mercenary looks exactly the same, whenever they are. He had been affable and helpful, checking that I knew how to work the slide and recharge the power unit before he left.

He also drank copious amounts of tea and spoke to Wilf with respect. I would have been happy to have him on my side and very worried if he was out tracking me on a dark night. Tom said he trusted him and he referred to the man as an old work colleague.

The mercenary, who had introduced himself as Dez, said he'd already been paid when I asked. I had tried really hard not to think precisely what that might mean. My conscience is cloudy most of the times I'm in.

AFTER A BIT of a tidy which drove both of them to making male noises of exasperation that would be recognisable in any language and any when, I was ready to go. I picked up my travel pack and checked the contents: medical kit, clean underwear, *and* reading matter, which caused slightly louder and more obvious comments. Wilf was sitting watching this from the comfort of the armchair and for a moment I wished I could light the fire against the cold spring evening and pull a book from the shelf. I did some sighing of my own.

THE TIME TRAVEL tree was quiet, which was odd. The caves that led off on the different sides of the central area were empty. Where there were usually cases of goods to be picked up by the stay puts, there was nothing. It seemed strange, I had never talked about it but I always felt a residue from other travellers, as if a door had just closed on someone leaving the room in an old house. I realised that both Tolly and Osric were on high alert.

Instead of us each using our own, I had made a narrow arch to the tree, however thick the pushback from time, travelling via one tunnel with Tolly was easiest. Though it still felt really strange. We moved on to the sanctuary.

I took a chance on getting a fine by not using the appropriate arrival concourse and opened an arch into Albert's living room in the apartment above his coffee shop.

We walked through and I used an extra push of energy to keep it open. Osric had made that seem easy, but it was really difficult. He put his hand on my shoulder for added strength, and I think comfort, but his fingers radiated worry.

Tolly had gone first and he was standing by the window looking down onto the sanctuary, his face paled to several shades past healthy. I went over to join him.

The whole area was empty. No trains, no people, nothing.

I HAVE NEVER FELT SO ALONE.

Osric sighed and said sadly, "This was something I was hoping not to see."

"Now I understand why they kept running the train engines," Tolly seemed oddly pragmatic.

"Where is everyone?" My voice was hoarse with apprehension, and the arch of my tunnel was shimmering like a wet cloud in the hot sunshine.

"At the next designated safe site." Osric sounded as practical as Tolly.

"And where *is* that exactly?" I was shaking and angry, clearly both of them knew something I didn't, again.

"I don't know," Osric said.

"No one does, except the one chosen elder," Tolly shrugged. "That's the point."

"How do we find them?" I was sweating by now and my time travel arch was almost invisible.

"We go back to the tree," Tolly said.

I could see that this was news to Osric but he kept quiet. I wondered what his strategy would have been. He obviously had one. I just couldn't understand why I didn't.

"Why don't *I* know how to find out where they are?"

"You're a straggler, you would get picked up eventually by someone you know, like me," Tolly spoke reassuringly.

"Thank you," I said weakly. I folded into a chair which was comfortingly very Albert. I wondered if he would miss his furniture, and then worried about the other things he might have taken with him. Hopefully no one was checking for illegal plastic contraband. The room was empty of all the personal stuff as if some warning had been given, but the items too large to move quickly, like furniture, were still around.

"I think we'd better get going," Osric was looking out of the window and he was puzzled. "I'm guessing, but I imagine this place is on a detonation timer."

"As in a *bomb*?" My voice was faint. I leaped to my feet and recharged the wavering arch back to the travel tree.

Tolly was once again through first. He checked two of the caves and I looked into a further three, while Osric examined the tree. The silence felt uncomfortable, as if the tree was listening for footsteps in the dark. After a moment of anxious reflection, I stood next to Osric and Tolly.

I had no idea what they were looking for but eventually Tolly pointed to a small red ribbon tied to a thin silvery twig and said, "Albert is with my family."

"Albert doesn't travel alone, he's a stay put!" I was incredulous.

"In an emergency he does; Albert and I agreed if there was one that we would meet at my place of safety. I think this qualifies," Tolly said dryly.

There was an odd sound, like the ripple on a calm sea. The tree shook slightly so that its silver leaves rustled in a non-existent wind. We were all holding our breath.

"I would say that was the destruction of the old sanctuary," Osric's voice was full of sadness.

"Has this happened before?" I had tears in my eyes. It seemed as if my home was gone, or I was, I couldn't work out which.

"Not in my time," Osric said, his face grey with pain and loss.

Tolly didn't seem so affected, but I could understand; his life was his family and his home was the plain surrounded by the Altai mountains. He didn't have the emotional tie that Osric and I experienced with the sanctuary.

I waited while Tolly opened his own tunnel. It was quite lengthy in as much as the exit was in shadow and curved around a slight bend. I waited until he had walked in, then I followed. Osric paused until we were halfway along before he entered, he was checking behind us, like the tail end Charlie of some long-ago army team. I knew the terminology because Tom the postie used it as part of his every day vernacular, and I figured he should know. It was comforting that Osric was watching our backs, but it also made me nervous to think that he needed to.

I WAS glad to get out of the viscous air into the cold evening of a Mongolian spring. There was still snow on the mountains and I shivered, then I put my pack down and fished around for a warm layer. I had never been through a tunnel I hadn't made. Though I trusted Tolly completely, we had gone through mine on the few occasions when we had travelled together instead of meeting at a designated time point. It was difficult to accept that it had been his genetic changes that had made it easier. I added two extra layers, a scarf and gloves. Osric was watching me with some amusement.

"Why are you grinning?" I said grumpily.

"What else do you have in there?" he snorted.

I was grateful for the ordinary conversation and the teasing, because my head was still full of the feeling that I was adrift on a very choppy sea, in a boat with no oars. The way the time travel tree reacted to the blasting of my once-sanctuary home was disturbing on a visceral level that spoke of a DNA relationship I didn't know I had.

"Has anyone studied the time travel tree?" I asked.

"With regard to what?" Osric was wearing his speculating expression, one that I recognised from the years we spent together when he was training me.

"Us," Tolly spoke quietly.

He must have been thinking about it for some while, whereas the thought had only just occurred to me.

"Let's cover that on another occasion," Osric said enigmatically.

I snorted, because that meant he had been doing some research on the subject but wasn't prepared to share his conclusions just yet. Osric could be quite secretive when it concerned his findings, something that I found irritating on several levels. More so at that moment, as it was becoming increasingly obvious to me that I was literally an open book when it came to hiding things.

THE LIGHTS from the ger camp were welcoming and I could hear voices around the central fire. A dog barked, but only in greeting. It came over to us and launched itself at Tolly, who staggered back under the welter of yips, barks and licks.

I heard a woman's voice, incredulous with hope, and then a small figure followed the dog on the launch pad of emotion. Tolly was inundated with female questions, the kind that meant no answers were required. In his Mongolian tongue they should have been unintelligible to me but they weren't. "Where have you been, we were so worried, we thought we had lost you too," are the same in any language.

We trailed his mother and two sisters back to the fire; the dog remained on guard in the shadows.

My knees were weak with suppressed shock and I sat down suddenly in a comfy chair that was shyly offered. Though no introductions were made and there was a sense of disquiet about our arrival, a hot milky drink had been placed into my hand and calm words encouraged me to drink. It burnt my tongue and clearly contained something very strong on the alcohol spectrum.

"Mama, where is Albert?" Tolly asked gently once we were all sitting down.

"He's inside the guest accommodation," his mum looked worried. "He was injured when he arrived." She stopped speaking as Tolly hurled himself out of his chair and ran to the ger. He pushed the door open and disappeared.

I sighed and got up. Gathering my pack, I went slowly after him. I pointed, "I might be able to help."

Tolly's mum nodded and smiled thinly, her continued reservations obvious. "He said you had a gift for healing."

"I'm not actually medically trained," I explained. "But I do have some skills, I'm just not sure healing is one of them."

"I have a doctorate in zoology, so I'm aware of the difference," she said dryly, sounding exactly like Tolly.

"I'm sorry," I said, "I wasn't trying to be flippant."

Osric snorted, "Call me if you need help."

"I'm pretty sure he won't be pregnant!" I stalked off after Tolly.

A faint remark wafted over the night air. "Oh no, not a bit flippant."

THE GER WAS DIMLY LIT and warm, all the creature comforts encompassed in a massive, sturdy, circular tent. The wood-burning stove was central and the flames flickered and danced behind a clear cover. It might have looked primitive but the equipment and fittings were modern and ecological. A bed on one side was balanced by a kitchen unit on the other, and the small bathroom was accessed at the back opposite the main entrance, which was a low, carved wood door. The foot of the bed faced the stove. Albert lay quietly, his breathing shallow but not laboured.

I walked over to where Tolly was standing looking down at him, holding his hand, his face suffused with barely controlled anxiety. Albert's eyes were closed but I could see that his fingers were curved in Tolly's.

I pointed at the bathroom. "How does that work?"

Tolly came out of his fugue state. "The main water supply and drainage are already underground and we just hook up when we arrive."

It was so prosaic an explanation, I was a little bit disappointed for a moment.

Albert sniggered, a sound that was literally music to my ears. "I'm going to need a surgeon," he wheezed.

I pulled back the thick covers. They were light, warm and very soft: the cashmere goats had been helping out. On the floor, nearly hidden under the bed, was a bloody lump of the illicit plastic wrap, with a straw and a water bottle made out of the same stuff. Albert watched my expression, his crude attempt at a chest tube had clearly been successful. I'd been able to bring them forward because for some reason, time was on our side. Hoping to avoid any awkward questions, I slid the illegal mess further out of sight with my foot.

The transparent dressing was sucking on a wound, attached to it was a tube that was circulating blood. I followed it to a small dialysis machine, which was in turn fixed to Albert's arm.

"Whoa," I whispered. "Why isn't this healing?"

"Something that was in the projectile is preventing it," Albert explained.

"Will a transfusion of blood from a donor help?" Tolly asked him.

"It might, but you can't do it, or you Galli," he said to me, as I opened my mouth to ask.

"What *can* I do, Albert?"

He looked at me, the dim light made his face unreadable but he sighed. "Open a tunnel to my home."

Tolly was horrified. "Are you sure they will help?"

"My mother is a doctor, she is also an exact genetic match for me, her blood will fix this."

It was my turn to be stunned. Albert was a clone.

"NOT TECHNICALLY," Albert explained. "I'm a bit of an experiment. It was more like a type of parthenogenesis. My mother is a geneticist, she was working for the global government on the usual quest to create a traveller—"

"Are you saying she succeeded?" I interjected.

"Galli!" Tolly was exasperated.

"My mother was an unwilling participant for a variety of reasons and would never have really tried, but she was able to make me. She has the recessive gene; her twin brother has the dominant one and was a time runner."

I contemplated that for a moment while I looked at the blood circulating. Even in the half-light I could see it was not a healthy colour.

Gene editing for congenital abnormalities or choosing the sex of the baby was not new, but cloning was frowned upon because it usually caused severe problems in most mammals. Mixing in the DNA of other species was highly illegal, though I was damn sure it went on. Most scientists employed the 'just because you can doesn't mean to say you should' rule, except where the traveller genes were concerned and then all bets were off.

"Do you have any medical problems from the process, Albert?"

"One or two, my immune system as you can see lacks a little something, so there's that, and of course the fact that I'm not entirely male," he said dryly.

I leaned out of the ger doorway and whispered loudly for Osric, who came striding over. The rest of Tolly's family and the dog stayed by the fire, though I could see his mum's eyes glinting in the light as she watched. I understood her reticence about our arrival, we were the unnecessary evil, and every time we turned up people died.

"We need to open a tunnel and send a message through. If I do the arch, can you stand by, just in case—"

"In case of what?" Osric interrupted me.

"We're going to send Albert to his mum," Tolly explained. "He needs a blood transfusion and she's a match."

"Is she now," Osric muttered. "I thought you had a death sentence on your head if you went back?"

Albert sighed, "It might be negotiable and I will die anyway if I stay here."

Osric held up the line with the now seriously discoloured blood running through it; he let it drop. "Right, what do we say?"

Albert gestured to a satchel that was lying on one of the low seats covered in carpet, scattered around the ger. I picked it up and brought it to him, he weakly fished around inside until Tolly took over, pulling out a variety of small objects, all designed to be fetishes, something that Albert supplied to new time runners. I thought I saw a flash of illicit red nylon troll hair, and winced. A small beautiful carving of a reindeer made Albert pause.

"This one," he said. "She'll know who it's from."

Albert gave me a set of place coordinates and a time grid and I opened the arch holding onto his hand, which was quicker than going via the tree but not safer. It was hard to hold it open, because as well as all the research I usually did, I have to be able to think myself somewhere as part of the third reference point and I was using him for that.

Tolly propped Albert up so he could see if I was in the right place. He nodded, too out of breath to speak, and Osric threw the fetish. It bounced and came to rest by the back of a chair. A small slim hand reached down and picked it up just as the tunnel arch closed.

Albert slumped back on the pillows, exhausted. Tolly's face was grey with worry.

"Why does this feel like a trap?" I whispered half to myself.

"Probably because it is," Osric said.

"How long do we wait?" I added, after the collective silence of many thinkers. A slight sound made me jump; Albert weakly indicated there was something under the bed. I moved the covers out of the way and with building trepidation, crouched down to look. "Juno!"

"Please take care of her for me?" Albert made it sound final. I scooped the disgruntled cat into my arms and she settled down and rumbled her thanks.

A tunnel suddenly shimmered by the bathroom doorway, and a short stocky man came through, his weapon held in front of him. We all stood still, fear making us rigid.

Tolly moved his hand slowly towards the flap of his del, I wondered for a second if he had borrowed something from my store before we left home. Then realised that he would not have needed to. Tolly was always prepared.

The man made a placating gesture and Albert seemed shocked for a second, and then resigned. They conversed for a few sentences in speech that none of us understood.

Mostly people used the common tongue, which was a mix of English, and a little Chinese and Spanish, to communicate, but the old languages were still spoken by the different tribes who clung precariously to the past.

"This is my, um, brother," Albert stumbled over the term, so I took that to mean his mum had not stopped with one version of the cloning-parthenogenesis attempt.

The man bowed. "I am Reggie."

Yes of course you are, I thought. As a made-up name it was fine. I waved with the hand that was free from cuddling Juno, but didn't introduce myself.

Tolly interjected before the stilted conversation deteriorated even further. "We need to move him now; can you help us with a tunnel that he can go through?"

Reggie nodded and an arch appeared behind him. I must have looked surprised and a little horrified because he gave me a wicked grin. A pirate with traveller abilities.

On the other side were three people, the older woman had long blonde hair an air of superiority and was dressed warmly in the decorative skins of a northerly tribe. I assumed this was Albert's mother. She appeared vaguely familiar to me but I couldn't place her, and I thought it was probably because she reminded me of Albert.

Standing next to her was a man with the weary air of an overworked medical doctor.

The third person was a very young woman who was an exact clone of her mother, but with the palest skin I have ever seen.

"Alice," Osric said, in his most sarcastic drawl, looking at Albert's mother, "how are you?"

I did a double take worthy of one of the televised comedies that Tom the postie made me watch. Osric was *furious*. I glanced at Tolly; he was neither surprised nor angry, just very sad.

I realised my mouth was open and I shut it, trying to maintain a bit of dignity.

"Osric," she drawled, "if that's what you're calling yourself these days, how nice to see you."

It was like watching a fourteenth-century bear baiting, I wondered if she had any idea how angry he was and just how dangerous it made him.

Albert spoke up, "This is what you wanted, but that's it, no one else."

I may be slow but I get there in the end.

IT WAS SOMETHING OF A STANDOFF, as we were one side of the arch which was beginning to waver and they were still on the other. Albert was pale but determined.

Osric sighed and his anger simmered somewhere slightly below boiling point. "I asked you to leave us alone, in return I have not interfered in your..." he hesitated over the word, "experiments."

Alice Dubrecht shrugged as if she didn't care what he thought, but I could see she was watching him intently. I found myself holding my breath and I exhaled slowly.

"Are you responsible for the death of Tolly's uncle?" Osric spat the words out.

"Sorry about that," she said turning to Tolly, "sometimes the staff can be a little overzealous."

"What about chasing him into his tunnel, and *shooting* him?" Osric added.

"Ditto," Alice smiled winningly, holding her hands out as if she was a little girl being told off for scrumping apples in a neighbour's orchard. "But you have to be impressed that we found one of the few travellers who could take a time gene-less person through their own tunnel?" She really did look as if she wanted Osric's approval. It was creepy and I shuddered. Alice Dubrecht was a psychopath.

She examined Tolly for his reaction, then her gaze slid over towards me. "This is your protégé Galli, I take it?"

I felt as if my skin was covered in spiders and tried not to look horrified. I must have squeezed Juno a little too tightly because she meowed in complaint, so I put her down and she scuttled under a low chair on the other side of the ger.

"Well brother, this has been nice but we really must be going. Albert and I have some catching up to do."

If I heard the word, I hadn't really taken it in, and Tolly didn't react so I just stood there like Barney trying to ignore Bessie when she was being provocative.

They moved swiftly through the arch and without speaking to us, took control of the bed and the equipment.

In no more than a matter of minutes, they were gone.

Tolly looked bereft. I reached for his hand and we stood there for a moment.

Osric sighed. "I'm so sorry."

Tolly's painful silence filled the ger.

"When did you know?" Osric asked him.

"I have been very close to Albert, some of it I heard from him and I worked out the rest." Tolly was whispering and he didn't look at me.

"Why didn't anyone tell me?" I asked sadly.

"It was to protect you," Tolly explained.

"I didn't know I needed protecting," I said to myself. Then, as if the word came back to me in a flash of memory and I suddenly realised she wasn't referring to his monk-like status. "*She's your twin sister?*"

"DO we have the coordinates for the new sanctuary now?" I asked, hoping it was something that Albert had known and passed on.

"No," Tolly said, "And even if we did, we can't go there."

"Where did that arch open from?" I'd no idea, as it wasn't to the same place as the one I had created to send the fetish through.

Neither of them answered me.

"WHAT DO WE DO NOW?" Tolly was speaking to Osric. The night was quiet, the family had gone to bed in the other ger. His sisters, who usually slept alone, decided to go with their mother. I didn't blame them.

I built up the fire. We drank hot creamy milk with cinnamon and ate hard cheese and crumbly biscuits made with the same yak milk, our tiredness and fear morphing into hunger.

"We go home," Osric was whispering, which made me nervous though all there was, were stars in a clear cold sky, the dog dozing peacefully, with one ear cocked for the safety of the goat herd, and Juno, curled into a sad furry ball on my lap.

"I *am* home," Tolly said. "What are the chances that they will come back here soon?"

We all knew to whom he was referring.

"I think Alice will concentrate on Albert." Osric shrugged.

The thought made me shudder and I was glad that I wouldn't be the focus of her attention. Then I felt guilty, because Albert had handed himself over so the rest of us could go free. In my head I added the thought, for now.

"But..." Osric said and then said nothing.

"It's only a matter of time," I was not helping anyone including myself, by stating the obvious.

I WENT 'HOME' the next day, via the tree. Very carefully opening an arch and closing it again, repeating the connection until I was sure there was no one waiting for us. Osric stood patiently while I completed the paranoid process to my satisfaction. He was preoccupied to the level of a deep, thought-filled silence, and he carried Juno for me.

Tolly and his sisters waved me goodbye. His mum had given me a worried but busy hug earlier that morning before going to check on the goats. I still hadn't been introduced to his family, no names were given or mentioned, something that I think Tolly's mum had insisted on.

He'd told me once, when we first met, that his mum had met his dad, who was studying to be a mining engineer, at university. Clearly his sisters were not from the same relationship. It was odd how we were such close friends but I hardly knew anything about him. I realised, with sadness, that my own life was just as hidden.

Leaving felt very ordinary, as if the day hadn't followed the awful, frightening night before, but something more prosaic.

The tree sat in its quiet cave, the leaves rustling in an unquantifiable breeze. There were no further messages from anyone, I checked over and over in the short space of time that I allowed myself to be there. If Osric carried out any examination of his own, I didn't notice.

Eventually with a sigh of sadness and frustration, I pinned a colourful piece of ribbon from my favourite chocolate shop in my place of safety time, on a small shimmery twig. There was one person I knew who would recognise it, she and I both having something of an addiction to their honey-bee variety.

Osric and I went through another arch, after carefully listening to the echoes of nothing in the passageways joining the tree cave.

He sat down in my living room chair, putting Juno gently on the floor and I went to the kitchen area and made tea. I found the tin of ginger biscuits had magically refilled and after a moment or two the cat flap pinged and Wilf arrived, his tail swishing in greeting and irritation about being left out of the excitement. He went straight over to Osric and waited, staring as only cats can with no patience at all, until Osric picked him up and began stroking his head. Wilf settled down and began to wash.

If my cat noticed Juno, he didn't acknowledge her. She eventually moved to lie on a corner of the carpet and did some fairly impressive ablutions of her own before curling up to sleep.

"Where do you think Alice will come first, here or Tolly's?" I sipped tea, sitting down in the other chair by the fireplace. I thought about lighting it but I was too tired and it wasn't that chilly.

"I imagine it's not that easy to stalk nomads through the Altai mountains, despite the memory map in the stolen fetish. I think it was probably something of a fluke that it worked before." Osric waited for me to catch up, then added, "It wasn't the tracker you left in 1348, it was pirates *and* a traveller who followed Tolly into his tunnel."

"She has one of us working for her," I added sadly.

He nodded in satisfaction, as if pleased with his pupil. I thought, letting my mind wander through the information we had accumulated and all the missing pieces. I sat up, shocked. "Travis! It's actually him, isn't it? Tolly and I thought he was another victim but he's the traitor."

For a moment I was truly horrified. Albert's behaviour I could somehow understand. His mother had hunted him as well as us, which was why he'd hardly ever gone anywhere away from the sanctuary, and I had every sympathy for his situation and the silence on his secrets. But Travis I'd admired, voted for and *trusted*. I had given him the stone horse fetish belonging to the government tracker I'd left in 1348. Alice Dubrecht and her pirates, one of whom had shot my friend, were connected to the elder I looked up to.

"There are people within the sanctuary who really believe we should negotiate with both the global government and the pirates." Osric was sad in his revelation.

"I didn't think I could feel any more betrayed, but you just made me realise I can." I was something else as well. Really *angry*.

"I need to speak to Tom," Osric said.

———

THE CONVERSATION with Tom was bizarre. Answering the ping on his iPad almost immediately, he blinked a few times and then said with an impressive level of irony, "It's a shame you missed your funeral, my eulogy was both humorous and interesting."

"I'm sorry I wasn't there for it too," Osric was equally dry.

"What do you need?" Tom switched to the point.

"We're going to get some unhelpful visitors."

I tried not to snort.

"Should I bring a work colleague?" Tom replied.

"Two would be better," Osric said.

"What about supplies?"

Osric looked at me enquiringly. I nodded. "We have plenty," he said.

"Good enough," Tom was texting while he spoke. "We'll be there in," he consulted the return text, "two hours."

Osric and Tom regarded each other, no thanks were necessary or forthcoming. I wondered, and not for the first time, what their history was. Clearly the respect went both ways. The communication ended without goodbyes.

———

THEY CAME in the early hours. Like wraiths, full of fear and shadows.

After Osric finished his conversation with Tom, I had a long bath, because a run-in with a psychopath was always much easier if you were clean. Then I checked the security space in the storage room and pulled out all the laser guns and power ammunition packs that I had.

Osric had changed out of his monk's robes into something easier to fight in, and after rummaging around in the detritus on his desk in the hidden cave, he came back with several small, innocuous-looking devices.

"These were just hanging around amongst the books?" I asked him, incredulous.

"Well, I was working on them and they're not dangerous unless you set the timer," he explained, far too calmly.

"Peachy!" I was scared, so sarcasm helped.

He snorted, and began plotting a series of moves on a scrap of paper with a pencil.

Tom and two of his colleagues arrived, one of whom I recognised from my foray into weapons requisition. Dez nodded to me and introduced his associate by pointing a thumb to the side, "Ray." The woman was short, blonde, unsmiling and similarly disarmingly unremarkable.

Dez and Ray set about checking my stock of guns and ammunition, conferring with Tom. They both made noises of interest and grudging admiration, though no actual words were discernible. I made lots and lots of tea.

Ray examined the planned drawing that Osric had left on the table. Her mouth was full of biscuit but I think she said, "Pen and paper, old school, good!" Thereafter there was information, conferring and confirmation.

Glancing at the drawing myself I sighed, went to the bookshelves and tapped a keypad beside each set: a neat shutter slid sideways over the vulnerable books. By the large glass French windows to the left of the main room another keypad sent a layer of transparent reinforced carbon fibre gliding into place. All of them watched for a moment then went back to talking about the plan. I covered the few bits of furniture that I had and rolled up the carpet. The talking stopped again for a second or two then resumed. Going up the stairs I did the same with the books in the bedroom and bathroom. I threw a protective cover over my bed and removed the paintings. The store next to the kitchen got the shutter treatment and after that the utility room. I went over it all for a second time, to make sure I hadn't missed anything.

"Impressive!" Dez said. He handed me a gun and watched while I checked that the safety was on before I removed the laser pack and examined the connections and charge.

I listened to the conversation but didn't join in.

"This one I want alive," Osric was showing them a holograph which spun lazily in the middle of the table. The technology for the image was emergent, but not readily available. No one commented, they were holding actual laser guns so I think they got it.

"This one?" Tom asked, pointing at another holograph. Osric shrugged and thought about it. He shook his head.

"What about anyone else?" Ray's tone was matter-of-fact, and the unspoken question clear.

"No." Osric said.

They all looked at each other and nodded. No one added anything, so they moved on to the tactics and positioning aspects of the plan.

I made more tea. Really, I have no idea where they put it, not one of them said no, we were all awash. I used up my entire store of chocolate biscuits and even my emergency stash, after Osric looked pointedly at the hiding place in the bottom drawer under the oven where I kept my pans.

Tom went out, sweeping up an armful of astonished tabby fur from their observation point on the kitchen counter, they both took the insubordination quite well under the circumstances. He moved the horses to the further field over the other side of the hidden cave. I never used it as I couldn't keep an eye on them and it was too far from the house for Maddie to do a casual check when I was away. There was, however, a small field shelter with a door that could be locked if necessary and it had a security camera feed to my computer. I could see that neither Barney or Bessie was particularly impressed with Tom or their alternative bijou accommodation. We could hear him assure them both that this was temporary. Dez snorted, making him sound exactly like Barney who did the same. The cats retreated to the loft above the stalls, where a plentiful supply of interesting things scratching around in the hay had caught their attention.

As the light began to change to dusk and then quickly to dark, Tom and Ray left to take up watch positions outside in the woods near the stables. Dez went into the bedroom and climbed out of the dormer window. There was an uncomfortable and very small flat area on the porch over the door to the utility area, where he could observe the side of the house not covered by Tom and Ray.

After some thought and a completely non-verbal conversation with Osric, who had decided on a more relaxed position next to the unlit fire in one of the chairs I had previously covered, with a gun and a book in his lap, I contacted Tolly. It was through a very fast arch, which I had opened and closed twice, once for the message, a screwed-up piece of paper around a lump of Altai rock, and then for his answer. He was awake and pacing close to the fire that seemed invitingly reassuring. Tolly stood on his side of the arch for a moment, in silence. His mother and sisters had gone to hide in some caves in the Altai mountains, which were an old and well-kept family secret. The fire was a lure and several members of his extensive tribe waited, hidden beyond the camp in the trees. Their own range of weapons were impressive.

"Send the signal through as soon as you know and I will come," he said simply, then walked away as I closed the tunnel.

All my illusions about my safe place were disintegrating as if snow had fallen on hot water.

So I made more tea.

AT FIRST THERE WAS A FEELING. I sat up from my uncomfortable position the other side of the cold fireplace, where I had been dozing. I could see the Osric shape in the darkness half out of his chair. He didn't make a sound, but we were both suddenly alert. Reaching for his bone-conduction earpiece, thoughtfully supplied by Tom, he tapped it twice, which was a pre-arranged sign. In my own ear I heard the return tapping. One for nothing, two for be aware.

Tap... tap. They were here.

My hand was gripping the gun in my lap and I slid the safety across. The sound of it clicking filled the waiting stillness like a thunderclap.

Osric turned to me just as Tom whispered, "Three at the side of the stables, coming your way."

"Three?" I whispered back.

"She's overconfident, and thinks that it's just you and me," Osric was scathing.

Tolly?" I added.

"I imagine he may be experiencing something similar." He went over to the French windows and silently did some very un-monk-like sneaking and peaking.

"Two more coming from this side," Dez's voice was a murmur in my ear.

"Not as overconfident as you thought," I said as quietly as I could, to Osric.

Tom spoke in a conversational tone, "Stand by."

We waited for Dez to give the signal that the two at the front were who we hoped them to be. The alternative plan included a lot of improvisation, and for my part some running around and screaming was not out of the question.

"Affirm," Dez whispered triumphantly.

"Fire," Tom said calmly.

There was the sound of shooting and flashes of laser light. The three at the back put up a good defence. I stayed propped up against the side of the kitchen cabinet, furthest away from the door to the utility room.

Dez shot the taller of the two in the first second, killing him, the other shadow made it into the house and used the doorway as cover to fire up to the roof where Dez was no longer hiding. He came through the window in the bedroom like a silent avenging ghost, and stopped at the top of the stairs. Osric was wearing the designated green light on his shoulder which indicated friend not foe, and it took no more than an additional second for Dez to check my location, then he lowered his weapon.

The house was dark but a gibbous moon shone through the windows and gave us enough light to distinguish each other from the non-malignant shadows, like the kitchen sink and the table. That and reasonable night vision, all of us having sat in the dark for several hours, waiting.

I could hear the person in the utility room checking a charge in the gun they carried. Suddenly the noise outside the back of the house stopped. It was over.

It wasn't much of a firefight, as no one wanted it to carry on inside the bothie. The expression FIBUA had been used at the briefing, which I had been told was fighting in built up areas, not exactly appropriate for a description of my home but I got the idea.

And I was hoping that the person in the utility room would have the sense to realise that they had lost.

The sound of a double tap of gunfire from outside made me wince. No wounded, no prisoners, no mercy. And no sleep while I remembered the echo of the thought.

A small noise from the utility room and then a scuffle. Tom and Ray had moved quietly.

The door opened and a ceiling light came on in the main room, making me wince with the sudden cold brilliance of it. Osric held my household remote control in his hand.

Ray pushed a small figure to the floor.

"Nice welcome, brother Osric," Alice Dubrecht said cheerfully.

I shook my head, either she had something else planned or she really didn't understand what a dangerous situation she was in. I was hoping it was the latter.

"We found these out by the stables," Tom said.

Osric paled; he moved his hand as if placating a rabid dog. "Gently Tom, put them down very carefully please."

"I defused them," Tom was matter-of-fact cool.

"They come with a booby trap as standard," Osric spoke with icy calm.

"I disabled that too," Tom smiled.

Alice's face went from cat that had got the cream, to furious psychopath, in an instant. I think she even hissed.

"Really for something so," Tom hunted for a word, confirming my suspicions about Osric's sharing of secrets, he eventually went with, "sophisticated, they are actually quite intuitive." He nodded his approval and Ray leaned in slightly for a closer look. She shrugged, clearly unimpressed.

Alice's expression was incredulous. That's the problem with psychopathy, absolutely no sense of humour.

"What now?" She asked Osric, getting to the point. For which I was oddly grateful, as my tiredness had overcome my adrenalin fear and I was wondering exactly that myself.

"We're going to have a chat," Osric told her.

If ever a statement sounded ominous it was this, not that Alice noticed. I shook my head, the woman still seemed to think she had the upper hand.

"Galli, I need you to open an arch into deep time."

At last, the words that made her stop smiling.

If I'd had the energy I would have gasped. From the expressions on the faces of Tom's work associates they clearly had no clue what it meant, but were curious.

"Osric, brother, you know you can't send a living person through?" Alice was back to confident.

"I have no intention of send anyone *living*," Osric said.

I DIDN'T WATCH as Tom and Dez moved the bodies of Alice's employees to an area behind the stables. Dez went back and picked up Travis from the front of the house. It was awful. Dawn had found us conferring, Osric explaining what he needed them to do and why. Alice observed with interest and speculation, much as you would a failed experiment. I began sorting out my house and waited for them to come and get me. Then I made tea, again.

It was early morning when Tom walked back into the kitchen and nodded to my unasked question.

The arch into deep time was a matter of rumour and gossip amongst travellers, I had never told anyone I was able to do it and never asked Tolly or anybody else if they could. That Osric was aware had come as something of a surprise to me.

I was exhausted and it took a great deal of power. Eventually the arch wavered and the cold smoke took shape. The other side was somewhen I'd never ventured, because I had thought it was likely I would have been eaten by something large and fast; now I knew it was another place time wouldn't let me go. It intrigued Ray. Dez held her shoulder when she leaned in.

"You're exactly no fun at all Dez," Ray muttered.

They rolled the bodies through, stripped of all dignity and I waited for time to spit them back. The arch faded as I sweated, and nothing happened. It made me wonder, and not for the first time, about Osric's own abilities.

There was a shout from the house and we all started running. Some of us, as in me, were panicking.

Dez and Ray circled around and into the utility room door and I went straight through the French windows, now open to the morning.

Tolly was lying on my sitting room floor, bleeding. I thought for an inappropriate moment, along with a strong sense of déjà vu, that I wished I hadn't already unrolled the carpet.

Alice smiled, her lips curved and her teeth on display, like a well-paid politician. I was really beginning to dislike her, which made a pleasant change from being afraid.

I knelt down next to Osric, who was holding his own hand over a spreading stain of blood in a worrying chest area on Tolly's body. He looked at me as my friend opened his eyes. "There were too many and they were good, several of my family were killed. I was coming to tell you when I was ambushed."

The psycho's smile widened even more.

"But we won in the end; they're all dead, even the one who did this." He fainted and his breath was becoming laboured.

Alice shrieked in fury, making Tom, who had arrived last, weirdly via my bathroom window, raise his gun and aim it at her. Even securely and incongruously tied to one of my kitchen table chairs, she felt dangerous.

Taking a chance, which was more of a calculated feeling than the edge of your seat kind. I said to Tom, "Ring the air ambulance!"

"Are you sure?" He asked me, his face betraying a knowledge that would have been disturbing if I hadn't been all out of worry.

"Now!" I shouted.

Osric leaned toward me, about to ask a question. I shook my head. Ray hurried over with her field kit and we went to work trying to pack the hole and stem the bleeding. We checked for the exit wound, and packed that too, using a combination of current time combat dressings and my own version of sphagnum moss-based coagulant gel.

I could hear Tom in the background giving information and then a grid reference to the controller. He explained that they had been doing a live fire exercise, inferring special forces were involved. I raised my eyebrows to Osric who nodded that, yes, he had it covered. The neighbours were going to be hearing about it, because it was a village and everyone knew everything. They would be either indignant or impressed, depending on how Tom could spin it.

"Four minutes out," my mystery postie said.

"Right." Osric got to his feet and went over to Alice. He untied her from the chair and gripping her arm, took her away. Alice's face was impassive and disconcertingly the confidence was back.

Almost exactly four minutes later, I heard the Eurocopter EC135's distinctive rotor blades as Tom guided it in to the field behind the barns. A small part of my brain was impressed because there isn't a bit of land on the moor that is in any way flat.

Tolly was lying still, his breathing laboured. I held his hand and whispered over and over, "Stay with me, please!" He squeezed my fingers, but his eyes were closed.

Two medics ran in with the heavy bags slung over their backs, one was a large dark-skinned young man with a reassuringly confident manner, the other a slim, very beautiful, Asian woman.

"Hi Rachel," I said.

"You two know each other?" The man asked, he pointed at himself, "Martin the paramedic, by the way."

"Hey Galli," Rachel grinned. She explained to the paramedic, "We both did some time in various voluntary children's organisations, and just kept bumping into each other." She shrugged. It was, for the most part, a true statement.

"Well, it's good to meet you Galli, and we're lucky to have Doctor Kavi training with us at Eaglescott this last two months." While he spoke, he worked on Tolly, cutting off his bloody clothing and checking the wound, much as we had done. He nodded his approval at the packing, handed Rachel an intubation tube, then began putting in an IV line for fluids. I could see Tolly's blood pressure rising to an acceptable level on the monitor and sighed with relief.

Tom came in. "She's burning and turning, ready when you are."

Something happened as he looked at Rachel. It was interesting, I mean, their eyes met and an indefinable moment occurred. Even Martin the paramedic noticed as he was setting up the stretcher.

"Your friends I take it," he indicated Ray and Dez, who were both standing quietly over by the stairs out of the way. No sign of the weapons that had been very much in evidence earlier, but still managing to look deadly.

"You haven't seen them and they were never here," Tom said to him.

"Got it boss," the paramedic answered, clearly having worn another type of uniform in his not-too-distant past. He was impressively unfazed by the blood, soldiers and the situation. "Ready?" he asked Rachel.

She took my hand. "It's good to see you Galli. Don't worry, we'll take care of Tolly."

As they were leaving, I heard Martin saying, "How do you know his name?" He snorted, "Wait, let me guess, don't ask!"

"Don't worry, I'll do the forms on the ride back," she answered.

Their voices receded and the helicopter took off. I looked out of the French windows at the rising sun's rays glinting off the rotor blades. It looked like the morning star.

"WHERE IS SHE?" I asked Osric when it was quiet for several minutes.

"Somewhere safe." He smiled.

He was right. If I had known of her whereabouts at that moment, my hands covered in the blood of my closest friend, the brother of my heart, her safety would most definitely have been in question.

"Anything we can do for you before we go?" Dez asked.

I looked around at my house. Apart from the carpet and a few muddy footprints there was no sign of any trouble. I went over to the kitchen cupboards and found some cleaning solution that I had made up from the ubiquitous sphagnum moss and scattered it over the bloodstains.

"Hey, can I get some of that?" Ray asked, looking down at the carpet, impressed with the almost immediate results.

"Sure, have this one, I've got some more in the store room," I sounded as out of it as I felt.

"You know what, I'm going to make tea," Tom said, looking at me.

"I'll do a perimeter sweep, two sugars please," Dez went out of the French windows.

"Any more of those biscuits to go with it?" Ray followed Dez out, "I'll sanitize the kill zone area, boss."

I didn't think her remark meant what I thought it did. Tom explained, which somehow made it worse, "Checking for traces of, um, us and them."

I looked at my hands again. "I think I'm going to wash."

The bathroom felt peaceful, and the bath looked like a haven of calm. I settled for cleaning the blood from under my nails after I'd transferred the tiny crystal information chip that Rachel had palmed into my hand before she left.

The laptop was on the side table in the bedroom. One of the techs I knew from the sanctuary had adapted it for me and time, obligingly, let me bring it home.

I used my own personal fingerprint and then input a code. A small holographic file emerged. It said, 'Don't go looking, it's not safe.'

"THAT'S IT?" Osric was exasperated.

"I imagine she didn't want to put anything else in there that would incriminate her or expose us." I was sad, empty and frightened. My sanctuary had moved and I didn't know where it was, but even if I did, I couldn't go there.

"I wonder what's going on?" Osric mused.

"Well," Tom said, delivering tea and buttered toast to the table, "you could ask her."

We both looked at him, me because I really didn't understand just how much of my life he'd become privy to and Osric who amazingly, hadn't seemed to have thought of it.

"She works at the air ambulance base, it's a few clicks in that direction," he pointed.

I ate the toast, Osric ambled off to the cave, plate in hand, to do some work, or so he said. Tom went home and returned in his normal off-duty postman clothes. Ray and Dez came to say goodbye after finishing whatever they were doing outside. Ray took some of my cleaning gel, pointing at a large, nasty looking, discoloured patch on her jacket. I was blood stain immune at that point.

Dez cleared his throat, "If you ever need me to check your ammunition packs, this is my private number." He handed me a scrap of paper. Ray shook her head and rolled her eyes.

They left and I heard her not too quiet whisper, "You could have asked her out for a drink!"

And Dez's ironic reply, "We just rolled some dead bodies through a time door, I didn't think that would cut it."

Eventually Osric stomped back into the kitchen and began making tea. He was furious and had a bruise over one eye. No explanation was offered and I assumed it was psycho twin sister Alice related. Tom sat at the table working on his laptop and I waited in my silent circle of worry.

THE PHONE CALL made all of us jump, not a good look for an ex-special forces operative and whatever category Osric fell into. For me though, it was absolutely fine. I answered and when Rachel spoke, I put her on speaker.

"He's going to be okay." She sounded exhausted.

"When can I see him?" My voice was trembling.

"Yes, it might be a good idea to move him to a private facility where he can recover at his own pace." Rachel answered, as if to a different question.

I got it. "I take it his healing rate is already causing some curiosity?"

"Of course, later on today will be okay, I'll be happy to accompany him."

I looked at Tom, he nodded and began tapping keys.

"The transport will be on the way as soon as Tom can organise it."

"I'll be in touch once I get his discharge paperwork done." She disconnected.

"Well," I said, after relief and no sleep were displaced once more with apprehension, "What was that about?"

"Rachel being careful?" Tom said hopefully. He tapped a final key. "Dez and Ray will pick him up at four this afternoon using a private ambulance."

"Where are they going to get hold of one of those?" I asked. He shrugged and Osric snorted.

ACCORDING TO RAY, Tolly complained most of the way and she had to threaten to sedate him before he stopped.

We put my friend in the cave after making up the sofa-bed, as Osric had decided he was going to look after him, the back and forward to 1330 being less obvious there. I sat on a chair and held Tolly's hand for a moment. Rachel and Tom came through to the cave after seeing Ray and Dez off for the second time in a day.

"I can't stay long," Rachel was tired.

"Please." Osric indicated a chair and we all made ourselves comfortable.

"What happened?" I asked her.

She sighed. "It's all gone."

"We know about the sanctuary." Osric's face showed his devastation.

I stumbled around to find the right words and settled on, "Who was it?"

"Do you remember the young boy I asked you about, the last time we saw each other?"

I had to think for a minute, the experiences of the previous two days and nights had stretched out in my mind to feel more like a week. But eventually I remembered, "Yes, a beautiful child but disturbingly blank?"

Rachel sighed. "He wasn't a time runner; he was a tracker."

"But he couldn't have been more than *eight*!" I was incredulous.

Osric and Tom were listening, one with the dubious benefit of experience, the other, with the interest of the newly involved.

"And a tracker with a difference," Rachel continued. "He led the global government team right to us."

"How could he have done that?" Osric was talking mainly to himself.

"He must have had a tank-mate who was high up in the organisation, to enable him to use emergency access coordinates." She shrugged. "Because they didn't come via the tree."

I thought about it while Tolly and Osric were comparing fury and fear. We'd become complacent; in the past we had always travelled via the tree, and it had given both the sanctuary and our own chosen times another layer of safety. It was one more set of coordinates to decipher. But lately the occasions when people came directly into either had increased and most of those had been elders, the ones who held all the sanctuary secrets.

"Are we saying that there's another elder who gave the global government the grid codes and Travis was working with Alice?" I think my levels of incredulity had peaked.

Rachel looked at me, puzzled.

"Did anyone get away?" Osric said sadly.

"Most of us had enough time to collect some things and travel to our places of safety," Rachel said.

"Who issued the warning?" Tolly asked her.

"Albert, he sent a cyphered message to nearly everyone and because he's so respected, people listened. We scattered, but fast. It was amazing, you should have seen it, people opening arches and tunnels just everywhere. One of the elders took most of the inexperienced children into one tunnel, I don't know how he was able to do that and I don't know where. I think that was the point Albert was most insistent on, that we kept our destinations to ourselves." Her voice was choked with emotion and pride.

I felt my eyes fill with tears. "Albert did more than that, he gave himself up to the pirates for us."

She stared at us with astonishment. "He said he had to go via the tree for some reason!" Osric, Tolly and I exchanged a glance. "I know he doesn't travel much." Rachel put her head in her hands. "And I should have waited for him."

"Then you would have been shot too," Osric spoke with finality. "Albert told us just enough when we saw him, so that we wouldn't worry or go charging off to try and look for the new sanctuary. What he hadn't realised was, we would check on the old one before we found his message."

She was horrified. "You didn't?"

"It was completely empty," I said. "We left again in a hurry via the tree and Tolly saw a coded symbol from Albert indicating that he was with Tolly's family. His injuries were life threatening and things got a little *complicated* after that," I paused, "Alice Dubrecht is his, er, mother, it seems she was working with Travis."

Rachel looked really frightened.

"Don't worry, neither of them will be bothering us again," Osric explained.

I didn't ask him about Alice's whereabouts, or more accurately when she was. Tom was curious, but he kept his questions to himself, though Osric's black eye was probably an indicator of her level of resistance to whenever it was. I was really hoping for a seriously unpleasant destination.

We sat in silence, contemplating the situation and trying to deal with our respective feelings.

Eventually I said, "But who told Albert?"

Tolly answered, "I think it was Reggie. I don't understand all the northern tribe language but Albert said 'thank you' to him for 'helping' when we were in the ger. I thought he was talking about coming to get him."

"Why would the pirates warn the sanctuary?" I was even more puzzled.

Osric snorted, "I don't think it was entirely altruistic, they have a vested interest in getting hold of our abilities and they can't do that if the global government have us."

I waited for the wave of incomprehension to sweep over and recede. We all needed the moment.

"Why did you come to this time?" I asked Rachel.

"It has good medical facilities, not too good security and lots of job opportunities," she grinned. "Besides, I knew you were here."

"How did you know?" Tolly was instantly suspicious.

She pointed to a box of chocolates with a distinctive checkerboard design sitting on the kitchen counter top. He rolled his eyes.

"Seriously?" Tolly asked.

"I don't think you understand the importance of chocolate," Rachel said gravely. "Look, I did quite a lot of my training here, I know this time."

I admitted, "I helped Rachel get a job locally when she needed to improve her trauma experience. And time doesn't seem to mind either of us being here."

Tolly nodded. "Do you ever get a sticky feeling if you try and stay too long in other place/times?"

Tom was intrigued. "*Sticky?*"

I shrugged. "It's a good description. Everything starts to feel like wading through syrup."

Tom nodded wisely, "I have the same problem when I've been in the pub after about three pints."

Rachel laughed then blushed. Osric squinted at both of them and I smiled.

We sat quietly for a while. Rachel became sad and I gave her a hug, then went to make the inevitable pot of tea in the little side kitchen.

"What now?" Tolly said.

"We live our lives," Osric replied with finality.

THAT NIGHT I lay awake in bed for a while thinking things through, despite the inevitable post trauma exhaustion. We'd talked about what we would do; I promised Osric that there wouldn't be any book hunting without him or Tolly. Rachel had made plans to complete her training with the air ambulance. The pirates were hopefully in disarray after losing Alice and Travis, but the global government's hunting programme would continue and it seemed they now had serious help. We would be careful though, and time was a big place.

I got up, and reaching out of the window, felt the rush of spring rain on my hands.

SEVERAL WEEKS LATER, I was back in my kitchen making tea after a very successful retrieval job. The library, that sadly had burned down later that night, had been relieved of several really important finds. I thought wryly about the plastic troll I'd bargained for with the little girl, on the reconnaissance visit I had done previously. I remembered Albert's absolute joy and was sad for a moment.

Tolly sat listening carefully while I explained my theory.

"I think if we go to the monastery, *you* could do some sneaking about. Empress Matilda's crown is definitely there!"

Tolly lowered his head and slowly began to bang it gently on the table.

ACKNOWLEDGMENTS

Robin Phillips of Author Help, for always making the impossible, possible. The 'Yoda' of the publishing world! (authorhelp.uk)

Henry Hyde for the amazing cover. (henryhyde.co.uk)

Gill Baderman and Sara Pearcy, old friends, for caring enough to ask, 'how is it going?' and listening to the answer.

Lorna Oldfield and Tim Clark for letting me use their 'removal stories,' the printable ones anyway!

Charlotte Wilson of Brendon Manor Stables, for all the wonderful rides out on the moor in the wind, rain and snow! And the one to the 'cottage' by the river which gave me the idea for the short story.

The real Tippi-teethi, for answering all my equine dentist questions, any mistakes in the procedures are mine.

P H A, for all the useful advice on anything weapons and sneaking around in the dark!

ALSO BY S. PARNAM-HARRIS

Dreamwalkers

A Short Book of the Dead

The Starfire Diaries

The Voice in the Mirror

Find out more at sparnam-harris.com.

www.ingramcontent.com/pod-product-compliance
Lightning Source LLC
Chambersburg PA
CBHW020533020726
47494CB00006B/1749